SHIELDED

Books by KayLynn Flanders

Shielded

Untethered

SHIELDED

KayLynn Flanders

EMBER

This is a work of fiction. Names, characters, places, and incidents either are the product of the author's imagination or are used fictitiously. Any resemblance to actual persons, living or dead, events, or locales is entirely coincidental.

Visit us on the Web! GetUnderlined.com

Educators and librarians, for a variety of teaching tools, visit us at RHTeachersLibrarians.com

The Library of Congress has cataloged the hardcover edition of this work as follows:
Names: Flanders, KayLynn, author.
Title: Shielded / KayLynn Flanders.
Description: First edition. | New York : Delacorte Press, [2020] | Audience: Ages 12 & up. | Audience: Grades 7–9. | Summary: "In a kingdom at war, the princess discovers a devastating truth and might be the key to saving not only those closest to her, but the kingdom itself, if she reveals the very secret that could destroy her"— Provided by publisher.
Identifiers: LCCN 2020007020 | ISBN 978-0-593-11853-5 (hardcover) | ISBN 978-0-593-11855-9 (ebook)
Subjects: CYAC: Magic—Fiction. | Secrets—Fiction. | Princesses—Fiction.
Classification: LCC PZ7.1.F5746 Sh 2020 | DDC [Fic]—dc23

ISBN 978-0-593-11856-6 (paperback)

Printed in the United States of America
10 9 8 7 6 5 4 3 2 1
First Ember Edition 2021

To Cameron.

No, *you're* the best.

✦ ✦ ✦

CHAPTER ONE

Even though my throat was as dry as the stone walls of the castle, a silvery ray of hope kept me anchored in the center of the crowded dining hall. Courtiers pressed in all around me, a sea of golden hair and sharp smiles. But not one of them was my brother. And not one of them was his best friend.

"Princess Jennesara!" a shrill voice rang out.

The conversations around me quieted. I ducked my head and pretended to fiddle with the delicate chain lacing the front of my too-tight bodice. A couple moved in front of me, and I took my chance to sidle away from the girl heading my way.

I'd endured Lady Isarr's poorly veiled interest in my brother through all four courses of dinner. I almost told her where she could corner Ren so she'd let me eat in peace. If he'd truly left me to fend for myself, maybe I still would.

I rose on tiptoe, my hand clenched in the soft wool skirt of my dress, dismissing one blond head after another.

"Pardon me," I murmured as I brushed by a lord and lady whose names I'd forgotten.

My seventeenth birthday was tomorrow, and most of my

father's court had come into Hálenborg when they'd learned we'd still be celebrating despite the attacks at our northern border that we couldn't seem to quell. Most people had thought the fighting would be over in a month. It'd already been seven.

The spectacle was not what I wanted. But the kingdom needed it, or so my father had told me. He'd said the celebration would be worth the resources it required, that Hálenborg could use a boost in morale.

Dwindling resources aside, I'd rather be manning the upper battlements of the castle in a blizzard than chatting or dancing with courtiers. Because even if the white streak in my fair hair was hidden—and I made sure it was always hidden—their discerning scrutiny always left me feeling exposed. But maybe it wouldn't be so bad this year. Maybe Cris would finally ask me to partner for a dance.

The haunting notes of the fidla players mingled with the voices of too many people trying to be heard, and pounded against my skull. My stomach flopped and churned, the delicious food weighing heavily now. Ren and Cris *weren't* here.

I touched my hair, making sure the elaborate plait was in place, and dodged around a woman's skirt, admiring the ornamental dagger at her waist. My hand rubbed against the skirt of my own dress, where I wished my sword hung. My father and his court didn't have a problem with women being soldiers—just with me being one.

Lady Isarr stopped near the Turian ambassador, his black hair and olive skin standing in sharp contrast to everyone else. Her eyes raked over the room.

I ducked down and squeezed between a courtier's dress and the cold wall.

"—first messenger of the season arrived from Turia, and the king sent him straight back again," the woman I was hiding behind said to her companion.

My ears pricked up at that. What message had my father been so eager to send to our southern neighbors?

"I heard . . . ," her companion said, but she stopped when she caught sight of me crouching nearby.

I jerked up and tried to sidestep out the door, but an iron sconce caught my braid, yanking me back. My attempt to extricate myself only tightened the sconce's hold on my hair. My cheeks heated, and some of Ren's more colorful curses ran through my mind. Maybe it was better he wasn't here—he'd tease me about this for the next ten years.

"Your Highness," a man from the kitchens said, interrupting my frantic tugging. The candle in the sconce wobbled. "Let me help."

I tugged harder, wincing as several hairs were torn loose. "No, no, I'm all right," I responded with a smile as fake as any courtier's. One final pull, and at last I was free.

Those closest watched me with surprised stares and barely concealed smirks. Or, worse, pity. I kept one hand at my hair and the other on my heavy skirt. My cheeks must have been flaming red. "Excuse me," I sputtered, and darted into the hallway. Had anyone seen the white strands?

Cool air blasted into me, sending shivers along my neck. Spring should have warmed the castle more by now.

"Princess!" Isarr's screech rang above the muted conversation in the hall behind me.

Did the girl never give up? I picked up my skirt and sprinted to the nearest door.

The latch stuck.

"Come on," I muttered with a glance over my shoulder. But instead of seeing Isarr, I spotted two men standing far down the hall. Was Cris here after all? The lighting was too dim for me to make out his features, but one of the men stood like him. Why were they conversing in the hall?

Isarr still searched, her nose up in the air, like a hound sniffing me out. My fingers threaded through my ruined plait. No one, not even Cris, could be allowed to see the white in my hair.

I rammed my shoulder into the door and slipped inside the retiring room, latching the lock carefully behind me. My heart tapped against my ribs as I leaned against the door. Isarr's feathery steps passed.

In the darkened room, I let loose a sigh that carried all the tension of the night. Being watched by so many was exhausting.

Here, alone, my defenses could soften. I loosened the strip of leather from my plaited hair and ran my fingers against my scalp, pulling outward until the strands untangled. I tilted my head one way, then the other, stretching my neck and letting my wavy hair fall over my shoulders.

Lingering traces of perfume and woodsmoke and old furniture finally settled me. My hands followed the motions they knew by heart, weaving my hair back into a braid that would conceal the white streak behind my temple again.

I'd kept it a secret my whole life and shown Ren only after our mother had died. Even then, when he was five and I was three, he'd known I was an impossibility. The discoloration was no bigger than a coin, yet it marked me as dangerous. A challenge to his claim to the throne—a throne I didn't want.

I ran my hand over the finished braid. There were too many risks to leave my hair loose for long.

My back and ribs ached from my heavy dress, and my bed called to me. Surely, no one would miss me if I didn't return to the dining hall.

Voices outside the door stopped me. "Did you see her hair?" one murmured, and another laughed. "She obviously braided it herself."

"Positively shameful," came the reply.

The voices faded to whispers but didn't disappear. I'd heard the comments before. I brushed my braid over my shoulder with a long exhale and moved to the dying embers in the fire. All sorts of rumors would snake through the castle if I emerged from a dark room by myself. I'd have to wait.

I found the fire iron and prodded the embers until a small flame ignited. A charred scrap of parchment the size of my palm fluttered against my dress, then to the floor.

I brushed a smudge of ash from the embroidery on my skirt, but it only smeared. "Glaciers," I muttered. I snatched up the offending bit of parchment, ready to cast it back into the fire. But the tiny flame dancing in the hearth illuminated a single word.

Magic

The hairs on my arms shot straight up, and a waterfall of shivers skittered down my back. I poked the fire iron through the rest of the warm embers, but nothing more of the note remained. Though the edges of the scrap were blackened, I could read another word: my father's name.

I angled the scrap to the low flame to see what else I could make out.

Magic may indeed be our only hope to stop the destruction.
—search for the mages' library has been unfruitful. The key must lie in Hálendi or—

A hole ringed with black had destroyed the next part, but then:

—strange magic on the front lines. Herds of cattle now husks in the fields, collapsed mines, villages—

The cold in the empty room wrapped around me, tightening until my bones ached. Did my father know about this? He must, but the note now cradled in my palm had been burned in the retiring room—not in his study, nor in the council room.

The muscles in my shoulders and neck tightened as if preparing for a fight. The magic of old had been banished ages ago. Now it was only supposed to be inherited by the heir to the throne of Hálendi, by my brother, Ren—his magic marked by the customary white streak of hair near the temple. How could there be magic on the front lines?

Unease prickled along my scalp. I'd spent my entire life hiding my magic. Who else out there was hiding magic as well?

I tucked the scrap into my pocket, then cleaned my blackened fingertips on the underside of the rug. I paused at the door, my hand on the latch, and closed my eyes.

In the quiet, I let my magic swirl to life. The tethers hummed inside me like silken cords emanating from just under my ribs, connecting me to my father and brother. As I focused on those threads, the soft hum of Ren's excitement and my father's anxiety seeped into me, mixing with my own feelings.

As far as I could tell, that was the extent of my magic—a one-way glimpse into their emotions. Nothing that could lend me an edge in battle. Nothing like Ren, who could heal others with his magic.

The door to the retiring room creaked as I eased into the now-empty hall. The gentle tug of the tethers pulled me down one hallway after another, the emotions of my remaining family threading tighter the closer I got.

The charred message sat heavily in my pocket with every step. When I reached my father's study, inky blackness coated the hall—the sconces hadn't been lit in this part of the castle. Muffled voices seeped through the crack under the door, and the tethers within me quivered. I knew who was inside.

With a furrowed brow, I stared hard at the door. What could they be meeting about with all of court in the dining hall? I pursed my lips, then tiptoed closer. It took only a moment to find the spot where the door had warped away from the frame. A wisp of my father's voice escaped through the gap.

"Our troops are spread too thin. No one can know of your journey to . . ."

The sound faded as though he'd turned away. My breath froze and withered in my lungs like the last rose in the first frost. Where was he sending Ren?

I pulled the door open, slipping inside before I could second-guess myself.

My father's study was sturdy and efficient and all hard

angles. He was standing behind his desk, the fire's light casting deep shadows on his face.

"What are you doing here?" A vein on his forehead bulged, and his anger blasted through his tether into me, followed by worry and the tiniest hint of . . . relief?

"Where are you sending Ren?" I asked before either of them could tell me to leave.

"You were not meant for this conversation, Jennesara." My father's sharp reprimand lashed toward me, but I stood firm, clinging to that hint of relief to keep his emotions from overwhelming my own.

"Maybe not, but I'm here now, and I deserve to know," I replied, my stance wide, ready for the fight. "Please?" I added when I felt him softening.

My father rubbed his temple. "You have to promise to guard this secret. You cannot breathe a word of it to anyone."

"I won't tell a soul, Father. I promise." I held on to my skirt to keep my trembling hands from betraying my desperation. If only he knew how well I could keep a secret.

He sat and gestured for me to sit next to Ren. My brother's blue eyes locked with mine as I slid into the chair, a barely concealed grin pulling at his cheeks. Yet underneath his excitement for whatever task my father had assigned him, a flicker of annoyance darkened his tether. I swallowed back the uncomfortable sensation and smiled back, though my expression faded quickly.

"It's been seven months, and we still haven't been able to pinpoint where the attacks at the border are coming from," my father said. "There are reports of a main camp within the borders of the Ice Deserts."

I tilted my head. "But only scattered bands of wanderers and banished criminals live in the Ice Deserts. How are they crossing into Hálendi?" Our border was protected by ancient magic. For anyone—let alone an army—to cross, was . . . unthinkable.

"I don't know." My father hesitated a moment and touched the Medallion that always hung around his neck. The runes engraved on the palm-sized surface were darkened and smooth with age. "But with Athären leading the troops closer to the front lines, we can finally get one step ahead of them."

I tightened my grip on the chair at the mention of his plans for my brother. "How close to the front lines?"

His jaw set, and he folded his hands on his desk, the picture of confidence. Yet a tiny seed of doubt seeped into me through his tether. "I am sending Athären to North Watch."

His words punched into me. Four days north, all the way to the border. I wanted Ren to tell me it was a joke, that he would never leave me behind, but he only sat taller, anticipation simmering through his tether, making my heart beat faster.

"But he's only nineteen!" I started. My thumb rubbed at a ribbon of embroidery on my skirt, up and down, again and again, as I scrambled for any excuse to keep my brother with me. "And I beat him in our last sparring match, and—"

"I can do it, Father," Ren said as he kicked my leg. "Thank you for trusting me with this."

I should be happy for him—he'd been training his entire life to become king, and now he had a chance to prove himself. But alongside my fear for his safety, a dark streak of envy grew inside me, twisting and tumbling like a stream overflowing with spring runoff.

"What about the magic being used against us?" I persisted. "Ren's magic is for healing, not fighting."

Both men stared at me like they didn't know what I was talking about. The fire sputtered in an unseen draft, unease filling the silence.

"What magic?" my father finally asked, leaning toward me over his desk.

I sat up straight. They didn't know? When I pulled the bit of parchment from my pocket, it cracked into two pieces, but I slid them to my father with a glance at Ren. "I found this tonight," I said slowly.

My father rubbed his hand across his forehead as he studied the note. Then he handed it to Ren.

"Where did you find it?" Ren asked.

"The retiring room fireplace. I thought it was an odd spot to find it, but . . . You really didn't know?" I gripped the edge of the desk and scooted my chair closer. "Have you ever heard of magic like this? Cattle left as husks? Mines collapsing?"

Dread filled my chest, heavy and sour, choking me until I realized most of the fear came from my father's tether. A few deep breaths, and my emotions were once again my own.

"What is this about a search for the mages' library?" Ren asked, pointing to the top of the fragment. "Did you authorize one? And what of a key?"

My father shook his head and rubbed his thumb over the Medallion, staring at the note without seeing it. I had heard the tale of the mages' library—everyone in the kingdom had. But it was a bedtime tale for children, a legend from a different time, when mages roamed the Continent across the sea. Every hundred years or so, someone would foolishly set out to find the mages' library, but no one returned with any success, *if* they returned at all. Why would someone waste time looking for it instead of focusing on the attacks?

I cleared my throat. "Surely, with magic being used, you won't send Ren."

My father settled the Medallion against his tunic and nodded. "This must be why my thoughts keep urging me to send Athären. His magic will turn the tide for us."

"I could help, too." The thought of my brother in danger and my not being there to guard his back made me ill. I took a deep breath. "I have m—"

A sharp pain in my foot cut my argument short. I glared at my brother.

"I will find out what's happening, Father," Ren interjected with a nod.

"You'll be safer if no one knows you've gone to North Watch," my father continued, his eyes fixed once again on the note.

"And when he's suddenly not in the castle anymore?" I asked, wondering how they planned to keep this from the courtiers, whose daughters constantly tracked Ren's movements in the castle so they could flirt with him. He'd never be able to leave without someone noticing.

"By then, it will be too late for anyone to interfere."

So not even the council knew, which could mean only one thing. "Who don't you trust, Father? Do you know who wrote the note?" The worry my father had been feeling for weeks tightened my shoulders.

"I do not want you involved in this, Jennesara," he snapped. He leaned toward me, and the Medallion around his neck swung forward. He caught it before it hit the desk.

Then he did something I'd never seen him do. He pulled the chain with the Medallion over his head and took it off. He brushed his thumb over the engravings on its surface and extended the artifact to Ren.

"Atháren, take the Medallion of Sight. As heir to the throne, its magic will be strong for you. It will keep your mind clear from deception and aid your decisions in North Watch."

Ren's wide eyes met mine before he deftly took hold of the Medallion, reverently slipping it around his neck and under his tunic. But over all of his astonishment and excitement, his determination is what made my stomach sink.

"Thank you, Father," he said. "I won't disappoint you."

The ache inside me spread. He *would* leave me behind, then. I started to stand. "I should—"

"Sit, Jennesara." My father shifted in his seat. Stood from his desk. Faced the window. "Atháren, you may go."

My brother hesitated and felt . . . unease? No, something else. Whatever it was, he knew what was coming.

"I— Yes, Father." He brushed his knuckles against his chin as he left, a subtle gesture he used countless times when he couldn't speak the words aloud—*chin up, Jenna.*

I kept my breathing steady, unwilling to break the silence. The click of the door stretched through the quiet of the study. But still my father faced the window.

"You will turn seventeen tomorrow," he finally said. I waited, cautiously opening myself to his tether, ready to pull away if it threatened to overwhelm me again. But his feelings were softer now. Tender. With the smooth edges of age-old sorrow and grief as deep as time. "I met your mother when she was your age."

I went perfectly still, my breath catching in my lungs. He never spoke of my mother.

"She was visiting Hálenborg with her parents. She'd lived on the coast her whole life, in Hálendi's only port city, and she brought the waves and wind of the sea with her into the castle." He swallowed hard. "You look just like her, you know."

He turned then and shuffled his feet. Swallowed again. "I know I haven't . . ." He straightened his shoulders and started again. The relief in his tether strengthened. "I'm glad you're here, because I have news. Last fall, King Marko sent an official betrothal request to join his eldest son to you in marriage."

I flinched at the change in subject, at the switch in his emotions from tenderness to unyielding determination. He continued before I could form a response. "I sent your acceptance before the pass closed. If—"

"What?" I blurted. My heart pounded so hard my hands started to shake. "I didn't accept anything."

He pursed his lips, and a hint of regret laced the determination in his tether. I didn't like that regret.

"You can't force me into a betrothal," I insisted. "It's—"

"It's done," he said as he rubbed his neck where the chain of the Medallion no longer rested.

My jaw hung open, but no words escaped. There were rules in place, centuries of customs that protected our citizens from forced marriages.

When I didn't respond, he cleared his throat. "A messenger arrived this afternoon. The prince invited you to Turia for the monthlong evaluation of the betrothal. I replied, agreeing to the invitation on your behalf."

The message he'd been so eager to send, it was *this*?

He stopped fidgeting and finally met my gaze. "If you find anything amiss, any reason to back out, I will support you."

I shook my head and shot to my feet. The hem of my dress caught under my boot, and I lurched to the side. I yanked the fabric away, crushing it in my fist. "Then why send an acceptance I didn't agree to in the first place? Why the secrecy?"

"The fighting at our border should have been resolved months ago, but it's only worsening. The majority of our people are not the warriors they once were. The courtiers—"

"It's not *my* fault those lazy courtiers won't lift a sword. What if *I* trained—"

His hand sliced through the air, batting my words away. "We need support from Turia, especially if magic is involved. And the Riigans are pressuring Marko into an alliance—one Marko doesn't want."

I folded my arms and widened my stance. "You agreed to the marriage months ago, before you knew magic was involved," I said, trying to stay calm, trying to make him see reason. "What aren't you telling me?"

My father sighed, deep and long. The moaning wind and the crackling fire filled the silence as I waited him out. "It's the Medallion." He began pacing, and his tether coiled so tight with anxiety I had to roll my shoulders back. "For weeks—months, if I'm being honest—it's been warning me."

"Warning you?" I asked, staying still in hopes he'd say more.

He'd never spoken to me about the Medallion before. "About the border?"

He nodded, then shook his head. "The Medallion of Sight doesn't reveal a defined path—more like impressions. Something's coming. I've done everything I can think of to protect our borders, but with this report of magic . . ." He stopped speaking, lost in thought.

I stepped forward eagerly. "Father, I can help."

"No." He sliced his hand through the air again. "I need you in Turia."

"I don't want to go to Turia!" My voice rose, the words tumbling out before I could catch them.

"I signed the documents!" My father slapped the desk, papers flying under his hand. "It is done. *This* is how you can help."

Then it clicked, the feeling I'd sensed in Ren. It was guilt. He'd known about the betrothal, but for how long? I pushed the prickling ache down—I'd get answers from my brother later.

"You will be safe in Turia," my father muttered as he rubbed his forehead.

I swallowed my angry retort. Instead, I drew inward until I could sort the emotions in his tether more clearly. Frustration, unease. *Regret*.

I sat in my forgotten chair and folded my hands in my lap. "You don't really want to send me away to Turia," I started softly. "I know you don't."

His eyes fell shut, and his brow furrowed.

I licked my lips, hoping I could prove my loyalty to Hálendi in another way. "I could go with Ren to North Watch, or—"

His eyes snapped open, his shoulders tense and his eyes

fierce. "I would not send you into a war unless you were the last able-bodied warrior in Hálendi." He turned away from me to study the tapestry behind his desk.

I controlled my frustration and measured my words carefully. "I want to help, Father. My skills are unmatched. Surely—"

"I know you are adept in a practice ring, but that's all it is, Jennesara. A practice ring." He pinched the bridge of his nose. "You have no real experience in battle, or even in training others."

I flew to my feet and braced myself on his desk with both hands. "Whose fault is that? All I've ever sought is to prove myself beyond our castle walls, and you've done everything you could to keep me from that. Now you tell me I'll be packed up and shipped away, married to a prince I've never met and pretending a foreign kingdom I've never visited is my home. I've done everything you've ever asked, and at the moment when I could be of use, could aid my brother and my kingdom, you dismiss me?"

"I cannot send you to the border!" he shouted. His eyes flashed; the tendons in his neck tightened. A wave of his frustration slammed against me.

He inhaled deeply and crossed his arms over his chest. His voice was quiet when he spoke again. "I cannot send you to the border." He looked down at his desk. "I will not." He lifted his head to face me again, deep pools of sorrow and exhaustion reflected in his eyes. "We are sending more troops to the north. Atháren will direct them where they are most needed to prevent attacks deeper within our borders."

An ache formed at the back of my throat, and a chill bled through me. "You just said we don't have enough troops."

"It is part of the betrothal agreement. When you set a date for the marriage, King Marko will send his troops to assist us."

I fell back into my chair. So the sooner I accepted my fate, the sooner my countrymen would cease dying on the border. I'd fallen through ice into a lake once and the cold washing over me now felt the same as it had then.

"You said you'd support me if I found a reason to break the betrothal," I said, the walls looming closer with every breath.

My father sagged into his own chair. "And I will. Should that happen."

But I could feel his hope. Hope that I would set a date and marry, and stay safely tucked away in Turia.

I clasped my hands in front of me. Anger, frustration, and sorrow leaked out of the tiny fissures widening within me. I wished I could hold on to anything other than the emptiness.

"When will I leave?" I asked, biting off the words like a bitter medicine.

"The day after your birthday. Ren will accompany you until you leave the outer villages of Hálenborg, then discreetly separate from the party."

The air whooshed from my lungs. "So soon?" I'd always loved my birthday—a day of freedom from my usual routine. And now it would be my last day at home.

"We cannot delay," he said, his spine bowing until he looked much older than he was. "This is what I need from you. What Hálendi needs."

His words struck me, their echo silencing the arguments I had ready. I stood and straightened my dress. My eyes stayed fixed on the edge of his desk.

"I am a princess of Hálendi. I will do my duty to my

kingdom," I said, echoing what he'd admonished me with so many times. The words tasted sour, and my voice crumbled until it was barely a whisper. "But you've known for months. My birthday is tomorrow. Why didn't you tell me before now?"

The dimming light of the fire reflected off the white streak in his silver hair and deepened the lines on his face.

"Jennesara, I—" He swallowed, then shrugged helplessly. "Because I'd hoped the kingdom could be put to rights by the time the pass opened. I needed options. But the note you brought is only further proof we've a traitor among us. We're out of time."

His logic made sense. It did. But it still hurt enough that I couldn't respond.

"We will announce the betrothal at the end of your birthday celebration tomorrow." He put his hand over his mouth as though he could take the words back. But he'd said them. He'd signed the agreement.

Bitterness and regret and anger fought inside me, both my own and my father's. "Good night, Your Majesty."

I walked slowly to the door, wishing he would say something, anything, to repair the cracks in my heart, but he was silent. I pushed his tether away. I couldn't bear to feel his emotions when my own were choking me.

My world was tipping, my shattered life scattering like glass across ice. How was I going to find my place in a new land when I couldn't find a place among my own people? How would I keep my magic a secret under the scrutiny of an entire new kingdom?

I passed through the castle in a daze, staying far away from the bright dining hall. The practice ring beckoned, calling me out into the night to fight the weight pressing down on my heart. But I couldn't win when my enemy was my own secret, my own father, my own kingdom. This was a battle I couldn't fight—my freedom for my kingdom's? It was an impossible choice.

I stalked upstairs to my chambers. A single log burned in the hearth, its warmth barely penetrating the room. My sword—one the weapons master had had made specifically for me before my father could forbid it—lay on the sofa near the glowing fireplace.

My mind returned to the note, to the worry and frustration and doubt my father had been feeling for months. And then I realized I'd asked the wrong question when I'd asked who had written the note. The real question was: Who had burned it?

CHAPTER TWO

Training with Master Hafa, the weapons master, always pulled me from bed early—usually before the sun had even crested the hills. Today, my birthday, I burrowed deeper into the down-filled blankets. My father had signed betrothal documents for me, the seamstresses had picked out my dress for the celebration tonight, but *I* would get up when I wanted.

My mind had traveled too many paths overnight, wondering who could have written the note, who had burned it, what I would find in Turia. I'd looked forward to this day for months, but now it was the day my betrothal to a complete stranger would be officially announced to the kingdom. I'd have to act as if everything were fine. As if I didn't now have a man waiting to marry me. As if I weren't leaving tomorrow. As if there weren't a traitor somewhere in the castle.

My door creaked open just after dawn, and three maids poured into my room. I groaned and pulled my pile of blankets higher around my ears.

"Don't know what he's about," one of the women muttered

to the other maids as they opened the door to the small room that served as my closet and walked right in.

I poked my head out, smoothing back my hair and glaring at the doorway to my closet. "What are you doing?" I croaked, my voice rough with sleep. "Where's Aleinn?"

The tallest of them shuffled out, her arms already full of dresses, and dumped them on the back of the chair by my mirror. "Your maid had other tasks assigned to her this morning. His Majesty asked us to prepare your things for a long journey. Only gave us *one* day, if you can imagine."

The other two emerged as well, one holding the fine gold and silver chains that laced the bodices of my dresses, the other with my most intricately engraved belts—all of which I wore only for special occasions. The three of them watched me, expressions carefully blank. I wasn't sure if they wanted gossip or if they were just annoyed at the lack of notice.

Excuses lay at the tip of my tongue, how I didn't want to go, that I was going for *them*, for all of Hálendi. For everyone but myself.

I didn't elaborate on the king's request. In my father's house, it didn't matter if you were daughter or servant, princess or peasant—you obeyed. Besides, if these servants knew the real reasons for my journey, word would spread around the castle before the day's end. Including to whoever had burned the note.

The maids sent each other a look, one I'd seen often but could never decipher, and bustled back to the closet to decide which pieces should be packed.

I groaned and snuggled into my pillow. I'd miss this pillow.

"Fine," I grumbled to myself, and yanked the blankets off,

shivering as my feet hit the woven rug. Better than the freezing floor, but not by much. My closet was fast emptying of dresses and wraps and dainty court shoes, but my gear for the practice ring lay untouched.

I frowned and threw on my oldest pair of trousers, a soft burgundy tunic, and my favorite sweater, which had an intricate snowflake design over one shoulder. Then I gathered a bundle of clothes the maids had skipped over—leather boots with the warmest lining, my best trousers, three tunics that I could move in easily—and tucked them into the maids' pile.

In my bathing chamber, I rebraided my hair to hide my white streak. If today was to be my last day here, I had a lot to do.

The dark corridors were striped with narrow strips of pink morning light as I jogged to keep warm. The castle's library inhabited the south corner of the keep, where several lifetimes' worth of knowledge slept. Knowledge that would help me decipher the note.

I slipped through the library's tall doors with a contented sigh. I couldn't help it. Even with the threats and changes looming, the quiet reverence of all these books settled my soul. I would miss this room more than my chambers. More, even, than the practice ring.

It was the loveliest room in the castle, with tall ceilings and wide windows, which framed the cottony clouds tinged with pink and orange spread over the light-blue sky. Here, light could filter in. Heavy blue drapes lined the windows to protect the leather-bound manuscripts from harsh lighting. The air tasted like a soup of tranquility and dust. I wandered to a shelf, brushing my fingers over the thick spines.

My feet guided me to a section I'd been forbidden from studying. There were only a few rows of books that referenced magic in the entire library—not even enough to fill an entire shelf. But when my father had caught me studying the history of mages, he'd slammed the book I was reading closed and said I would be barred from the southern wing entirely if he caught me studying magic again.

I hated it, but I couldn't risk my secret getting out. I was a princess who fought like a soldier, who stayed cooped up in the castle. Having an interest in magic would tip the scale of opinion from eccentric to dangerous.

But now I was leaving. And soon I would no longer be a Hálendian princess at all.

I hefted a stack of books off the shelf and sat tucked away at a wooden table in an alcove near a window. I flipped through page after page, scanning for any reference to the mages' library or a key.

During my restless night, I'd come to a depressing conclusion. The mystery of the burned note wasn't my burden to solve. There was no way for me to figure out who wrote it, even less of a chance I'd find out who burned it. Not in one day.

But I could find out more about the mages' library. If I could ease Ren's burdens in North Watch, or my father's worries, I would do it.

I snapped one book closed and pulled another, then another. Everywhere I searched, the mages' library was mentioned only in passing as a stronghold for magical texts and artifacts after magic was banished from the Continent after the Great War.

I'd been allowed to study the war—its end had been the

birth of Hálendi. When the first emperor finally defeated the power-hungry mages tearing the Continent apart, he'd exiled everything to do with magic—all the manuscripts, artifacts, any source of knowledge—across the sea, here to the Plateau. His son had been the first Hálendian king.

My hand stopped when I pulled out the next book. *Turia*. Had it been shelved in the wrong place? My brow furrowed, but I cracked open the worn cover, and its scent, like an ancient, musky forest, wafted up. The pages were so old the parchment was almost translucent.

I'd studied the kingdom south of ours with my tutors; I knew how much grain they produced in a year, how much fruit their orchards yielded. Their healers were the best on the Plateau, maybe even better than those on the Continent.

I knew so many things about Turians, yet I couldn't fathom myself among them. Although with Ren leaving for North Watch, I wasn't sure I could picture myself here without him, either.

My fingers ghosted over the pages, skimming over faded ink. A brief mention of magic caught my eye. I went back to the top of the page and read more carefully, but it was only a mention of a Turian scribe named Jershi who studied magical history and lore. His writings were in Turania's palace library. Perhaps I could continue my study there and send on any information I might find about the mages' library. My stomach twisted into another knot, and I kept reading.

There were notes on Turians' skill in making pottery and bronze statuary, their preferred weapons and style of government, and how their language had changed over the years because of Hálendi's influence. A flash of gold popped out as I flipped through the pages, and I thumbed back until I found the glint that had caught my eye.

It was an illustration of a Turian family. I glanced at a note in tiny script underneath. *Royal Family,* it read, and was dated over one hundred years ago. I gulped, unable to look away. Four boys with dark hair, all gangly limbs, stood stoically around a woman with tightly curled hair seated next to a man with thick eyebrows. I rested my chin in my hand to keep it from trembling. They all had rather unfortunate noses.

I swallowed and studied the family closer. The boys wore loose shirts with only three buttons at the top, and no collar. Their shirts were tucked into their straight trousers, and their trousers were tucked into knee-high boots. They wore ornately embroidered vests, all shades of brown and gold. Their features weren't as angular and harsh as those I'd seen on the men around me, and their eyes were a deep brown.

I ran my fingers over the page. A rustle of excitement started in my belly. I'd rarely been allowed outside the castle walls. My mother and I had been on a trip to her hometown when she'd suddenly fallen ill and died. Ever since, my father had refused to let me venture far—or anywhere, really. I'd been in the city surrounding the castle only a handful of times.

While I hated it, I understood the fear and anguish that backed my father's demands. I felt them with him through the tethers. It was the same fear that now drove him to send me to Turia.

Everything I knew about the world beyond was because of these books and Mistress Edda, the guardian of the library and my tutor since before I could hold a sword. I didn't know what I'd do without her and her abundant patience with my questions. But no matter how much she taught me, my heart ached to see more than golden hair and white snow and the occasional visitor from afar.

A hand dropped onto my shoulder. Without thinking, I twisted away and grabbed the wrist, pulling hard toward the table and pushing my chair back into whoever had crept up behind me.

"Whoa!"

I pursed my lips and let go of my brother's wrist, taking a deep breath to calm my stuttering heart. "How many times do I have to tell you not to sneak up on me?" I asked, more sharply than I meant to.

Even though his appearance hadn't changed since yesterday, I hadn't noticed until now that Ren no longer looked like the boy who had taught me to fight when we were little. He was tall and broad-shouldered, his blond hair long enough to brush his collar, his white streak prominently displayed. He was kind and charismatic. He was a leader. Our paths were always meant to diverge—with him as king and me as . . . something else. But I thought we'd have more time.

He'd also failed to tell me about the betrothal.

Ren tilted his head at my tone, then pushed me aside so he could sit at the table. "I like the challenge."

"You have a death wish," I said as I piled other books on top of the Turian royal family with long noses.

"Aren't princesses supposed to be demure?" he asked, batting his eyes.

I snorted. "I'm a princess of warriors. Don't ambush me."

He leaned back and stretched his legs under the table. "That's why Father wants you in a dress, you know. Fewer places to hide weapons and less of a chance you'll accidentally stab someone when you aren't paying attention."

He grabbed the corner of the top book and angled it so he could see the title stamped on the cover. "*History of the Great War*?" he asked. "Delving into the forbidden shelf, are we?"

I pursed my lips and fought down a wave of nerves. "What could Father possibly punish me with? He's already sending me away."

Ren shifted in his chair. The emotions from his tether, always deep in the background, rose up, though I didn't need magic to sense his unease. "At least we get to go together," he said with a glance around the empty library.

I rubbed at a black knot in the dark wood table. "How long have you known?"

"About the betrothal? Not until yesterday afternoon. No one did."

I swallowed. At least he hadn't kept the secret for long. "Who else did he tell? And why wasn't I there when he told them? Why didn't you warn me?"

Ren squirmed. "It was only me and General Leland. I was meeting with Father when the general arrived from North Watch. Father told him he'd be escorting you to Turia, and it just sort of came out. He said he was about to look for you." He sighed. "I'm sorry. I should have told you first."

I nodded, accepting his apology. "You didn't want to be the one to break the news." I exhaled a long breath. "I guess

I wouldn't want to, either, if I were you." I brushed the pages of the nearest book open to a map of the Plateau, running my finger over the Wastelands west of the Wild. "Do you know who it is that Father doesn't trust?"

Ren shook his head, uncharacteristically serious. "He's been worried about the border, but I didn't realize he didn't trust his own council."

We sat in silence for a long moment. "I don't think you should go to North Watch," I said quietly. His annoyance immediately flared. "It's not because I don't think you can do it," I hurried to add.

He squinted at me. "Don't read my emotions like that—it's not fair."

I shrugged one shoulder. "It's the only thing my magic can do. I might as well use it if I'm going to all the trouble to hide it," I grumbled. "If we told Father about the tethers, we could find out if it's more than just the connection, or if I could use my magic to help in North—"

"No." Ren's quiet voice cut into my argument. "Absolutely not. He is bound by the laws and the people."

"But I would *never* try to take the throne from you! I know some madwoman two hundred years ago inherited magic and tried to kill her brother, but that doesn't mean I'll do the same."

Ren leaned closer, his elbows on the table. "We've talked about this. Someone else could claim you should be on the throne. With the raids in the north, we cannot afford even a hint of division."

My head began to ache. "I know." I paused, weighing my words before speaking. "Ren, why hasn't father used his magic to end the raids?"

I had vague memories of him pushing boulders and digging holes without a shovel. But it had been years. Whispers floated around court about him, though, about how there hadn't been a king who could move earth in ages, maybe since Kais himself, the first king.

My brother shifted in his seat and scratched at the chain that now hung around his neck. "Father's magic is weak. He hasn't had to use it in years. He depends on the magic of the Medallion to guide him."

I licked my lips and stared at his chest. "What's it like?" I asked reverently.

Ren grinned and untucked the Medallion from his shirt. He leaned closer and held it out to me, though he kept the chain around his neck.

My eyes widened, and I matched his grin. At first touch, a tingle sparked in my fingertips. My breath hitched. I traced the aged runes on the front.

"I didn't know there was anything on the back," I said as I turned it over and studied the sporadic markings, rubbing the pads of my fingers over them. "Do you know what they mean?"

He shrugged. "Maker's marks, I think."

"Do you feel different? Wearing it?" I reluctantly set the Medallion in his palm, and he tucked it back under his shirt.

A hint of uncertainty danced on his tether. He shrugged. "Maybe a little. Father says I'll learn to trust it in time."

My shoulders fell. "I wish I could be here for that." A lump formed in my throat. I put my head in my hands. "I kept the tethers a secret my whole life so I wouldn't be sent away. And now I'm being shipped off regardless."

Ren's grin faded. He rubbed the leg of his trousers for a

moment, then reached for a book in front of us. "Did you find anything useful?" he asked as he scanned the open pages.

I shrugged. "Not really. Everyone's already heard the legend of how the mages' library contains their magcial secrets and is protected by enchantments. Nothing about a key. No hint at where it is."

Ren shifted the stack until the Turian royal family peeked out. I tried to shut that book, but he grabbed it from my hands and pulled it closer.

"Researching magic, huh?" His smile grew crooked. "Magic . . . and Turian men?"

A blush burned in my cheeks, and I dropped my forehead on the table with a thunk. "How am I going to face this alone?"

"I think the whole point of a betrothal is that you *won't* be alone."

I scowled at him, but he only waggled his eyebrows at me, eyes sparkling.

I pushed him, hard enough to knock him out of his chair, but he held tight to the table. Underneath his teasing exterior, his tether flared with worry.

"I'm serious, Ren. I know a bit about their customs, but not enough to marry their prince. I . . ." I fiddled with the end of my braid. "Will I have to hide it still?"

Ren pursed his lips and stared out the large windows. "You can never tell anyone about your magic," he whispered, so quietly I almost missed his words.

My fingers, suddenly cold, shut the book on the Turians. I'd kept my secret for seventeen years; I would have to continue keeping it. But the thought of not having Ren there, not having a confidant, made the burden heavy.

Ren cleared his throat and bumped my shoulder. "Just ignore everyone like you always do. He's a better choice than marrying some fish-head from Riiga."

I tried to shake off my mood. This was the last day we had at home. "Even if his nose is too long for his face?"

Ren's laughter burst out in the silence of the library. "He's not as handsome as me, but I think the Turian royals may have grown into their noses over time."

I rolled my eyes. "So." I licked my lips. "Do you approve of the arrangement?" Ren had met the Turian heir, Prince Enzo, once on a state visit, but I'd been too busy training to care.

Ren rubbed the back of his neck. "Honestly, he's kind of boring. And pretentious."

I groaned.

"But you'll be queen of an entire kingdom. And if we get the northern border under control—"

"The contract is signed. And you need the troops."

He scratched behind his ear. "I could always threaten to abdicate and live in the countryside with you." He smiled and raised his eyebrows, but I felt his stress—stretched between my father and me, between his duty and his desires.

"The countryside would be wasted on you, Ren." Thinking of him anywhere near fighting made me sick, but I wouldn't be the one to keep him from his task. "You'll be brilliant in North Watch. Probably end the whole thing in a week." I managed to pull one side of my face into a smile.

His eyes crinkled with a smile in return. "A week? I give it five days."

A single laugh escaped me. I swallowed before it could turn into anything else.

"I'm still worried for you," I whispered.

He lowered his voice, all traces of levity gone. "I know, Jenna. But you'll have the tethers to make sure I'm okay. Or," he added, lips quirking, "to let you know the exact moment of my death. Either way."

I elbowed him in the stomach. "Not funny, Ren. Not even close."

He leaned away to dodge the blow, and his chair tipped over, dumping him onto the floor in a heap. My laugh echoed through the library as he stood and brushed himself off with a grin.

"Hey." He touched my shoulder and pulled out a small parcel wrapped in blue cloth. "For your birthday."

My lips spread in a slow smile as I took the gift. It was small and rectangular, about the size of my hand.

"Go on," Ren urged.

I bit my lip and peeled back the wrapping. It was a tiny leather-bound book. *Flora and Fauna of the Wild*. "Thank you," I said, holding it to my chest.

He shrugged, but a hint of pink tinged his cheekbones. "Leland will keep you safe in the Wild as long as you stay on the road, but this way you won't have to ask them what every strange plant or unearthly creature is."

My fingers itched to open its pages and see what kind of creatures he meant. "It's perfect."

Ren cleared his throat and set his hands on his hips. "No more melancholy things on your birthday. Breakfast should be ready soon, and—"

"Glaciers!" I shot out of my chair and scrambled to close the books. "I can't. Master Hafa is expecting me in the ring!"

Ren took the books I was gathering out of my arms. "I'll take your gift to your chambers. You'd better go. If you're late, he'll make you run laps around the palace all day, birthday or not."

"Thank you!" I called as I sprinted into the corridor.

While the servants were up and busy at this hour, at least no courtiers would see me racing through the halls, past the kitchens with fresh bread cooling on racks, and into the yard.

The white granite wall glowed in the rays of morning light as I ran the slushy paths to the round barracks building. I kicked my boots against the door, shook off the bite of the early morning air, and stepped inside.

The practice area was as large as the dining hall in the castle, but circular. The rough stone walls had stood for centuries, but the wood doors and shutters over the long, thin slots nestled at the roofline were newer. It was drafty, but as Master Hafa liked to point out, battles were rarely conducted inside. Two practice rings outlined with short wooden fencing took the majority of the space—a large oval to the left for enlisted soldiers, and a small ring on the right for nobility. The latter would have been filled fifty years ago, but it was always empty these days.

I wove my way through the small crowd already gathered around the larger ring, looking for Master Hafa. I felt eyes on me, a slight itch between my shoulder blades. When I turned, no one was staring, but General Leland, my father's highest-ranking commander, and his advisor and friend, stood against the wall, his focus on the main contest. A jolt reminded me that he knew I'd be leaving. He knew of my betrothal. How many others here had heard of it already?

I eased my way through the crowd around the large ring in time to see Cris land the final blow to his sparring partner. Everyone celebrated his victory, but I'd been caught in his gaze.

"Jennesara!" he called out, his chest heaving from the match. "Shall we spar? You may actually stand a chance now that I have already beaten three others!" The crowd laughed and jeered.

A blush heated my neck at his attention. "You know I can't turn down a challenge like that, Cris!"

The men and women in uniform started calling out encouragement to their respective favorites, but the cries for Cris were noticeably louder. Most usually rooted against me—I'd beaten everyone except Master Hafa. But today, their lack of favor stung. This was the place I most felt at home, and it was the last time I would stand in the dust to sweat and fight with them.

I pulled off my sweater and draped it over the fencing surrounding the ring and blew on my hands to warm them. I arched one arm behind my neck, then the other, stretching my legs and bouncing on my toes. It would be a good day to swing a sword at someone's head.

Master Hafa emerged from the crowd, handed me a long wooden staff, and nodded toward Cris. "You may start with this one," he announced in his gravelly voice.

I made a fist, placed it on the opposite shoulder, bowed, and took the staff. As I tested its weight, I couldn't keep from grinning. When I was five, Ren had taught me to use my stature and speed to my advantage, and staff combat was still one of my favorite ways to fight.

Ren is leaving.

The thought came unbidden, and I struggled to shake it

free. I needed to let all emotions fall away as my opponent and I faced off.

Cris was taller and stronger—and very distracting—but I was faster and born to fight.

I found my grip and adjusted my stance, breathing in the scent of dirt, sweat, and the thrill of a fight. Cris grinned at me from the other side of the ring as we started circling each other. I smirked back.

Finally, he stepped forward and took the first swing, sweeping at my legs. Everything seemed to slow. The clarity that always came to me in a fight dawned—my vision sharpened, sounds magnified, and I felt every breath, every breeze from my enemy's weapon. I welcomed the jarring of my bones as our staffs connected, and I quickly jumped and spun in the air, catching Cris with a hit to the shoulder. I connected, but he used the momentum to roll away and regroup, readying for the next move.

"You don't need to go easy on me," he taunted, trying not to smile and failing.

"I didn't want to mess up your face any more than it already is. I know it's your most prized possession," I shot back, then blocked his staff as he swung at my ribs. "Besides," I grunted, shoving him off, "my brother needs at least one friend with his face intact to keep his ego in check."

His next jab was high, and I dodged left, jamming my staff into his foot as I turned. He yelped and sprang back to avoid my strike at his neck.

"Why, Princess, did you just call me handsome?"

I scoffed and aimed for his knees. Cris's staff grazed my shoulder. I parried his next swing and danced away from him.

The crowd around the ring was shouting and cheering, but to me it sounded like the pounding of heavy rain—one indistinguishable rumble.

I am betrothed.

Anger and frustration flared in my chest. Losing wasn't an option. Not today.

I was several paces back from Cris, and he was still grinning, waiting for me to take the offensive, broad shoulders straight and uniform neat despite his previous frays. So I ran at him. His eyes widened, and he pulled his staff in closer. I yelled as I took my last step, using my staff as a pole to push myself higher than I could jump on my own. He dropped his staff and grabbed my foot before it could slam into his sternum, holding on tight and pulling me down. I twisted around and used our combined momentum to pin him to the ground, pushing my shaft under his jaw against his neck.

As the dust settled around me and Chris, the only sound was our labored breathing. Then the crowd erupted.

I couldn't keep the grin of victory off my face as I pulled my staff from Cris's neck and rolled away. He lay there with wide eyes, propped on his elbows. He ran a hand through his hair and held it back a moment before releasing it with a disbelieving chuckle. I held out my hand, and his surprise transformed into something more like admiration.

He grasped my palm, and I hauled him up. Instead of letting go, though, he pulled me closer. "Ice and snow, Jenna, where did you learn *that* trick?" He caressed the back of my hand with his thumb. To any spectators, it would only appear as a congratulatory remark and handshake.

I tugged my hand free and shrugged, my stomach turning over from nerves, and something else that threatened to send a shiver down my spine. "I can't tell you *all* my secrets. You'll have to figure out how to beat me on your own."

"Princess Jennesara," someone said, cutting in. I pulled my eyes from Cris's as General Leland approached, nodding respectfully to me.

"General Leland," I replied, straightening my tunic. "I'm glad to see you've returned safe from North Watch."

I'd been afraid of the general when I was little—his near-colossal height and the permanent stern look on his face had always stirred my unease. Ren had told me again and again that my fears were unfounded, and I had to admit that Leland only ever treated me well.

Leland's strained smile accentuated the hollows under his eyes. "I arrived just yesterday. I could not miss your birthday." I swallowed and kept my shoulders from slumping at his hidden meaning. He'd returned to escort me to Turia. He turned to Cris. "Lord Cris, I would like to speak with you."

I attempted a smile and took a step back.

A muscle in Cris's jaw flexed, but he bowed before exiting the ring and walking off with the general, their voices dropped low. Cris's mother had passed away several years ago, and since he'd never known his father, Leland had taken him under his wing. That, more than anything, was what eventually softened my view of the general.

I rubbed a hand against my stomach, uneasy for another reason. Would Leland tell Cris I was leaving? Would he tell him about the betrothal? A disappointment I hadn't let myself feel swelled inside me. A hope I had never let myself entertain sputtered out—the hope of Cris becoming more than just my brother's best friend.

I am leaving tomorrow.

I turned and handed Master Hafa the staff, picked up my sweater, then trudged back to the castle.

Everything I did today would be the last time. I was glad I had a last chance, but I also regretted all the future chances I would never have. And underneath it all, there were weightier matters to worry over. The blackened edges of a note that shouldn't have been burned, a note that shouldn't have been written.

But Leland would look after my father, and Cris would look after Ren. And I'd find out everything I could in Turia's library before the trouble at the border escalated any more than it already had.

In the Borderlands of the Ice Deserts

A pair of tall, cloaked figures stood brazenly in the middle of a burned-out town covered in ash and snow. The pre-dawn glow in the east barely illuminated them through the billowing smoke.

"Where is Redalia?"

"She has her instructions," the one with drooping shoulders replied. A small trickle of blood seeped from his nose.

"And why was I not privy to those, Graymere?" At the edge of the street, a new fire flared up in a collapsed building.

"You are alive because of me. You will follow my orders, as will Redalia."

The man grunted. "And what of your new ally?"

"He won't fail."

"They are more powerful than I would have expected after so many years."

A slow smile spread across Graymere's face, his gray teeth reflecting the firelight around them. "Soon it won't matter what magic their line has manifested." He whistled, and a broad gray horse cantered into view.

The other man tilted his head. “Do not underestimate our enemy. We have waited too long to fail now.”

Graymere’s shadow seemed to grow despite the lack of light. “A *dead* enemy cannot be underestimated. I will have my revenge on Kais’s line.”

“What of Kais’s bond? They will know your plan.”

“No.” Graymere mounted his gray horse. “I will take care of the bond—with her blood.”

CHAPTER THREE

My boots left muddy prints as I ran down the hall. I'd stayed in the garden longer than I'd intended, and the two seamstresses who were waiting to dress me would be even grumpier than usual. I skidded around the corner to the family wing of the castle and almost slammed into my handmaiden.

"There you are," Aleinn scolded. While only four years my senior, she'd taken to mothering me from the first day she was assigned to me. "I've been looking for you everywhere." She wrinkled her nose as she caught the scent of sweat and dirt wafting from my tunic. "You'll need a bath before tonight, as well."

I frowned but nodded. Though messages from Hálenborg could reach Turia's capital, Turiana, in eight days by switching horses and riders at the border outposts, it took twelve days to travel by caravan. Twelve days until another warm bath. Twelve days until I could look for answers about the mages' library. Twelve days until Hálendi was no longer my home.

Aleinn held her hand out to lead me to my chambers. As we

walked, she kept pace but remained one step behind out of deference. She was the closest person to a friend I had in the castle, and I understood why she kept space between us, but I couldn't help but resent it.

"How is your brother faring in the stables?" I asked, hoping to close the gap in another way.

"He loves the horses, but not the mucking," she replied softly.

"No one likes mucking. That's why they make the newest stable boys do it."

She laughed. "He says the stable masters claim it builds character."

"And keeps *them* from having to do it."

I touched her arm, and we paused in front of the chamber doors. "I'm going to miss you, Aleinn."

She patted my hand. "Haven't you heard? I'm to accompany you."

Hope flared inside me, though guilt tried to stamp it out. "But . . . your brother. Your family . . ."

Her smile was soft but genuine. "I don't mind. Seeing more of the Plateau will be something of an adventure. I've heard so many tales about the strangeness of the Wild, and we'll get to journey through the heart of it!"

I pursed my lips to keep back a smile. Was she really excited to sleep in a tent and travel through the unknown, or was she just trying to make me feel better? "You only have to stay until I've gotten settled."

And then she'd return home. But I never would, not really. My shoulders drooped, and her smile dimmed the smallest bit.

"This journey," she said, "is it . . ."

I pasted on a smile and tilted my head toward my chambers and the waiting seamstresses. "How mad do you think they'll be when they learn I still need to bathe?" I didn't want to answer questions about rumors—especially not in the hall—and I hoped she understood.

Her pale-blue eyes studied my face. I didn't flinch, didn't waver. With a nod, she opened the door and gestured for me to enter. "Why don't you go find out?"

✦ ✦ ✦

My bedchamber was still full of maids frantically folding and packing when I'd finished scrubbing the dirt and sweat away, donned a robe, and rebraided my hair. Aleinn and I stayed out of their way in my sitting room.

The fire roared, but my skin raised in gooseflesh in the brief span between when I removed my robe and when the seamstresses hefted the dress over my head. I was lost to a world of rustling fabric, cocooned in filtered silver and blue light, until they got it settled correctly. They helped me onto a short stool in the middle of the room, and then they were off, checking every hem, every bead, every seam, making any last-minute changes they deemed necessary.

My stomach churned and rolled. The next time I'd be fitted for a dress this spectacular would be for my wedding. Another jolt passed through me at that thought, and I breathed through my nose to steady my nerves.

"Arms higher, Princess." Aleinn's soft voice floated into my thoughts, and I adjusted my arms so she could wrap a thick ribbon of blue with intricate silver embroidery around my waist, its ties draping down the side of the skirt.

"You'll be sure to catch everyone's attention in this," Aleinn said with a knowing gleam in her eye, one I wasn't familiar with.

"Who are you— Ouch!" I yelped, with a glare at the woman stitching something at my side. Her cheeks went red, but she kept her head down.

My teeth clenched as I remembered the note. The traitor could be anyone, could have eyes and ears anywhere. I exhaled slowly and let the seamstresses circle me like hungry wolves. Leaving my father here to deal with a council he didn't trust fought with every instinct I had, but he'd given me my orders.

"Oh, Princess, you look lovely," Aleinn murmured.

I did not doubt the seamstresses' skill. The dress was a masterful work of art—the midnight-blue fabric was so finely woven it shimmered, and the embroidery at the edge of the long skirt swirled with a life of its own. But I had always had a hard time with dresses. Formal gowns were the worst: the skirts were heavier and the bodices tighter, and they weren't made to stash weapons.

I'd once tried to explain to Aleinn the reason I often wore trousers around the castle, but she couldn't understand why I would need to reach a knife strapped to my ankle. My point was that if something happened, I couldn't get to it if I was laced tightly into a dress.

My mind snapped back to the present when the shorter seamstress fingered my golden braid, still wet, at my back.

"Princess, we can help set your hair so it won't cover the

jewels at the collar. You are planning on leaving it down for the ball, aren't you? Take it down now, and we can see how it will accent the dress."

I shifted and clenched my hands into fists to keep from wiping them against the fine fabric of my skirt. "My braid reminds me of my mother. I think I ought to have a bit of her with me on my birthday, don't you?"

A tiny trickle of sweat started between my shoulders. It had been ages since anyone had questioned me about why I didn't let Aleinn style my hair. When I was young, my mother had always arranged it. After her death, I'd insisted on taking care of it myself. The servants looked at me funny, and the nobility laughed behind my back at the simplicity of my appearance—I'd managed to master only a handful of styles that hid the streak, and none of them were appropriate for the announcement of a betrothal. Still, everyone seemed to accept it as one more oddity about the princess who didn't act as they thought a princess should.

But would they be so forgiving in Turia? My ribs ached against my lacings. I'd be married to the prince heir. I'd be a queen, eventually. There was no way I'd be able to convince the Turians to let me arrange my own hair.

The shorter seamstress pursed her lips, still staring at the neckline like she hadn't heard my reply, and started unlacing the fine silver chain at the front of the bodice. "Miss Aleinn, could you help us?"

My mouth went dry. "Wh-why are you unlacing?"

They all ignored me.

"The glass beads on the bodice were imported from the Continent and chosen specifically to match your eyes," Aleinn said as she came to stand behind me. "They'll be wasted if your hair covers them."

I'd been told I had my mother's eyes—ice blue with a ring of navy around the iris. The beads glimmered with the same intensity.

"We need to see where your hair falls at the back," the seamstress said, nodding to Aleinn, who reached for the tie at the end of my braid.

"I know the most wonderful style that would suit this dress perfectly. Perhaps I could arrange your hair—just for tonight, since it *is* your birthday," Aleinn said. "We'll make sure no one can resist you," she added with that new knowing gleam in her eyes again.

I did want to dance with Cris, but with Ren's fresh warning, I knew I couldn't let my secret out, even if I was leaving tomorrow.

My breaths came fast as I tried to think of an excuse that wouldn't raise more suspicion. A strange feeling started between my stomach and my rib cage. It was almost like the sensation you get from sitting too long on the hard chairs in the library. Like when you land on your back with the wind knocked out of you. It wasn't exactly painful, but it startled me enough that I sucked in a breath and lost my balance on the stool. Time seemed to slow as I fell, and the strange feeling spread.

"Easy, Princess. You won't get out of it that easily." The taller seamstress caught me before I made a complete disaster of everything. And with her words, the strange feeling dissipated like smoke in the wind. It had felt so substantial, yet it fled like a dream.

All the blood drained from my face. Aleinn gripped my arm,

holding me steady. "We can leave her hair as it is for now. The princess needs to rest before tonight."

Relief washed over me until the taller seamstress huffed.

"If you are finished, you are dismissed," Aleinn said with a wave of her hand.

But the shorter seamstress wasn't done. "We have been commissioned by King Shraeus to . . ."

I pulled my skirts closer to me and stared the woman down. She stepped away one pace, a hint of fear in her eyes. I took a breath to make sure my voice was steady.

"You will address my attendant with the respect she deserves. You may finish, or I'll go as I am."

"Of course, Princess," she mumbled, unwilling to directly disobey my orders. They laced the silver chain back into place and checked the hem one last time before gathering their things and scurrying into the hall.

An ache bloomed behind my eyes, and my legs shook under the added weight of the skirts. "Could you dismiss everyone else as well?" I asked Aleinn in a faint voice. "They can return once the dance has begun."

Aleinn shooed everyone else out, and finally my chambers were calm. I brushed a dressing robe aside and eased into a chair near the blazing fireplace, careful not to slouch—not that I could. My thoughts flew over what had happened, and the feeling that had dissipated so quickly.

"Jennesara, are you well?" Aleinn glanced at my braid and fidgeted with her skirt.

I brushed my hair over my shoulder and steadied my voice. "I'm fine. Just a little nervous, I suppose."

"I . . ." She swallowed, and I hated that her eyes stayed on the floor at my feet. "I'm sorry for pushing. I thought perhaps Lord Cris might—"

"I'm going to Turia because my father signed a betrothal agreement with the prince heir," I blurted out. I shook my head and rubbed my forehead. The fire crackled in the silence. When I could finally meet Aleinn's eyes, they were laced with pity. "It's for the best," I added in a whisper, the clamp over my heart tightening.

"The best for who?" she asked, her hands folded in front of her, her voice so gentle it made me want to cry.

My lips twisted as I tamped down the pain of my father's deception. "For everyone." I sniffed and stood a little too fast, making my head spin. "I'll arrange my hair more suitably and make sure the jewels aren't covered," I said. A dismissal.

She walked to the door and paused. "Princess, I didn't mean to . . ."

I fiddled with the end of my braid, a sad smile lifting one side of my lips. "I know."

✦ ✦ ✦

The sky slid from pink to purple to black as I stood at the tiny slit of a window in the sitting room of my chambers between two open trunks, their contents spilling out. The ball would start soon, followed by the announcement. I'd leave in the morning. And nothing would ever be the same.

For once, I looked the part of a princess, in my midnight-blue and silver confection. Sparkling glass beads trailed the seams of the bodice, and the snowy-white blouse underneath was of the finest linen, with flowing sleeves and long cuffs at my wrists. The traditional navy-blue medallions with the royal sword and shield engraved on them were pinned to the fabric just under my collarbone, and three strands of sparkling sapphires were strung between the medallions.

My hair ran in an elaborate plait from one temple to the opposite ear, with the long tail pinned up. By the time I placed the unadorned silver circlet on my head, I didn't look like myself. I didn't feel like myself.

The tethers called to me, but I dismissed my brother's and father's, instead focusing on a third. I ached for my mother, and even though what was left of her tether wasn't much, I treasured it.

I didn't have many memories of her, but I still remembered feeling her tether break, though I was only three. After a week of travel, we'd played in the frigid ocean in Osta, her hometown, the last morning before we left for Hálenborg. The white cliffs had sparkled as much as the sun glinting off the waves, and the seabirds dove in and out of the water, their silver-tipped wings slicing through the air.

Halfway to home, we set up our tents. The moon was high when I awoke with a terrible feeling. Messengers came and went through the night, trying to find a healer, as my mother's health rapidly declined without warning. Her maids banned me from her tent, for fear I'd catch the mysterious illness myself, so I snuck around the back. If I could just see that she was okay, I thought, maybe the strange feeling inside me would go away.

I peeked through the canvas and saw her lying on a bed of pillows, her face ashen, deep purple rings beneath her eyes, her golden hair fanned out around her. I crept in and curled next to her. She'd brushed her hand weakly over my hair then and made me promise to hide the white streak.

I watched over her all night, helpless against the sickness within her. Minutes before dawn, the delicate tether connecting us snapped, and she was gone. I'd wailed at the pain I felt. I was confused, alone. The servants assumed I was distraught because my mother was gone. But it was the snapped tether causing my cries, an injury I couldn't understand.

The broken thread lay deep within me even now, like a torn pennant over an empty battlefield, reminding me of an emptiness that used to be full. Reminding me of how it felt to lose someone I loved.

A tap at my door brought my focus back.

"Enter," I called, knowing who was waiting in the hall.

My father came in and stood next to the chair by the fire, his hands behind his back. I watched the stars brighten the dark sky.

The silence lengthened between us, but I didn't push his tether away like I usually did. In the stillness, his emotions settled into the deep ache of longing. Beneath the weight of his kingdom, his steel and harsh angles, he was a man who desperately missed his wife. I looked more like her now than ever, and he was about to say goodbye to me, too. I didn't speak; I couldn't. I understood him more in that moment than I had in years.

"I have a present for you." He held out a long bundle wrapped in silk so fine it flowed like water.

I stared at him, wishing things could be different, that I could stay. "A present?"

"With the fighting moving deeper into our borders, I need to know you will be safe crossing into Turia—"

"Because sending Ren and General Leland wasn't enough?" I said as I came to stand in front of him.

His shoulder lifted in a shrug. "I had these pulled from the treasury for you."

He settled the bundle on the sofa in front of us and pulled one side of the faded cloth away, then the other. An old sword sheathed in a tattered brown scabbard lay within. My eyes landed on the hilt. A clear blue stone embedded in the cross guard emitted a soft glow.

My father carefully unsheathed the sword, and the chaotic mounds of unpacked clothes around us faded away. The steel-blue blade wasn't overly long, and was so intricately etched it looked almost as if it were made of stone. Ancient leather strips wrapped the hilt. Tied to one of the leather strips was a ring, with a smaller version of the stone from the sword and the same intricate carvings.

"It's beautiful," I breathed. "I've never seen anything like it." I tentatively put my hand out, silently asking my father for permission.

He nodded, a hint of a smile in his eyes.

I gripped the sword by the hilt. It was lighter than I expected, but perfectly balanced. I drew the blade closer so I could inspect the markings. The blue stone seemed to brighten, but the heat in my hand as I hefted the weight distracted me from the light. I stepped back and swung the sword a few times, as best I could in my dress. It felt like no sword I had ever wielded—it was almost an extension of my arm.

"And the ring, Jennesara." My father slid it onto the middle finger of my left hand. Something like a lightning bolt raced up my arm and into my chest.

My brow furrowed at the perfect fit, and my father chuckled. "What are these gifts, Father?"

He nodded toward the sword, hands clasped behind his back again. "They are ancient artifacts passed down through the line of kings. These particular pieces are rumored to have belonged to Kais."

My eyes widened, and I gripped the gift tighter. The first king of Hálendi had been a powerful enough mage to enchant the border between Hálendi and the Ice Deserts. These were his? What else was hidden in the treasury?

He pointed out the engravings running the length of the blade. "These runes tell of the powers this instrument yields. Here at the tip, swiftness and power to strike true." My father's finger trailed down the markings toward the hilt. "These speak of destruction, of protection when wielded by one in the line of Hálendian kings."

My father took my left hand and held the ring up between us. "This can absorb and store magic. The sword can then wield that energy."

"The magic is in North Watch, though, not in Turia. Why not send these with Ren?"

My father sighed and . . . did he glance at my hair? "The Medallion of Sight will be enough for him. Besides, I gave these to your mother when we were wed. She would want you to have them."

My thoughts jumped and tumbled over each other as I tried

to take in the revelation, as I pulled the sword closer to my body. I took a breath and a leap of courage. "Mother could wield magic with this?"

He let my hand drop, his sadness raining against me through the tethers. His eyes grew distant. "She wore them always, but there was no opportunity for her to harness magic. But you—" He swallowed, and his nervous energy had my fingers tapping against my leg. "You can."

My heart pounded so loud I could barely hear him. "I can . . . what?"

He sighed. Glanced back at the door. "I know, Jennesara." He touched the white streak in his hair. My lips parted, and I almost choked.

"All this time?" I whispered.

He didn't smile, but his expression softened. "I'm your father. Of course I knew."

"But . . ." My mind ground to a halt. "You kept me here. I thought you'd have to banish me if—"

"I'd never."

He sat on the chair behind him as though his legs couldn't bear the weight of his words. Because he sort of *was* banishing me.

"I kept you from learning about magic to protect you," he said. "Kept you close so rumors wouldn't spread. It maybe wasn't the best way to keep you safe, but it was all I could do." He ran his fingers through his hair and smiled. "I'm proud of you. You are a daughter of Hálendi, and you will bring us honor in Turia."

Tears pricked the corners of my eyes. Years of memories

shifted in my mind, changing him from an overbearing, strict man trying to control me to a father desperate to protect me.

I sheathed the blade, then threw my arms around him. "Thank you," I whispered. "For the gift."

He embraced me tight, and I inhaled his scent, which reminded me of childhood, of safety, of strength. He held me at arm's length.

My mouth opened and closed, and I laughed a little. "Tell me *everything*."

His chuckle rumbled in his chest, and he gestured to the sofa so we could sit comfortably.

"I don't think we'll have time to cover quite that much," he said, and I shook my head, remembering the dance. The betrothal. But he continued speaking, and all other thoughts fled. "What's most important, though, is that everything has a force within it that makes it what it is, whether it be person, animal, or element. This energy, this life force, has always existed in our world. It has from the beginning and will until the end. It cannot be created or destroyed, but it can be manipulated."

I leaned forward, eager to learn about this after a lifetime of being forbidden. "And this 'energy' is magic?"

"Those who are said to have 'magic,' as it is termed, are simply those who possess the ability to manipulate the energies around them. Everyone experiences magic differently, and it is up to you to learn how you can harness it. Usually, but not always, one type of life force connects with your magic more than others."

So even if my father had told me he knew of my magic before now, it wasn't as if he could have told me how to coax it out and test its potential. That would have had to be done on my own. I'd asked Ren once, when we were younger, how he learned magic, and he'd tried to describe it then, but I hadn't understood. I thought he'd been keeping it from me on purpose, but perhaps it was too personal to really be able to share.

I fingered the leather strips on the hilt. I couldn't move mountains or heal someone. Were the tethers even magic? Or just a curse?

"I—" I swallowed, not sure I could force the words out after keeping them inside for so long. "My magic is different than that," I said, and my father leaned forward, hands on his knees. "I can sense emotions. Not everyone's," I hurried to add. "Just yours and Ren's. And Mother's, when she was alive."

He blinked, and his mouth hung open. Then he snapped it closed. "So all this time, you could . . ." I nodded, and he huffed out a sigh. "Well." A slow smile started.

"Sorry?"

He shook his head and laughed a little, then folded his arms like he always did when he was pondering something. "It could be a remnant of Kais's bond. He created a magical connection to his family so he could always know when they were in danger or needed protection. Perhaps you were meant to have this so you could stay close to us while in Turia."

I nodded as he spoke, remembering times when Ren had been in trouble or my father particularly worried.

"Nothing else?" my father asked. "No other form of magic has manifested? Not moving earth or healing or . . . ?"

I shook my head. "No, just the tethers. The bond. But maybe with this"—I held up the sword—"I'll be able to do more."

He slowly shook his head. "I don't think so. These tools can only channel and store magic. There is no more and no less magic within you than there has always been." He swallowed. "I should have prepared you more. I thought we'd contain the trouble at the border. . . ."

My fingers traced the old scabbard and the blue stone. I couldn't be disappointed about this. I wouldn't. If I had to travel to Turia and leave everything behind, at least I'd be taking a piece of my mother with me.

He cleared his throat and stood, the mantle of king falling around his shoulders once again. "I hope you'll never have to fight with these, but I need to know you'll be safe on your way to Turia. Master Hafa will accompany you as your protector, and train you with your new weapon."

My eyebrows shot up. "Ren, General Leland, Kais's sword, *and* Master Hafa?"

His expression remained stoic, but his eyes sparkled. "You *will* be safe on your journey." He held out his hand to help me stand, and I took it.

I tugged on a loose strip of leather on the hilt. "Can I wear it tonight?" I asked, holding the sword up a little.

"No," he said immediately.

"It was worth a try," I said as I tucked it under the sofa cushion, where I stored my other sword.

He held out his elbow and I slipped my hand through.

He paused before he opened the door. "You look beautiful tonight, Jennesara," he said, and with a sad smile he led me toward my last Hálendian celebration.

✦✦✦

The ballroom was the most ornate room in the austere castle, with a large fireplace at either end, elaborate silver sconces along the wall, and a gray marble floor with silver and navy veins.

The glittering lights, cascading music, and swirling gowns paired with charcoal-gray double-buttoned coats counted down my last night in Hálendi. My last night home.

I usually avoided anything that involved courtiers scrutinizing me and finding me lacking, but tonight I would show my people who I was. That I was loyal to my brother and to Hálendi. The work the seamstresses did was worth it, given the approving looks I received from even the most judgmental nobles.

As always, Ren looked stately in his navy coat with the band collar and two rows of silver buttons marching down the front. He also had the traditional Hálendian medallions at his shoulders, three silver chains strung between them. Courtiers surrounded him the entire night—women in general, and Lady Isarr in particular—but every now and then, he'd catch my eye and his admiration and pride burned in the tethers.

Time both stretched interminably and flew by. I longed to catch Cris's eye. Even if only for one dance, I wanted one memory I could hold on to from my last night home. But he always seemed to be on the far side of the room as I was swept up by one courtier after another.

My taut neck ached as much as my feet by the time my father signaled me off the dance floor for the announcement. Ren met me on my way to the dais, with a brief brush of his fingers to his chin before his hand was at my back. *Chin up, Jenna.* I nodded in acknowledgment, my brother's words repeating in my mind as my father rose from his seat and Ren took his place at our father's right. All eyes turned to the dais, and conversations died in every corner of the room.

"Tonight, we celebrate the seventeenth year of my beloved daughter, Jennesara." My father looked down, his hard features softening in the flickering candlelight.

Everyone clapped politely. Whispers filtered through the room. I straightened my shoulders under the scrutiny and took a deep breath, willing my nervousness to calm. I could not—would not—show any weakness.

I studied faces, wishing I could pick out the person my father shouldn't trust. Wishing my bond, my magic, could ferret out the traitor in our midst.

"It is also my great joy to announce a new opportunity for Hálendi, one that will further bolster our great nation in these trying times."

The whispers that had started died out.

"I am proud and pleased to announce the betrothal of my daughter, Princess Jennesara of Hálendi, to Prince Enzo of Turia."

There was a breath of silence, a swell of anticipation before the wave crashed into exclamations and whispered conversations. My eyes snapped to Cris, standing next to a beautiful courtier. His jaw was tight, and he wore a slight frown.

I tore my gaze from him, my face frozen somewhere between happy and complacent. It was too late—we'd never have a first dance. My heart beat faster as I realized how close the end really was. The end of the celebration. The end of my childhood.

My father put his arm around me. This was my duty. I

would perform it to exactness, and Hálendi's troops would get the support they needed. But every stare, every conversation, pressed down on me as I focused on the opposite wall.

My father's tether thrummed with anxiety, but also with something softer. He cleared his throat and raised the arm that wasn't around my shoulders.

"Please join me in toasting not only the princess's birthday, but her betrothal, and the strengthening of Hálendi!"

As the masses clapped and cheered, I lifted my chin and smiled like I had just conquered the world. But inside, I was crumbling. My father knew about my magic. A traitor was hiding somewhere in the castle. Ren would soon be on the front lines facing magic he might not be able to fend off. Tomorrow I'd be gone.

Alone. To face an entire kingdom on my own.

CHAPTER FOUR

My carriage swayed one way, then the other, in a strange sort of dance to the beat of muffled hoofbeats against cobblestone. In twelve days, I'd be in a new home watching strangers unpack my belongings.

The journey wasn't long enough to fill in all the gaps, but I'd spent my life reading about the world beyond Hálenborg, and I was finally getting to experience it on my own. Well, without an entire kingdom watching, anyway.

"Princess," Aleinn admonished for the third time as the carriage rumbled over the main road out of Hálenborg. "They will see you gawking at them."

I pulled away from the narrow pane of glass a little, but my eyes never left the streets outside. "What if this is the last time I see my city? My home?"

She rested her hand on my knee. "I'm sure you'll return."

The stark image of my room as I'd left it played in my mind. Bits and pieces of my life not deemed worthy to accompany me to Turia in scattered mounds. The sputtering fire in the blackened grate losing the fight against the unusually cold morning. I bit my lip. "It won't be the same."

Aleinn sat back again, burrowing into the cushions. "Nothing is ever the same, even from one day to the next."

But I'd caught her taking one last look at the sights as well. Early this morning, she'd said goodbye to her brother and given him a letter to give to their parents. She'd squeezed him tight and told him to mind the stable master. Her hands were trembling when she'd let him go.

She was accompanying me only until I was settled. Then she'd return. Then I'd let her go.

"I guess you're right," I said with a small smile. "But I still don't want to miss it."

She sighed and took up some mending while I watched the city awaken. Seeing the early stirrings was new for me, as I'd only been allowed into Hálenborg a few times, on big market days and for the celebrations of first and last frost after I'd turned eleven.

Doorways flicked by, brightly painted smears in a wash of gray buildings that merged with a blanket of gray clouds in the sky. Spring's first flowers struggling against the extra chill peeked out of window boxes. I caught snippets of men and women bundled in thick coats, their fair hair covered with warm hats, working at one task or another to prepare for the day. It was only a flash of their life as our caravan passed, a slice of who they were.

We passed a bold yellow door, and I sat forward, craning my neck until the door was out of sight. I let loose a little whoop. Aleinn raised her eyebrows, her needle paused midstitch.

My breath fogged a corner of the window. "This is the farthest I've been from the castle since my mother died."

Aleinn's lips pursed like she was trying not to smile. She finally set her mending aside with a shake of her head and leaned closer so we could look out the window together. "And now *this* is the farthest," she said, and bumped my shoulder with hers.

I chuckled. "You're full of wisdom today, aren't you?"

She tilted her head. "I'm always full of wisdom. You are just too busy swinging a sword or running to the library to notice."

I opened my mouth to respond, but I had no rebuttal. She wasn't wrong.

We were both so engrossed in the passing view, we both squeaked when a dark shape darted by. A horse and rider—Cris. My cheeks heated, but he didn't look in. Of course he wouldn't. Earlier this morning before we'd left, I'd caught his eye and sent him a tight smile. He'd looked away as if he hadn't seen.

The courtyard of the castle was brimming for our departure—with horses snorting white puffs and churning up the new grass, men and women calling to each other, runners going back into the castle for that last item that hadn't been packed. My father stood back, studying the chaos from afar. He'd given me a stiff hug and handed me into the carriage, formal to the last.

"Look!" Aleinn pointed with a laugh. A dog with curly black hair and his tongue hanging from the side of his mouth trotted next to the carriage, barking and leaping at our entourage. I pressed my face to the glass to keep him in sight longer. I silently cursed the barrier between me and the world, and vowed I wouldn't spend every day of our travels behind yet another wall.

✦✦✦

The city was long behind us when we stopped for our midday meal. There was no village nearby, so we pulled to the side of the road. I opened the door and hopped from the carriage before it stopped rolling. A sharp wind whipped through my braid as I filled my lungs and stretched under the open sky.

I turned in a slow circle, marveling at the vastness, at the emptiness extending in every direction. Only a few patches of low, scrubby trees stood in the whole landscape. Jagged rocks and tiny purple-and-white wildflowers stuck up from the yellowed grasses still bent with the weight of winter. Gently rolling hills mirrored the clouds, a sea of waves above and below. In the deepest shadows, bits of crusty snow hid from spring's grasp. Our party, which had clogged the streets of Hálenborg and filled the castle grounds with enough noise to make the dogs howl, was only a speck here.

The sense of freedom was intoxicating. But if I wanted to be free of my barriers when we started traveling again, I'd need permission.

General Leland stood chatting with Master Hafa, Ren, and Cris. The general never seemed to be alone, so if I wanted to ask, I'd have to interrupt their conversation.

"May I ride Gentry instead of in the carriage?" I asked the general, as I was eager to get on my palomino.

Everyone except Cris stared at me; he found something near his boot to inspect, adding a sheen of awkwardness to the answering silence.

My insides twisted and squirmed. I sounded like a five-year-old asking to play in the snow, but a half day of being cooped up was enough. I was finally out of the castle, and I wanted to breathe the world in—the wind freezing my ears, the brisk pine scent, the dappled shadows and bright sunlight. Everything.

General Leland took off his riding gloves and rubbed his jaw. "It would be an easier journey if you stayed in the carriage."

Easier for me or for them? I folded my arms, careful not to shiver as a gust of wind lifted the skirt of my dress. "I won't slow anyone down. I won't complain."

Ren's tether sparked with a bouncing feeling that always made me think he was laughing inside.

"Yes," Master Hafa interjected. "It would be best if you remained where you were."

"You'll stand out in all that finery," Leland added, to get in the last word. He motioned to the dress and cloak Aleinn had chosen for me.

"I'll wear a guards' uniform," I replied. "Surely someone has an extra."

The others in the party wore a finely woven undershirt below a thick wool shirt, and a heavy tunic overtop belted over thick trousers, with a cloak to protect from the weather. I tamped down the smirk fighting to emerge—their clothing was much more suited to traveling.

"She's fooling us all, you know," my brother cut in. "She doesn't care about riding. She just wants to wear trousers."

I jabbed my elbow into Ren as he and his best friend snickered. Cris's laugh had an edge that hadn't been there before. My teeth ground together. None of this was my fault. I was tired of everyone acting like it was.

"My brother will ride by my side," I offered. Ren started

to protest, and I glared at him. "He owes me a favor," I said slowly, enunciating each word. The sting of his knowing about my betrothal before I did was still there; he owed me about a thousand favors.

Ren swatted his gloves against his trousers and nodded once. "I'll stay with her."

Leland couldn't contradict the prince heir, but he frowned with fatherly concern. "You must ride close to the carriage," he said. "I won't have you getting lost."

I clasped my hands together, my head bobbing.

Master Hafa folded his arms across his chest but didn't object, and I breathed a tiny sigh of relief. No one ever contradicted Hafa, not even my father. I didn't think any amount of pleading would get him to change his mind once it was set.

General Leland reached out his hand to strike a bargain. He tightened his grip before I could let go. "Your father wouldn't want anything to happen to you."

I tightened my own grip. "I'll be fine, General, but thank you for your concern."

✦ ✦ ✦

Gentry danced under me as we resumed our trek south. I patted her golden neck and breathed deep, settling my own excitement. The carriage lumbered along in front of us, and a persistent breeze nipped at my cheeks.

"I owe you?" Ren asked as he brought his horse next to mine. The others gave us our space, riding several lengths away.

I raised my eyebrows and shrugged. "You owe me a lot of

favors. I'm just cashing in now. I figured you'd be *happy* to escort me as we ride toward my *betrothed*."

He chuckled, and clucked for his stallion to match the carriage's pace. Gentry followed his lead, leaving me free to close my eyes and tilt my face to the sky. I'd always wondered if I'd feel different away from home, truly free from the castle walls that kept me contained.

The answer was more complicated than I'd expected. I was still me, but *I'd* expanded as well, to fit more of the world inside.

"You won't be smiling by the end of the day, you know," Ren said. He shifted in his saddle.

I grinned wider. "I don't care if I'm smiling or not, as long as I don't have to get back in the carriage." Huge black birds circled high above, but other than the grasses in the wind, the entire landscape remained still. I glanced behind us. "Can . . . can we talk?"

Ren smirked. "The day would be long indeed if we didn't converse at least a little."

I rolled my eyes and lowered my voice until it barely carried beyond the dirt crunching beneath our horse's hooves. "Father knew—I mean, he knows about my magic."

Ren's head jerked. He blinked and adjusted the reins in his grip, resettling his prancing horse. "Are you sure?"

I nodded. "He told me when he gave me Mother's sword and ring."

He flapped his mouth a few times, looking for a response. "I . . . Glaciers."

"Yeah. But I don't know what I'm supposed to do with the gifts. He said the ring could absorb magic, and the sword could wield it. But the tethers—"

"Aren't really something you can manipulate," he finished for me. He rubbed his jaw with one hand.

"What does healing feel like for you?"

My brother's magic, though a big part of his life, was a taboo topic between us. We'd been so young when I'd plied him for information. I'd thought that since he was the heir and I was technically his competition, he'd been confusing on purpose, and I hadn't asked again.

He'd healed my arm once when I'd broken it after he dared me to jump from a tree, but other than having felt the searing heat from his hand over my bone, I knew only what I could glean from the courtiers' gossip. But now, after my father had told me everyone experiences magic differently, I was desperate to learn more.

"It feels . . ." He touched his torso, between his heart and his stomach. "It feels like rushing."

"Rushing?" I asked.

He returned both hands to the reins. "Like when you're galloping as fast as you can? Or when you get the final hit on a tough opponent?"

I nodded slowly. There was no better feeling than winning a sparring match.

"It's like that, but more focused."

"When did you first notice it? And how did you know what type of magic you had? Why—"

"Whoa," he said, and his horse flicked his ears back and jerked to a stop.

My laugh rang out. Ren settled back in his saddle and grumbled something under his breath about sisters.

"Not a word," he muttered when he caught up to me. My

laugh turned to a cough, and I pressed my lips together. He dragged the silence out.

"Come on," I said. "You know you want to tell me."

He hid his smile and raised his eyebrows dramatically. "The first time I used magic was an accident."

My awareness of the rest of the party, of the wind riffling the grasses and my hair, faded to nothing.

"I'd scraped my knee after Father's horse tossed me—"

I snorted. "The one you were forbidden to ride?"

"Exactly," he said, chuckling. "I sat on the ground, stunned, with a bleeding knee, and something moved inside me. I thought I was going to be sick, but instead, this rushing, twisting feeling spread to my knees. My skin knit itself back together faster than Hafa could best Lady Isarr."

I snorted and adjusted my seat to relieve my already aching hips. "Okay, but then how did you figure out how to heal others?"

He shrugged, a little put out I hadn't made the proper exclamations of wonder. "Father encouraged me to practice with it, and once I was fully aware of the magic within me, it became easy to focus and direct it."

Of course it would be easy for him. I shook the bitterness away, keeping my features smooth. "But you still had to train?"

He swatted at a bug buzzing near his face. "Father once said it's like a muscle, one you have to exercise to improve."

We rode in silence a few paces. I played with the end of my braid. "So Father can't end the fighting at the border on his own?"

Ren nodded, shoulders drooping. "Father asked me to try

to do other sorts of magic, working with the elements, like he can, or moving objects. But nothing came as naturally as healing."

My mind churned over this new information. "But you *could* do other things?"

"Not very well. Father said that some things were more willing to change than others, and that some things responded better to a certain person than others. A lot of knowledge about magic has been lost over time—we have only bits and pieces of what used to be known. Father told me of a historian who studied magic, but most of his works aren't in our library."

We were the kingdom known for our magic; why weren't they in *our* library? I guided my horse around a patch of mud. Maybe it was good they weren't—I didn't know when I'd get to return home. Would Turia's library have more than a row or two of books on magic?

My stomach dropped like a falling icicle. The palace awaiting me at the end of these twelve days—specifically the prince who lived in the palace—was not something I wanted to dwell on.

The wind picked up, brushing my braid over my shoulder, and a few drops of water splashed onto my cheek.

"Oh, you've done it now, Jenna," my brother said as he snatched the hood of his cloak and jammed it over his head. "You think Hafa will let *me* ride in the carriage?"

I raised my own hood as the rain began to pound down so hard I had to speak louder to be heard. "Hafa would let you, but I doubt Aleinn would."

My brother directed his horse closer to mine, so that we rode knee to knee. "I'd rather be out here anyway," he said in a low voice as I wiped rain from my face and tugged my hood lower.

Twelve days. Only one more with Ren.

For the first time, I wished I could send my emotions back through the tethers so my brother and father could feel all my love. “Me too,” I murmured.

✦ ✦ ✦

When you had to stay within the outer walls of the castle, there wasn’t much motivation to perfect the art of riding. Ren was right—by the time evening fell, I desperately wanted to get off my horse.

The rain finally let up an hour before we came to a small town of thatch-covered roundhouses. Ren and I had talked of everything and nothing, reliving memories for as long as we could, avoiding the uncertain future that sprawled before us. We didn’t speak of North Watch or the note.

We’d passed a few villages, tucked into valleys away from the incessant wind. There were also cattle ranges and glimpses of small farms. Old-fashioned turf houses—their bright doors peeking out from the mounds that hid them—dotted the countryside the closer we came to the town.

When Leland finally called us to a halt in front of a tiny roundhouse with a beautifully carved sign planted in front of it, I almost fell off my horse in my haste to dismount. I leaned on Gentry, patting her side while surreptitiously stretching my back.

“Told you,” Ren whispered as he led his horse to the stables in the back. I was too tired to kick mud at him.

Instead, I let the inn's groom take Gentry's reins and lead her away. The scents of roasted meat and onions and carrots and spices—sure to be a warm stew—wafted through the open door, and a warm orange glow beckoned.

I didn't think I could take a single step, but my stomach got my feet moving toward the inn. Then a dark shape stepped in front of me, and I skidded to a stop.

"Tonight we train, Princess." Master Hafa stood there stoically with his hand on the hilt of his sword.

All the excuses inside me died along with my hope for a warm fire anytime soon. I'd forgotten that my father had said Hafa would train me with my sword.

What was left of the day was fading fast. Yet if this was the price for riding, I'd pay it. He led me around the roundhouse to a small pen for horses. The whole thing was mud.

I placed my fist on the opposite shoulder and bowed respectfully. I reached for my sword, but Hafa shook his head.

"We will wait to train with that until we are farther from Hálenborg," he said as he picked up two wooden practice swords from where they leaned against the fence, handed them both to me, and gestured to the makeshift ring.

Farther from Hálenborg. Even here, the farthest I'd ever been from the castle, the burned note followed me. And the lack of trust among my father's advisors. Would that distrust extend all the way to Turia?

I delved inside for my tethers. Ren's was strong and steady, an anchor as always. Distance had rendered my father's tether duller, a murmur of what it usually was. But he was safe. He was well.

I shrugged off my cloak and overcoat, unbuckled my own

sword, and gingerly set these to the side. Master Hafa sent two guards, Geoff and Melsa, into the ring. I'd fought them both before, beat them both. But never at the same time.

My opponents adjusted their stances, moving to the balls of their feet and assessing me. I assessed them in turn when I joined them. They came forward, and I went back, matching them step for step in the deep muck of the field. My legs were already trembling. But Master Hafa's words reverberated within: *In a real fight, the goal is to end it as soon as possible.*

The ache in my body kept my mind from falling into focus. I paced the perimeter, keeping my wooden swords ready and my attackers at a distance. I needed to disarm one, or somehow get them so close together that they would trip themselves up.

My back brushed against a rough fence. Before I could move away, I felt something hard being tucked into the back of my trousers.

My lips twitched. Both attackers started toward me. Instead of engaging, I took two quick steps to the side, then threw one of my swords at Geoff's shoulder with a grunt.

"Whoa!" He lurched in the other direction but managed to reach across his body to knock my sword away. Before it had even hit the mud, I gripped the wooden dagger that had been slipped into my waistband and launched it at his hand. Geoff dropped his sword and fell backward into the sludge with a shout.

Melsa ran at me, swinging her blade at my chest. I blocked her attack and twisted, swiping her feet out from under her and pressing my remaining sword to her throat.

Mud dripping from my knees, I looked up in triumph at Master Hafa, but he only scowled at me, his steel-gray eyes flashing.

"Jennesara, you cannot cheat in real battle. And Atháren"—he turned to address my brother, who was watching us with a grin—"you will not always be there to help your sister. Both of you, run to the river and back!"

"But," Ren started, "it's nearly dinner—"

"Twice," Hafa said, ending the debate.

Ren clamped his mouth shut. I tossed my practice sword to Geoff and took off. A frigid wind sliced through my wool shirt and burned my lungs. But as punishments went, running wasn't so bad.

By the time we had returned, the sun had set and we were both covered in mud and sweat. But my legs and back didn't hurt quite so much. We hadn't spoken much during our run, but the bittersweet feeling coming through Ren's tether told me enough. This would be the last time we'd run together like this.

When we entered the tiny roundhouse, most of our party was lounging on cushions, eating and playing games. The noise of so many people crammed into such a small space rang in my ears. Ren sat with Cris in a circle of guards between the fire in the center of the room and the door. I sat next to Aleinn near the fire and slurped up a meaty stew; it was simple, but better than I'd had in ages.

I surreptitiously watched everyone, intrigued yet overwhelmed by how easily they laughed and spoke with each other. This kind of casualness, I'd never seen. In the palace, formality ruled, a precise respect. But out here . . . everyone was relaxed. I liked it.

✦✦✦

I didn't dream that night. When it was full dark a shot of anticipation coursed through me, and I jolted awake. I stayed still. Aleinn's elbow was sharp in my back.

My focus tightened on the tethers. My father was calm. Asleep, probably. Ren fairly bounced inside me. I didn't need the low embers of the fire to pick out his movement through the room as he and five guards snuck their way to the door.

Once they'd gone, I eased away from Aleinn, tucking the blanket tight around her. I stood under the front eave of the doorway and watched as Ren and his men gathered their horses and moved silently around the inn, ghosts in gray uniforms leading black demons through the night.

A rustle of clothing sounded behind me. Cris brushed by on his way out of the roundhouse, his pack over his shoulder, the last of the group. I reached out, grabbing his arm. The contact sent a shiver through me, but I held tight. He gazed down at me, his normally bright eyes now shadowy caverns in the night, jaw tight.

"Look out for him, Cris," I whispered. "Keep him safe."

Cris's shoulders rose and fell with a deep breath, but his arm relaxed under my grip. "I will." He swallowed hard enough that I could see his throat move.

Ren spotted us and jogged over. Cris nodded farewell and went to ready his horse.

"It's almost time." Ren put his arm around my shoulder, but his attention flitted between me and the men he'd be traveling with.

"I'll miss you," I whispered as a shudder coursed down my spine. The evening's chill was seeping through my sleep-warmed layers.

Ren's arm tightened as he leaned his head against mine. "I'll miss you too, Jenna."

"Be safe. Come home." My breath hitched on the last word, before I ducked my head.

"I promise."

He kissed my forehead and pulled away first, knowing I might never let him go. He didn't say anything more, just brushed his knuckles under my chin—*chin up, Jenna*—walked to his horse, mounted, and rode into the night. Just before he passed through the inn's gate and out of sight, he turned, waved once, and touched his hand to his middle.

I turned my focus inward and reached for his tether. His hope, his excitement, his worry, and, most of all, his love for me flowed in like warmth and pure light—a farewell stronger than any words would have been.

When he'd blended into the darkness, I touched the small rectangle in my pocket, brushing the soft cover of the little book. I hoped Ren's parting gift would be more interesting than useful.

Branches screeched against each other at the edge of the property, and I worried that wouldn't be the case. I'd heard tales of the Wild: how it spit out anyone who tried to leave the road and traverse its depths. Or, worse, how the few who'd managed to enter it had never returned.

A deep breath calmed my fluttering pulse. We'd stay on the road. We'd be safe.

Four more days through Hálendi's villages and fields. Four through the thinnest part of the Wild. Three to Turiana. Eleven days to the prince—and to the library where I would find my answers.

In the Throne Room

The laugh lines etched around the king's eyes and mouth were faint, unused in recent years. He sat surrounded by gilded smiles and too much wine and the faintly metallic scent of rotting fish that had invaded his palace yet again.

The unyielding stone of his throne bit into him despite the cushions he replaced monthly. Yet he didn't lower himself from his dais, didn't partake in the revelry of his court. Instead, he watched from his rightful place. From above.

A door opened at the side of the hall, and the king's hands clenched. Advisor Blaire scurried across the throne room, robes twisted in his fists, a sheen of sweat glinting in the dim light filtering in through grimy windows.

Blaire was a man who might have been handsome once, but he'd spent too long giving in to the desires of others, losing too many pieces of himself over the years. He was also shorter than the king, which was part of the reason he had been chosen as an advisor—the king didn't have to be sitting on his dais to look down at him.

Blaire bent at the waist in a deep bow when he reached the edge of the platform. Too deep.

The king's beady eyes narrowed, and the lines around his mouth intensified. "Well?"

"Your Majesty, I am afraid—"

"You said you could reach the mages, Blaire," he said, his voice dangerously low. The king took a controlled breath and looked down at his fingernails digging into his palm.

"One messenger has returned from the Ice Deserts." Blaire bowed his head. He wiped his sweaty hands down his robe. "But only one. And he is . . ."

"What?" the king snapped.

Blaire swallowed. "He is unfit to be summoned to the throne, Your Majesty."

The king looked up, his gaze calculating and measuring. A smile stretched across his face. "Well then." He rose from his throne and nodded to the servant. "Take me to the messenger."

CHAPTER FIVE

General Leland was far from pleased to wake up to the prince heir and six of his men missing.

"Why would Shraeus command such a thing? It isn't *safe*." He paced at one end of the room, refusing to take a letter that Master Hafa was calmly holding out.

Most of the men and women had scattered to finish their preparations in the cool morning, rather than risk Leland's wrath. But I stayed, rolling up my sleeping mat as my insides rolled tighter as well. Not even Leland or Hafa knew of the plan?

I tied off my mat and closed my eyes, focusing on my father's tether. No spikes, no more worry than usual. Exhaustion dulled the edge of Ren's excitement, but nothing alarming there, either. I blew out a long, slow breath and stood.

"He says it was imperative Ren return right away," Master Hafa explained for the third time.

Leland glared at him. "We could send you after them."

"King Shraeus specifically asked me to stay with the

princess." Hafa glowered back. "And you know Hálendi can't afford any delay."

I ground my teeth and yanked yet another knot into the strip of leather around my mat. The dying fire popped in the oppressive silence as they glowered at each other. My father had planned Ren's departure like this for a reason. I couldn't let Leland intervene, no matter his good intentions.

My heart picked up speed, and I stood, brushing the dust from my hands. "Cris will watch out for him."

Leland stumbled over a fur someone had left in his path and stopped his frantic pacing, hands on his hips, facing the wall. He released a huge breath and turned to face Hafa. "We have our orders. We continue on."

Hafa jerked his head in a nod, but the tension between them didn't quite dissipate. I hoped my father had been right to send Ren away in secret.

✦✦✦

The crisp spring air warmed as we continued south. The grass poking out of the snow appeared green now instead of yellow, and the road had turned to mud. Then the rolling hills, filled with sheep and cattle, shifted into forest. It was early in the season for most travelers, and any that we did pass were wary of our large party of warriors and servants.

Leland led the way, still fuming and snapping at anyone who drew his eye. Hafa's perpetual scowl burned a hole in my back the entire morning. Everything ached.

When the sun had reached its peak, we stopped in the middle

of the road for our noon meal. Tall evergreens bordered either side, and big black birds assessed us from the branches while tiny squirrels chattered nearby.

I watched from afar as several people gathered small sticks and hewed logs, digging a small pit and lining it with rocks faster than I could ease my weary bones down to sit. The small bush growing next to me held tiny white flowers and a type of little red berry I'd never seen.

I pulled my book out of my pocket, reaching out for the tethers again. I'd lost track of how many times I'd checked in on my father and brother, but both were well, and the connection was still there, despite the distance between us.

I flipped through several pages, seeing if I could identify the plant, but my stomach rumbled, and I gave up searching through the tiny words and intricate pictures.

As I plucked a handful of berries from the branch, Hafa's foot connected with my wrist. Not hard, just enough to startle me into dropping them.

"I wouldn't touch those if I were you, Princess."

I shook out my hand. "Why not? They're beautiful."

He grunted. "Because those beautiful berries are poisonous."

I brushed every remnant from my palm and scooted away. "How can you tell?"

He pointed out the leaves, the color, and the clustering of the berries. "It's common sense," he muttered, and though I don't think I was meant to hear, I did.

My fingers tightened around my book. "It's not common sense *to me*." The words came out before I could stop them. Hafa raised an eyebrow. I swallowed and continued. "I only have ten days, Master Hafa," I said, a hint of the panic I was trying to keep suppressed leaking out.

His lips pursed into a thin line; then he let out a gusty sigh. He sat down, all grace and power, resting his forearms on his knees. "Being in the wilderness is exactly like a sparring match. But the opponent is Nature, and she'll kill you the first chance she gets. So pay attention to your surroundings." He studied me a moment, and I wasn't sure what he saw, but he called out to a small group of soldiers, who came to sit with us.

As the others settled, my already aching back stiffened. A rock was poking into my leg, and I was pretty sure half of my backside sat in a puddle. None of the men or women changed their demeanor even though I was part of the circle. They threw themselves to the ground, laughing about a story they'd been halfway through when Hafa had summoned them.

"And when I turned around, a giant bear sat right there on his haunches in front of the river, watching me undress!" The man telling the story—Thomas was his name—finished with a roar of laughter that echoed through the trees.

The others joined in while pulling out their meals from their saddlebags. A squirrel shrieked above us, and a shower of dirt and pine needles coated me. My bags were still on Gentry. I bit my lip, but as I looked down the road to where the horses were being fed and watered, I saw that someone else was taking care of her.

Story time halted while everyone's mouths stayed busy with the food. Except mine. Aleinn was preparing my meal near the front of the group, and suddenly I didn't know what to do with myself.

I cleared my throat and scooted out of the puddle. "What happened next?" I asked.

Thomas blinked a few times with a furrowed brow, his cheeks stuffed with bread.

I cleared my throat again. "With the bear, I mean." My eyes darted around the group. Everyone stared at me, the various bits of half-chewed food in their mouths seemingly forgotten. "How did you get away?"

Thomas swallowed his too-big chunk of bread with a wince. His eyes flicked to Hafa, who nodded almost imperceptibly.

"Well," he started, leaning forward. "The thing about bears is they don't like to be startled. So I did what any grown soldier would do." He paused, and a few snickers rolled along the edges of the circle. "I screamed like a new baby taking his first breath and jumped into the river. The poor bear leapt up and ran off into the forest."

"Aw," said Kels, a woman to my right. "You mean the poor bear startled at the sight of you in your *bare* skin. You probably blinded her."

Laughter erupted from the guards, echoing and returning again and again. Kels leaned forward. "Listen, Princess. Most animals don't want to be bothered by the likes of us. If you make enough noise, they'll stay away."

The tightness in my back eased a little. "What about at night? We can't exactly keep making noise in our sleep."

Thomas guffawed. "You can if you're Kels. She snores like—"

She shoved him, but both were smiling.

I asked question after question as we ate. My cheeks heated

when Aleinn brought my meal, which was a good deal more robust than theirs, but they didn't complain or point it out. Somehow, I was now part of their group.

Just as we were getting up to go back to our mounts, Hafa touched my shoulder. He stared into the dense foliage across the road, and I followed his gaze. It took me a moment, but eventually I picked out what he'd seen. A mother deer, her ears perked up, watching us right back. And at her feet, her fawn staggering with spindly legs as he ate up the new spring grass.

Everyone else hurried to get ready before Leland's whistle—he was still mad about Ren leaving. But just beyond the edge of the road, I'd caught a glimpse of another world. One untouched by villagers or traveling caravans.

For the rest of that afternoon, after I'd loaded my own bags back on Gentry's saddle, I kept a sharp eye for another glimpse into that world.

✦✦✦

By evening, my muscles had congealed into mush from riding two days in a row. When Aleinn jumped down from the carriage, ready to assist me as usual, I'd already unloaded my bags from Gentry and had started hauling our tent to the place Leland's captain had pointed out at the side of the road.

The road cut a path through tall evergreens and budding foliage threatening to overtake everything. There would be no roundhouse tonight.

As I dumped the bundle of canvas and poles to the ground, warm dust billowed up around me, sticking to my face and neck. I arched my back, my hands behind my neck, and stared at the sunset's orange haze painting the sky above the tree line. The wind didn't bite as much the farther south we traveled, and the flowers were brighter, more varied. Spring held the land firmly in her grasp.

It took Aleinn and me three tries to get our tent up, with only vague instructions from Hafa. The soldiers, who already had theirs staked, laughed as the canvas fell down around us. They called out advice—some helpful, some meant to make our poles fall faster.

At dinnertime, Aleinn tried to step in as I stirred our meal over the fire, but I didn't let her. The meat burned, but she didn't complain.

After dinner, Hafa took me to a small meadow just beyond the trees lining the road. He bent and brushed his hand along the ground, then turned.

He pulled his arm back as if to throw something, and a second later, a sharp pain registered in my shoulder. I jumped back and squinted in the fading light at what had hit me. A pebble.

"Did you just throw a—"

Another rock hit my leg. Then my stomach.

"Ow! Stop—"

He pulled his arm back again. I ducked away, my hands covering my head. A rock scratched my right hand.

"Block them, Princess," he growled.

"I can't block them if I can't see them," I growled back, jumping to the side as he launched yet another.

"If someone attacks you with magic, you won't see it, either."

His casual reference to magic jerked me to a stop. He threw another rock—hard—but this time my hand came up on its own and batted it down, all my focus on him, on his face. Hoping for and dreading his next words.

"Your father gave you that sword and ring to protect you against magical attack." Another pebble pinged against my ribs—I'd failed to block it. "So we train with both weapons." He unsheathed his sword, and the sound rang through the night. A steel blade. Not a practice sword.

I swallowed thickly and drew my own.

Hafa ran at me, swift and silent, his sword arcing toward my head as he threw another pebble. My left hand—with the ring on the middle finger—came up a fraction too late, and the rock hit my stomach while I sloppily deflected his sword.

He retreated a step, a frown marring his features. "You can do better. You must do better."

Thoughts of the traitor, of the note, of Ren facing magic on the border rippled through me. I rolled my shoulders back. Adjusted my grip on my sword. Widened my stance.

This time I dodged the pebble and met him sword for sword, but the tip of his blade cut into the fabric of my tunic.

"Again," he commanded.

He kept attacking until only the stars lit our battleground. Too many tiny bruises to count ached where I'd failed to deflect Hafa's "magic," and my tunic had two more tears that would need to be mended.

When he finally said I'd had enough, my dirty skin itched and loose strands of hair stuck to my face and neck. Muscles I didn't know I had screamed at me for relief. There was a reason no one sparred with Hafa, including me: He was unbeatable. In all the years I'd trained, no one had won a match against him.

He started back to camp, but when I didn't follow he turned. "You need rest."

"I know," I replied, chest heaving, out of breath. But instead of going with him, I lay down in the grass. "I just want to watch the stars for a bit, then I'll wash up and come back."

Hafa studied my face, then nodded and left.

Dark triangle tops of evergreens framed the canvas of the sky. The stars were mere pinpricks of light, yet they bathed the world in their glory. No moon overwhelmed them tonight. But the sounds? The sounds were deafening. Frogs sang out to each other by the river across the road. Crickets played their haunting harmony. Families of little creatures nestled together in the brush or up in the trees.

The air had finally cooled, but I found I missed the bite of the wind back home. I missed the sanctity of the library. I even missed the white walls of the castle. Mostly, though, I missed Ren. And my father. Their tethers were nothing more than a gentle hum inside me, but both held an ache that resonated with my own. I cradled the connection, amplifying my homesickness yet soothing it as well, in its own way.

When the chill had fully seeped into my back and my breath had settled into a normal rhythm, I stood with a sigh, brushing off the bits of leaves and dirt sticking to my uniform. Hushed murmuring came from the camp settling in for the night. I picked my way over the road and through the stand of trees separating the road from the river.

My hair and hands were filthier than they'd ever been. But I was finally alone for the first time in two days. Squatting on the muddy riverbank, I untied my braid and ran my fingers through the mass of tangles. Dirt scattered as I shook out the strands, but I still took care to keep the white streak hidden. Even now. Even when there was no one else to see.

The icy river water smelled like home. It sent shivers up and down my skin as I dipped my hands and washed my face, as I dipped them again and again to rinse out as much of my hair as I could. By the time I'd finished, my fingers were numb and my eyes half-closed from exhaustion, but my braid was tight again.

A branch snapped somewhere behind me. Drops of ice slid from my hair into my tunic. The little noises of the forest had dimmed. No more frogs. No more crickets. No chirping insects. Just my breath puffing out. My hand wrapped around the hilt of my sword.

"Princess."

The voice came from the darkness to my left. I jumped back, my mother's sword drawn and ready. But it was only General Leland who stepped out of the shadows.

"Glaciers, General, you startled me," I said, clutching my tunic over my heart.

"Forgive me, Princess," he said with a slight bow. Had he finally recovered from Ren's departure? His face remained shadowed and his voice was flat, giving away nothing.

He jerked his chin toward my sword, which I sheathed, my heart still thumping against my ribs. "I've noticed some of the soldiers eyeing that weapon of yours." He lowered his voice, and the haunting notes of an owl's call swam through the trees above us. "Take care. You wouldn't want to lose such a valuable item."

Shadows flickered against the black trees from the meager firelight that had made it across the road. Another branch snapped nearby. "I will. Thank you."

My back itched right between my shoulder blades with every step until I finally made it back to camp. The sensation didn't go away until I was safe in my tent, where Aleinn snored lightly, burrowed under a thick blanket.

Only then did I unsheathe my sword to finger the etchings and the blue stone. I couldn't see them, but I remembered with almost perfect clarity their hue and depth and shine.

I unwrapped and rewrapped the leather strips on the hilt to cover the stone in the cross guard. Like this, it looked like an old, beat-up blade. I hoped I wouldn't have to draw it at all, let alone on one of the soldiers in our group.

✦ ✦ ✦

I kept vigilant watch over the next three days, but the journey continued on the same. Endless riding through patches of forest or rolling hills dotted with sheep. Leland snapping at anyone who stepped in his path. Hafa watching me like he would an enemy. Or a friend. It was hard to tell with him.

Our nightly practices kept getting harder. Welts covered my hands, and I ached more from the rocks than I did from the riding.

Our last night in Hálendi, our last night before we crossed the border into the Wild, we stayed in the largest inn yet. A bustling town was nestled on the plain a few hours' ride from the looming forest of the Wild, a place of refuge and rest for those preparing to enter or leave.

Leland stomped around ordering that more supplies be loaded, his captains supervising the packing and preparations. Hafa had beaten me faster tonight than ever before, and I sat—

admittedly sulking—near a fire in the courtyard, my saddlebag at my feet. A cool wind came from the direction of the Wild with a chill that shouldn't have been in the air this deep into spring.

The tethers of both my father and my brother flickered with worry, popping and snapping along with the flames of the fire. But I didn't know *why* they were worried. Was it because they knew my journey through the Wild would begin tomorrow? Because of something uncovered about the note? The traitor? Something happening near North Watch? Ren would almost be there by now. Would soon be taking command, leading the people as he was always meant to.

Hafa settled in next to me with a gusty sigh. "Moping won't change anything," he said, shedding his outer coat. He meant our practice fight, but he was right about more than that. I couldn't dwell on Hálendi anymore. But once in Turia, perhaps . . . I sighed. I didn't know what I'd do, what I'd find.

I scrubbed my hands over my face. "I know. Nothing I do will change anything," I muttered dejectedly.

The firelight reflected off the silver bits in his beard and the steel in his eyes. "You don't actually believe that, do you?" he asked in the softest voice I'd ever heard him use.

My scalp itched. I didn't scratch it—didn't want to draw attention to my hair. *I can't do this,* I wanted to tell him. Instead, I unbuckled my sword from my hip and held it in my lap. My fingers brushed against the now-hidden stone in the cross guard.

"Throwing rocks won't prepare me for what I'll face in Turia. *That* threat is at the northern border." If Hafa was entrusted by my father to accompany me, he probably knew about the magic being used by our enemies.

Hafa drew his sword from its sheath and his sharpening stone from his bag. "There is always a threat nearby. You have forgotten your lessons so soon?" He drew the blade along the flat surface, its shushing drowning out the surrounding chatter.

"My lessons never included magic," I said in a low voice, wary of the topic even though the few people nearby were being ordered around by Leland.

"Maybe they should have."

Someone dropped a crate and cursed loudly. Neither of us reacted. A single question looped through my mind: *How could he know about my magic?*

Hafa kept his head down. Pulled a rag from his pocket to polish his blade. My head still itched. I scratched my neck instead. But I couldn't speak. Not a single word.

He nodded to my sword. "If the king is giving you magical artifacts, he should have had the foresight to teach you about magic."

Oh. My breath left me in a rush. "I—" My throat caught on my relief that he only meant my sword and ring, and I tried again. "It was just a precaution. I don't think my father thought I'd ever have to use them."

"Even though he's sending you through the cursed depths of the Wild?" he muttered, jerking his sword against the stone.

I swallowed. "If we stay on the road, the Wild's magic won't touch us." My voice wavered the tiniest bit. Was I trying to convince him or me?

Hafa raised an eyebrow, gaze still fixed on his sword. "So you don't want to know more about your weapon?"

"Wha . . . ? Yes!"

Leland looked at us quizzically from across the yard but

continued yelling at some poor soldier. I cleared my throat. Focused on Hafa. "I mean, yes. I would love to learn more about my sword . . . and the Wild."

"To know about a magical artifact, you must know where it hails from." The fire popped and danced as I settled in. "Ages ago, before our ancestors came across the Many Seas to the Plateau, there was a great war on the Continent."

I knew about the Great War, but I nodded and stayed quiet to show him I was listening. He always gave information in a roundabout way.

"There were many kingdoms on the Continent, all squabbling for power over each other—even worse than now. When the first mages found that they could manipulate their surroundings or even enhance their own abilities, the fighting became widespread. Their original intentions were unclear, but someone who has power over others will always want more of it. Some push this desire away. Others embrace it.

"Many who held this power began following one called the Black Mage. They took all they could—invading kingdoms, recruiting followers, and enslaving others until their presence overwhelmed the entire Continent. Those not gifted with this magic banded with the mages who denied loyalty to the Black Mage, to fight against him and their other oppressors."

Hafa's tale, told by one who'd spent his life studying Hálendi's military, wove around me like wool threads pulling tighter, intertwining.

"They fought even with no chance of winning?" I asked.

He shook his head. "Do not underestimate the power of desperation."

I didn't respond. With one week left until we reached Turia's capital, and my wedding awaiting me there, desperation and I were becoming fast friends.

"After many years of battle," he continued, "a man named Gero, destined to become the Continent's first emperor, finally defeated the Black Mage. Gero's youngest son, Kais, along with his army, pursued the Black Mage's surviving followers across the Many Seas until they reached a new land, its sheer cliffs jutting out of the water. When they found a way up, they tracked the mages over snow-covered hills, through forests, and into the Ice Deserts. Many in Kais's army died from exposure, and eventually, Kais could no longer track the mages over the ice, so he left them there to die.

"Fearing another Continent-wide war, Gero banished all knowledge of magic across the sea. He exiled all artifacts with magic—his own, as well as those he'd taken from the Black Mage and his followers—to the edge of the world to be forgotten."

I sucked in a breath. "My sword came from the mages' library?" I asked, though I knew Master Hafa didn't like to be interrupted.

"Not exactly." He sheathed his sword, then drew a dagger from his boot to clean. "Kais spared a very few magical artifacts from banishment. He felt they would be necessary to combat the power of the mages, should they survive and emerge from the Ice Deserts."

"But they never did," I said, holding my sword with a new reverence. My father's Medallion must be one of those artifacts too. If these had been kept out, what other marvels did the mages' library hold? No wonder someone on the front lines was looking for it. And, perhaps, even Hálendi could gain an advantage themselves. "And what of a key to their library?"

Hafa's hands paused over the knife before he returned it to his boot and turned the full force of his gaze on me. "A key?"

I ran my fingers down my braid, smoothing its strands. Father had trusted Hafa to bring me to Turia. I'd never had any reason to doubt him. Still, I hesitated. "I recently heard there was a key, but I wasn't sure what that meant."

Hafa's beard twitched as it always did when he was thinking. "I haven't heard of a key, though it's been many years since anyone fancied themselves an explorer and went digging up the past."

My lips twisted up in a wry smile. If only that were true. "So Kais hid away everything to do with magic? Why not use the mages' own weapons against them to defeat them entirely?"

Hafa let out a gusty sigh. "The Ice Deserts are too unforgiving, and the mages either died or were lost for good. But also, Kais and his father worried about *anyone* having that much power, that much knowledge to manipulate the world and, in turn, those around them."

"But magic is just magic," I said, his words hitting a little too close. I brushed my braid over my shoulder. "The same magic used to gain power over others and cause suffering can be used wisely with good intentions and a pure heart." It was something Ren had told me over and over when I'd worried incessantly that having magic would make me act like the sister who'd tried to kill her brother and take the throne.

Hafa's beard twitched. "You are correct, Princess. But they

had just spent decades fighting. Emperor Gero believed the quickest way to start healing from the poison of war was to push the cause of the turmoil as far away as he could. He invited anyone with magical abilities to either renounce all use of magic or accept banishment to the Ice Deserts. Those living on the Plateau—the Turians—gave the land north of the Fjall Mountains to Kais, who became the first king of Hálendi—your ancestor. Our land, our entire purpose, is to protect the Turians from the plague of magic Gero sent here."

My mind spun as the yard around us quieted. Leland had finally gone inside the roundhouse, and there wasn't much more to pack. But Hafa had said something I'd never heard before. "Gero banished other mages to the Ice Deserts?"

Hafa nodded, waiting for me to make the connection.

It connected like a punch in my gut. "You think they survived and their ancestors are the ones invading from the north."

Hafa held his hands out to the fire in a show of warming them in case anyone was watching, and spoke, his voice low and urgent. "There are rumors of strange occurrences on the front lines. Odd enough to make me wonder."

He hadn't said it directly, but he agreed. *Glaciers.* Mages hiding away in the Ice Deserts all this time.

"How did they escape the enchantments Kais placed on the border? No one is supposed to be able to break through and return from banishment."

Hafa's expression darkened, the angles and planes of his face sharpening. "They *can* return. If they're summoned."

"Glaciers," I exhaled, aloud this time. The traitor. The

burned note. And my father was now alone at the castle. Hafa and Leland were with me. Ren was in North Watch.

I stood and began pacing, buckling my sheath around my waist. "I can't go to Turia, Master Hafa. I can't. What if—" I swallowed the knot of dread rising from my stomach. "What if it was someone within Hálendi's borders who summoned them?"

Hafa shook his head and stopped my frantic steps with his hand on my arm. "Whoever did that, whatever their purpose, we need troops if we are to face them."

I winced at the reminder. *My* purpose was to be traded for something more useful than I could be on my own. My hands shook at my sides, so I tucked them into my pockets and sat.

"You'll be safe in Turia," he said.

But it wasn't my safety I was worried about. It was my secret. I squeezed my eyes shut and breathed deep.

Seven days. One week. And then the blank slate of my future would be set.

"Are Turians afraid of magic?" I asked. "It must be so foreign to them. Will I have to hide my sword?"

Hafa shrugged back into his coat. Night had truly fallen around us, and though the yard had quieted, the night creatures had awoken. "Not afraid, only wary. They understand its purpose on the Plateau. Our purpose."

I rested my head in my hands, elbows on my knees. He'd answered me without answering.

"And the Wild?" I asked, sensing our conversation was almost over.

Hafa grew very still, his gaze fixed on the flames. A bat swooped and darted overhead, a jerking, chaotic flight.

He cleared his throat, but a thin layer of calm now coated him. Practiced.

"There is balance between the three kingdoms of the Plateau. Hálendi is a land of mountains and snow, with warriors trained to protect and defend, fields for cattle, and mines that provide us with precious gems to trade. Turia has wide valleys and fertile plains and a long growing season, as well as caches of hard ore to furnish us with weapons. Riiga's cunning merchants have access to the seas and the Continent that the other two kingdoms lack because of the cliffs surrounding the Plateau.

"With the balance in trade and economy, there is also balance in magic," he continued. "As magic presents itself in the line of the kings of our kingdom, so it does, to a lesser degree, in the rulers of the other kingdoms."

"Ice and snow," I muttered. Ren was the only one who was supposed to have magic. Yet I had magic. Wanderers in the Ice Deserts were apparently using magic to attack us. And now this?

"Magic, Jennesara, is not always predictable. Not according to our understanding of it, at least," he said before I could form a response. "There have always been those using magic for evil, and it is balanced by those using it for good. The land here is the same. It strives for harmony. And when Kais enchanted the Ice Deserts, the Wild was inadvertently affected as well."

My mind churned. Laughter spilled out of the tavern next to the inn, jarring the quiet of the night. "So you're saying the Wild has magic that equals the magic that surrounds the Ice Deserts?"

Hafa grunted. "Not sure what the land was thinking, but yes."

I swallowed. "What kind of magic is in the Wild?"

Hafa's steel-gray eyes bore into me. "I don't know, but at all costs, don't go off the road."

A beat of silence stretched into two. Even the drunks next door quieted. He stood, brushing off his trousers. Adjusted the sword at his waist.

"Jennesara, Hálendi's first king swore an oath to protect the people of the Plateau from threats both physical and magical. This is why we are a warrior people, and why we thrive in the cold, harsh winters. It is our legacy to survive and protect."

I dug the toe of my boot into the ash at the edge of the fire. I heard what he didn't say. That my role in protecting the Plateau was to marry the prince. To ensure that Ren had enough troops. I pressed my thumb into the cross guard of my sword. A faint zing shot up my arm, so subtle I almost missed it.

"Princess," Aleinn called from the door of the roundhouse. "It's far past time to retire." Light spilled into the yard, Aleinn's form a dark outline. I waved to her to show that I'd heard. A breeze carried the fire's heat into the black sky, and I shivered.

"Thank you for telling me this," I whispered to Hafa, my voice barely carrying over the raucous shouting from the tavern.

Hafa pursed his lips like he wanted to say something else. His beard twitched, but he only bowed at the waist and gestured for me to precede him to the door of the inn. I lifted the flap on my saddlebag, took out my hunting knife, and slipped it into my boot before slinging the bag over my shoulder.

We'd only be in the Wild for four days. We'd have no reason to leave the road. We'd be fine.

✦ ✦ ✦

The next day, when we crossed into the Wild, something changed in the air. The endless trees grew taller here, their color richer. Spiny underbrush climbed their trunks like a spider's web warning visitors away. More bits of snow were crusted in the shadows, even this far south in spring.

As we rode down the center of the road, no one venturing near the edge, I began to feel a charge. Something crackling inside me. The same as when I brushed my hair too much, and some strands snapped and rose into the air.

We rounded a bend near midday, and the road passed through a small grassy meadow, the spines and trees removed enough to allow space to breathe.

"We stop here!" Leland called out from the front of our group. His shout didn't echo like it should have.

Everyone dismounted and hobbled their horses so they could graze in the grass. I hefted my bag from Gentry's saddle, then joined the others in the middle of the road. Aleinn sat next to me, talking quietly with another woman next to her.

The food was fresh—packed this morning—yet the flavors barely registered. Ren's tether, and my father's, had sharpened. Their emotions, which had been growing hazier, tightened like we were in the castle together again. Ren's excitement burned away his weariness—he was nearly at North Watch; I could feel it. Was Father close to discovering the traitor? I hoped so, but his worry seemed to increase with every inch the sun traveled across the sky.

The clarity in the tethers didn't ease the ache of missing them that stayed wrapped around my chest all the time. One more day of travel until we'd reach the Fjalls. One day up and over the pass, one more through the Wild on the edge of Turia, then we'd be on easy roads all the way to the palace.

As we packed up lunch and started riding again, a bright flash of orange darted behind the tree line in the corner of my vision. I turned sharply to see what had flown by, but nothing was there.

It kept happening as we plodded along. Reds, yellows, pinks. And even a green I'd never seen before in my life. But every time, the flashes disappeared when I turned to look. Others saw them, too; I was sure of it. But by evening, everyone had stopped twisting about, trying to see what made the colors.

We stopped in a wide clearing for the night. No stumps marred the area, and the smooth ground made setting up our tents easy, despite the growing unease among our group from the day's travels.

"Has this clearing always been like this?" I asked Hafa as we unloaded the dinner gear from the back harness on the carriage. Aleinn helped us, a routine we'd perfected over the last few days.

Hafa's knuckles whitened around the ax he held. "Yes."

A wolf howled far in the distance, and Aleinn edged closer to me. "Who maintains the road?" she asked, the box filled with wooden bowls forgotten in her hands.

Hafa's lips pursed. "No one. It just stays clear."

"No fallen trees?" I asked. "No new growth that needs to be cut back?"

His head jerked side to side. "No."

"Glaciers," Aleinn muttered.

"Glaciers," I agreed.

Hafa's jaw unclenched, and he handed his load to another

soldier behind us. "Come, Princess. There is enough light to practice again."

I swallowed back my groan, the welts on my hands stinging in anticipation.

"There isn't much point in practicing," General Leland said to Hafa and me from near the front of the carriage. "In a few days' time, she'll be tucked safely away in Turia's palace. You may as well be helpful and gather kindling instead." His words carried an edge sharper than he'd used the whole trip.

The activity around us stopped and my muscles went rigid. No one spoke to Hafa that way. No one spoke to *me* that way. Not to my face, at least.

Hafa stilled. He'd *always* demanded my training. Even when my father tried to forbid it when I was thirteen and had twisted my ankle jumping off the fence surrounding the sparring ring.

Hafa stood like a stone column in the face of a storm. "Jennesara can decide how she would like to spend her time."

Aleinn and Hafa and Leland and everyone stared at me. A flush of heat rose in my cheeks at the attention, and that snapping, jittery feeling inside me intensified. Master Hafa had called me by my name only. No title. What did *I* want? "I want to continue training," I said.

Leland turned away, a mask of indifference, directing others to the place he wanted them to put his tent. Hafa led me back down the road, a slight bend hiding us from sight.

We followed our routine—swords and stones, and me landing hard when Hafa bested me, though I did better at prolonging most of the fights.

"Get up, Princess," he said when he'd won the fourth time.

I lay flat on my stomach and caught my breath. Sweat soaked into my shirt, and the last rays of evening light settled through the trees around me. Master Hafa gathered more pebbles. Smaller ones. The kind that stung the most when I lost track of them in the twilight.

"How will I even know if someone has magic?" I asked. "Won't it be too late by the time I figure it out?"

He nudged me with his foot until I ungracefully got up and he circled, ready to strike again. "That is why we practice. Your instincts in any fight are the line between life and death."

He flicked a pebble at my head before he'd finished speaking, and I blocked it without a thought, my palm stinging from the impact. I stood, stunned, at where the speck of gray now rested at my feet.

He dipped his shoulder down and dug his foot into the dirt. "Better, but you can be faster." His blade charged forward. He liked the element of surprise, but he'd trained me well enough to expect that.

Rock after rock, swing after swing, we fell into a rhythm of attacking and defending. I had jumped aside to avoid his sword at my shoulder when a choking fury stopped me cold. A rock slammed into my temple, and I yelped and stumbled away.

My father's tether.

I swallowed back a metallic taste and focused, the snapping tension easing as my father's anger softened.

"You are not trying, Princess," Hafa growled.

"I *am* trying," I replied, lungs aching to pull in enough air.

He shook his head and came at me again. "You're fighting with your mind. Fight with your heart—for your brother, your father, your kingdom." He punctuated each word by swinging his sword, forcing me backward until I stumbled into mud at the edge of the road.

I rolled away from him and cursed under my breath. My focus narrowed—no tethers, no Wild, no prince. Just Hafa's inhale, my exhale. The tang of metal and dirt and snow and pine.

I raised my sword, and everything else melted away. Crackling energy stirred in my middle. The feeling spread throughout my body, into my hands and feet. *Focus.* I pulled a breath deep into my lungs and attacked.

My blade whistled as I countered Hafa's blows. Half his pebbles still hit me. He attacked high, and I saw a hole in his guard and countered. But my sword whiffed through air. I fell forward and hit the ground before I'd realized what had happened.

"Timing!" Hafa barked, and I rolled over my shoulder and up. I'd been too early. Too fast.

On my feet again, I moved more fluidly than water, dodging Hafa's blade and deflecting more rocks, dancing around him until I found the opening I needed. *Timing.* I slid onto my knees. My sword moved up, almost of its own accord, its edge sliding under his cross guard to flick his weapon out of his grasp. I hooked my leg behind his knees and shoved against his chest. He and his sword hit the ground at the same time.

Somewhere in the trees beyond, a sharp trill broke through the barrier between us and the Wild. Master Hafa lay with the tip of my sword at his chest, grinning, his blade just beyond his reach. I exhaled and shook off my intense focus. Noises sharpened. The smell of dust and sweat and pine returned.

Slow clapping began.

Most of the camp was crowded at the road's bend watching our fight.

I sheathed my sword and turned to help Hafa up, but he was already standing, brushing mud off his uniform.

"How did that feel?" he asked as he gathered his sword.

It feels like rushing, Ren had said. I shook the thought away. "Clarity," I said instead, tucking my braid to the side. "It felt like clarity."

Hafa's eyes gleamed as night fell around us. "Remember that feeling, Princess. That is what it will take to win." He clapped me on the back. "Come. We need an early start tomorrow. My bones say a storm is coming."

I fell into step next to him, accepting congratulations from the soldiers, laughing when Aleinn pulled me into a tight hug. Yet as we ate dinner, circled tight around the fire, my euphoria shrank. How would my artifacts help me with a prince I had to marry? A traitor I'd never reach in time? A war on a border I'd never see?

On either side of the road, where the trees met the brush, there was nothing but a wall of black. Not one bit of light from the fire penetrated into the Wild. And when I crawled into my tent, my back itched between my shoulder blades. It didn't matter how many times I told myself we were safe on the road. Something was lurking out there in the Wild. And it wasn't just the wolves.

CHAPTER SIX

"The animals will warn you of foul weather, if you pay attention," Hafa said as we slogged along behind the carriage. We'd woken to a light dusting of snow, tiny white crystals covering everything from the tips of the sky-high evergreens to the spiny underbrush that was now taller than me. The snow had turned to rain by breakfast.

"What if there aren't any animals around?" I asked, tightening my cloak at the shoulders so the chill wind couldn't sneak down my neck. My hood was already pulled so low all I could see was the churned mud of the road directly beneath Gentry's hooves, and the rain soaking my gloves.

The precipitation did nothing to dampen the crackling charge inside me. It only intensified as we got closer to the Fjalls. I didn't have to focus to access the tethers anymore—my father and brother were always there, simmering below my own emotions.

Hafa sneezed. "If there are no animals, you'd best be on high alert. There are always little creatures foraging in the forest. Unless something bad's afoot."

I wiped my dripping nose and shivered. It shouldn't have been this cold. Was it a trick of the Wild? Or because we were climbing toward the mountains?

A jolt punched into me from the tethers so hard my hands jerked the reins. Gentry snorted, tossing her wet mane. I pressed my hand against my middle and raised my head. Ice-cold water dripped down my face and slipped under my collar.

My father's tether screamed with something I'd never felt from him: fear. A deep pit opened in my stomach. I doubled over, swallowing down its rising contents.

"Princess?" Hafa said, stopping his horse next to mine. His hand gripped the hilt of his sword.

I yanked off my thick gloves, stuffing them in Gentry's saddle, then tipped my hood back, gasping for air and letting the rain cool my face. "It's not—"

"Sir, make way!" Leland called from ahead, his deep voice an explosion of sound. The carriage sighed to a halt, the wheels sinking deep into the black, muddy road.

Complete, deafening silence cloaked the woods. Even the stream next to the road didn't make a sound. There were no birds calling, no wind in the trees. No raindrops pinging against leaves.

Hafa reached out and jerked my hood up again. He drew his sword slowly and put a finger to his lips. My father's tether didn't calm; it twisted into more knots. My eyes watered from trying to control my breathing, to relax. I nodded and stayed close as Hafa edged around the carriage.

A lone figure mounted on a horse stood on the trail ahead of us, gray cloak billowing in a wind I could no longer hear.

I squeezed my eyes shut, pushing away my father's tether. A hood obscured the figure's face, but I thought it was a man. The space inside me where the tethers lived jumped and danced like a raging fire. My ears felt full of cotton.

The man didn't respond to Leland's call, didn't move. Was he a trick of the Wild?

Gentry's ears flicked back, and her eyes rolled.

Hafa studied the trees around us, a wall of emerald. A tremor of panic shook my father's tether. My heartbeat pounded through my skull, throbbed in my fingertips. *No*. My father was in trouble, and I was too far away to help.

Leland drew his sword and the rasp of metal echoed deep into the trees. "Move, or we shall use force!"

Something was *wrong*. This man on the road. My father's tether. Hafa's words from last night came back to me. *Timing*. My head commanded that I run. Flee. Escape. I shoved the thoughts away and gripped the hilt of my sheathed sword.

The figure raised his hand, palm forward. An invisible wave enveloped the road, swallowing us all. The air vibrated with power unlike anything I'd ever felt.

Filthy men streamed out of the woods—some on horseback, most on foot—and surrounded us with clubs and swords. But no one moved or tried to fight free. Next to me, Master Hafa was frozen in place, eyes wide, hand clenched around the hilt of his sword.

My chest rose and fell fast. My breaths came loud. Hafa wasn't waiting for the right moment—he was immobile. I scanned our entire group. Everyone was.

Except me.

I exhaled slowly, relaxed every muscle from my head down to my feet, and kept my hand on my sword. I needed to blend in. For now.

The men's circle around us tightened. They were near enough for me to see their empty eyes, to smell death on their skin. The gray figure approached. Mud covered his horse's legs, splattered over its belly.

He was a smudge of gray. Gray cloak, gray horse, as if all the light and color had been leached out of him. He waved his hand, almost as if in greeting. But this minor motion knocked Leland and everyone in the front of the caravan aside, like a giant hand sweeping them away, clearing a path to the door of the carriage.

The gray man was a mage.

And he was coming for me.

Pressure built in my ears until my heartbeat drowned out everything else. My father's tether tightened, winding around and around my ribs, crushing me from the inside. My muscles shook with the effort to stay still. To blend in.

Surprising the mage was my only chance.

My heart pounded. The mage dismounted and stalked to the carriage, my view of him now gone.

The rain turned to a drizzle, then the clouds broke apart. Sunlight seeped through as a power thrummed over and around us, like a river rushing past a boulder in the middle of a stream. My ring warmed, its gem glowing brighter, absorbing the magic pressing harder against my body as the mage stalked closer.

My hood blocked most of my vision, and the carriage

blocked more. But I could see the mage's shadow pass by the warped glass of the carriage window.

He forced the door open and grabbed Aleinn by the throat, dragging her out and tossing her in the mud at the hooves of his gray horse. My mouth went dry. Would he question her to get to me?

"Stand." The mage's deep voice grated down my spine like a dull knife.

No longer held by magic, Aleinn pulled herself up with calm dignity. From hem to hood, deep-brown stains marred the silver embroidery of her cloak.

No, not her cloak. *My* cloak. The one I had traded for her cloak of plain gray.

I choked back a gasp. Ren's tether spiraled into an anxiety that scraped at the bottom of my stomach. My father's squeezed like a noose around me.

Aleinn didn't sob or plead or even tremble. She stood with her shoulders back, face shadowed. The trees on either side of the road swayed and shook, yet the wind never managed to reach us.

But the gray figure didn't attack. He instead dropped the cowl obscuring his face. His profile was normal enough—strong nose, sharp cheekbones. Yet everything about him was blurred at the edges, as if he were neither here nor there. An empty scabbard was buckled at his waist, but he pulled a silver dagger from within his cloak. He turned Aleinn to face those of us he hadn't swept aside. He drew back the hood of her cloak and grabbed her hair, forcing her chin into the air. She gasped but still didn't speak. Mud smeared her face. Deliberate swaths.

No.

"King Marko of Turia has asked me to deliver a message." The mage's voice echoed off the trees, the silence amplified after its absence. "The rulers of Hálendi are dead."

My mind emptied for a terrifying moment. The tethers had sharpened to near-perfect clarity since entering the Wild. Father's fear had changed to determination, the cord a band of thick steel. The mage was lying.

But the mage grinned, showing too many gray teeth. Suddenly, his whole being sharpened into focus.

And then my father's tether snapped.

Gone. Like a thick branch breaking from its tree. Like a limb.

Blistering pain radiated from my middle out to the tips of my fingers and toes. I couldn't breathe, couldn't force air into my lungs. Just like that, my father—

My eyes locked on the mage, and even though his magic still didn't affect me, I was as frozen as everyone else.

Ren.

I focused on his tether with everything I had.

Still alive.

Nothing existed beyond this connection with my brother. Not the earthy smell of the mud after the rain, not the puffs of men and women straining against an invisible force immobilizing them. Nothing.

The mage's face twisted in fury, and then I felt it. First a slight tug on the invisible cord connecting me to my brother, like the pluck of a string on a fidla. Then the tether shredded into an unrecognizable mess, a yawning agony at my core.

Ren had been ripped from me, too.

My vision blackened around the edges, and I swayed on my horse. The mage's head snapped up, and he swept his gaze over the crowd. *Stay still.* I had to blend in. Had to.

A deep coldness saturated my extremities. An excruciating throbbing marked the jagged edges of the broken tethers.

They were dead. My father and brother were dead.

And I was next.

The heavy blanket of magic flickered. Birds shrieked in the Wild, but the sound was muffled, barely reaching me. My ragged intake of breath broke the final beat of silence.

The soldiers on the road, who had been thrown from the mage's path, finally scrambled up with a shout, rushing toward the empty-eyed attackers surrounding us. Magic flickered in the clearing again, then disappeared like a snuffed-out candle.

The clang of metal on metal tore through the clearing as everyone around me charged into action. Boots stuck and slipped in the slushy mud; the coppery scent of blood already tinged the air as our attackers crashed against us. Hafa stayed by my side, waiting to strike anyone who came near.

I couldn't pull my eyes from the mage. Couldn't move. He jerked his fistful of Aleinn's hair so her head tipped to the side. He leaned in. His lips moved. He spoke to her, words only she could hear. Liquid ore pulsed in my veins instead of blood.

She met my gaze and quirked her lips up, almost a smile, then closed her eyes against the sun's brightness and relaxed in its warmth.

The mage's face twisted into a snarl, and he dragged his knife across her throat.

My mouth opened in a silent scream. Something small and

fragile inside me snapped—a tether I hadn't even known existed. Blood now mixed with the mud on her clothing. She'd never open her eyes again.

I knew what she had done. Our coloring and build were similar. She was wearing my cloak. She'd smeared mud on her face.

She had traded her life for mine.

No. She couldn't have. She hadn't even said goodbye to her parents. There hadn't been time before we left. It was supposed to be only until I got settled. Then she'd return. See her brother again. Her family.

I knew their pain. It lived raw inside me.

A piercing scream clawed its way from my throat. The mage released Aleinn's hair, and she sagged to the ground.

No.

I kicked my horse toward her limp body, but someone grabbed my reins and pulled. A hand roughly squeezed my shoulder. Leland. Dark-red blood smeared across half of his face from a gash in his cheek. He shouted something, but I couldn't hear over the high-pitched ringing in my ears.

I shook my head. Chaos surrounded me. Soldiers, servants, and the mage's army fought and fell and cried all at once. Master Hafa, still at my side, swung at anything he could reach.

I hadn't even drawn my sword yet.

"Jennesara, listen to me!" Leland yelled.

A ring of our muddy soldiers pushed off wave after wave of the mage's army. I sat in the middle like the bull's-eye of a target.

If everyone was protecting me, I realized, the mage might see that he hadn't killed the right girl.

Leland still held my horse's reins. "Jenna!"

My gaze snapped to his.

Father. Ren. Aleinn.

Dead.

"We can try to outrun them," Hafa shouted.

Leland cursed and yanked my horse closer. "There are too many. But Jennesara might outrun them in the Wild. I'll go with—"

"No!" Hafa bellowed beside me as he swung at the clubs beating at his horse. "She'll never make it!"

"You think I don't know that?" Leland screamed. He hacked at something I couldn't see on the other side of him.

Someone crashed into Gentry from behind, and she kicked out. I snatched my reins from Leland. *Don't go off the road. Don't go . . .*

Master Hafa's beard twitched, sweat running down his face and smearing specks of blood and mud into a canvas of war. "Go," he finally rasped to me. His expression turned to stone. "Survive, or that gray monstrosity wins."

I knew his look. The one that said failure was not an option. But I also saw how tight he gripped his sword. How his horse shuddered beneath him.

"Go!" he yelled again.

I reined in my sidestepping horse. The shredded tethers shrieked inside me. My numb mind latched on to Hafa's command. Death would surely come here, or death might find me in the Wild. But I was the only one left in my family. The sole heir.

"I'm sorry," I choked out.

I turned my horse, found a gap in the fighting, and escaped into the brush. Thorns scraped against my cheeks, latched on to my trousers and cloak as if to pull me back to the road.

Once I was through, the clashes of metal and cries of battle were immediately muted behind me, as though a thick wall stood between me and the fighting. Hafa's bellow rose above everything else, and I turned Gentry so I could peek through the foliage. Hafa had spotted the mage.

They were impossibly fast as they tore into each other. A wide circle opened around them to avoid their wild blades. The mage used a dirty sword from one of his men. Hafa swung again and again, pushing the mage back a step with each attack. I gripped my sword. Even outnumbered by their men, maybe I could help kill the mage.

And then the mage's blade found Hafa's chest. A move he never saw coming. A move I never saw coming. Hafa fell to his knees in the mud, then toppled to the side.

The greenery spun around me. I gasped in a breath. How long ago had I stopped breathing? Leland burst through the brush with a murderous gaze fixed on my still form. I understood then why others feared him in battle.

"What—" he screamed, but three of the mage's men spilled in after him.

I put my head down, turned Gentry toward the Wild, and kicked her flanks. Branches and wet leaves whipped at my face and snagged my cloak. A few strides beyond the trees, the shrieking faded. Crunching hoofbeats followed fast behind, though. *Hafa. Aleinn. Ren. Father.* I dug my knees into Gentry and pushed her harder.

No matter what turn I made, how fast we ran, I couldn't lose my pursuer. We pressed into the Wild for what felt like hours. Days, maybe. Gentry's sides heaved, matching my own gasping breaths. She found a narrow path up a hill, widening our lead. We broke through a line of trees, and the land in front of us dropped away. Sheer rock walls lined a deep, narrow ravine with more forest looming on the other side.

I yanked the reins hard to the right. Gentry's hooves slid for a moment, but she found traction and raced along the cliff. We pounded across fifty feet of open ledge as stones skittered over the side. I peeked down and saw a raging river swollen with snow runoff twenty feet below. Steep, smooth rock walls lined the chasm. I could push back into the forest, but Gentry would tire eventually and I knew I'd be caught. If it was the mage following, I'd be dead.

Survive, or that gray monstrosity wins.

There was no time to think. No time to decide. My instincts were all I had left.

The Wild hadn't spit me out yet. I steered Gentry as close as I could get her to the cliff's edge, then wrapped her reins around the pommel of her saddle and pulled my feet out of the stirrups. "Be safe, girl," I whispered.

Then I slapped her flank to keep her running, and I jumped.

✦ ✦ ✦

Icy water engulfed me. I tucked my knees up to my chest, but I didn't hit bottom straight off. The current dragged my body along, tossing me end over end as my cloak and boots and sword and layers of clothes dragged me deeper. My ears and face and hands ached with the cold. My lungs screamed for air as my heart pounded in my chest.

I kicked my legs but couldn't find a foothold to push off from, wasn't even sure which way was up. My mind numbed along with my body. Even the hole where the tethers used to be wasn't as painful.

My cloak suddenly tightened around my neck. I wrenched at it, trying to free it from whatever had caught hold of it. I reached back and followed the cloth, hand over hand. A log. It was snagged on a log.

Logs float.

My hands scraped against the jagged bark and pulled me up, gasping and sputtering when I broke the river's surface.

I got in an entire lungful of air. Two. And then a black horse and its rider appeared on the cliff's edge, barreling toward the forest where Gentry had disappeared.

I dunked myself underwater, keeping a tight hold on the log, which was wedged between a boulder and the wall of the canyon. My legs kicked against the current so I could move under the log to the other side. I surfaced in time to see my pursuer swallowed by the Wild once again.

My teeth chattered as I clung to the log. The rock walls were too slick to scale—I had only one path to escape. I needed to move before the rider realized I wasn't on my horse.

I braced myself against the canyon wall and pushed the log. It didn't budge. The current clawed at my cloak and boots to drag me beneath the surface. I filled my lungs and sank below the rushing water, keeping my grip tight on the wood as I followed it to the boulder and the wall it was wedged between. I got underneath it, eyes shut tight against the icy water, moving by touch alone. Rushing filled my ears, and my chest ached. But I found a foothold and pushed again.

The log shuddered, then dislodged and started spinning with the current. Kicking to stay afloat, I wrapped my cloak around myself to keep it from catching once more and put both arms around the log, pressing my face into it as I bounced up and down on the river's current. After several tries, I found a spot I could hold on to and keep my head above water.

The canyon walls eventually tapered down, and the river widened and slowed. Thick trees jutted into the sky from the edge of a sandy shore. The forest was bursting with noise: the river's lap against the bank, birds above and animals below. But no sign of the rider.

The sun's harsh light signaled its descent into evening. I had no tent. No fire. If I didn't get out of the river and dry off, I could freeze to death, and what good would my escape be then?

I waited for a rocky shore before leaving the water, remembering Master Hafa's warnings about footprints in sand. In a lurching, stumbling crawl, I dragged myself out of the river.

Dead.

Dead.

Dead.

Three beats pounded in my head for my father, my brother, and Aleinn. I clutched at my damp tunic, trying to ease the pain in my chest. *Master Hafa. General Leland. All those soldiers and servants. They're . . .* I couldn't even finish the thought.

I was alone.

Survive, or that gray monstrosity wins.

Master Hafa's voice penetrated the fog clouding my thoughts. *Survive.*

I pushed my wet hair out of my face and forced my legs to stand. Evergreens towered above, and the underbrush was no longer spiny like it was near the road. Now, soft ferns blanketed the forest floor in innumerable shades of green. My shivering abated—the air was warm. Unnaturally warm.

A bird darted overhead, its long blue-green wings a blend of the sky above and the woods below. I craned my neck, watching until it flew back into the trees.

I'd never in my life seen a bird that color. I'd never even read about one. I closed my eyes as the events of the day hit me hard all over again.

I was alone *in the Wild*.

On the other bank of the river, the emerald mass of trees and brush could conceal any number of threats. Even the mage's entire army. I shuddered and wrung out my cloak, then held it so its damp weight wouldn't strangle me. I needed to get away from the river—the last connection to my pursuer.

With my first steps into the shadows, my boots sank into tender soil. The chattering squirrels quieted, and I sensed eyes watching me. I inhaled air that smelled like fresh rain and tasted like berries, but the leaves and ground were dry. The ferns caressed me, welcoming me into the Wild's embrace, yet every kindness sharpened my agony.

I hiked as far as my shaking, battered legs would go, while the sun dipped toward the horizon. I carried my sword to dry it off. And to stay alert.

A steady beat against my skull kept time for my shuffling march. Sweat dripped down my temples and soaked my collar. I kept my eyes trained on the ground in the fading light as I dragged one foot in front of the other—until I slammed into something hard and landed in a bed of tiny pink flowers. Flowers that bloomed only in late summer. A fallen tree lay across my path, its trunk wider than I was tall. Smaller trees grew from its remains, thin branches unfurling over the wreckage.

My spent legs wouldn't hold me up again.

One thought carved into me despite my exhaustion: I shouldn't have run away. Leland and Master Hafa had commanded it, but if I'd stayed, fought the mage *with* Master Hafa, perhaps . . . I shoved the thought, the memory, away. I couldn't think about it. Couldn't bear it.

Master Hafa always told me to listen to my instincts and trust them, but nothing here made sense. I felt for the tethers, pushing through the curtain of pain, hoping there had been some mistake. But they were still torn and broken, just as my mother's had been.

I had no one left, nowhere safe to go. Would anyone even care if I somehow managed to make it out of the Wild alive?

I slumped over and burrowed out a small hole in the leaves and dirt at the tree trunk's base, overshadowed by its wide girth. I wrapped my damp cloak around me and lay in the hole, covering myself with as much displaced dirt and leaves as I could.

When I curled up, my sword remained in my hand at the ready. I still hadn't used it. But I would.

In the Wild

"You let him escape?" Graymere's hood perfectly concealed his face in shadow. The man in front of him crossed his arms to keep his trembling hands from showing.

"I gave chase for miles only to find the Wild had snatched him from his horse. There was no sign of him along the river, either." His eyes ricocheted off every surface, landing on anything but the mage in front of him.

"That is not how the Wild works." Graymere rubbed his temple. "I know this magic." He grasped the branch of an evergreen with one hand, crushing its needles in his grip.

A breeze stirred, and the shadows began shimmering around them before condensing and swirling into four vague outlines of men cloaked in night. Graymere lifted his other hand, and the figures rose from the ground as if pulled by invisible strings. He exhaled. Black blades sprouted from their hands, glinting in the filtered light of the forest as the blades and men became more than mere shadow.

Graymere released the tree branch and shook out his hand.

The man trembled as he stared at the massive evergreen, now only a brown husk. "I-I'm the best tracker of our village," he stammered. "If you kill me, you'll never find him."

"Yes," Graymere said as he turned to the man, arm outstretched, palm forward. The man fell to his knees, mouth open in a silent scream. Graymere clenched his hand into a fist, and the man crumpled. "I will."

A vine twisted around Graymere's ankle as he mounted his horse. He shuddered and kicked the Wild's tentacle away. "Find the Hálendian who escaped, and kill him," he commanded his four new minions before snapping his reins. As one, his creations turned and prowled into the forest.

CHAPTER SEVEN

I drifted in and out of nightmares, shivering and jumping at every sound in the forest until the sun rose. I was still mostly damp and freezing, buried next to the tree, but I was alive. The throbbing remnants of the tethers had dulled into a sharp ache. But while that pain had eased, I now felt every single bruise and scrape from my escape yesterday.

The pink light of dawn feathered down to my hiding spot as I listened to the song of the forest, trying to pick out anything that didn't belong. Tiny footprints surrounded my hideaway. Footprints that hadn't been there when I'd fallen asleep.

I dragged myself out from under the tree with a shiver. Cotton and dust coated my mouth. I brushed dirt from the blade of my sword, and the memory of the mage's knife sliding across Aleinn's throat flooded my mind. I flinched and squeezed my eyes closed, trying to block out the vision, but that only made it worse. Now a sea of blue and green eyes stared at an empty sky from the mud. I rolled over and heaved the meager contents of my stomach into the hole I'd slept in.

I stayed on my hands and knees until the world stopped spinning. I had no idea where the road was or how to find it, or if I could get back to Hálendi. Or, rather, if I even should go back.

I wiped my mouth with a corner of my cloak and curled up on the ground. But something dug into my leg. I gasped aloud—Ren's book! I righted myself and pulled it out, cradling it in my hands. *Flora and Fauna of the Wild.* It could tell me what was poisonous, what I could eat. Help me survive.

I reverently brushed the cover and opened it to the first page. But it was blank. My brow furrowed, and I turned one page after another. All blank. I could faintly see Ren's name on the inside corner of the cover, but that was it. The ink had washed away.

"No," I whispered. The sound jarred against the rhythm of the world around me as though the trees rejected my words. A tear splashed onto the page, and I slumped to the ground, pressing the book to my heart.

Eventually I rolled onto my back, my tears running into my ears and hair. Birds flitted from one branch to the next above me, flashes of red and orange and black and yellow. A family of rabbits hopped by, the father leading a slew of tiny bouncing fur balls. Nothing eased the emptiness spreading within.

Eventually I sat up and wiped my cheeks. I pulled the hunting knife from my boot and set Ren's book next to it. This, along with my sword, was it. Everything I had to survive.

I'd made it through my first night in the Wild, so now the question was: What should I do? With the death of my father and brother, the council would rule Hálendi, with General Leland—if he'd survived—at its head. And a traitor somewhere in their midst. If this was the traitor's work, I'd be killed the moment I got home. And there were probably spies—or the mage himself—watching for my return.

But why would a *mage* be in the middle of the Wild to attack *me*? There were much stronger fortifications around my father, and no one even knew Ren was planning to leave for North Watch. Another thought hit me: Did this mage have anything to do with the magic reported at the border?

I slipped the knife back into my boot, and the book into my pocket, wincing when the pain in my chest flared. My instincts told me not to return to Hálendi, but the mage himself had said King Marko had sent him. Perhaps Turia's marriage negotiations were only a ploy, then. But why would Marko attack when our kingdoms had been at peace for centuries?

I scanned the sky and turned until I was headed in a general western direction, and began walking.

I'd be killed if I went back to Hálendi, but I could also be killed going to Turia. Logic warred with the steady beat in my mind. All around me, the Wild's vivid colors danced in a warm breeze. And when I watched the gentle sway of leaves, the tethers hurt less. Peace pervaded, and the Wild itself seemed to whisper, *Stay.*

Animals came to investigate my trail. Foxes and rabbits and even an animal I'd never seen that had luminous eyes, tall ears, and a long, fluffy tail that swished behind it when it ran.

Hours and hours passed with only the animals as company as I journeyed west—I hoped. I should have been tired as I pushed through the underbrush. My muscles ached a little, but the buzzing energy inside, the spark that had ignited when

I'd entered the Wild, seemed to fill me up the longer I walked. I wasn't hungry, but I ate some wild strawberries I came across. The pulsing headache diminished, and a drink from a tumbling stream eased it even more.

As I stood to wipe the cool water dribbling from my chin, a black shadow drew my eye from farther upstream. I froze like a deer who'd caught a predator's scent. And slowly, so slowly, the shadow turned. Faced me. A jolt of recognition, of *otherness,* swept through me at the sight of the man. It wasn't the mage, but it *felt* like him.

Run, a voice on the wind whispered. And I did.

I jumped over the stream and took off, scrambling up a small incline and pushing myself into a sprint the moment the land flattened out. Leaves slapped against me and I held my hands in front of my face to protect it. I risked a glance over my shoulder, but I couldn't see him following—the foliage had knit together in my wake. But I could feel him following, too close for my liking.

I veered to the left, dodging trees, ferns slapping against my legs, marking my passage. I turned right, and the ground beneath me gave way. I tumbled down and slid to a stop next to a great tree, each of its broad green leaves almost as big as my head. My elbow throbbed where it had collided with a gnarled root, exposed from the ground like a grasping hand.

Hide, the same voice whispered.

I dove into a pocket under the exposed root, burrowing in until I could barely see out. The man appeared at the top of the ridge. He stopped, scanning the forest. His cloak was darker than black, a hue that pulled from the shadows around it.

Under the cowl, there was no hint of the man underneath—no glinting eyes, no hooked nose. Nothing. He had no face, like he was made of smoke.

He glided down the hill toward my tree, never slipping despite the cascading dirt. When he neared my spot, an echo reverberated through the forest. He jerked upright, head cocked toward the sound, and took off running. His footfalls made no noise.

And I could have sworn the echo he'd chased sounded like . . .

Like me.

I exhaled long and slow, dizzy from holding my breath. When I squeezed out from under the tree, it seemed tighter than when I'd hidden. I gripped my sword with one hand, ready to run, but stopped suddenly.

The ground. Where the shadowman had walked, the grass, once green, was brown. Any tiny flowers were wilted. Within the verdant forest teeming with life, a path of destruction stretched everywhere he'd been.

I fled, sprinting as far and as fast as I could in the opposite direction, listening for the whisper on the wind, but not hearing it again.

When I finally stopped to rest my hands on my knees and catch my breath, sticks and leaves stuck in my hair and clothes. I was more turned around than ever, and the sun had dipped below the trees, washing the sky in orange.

I found another spot for the night—a tree that had fallen onto another tree, creating an alcove underneath.

As I lay waiting for sleep to claim me, sifting through my

options, the one thing I'd figured out was that something didn't add up between the traitor, the mage, and now King Marko. I had two paths: Hálendi or Turia. My empty stomach turned. I couldn't go home—I didn't know the traitor's identity or the mage's next move. At least in Turia I knew the threat. And there was a chance I could find answers about the mage in the palace library.

I sighed, deep and long. Death hadn't found me yet, so I'd go to Turia. No matter the risk, I would search from the Fjalls to the cliffs if I had to. I *would* unearth who was responsible and avenge my family, protect my kingdom.

If, that is, I could find my way out of the Wild.

✦ ✦ ✦

My tutors had made me study maps of the Plateau for hours and hours. I'd always resented it: seeing how wide the world was and never getting to experience it. But as I picked my way through the Wild the next day, making steady progress northwest, I thanked each of them by name. The Fjalls split the Wild, and acted as a natural border between Hálendi and Turia. And while the main pass was the safest, most-used road over the mountain, there was another.

I found a long, sturdy branch and, after cutting off the shoots with my knife, used it as a staff as I walked. The ragged wound from the tethers still bled into me, a constant, dripping pain. Ren's book stayed in my pocket. Even though it wouldn't help me survive, I kept it as close as I could while keeping my hands free to climb and venture through the underbrush.

But the farther I traveled into the Wild, the less the tethers hurt in my chest. The Wild filled me instead, easing my burdens and healing the cracks around my heart.

I let the forest guide me, taking whichever path presented itself. It tended to be uphill, but I didn't care, as long as it led northwest. I'd need to cross the Fjalls via a path, and Miners' Pass, though small and dangerous, was my best chance to avoid the mage and his men. Then I'd be in Turia, and each step forward would lead me closer to answers. I hoped.

Near midday, a meadow spread out before me, with a gurgling stream cascading down from a cluster of rocks, pooling in a small basin, then continuing into the forest. At the edge of the meadow, the peak of the mountain I'd climbed all morning jutted out, a field of boulders leading to the top, no trees to impede the view.

I scrambled up, careful of loose rocks that would send me plummeting back down. Sharp edges chafed against my palms, and my arms shook as I climbed. A small animal with bushy brown fur scampered by, watching curiously. When I reached as high as I could climb, I stood among the boulders on a wide, flat rock, breathing heavily with my hands behind my head, the evergreen-scented wind whipping strands of hair from my matted braid.

Endless forest stretched in every direction as far as I could see. The land rose and fell, mountains and hills and gullies, but all green. Shining lakes dotted the expanse, reflecting the perfect blue of the sky that cradled everything from above. Pillowy clouds offered patches of shade as they migrated from one side of the world to the other.

My hands fell to my sides, and my shoulders dropped. My

eyes stung in the wind. I wished Ren could be here, standing next to me, seeing what I saw. But he'd never stand beside me again. My hand fastened around the book in my pocket, and I turned to face ahead. To the path I hadn't yet traveled.

The Fjalls rose like dark monsters from a sea of green. Or maybe the forest was the monster, and the Fjalls a row of rotting black teeth. Either way, I'd have to find my way across them.

✦✦✦

The forest was quite loud, once it got used to you. Birdsong, chirping calls, and the whisper of crickets and buzzing insects wove together into the tapestry of greens and purples and yellows.

As I walked the next day, there always seemed to be a stream in my path when I needed water. I hiked for as long as I could, rarely stopping for food. My limbs shook only a little; the Wild's energy filled me, a buzzing, crackling *satisfaction* I'd never experienced with food.

My mind spun in circles—thinking of anything and everything to keep memories of the mage's attack away. I realized we'd had only two days' notice before setting out to Turia. Yet the mage had been waiting for us. Expecting us. I cursed whoever had betrayed us to an icy death and swung my staff at a low-hanging vine in my path. It recoiled from the hit before resuming its position, and I swallowed back my anger and stepped more carefully.

As the sun began its descent into evening, a line of gray cut through the path I took. Everything in its wake had died. Birds didn't sing here, and a hint of charred wood hung in the air. I jumped over the path, unwilling to touch anywhere a shadowman may have crossed.

As the sun set, casting the sky in pinks and oranges, the foliage opened to reveal a wide meadow. The scent hit me first, a perfume so exquisite, so powerful, I stopped right at the edge and drank it in. A shining lake rested in the middle of the clearing, white sand enveloping its shore.

A grove of trees grew next to the water—trees I'd never before seen. Delicate white flowers bunched along the branches, and the branches curled and bounced like ribbons. I sighed as I approached the lake—the tethers didn't hurt at all here. Nothing did. I set my staff against a ribbon tree, brushing my finger through the soft grass at its base.

A small tug in the back of my mind warned me not to touch the lake, but the pull of its calm surface drew me in. A respite from pain. From the memories haunting every step. I knelt and dipped my hands, expecting the same cold water from the streams. But it was warm. Deliciously warm.

I drank my fill, then untied my hair, combing through the snarled mass as best I could. My scalp itched with dried mud, so I dunked my head underwater to scrub it. And though the water was warm, it had the same effect as jumping into a river of glacier runoff. Sharp prickles, numbness, then heat all over. But the heat didn't burn; it felt more like a cat stretching in the sun.

Though there was still maybe an hour of light left, I decided to stay. I lay on the soft sand of the shore and watched the stars appear one by one, until I was covered by a blanket of them. Safe under their protection.

✦ ✦ ✦

When the silver lake reflected the blush of dawn, I stood to gather my belongings, and dizziness overwhelmed me. I waited, hands on knees, until it faded. My sword lay on the ground next to my staff. I didn't remember removing it. I shook off my confusion, buckled it on, and headed toward the edge of the meadow. A small family of deer peered out from the trees beyond. I sighed and stared over the beautiful scene one last time.

As I hiked uphill, away from the lake, something dug into my leg. What was in my pocket? I pulled it out and startled. Ren's book. My brow furrowed. *Right.*

After looking back more than once with a wistful sigh, I dug my staff into the ground and forced myself to leave the haven. The energy inside me was jumping more today, tugging frantically. The forest was more frenzied, too; I had to use the dagger from my boot to cut away thick brush in my path. But I continued pushing toward the Fjalls.

Later in the day, a broad leaf sliced against my cheek. I stopped with a gasp and held my hand to the thin cut. Only a bit of blood seeped out, so I continued on. But then the land dropped at a steep cliff. Too sharp to climb down, too tall to risk falling from. I huffed and wiped sweat from my forehead. Another obstacle. One more in a string of fallen trees and rivers and mountains.

But something moved in the ravine.

A shadow. With a trail of death following in its wake.

I jumped back from the edge and fled into the forest, running as fast as I could. The Wild pressed me on, guiding me away from the shadowman and toward the Fjalls, but when I sprinted into a meadow, I skidded to a stop.

A shining lake. Ribbon trees.

It was the same meadow as yesterday. Had I been running in the wrong direction?

I clasped my hands behind my neck as I caught my breath. A dizzy sensation overwhelmed me. Maybe I just needed food. An ache within told me my legs needed rest, too. It couldn't hurt to sit for a few minutes. I took up my staff and headed toward the ribbon tree grove.

In the Palace Dungeon

"He killed them. He killed them all." The filthy man curled into himself, rocking back and forth on the wet, moldering floor.

The king leaned against the doorway and tapped the letter against his thigh as Blaire tried to get the messenger to speak of anything else. It wasn't the first time they had tried to get this story from him. But it would be the last.

He read the letter again.

The tariffs are not affecting them as we had hoped. I will find a way to connect the royals to us. I need only time and loyalty in the right places.

The king tapped the letter against his palm and shut the door with a click. "There's no more time to waste. Do it, Blaire."

Blaire released the man's shirt and turned to the king with hesitant, wide eyes. "Are you sure? H-he may not ever be the same."

The king narrowed his eyes at Blaire's reluctance and glanced at the outline of the potion in his pocket. "I would hear the message he was intended to deliver. If you are unwilling, I'm sure Lord—"

"I will do it, Your Majesty."

The king tucked the letter away as Blaire pulled a small vial of amber liquid from within his robe and knelt over the prostrate messenger. He forced the man's jaw open and emptied the vial, holding the man's mouth closed until he swallowed. The man coughed and sputtered, then lay still.

A moment later, the man jerked upright. Blaire jumped back, but the man only stared at the wall to his left. Blaire's eyes flicked between the man and the king before he sputtered out, "Tell us the message you have to deliver."

"We are coming." The man's detached voice echoed in the bare cell. "Have the location ready." He slumped against the wall, eyes unblinking, his stare now lifeless.

The king's eyes gleamed in the darkness. Sweat started beading on Blaire's forehead. "Your Majesty, I don't—"

"This will work." He grabbed Blaire by the front of his robes. "You still have the location?"

Blaire tugged at the collar of his robe. "Yes, but—"

He pushed Blaire away. "Then stop worrying. The plan will work."

Blaire used a handkerchief to wipe the sweat and greasy hair from his face, and bobbed his head. "Yes, of course, Your Majesty."

CHAPTER EIGHT

Soft grass caressed my bare arms as I lay on my back in the meadow. I'd washed my tunic, trousers, and undershirt, and scrubbed the salt and dirt from every inch of my skin. Sunshine beat down on me from a cloudless sky, its rays penetrating deep into my bones like I'd become part of the Wild itself. No more pain. No more hunger or thirst. No more questions. Somehow I knew the sun wouldn't even burn my skin, like it usually did when I was outside too long.

A tiny orange frog hopped along my line of vision. My clothes had been dry for . . . a while. How long? I couldn't remember, but it was warm enough that I didn't need the extra protective layers.

A tiny buzzing tickled my mind, some instinct long buried. I closed my eyes, but the buzzing continued, so I got up, stumbling when the ground shifted under me, and ran my fingers through the rippling silver lake on my way to the grove of trees. To my soft nook, nestled between the roots of the largest ribbon tree.

The ring on my left hand still had dirt in its engravings. Maybe if I took it off to wash it . . .

The buzzing pressed harder against my mind. My bare foot kicked against something hidden in the grass. When I bent to reach the small brown rectangle, my hand froze. A book? A dull ache started behind my eyes. I shook my head, trying to remember something. Hadn't this happened before?

"What is going on?" I whispered, and picked up the book.

A swirling wave of understanding crashed into me, followed closely by guilt. *Ren.* Then the pain came. The tethers throbbed worse than ever before, my stomach a rock of hunger. The cut on my cheek. My dry throat. What was happening? I looked down and blinked—I was in only my underthings, and my skin was decidedly pink from the sun.

"Glaciers." My fingers clung to the book like a lifeline. I snatched up my clothes and put them on. Searched the base of each tree until I found my sword. I buckled it around my waist, muttering every curse I knew, grabbed my staff, and ran.

How much time had I lost? I searched my memories as I went, using my staff to push away the ferns slapping against me at every step. Hazy recollections of sitting under the ribbon trees played in a loop—a day. I think I'd lost only a day.

As I distanced myself from the meadow, its tentacles held tight to the corners of my mind, urging me to turn back. Wrapping around the broken tethers and squeezing. The world spun, but I continued forward, a firm grip on my sword and Ren's book.

At midday, I stumbled into a stream and slurped up as much water as I could. Wild blackberries grew from the mud on the bank. I hesitated, wondering if they'd make me forget, but my stomach took control and I gathered as many as I could, eating until I had to sit a moment so they wouldn't come back up. Wretched Wild. How long had it been since I'd eaten?

I kept a few berries to take with me. I wouldn't forget again.

✦✦✦

That night, I dreamed of the shining lake. Of peace and painlessness. I sat up with a jolt at first light, disturbed at the strong presence that still lingered. Vines were twisted around me, fuzzy leaves caressing my cheeks, tightening so slowly I hadn't noticed I could barely breathe.

The green ropes had pinned my arms to my sides, and the more I struggled, the more they tightened. Cords wrapped around my stomach, squeezing. Where was my sword? Not in its sheath. I cast my eyes around until I saw it—also embedded in a tangle of vines.

I squirmed from side to side until I could bring my knees to my chest. I whipped the knife from my boot and, sucking in a deep breath, cut the cords around my stomach. Then I worked on those holding my arms, trying not to slice myself in the process. Three vines snapped under my blade, and then the others unraveled and retreated back into the forest.

The ones holding my sword dragged it away, and I jumped up, hacking at them until they released it. I stood, gasping in lungfuls of air, and wiped my hand down my face.

I found my direction and set forth again. I needed to get out of this place.

Where it had drawn me in with open arms, now the Wild turned against me, ripping into my skin and snagging my clothes with every step. Beady eyes watched from above, an army of garish birds keeping pace with my strides, screeching at me to turn back.

Everywhere I turned, rivers overflowing with spring runoff from the mountains crossed my path, which meant more water, but it also meant I had to follow them until I found a safe place to cross. Fields of boulders kept me scrambling on my hands. My tender skin chafed against my clothes. But the pain anchored me, kept me from thinking about the shining lake as I hiked through the night. I didn't dare sleep; I didn't have enough strength to fight off the vines again. My thoughts simplified to the bare necessities for survival: food, water.

Just before dawn, as I staggered through a swath of mud, I reached the Fjalls.

A meadow filled with tall blue flowers opened from the trees, and a wall of black rock jutted from the earth. Patches of green on shards of ledges broke the smooth surface. Even the Wild was quiet at the base of these mountains.

Magic hummed everywhere, vibrating through me until I could barely focus. I gripped Ren's book in one hand and the staff in my other, and followed the mountains, the black wall to my left, the Wild to my right. The road to Miners' Pass couldn't be more than a day away. Then it would be one day over the pass, one day in the Wild on Turia's side, and then I'd be out.

The land rose steadily, and my breath grew shorter the higher I climbed. Eventually I was so high on the benches of the mountains that the misting rain turned to crystals of ice suspended in the air, which stuck to my skin as I walked through them. Even with my Hálendian blood, the cold seeped into my bones until I thought they'd shatter with every step. I tore strips from the wool shirt under my tunic and wrapped them around my exposed hands.

My chin was drooping to my chest, my eyes falling closed, when I stumbled onto the trail I had been seeking. Wary of other travelers, or of the shadowman, I stayed off the road. And by late afternoon, I couldn't take another step. My sleepless night was catching up to me. Then the wind changed, and the animals who'd been following now settled in early. A storm was coming.

One peak of the mountain stretched jagged into the sky, higher than the rest. The pass. Tomorrow. I'd summit tomorrow.

I'd come across only a few bushes with meager berries I recognized, and my stomach ached with hunger. I ate all I could and found a wide, flat rock—no vines—under a rocky overhang to sleep on, before closing my eyes. Water filled my dreams again. Ren's book never left my hand.

◆◆◆

A glaze of snow dusted everything when I woke. The white sky blanketed the mountains, with fingers of wispy clouds reaching toward me like smoke through the trees. The storm wasn't done yet.

I tied the hood of my cloak tight around my face. Heavy snowflakes began to fall as I reached the road. Could I survive the pass in a storm? I looked up the steep, winding path shrouded in white, and back into the Wild, where clouds, building against the black wall, hid the tops of the trees.

The Wild called to me. Alluring, safe. Painless.

I ran a trembling hand over my face and shook away the desire to return. I wouldn't forget. Wouldn't give up.

My steps crunched along the steep trail, irreverent in the graveyard silence within the short, scrubby trees. I turned another broken branch into a staff to keep my traction in the mud and rocks. I didn't want to relinquish Ren's book to my pocket, but I needed the help to balance, especially if the wind worsened. The trail wove back and forth as it climbed, the next turn always hidden.

I pushed for hours, my calves and lungs burning from the uphill battle. Snow drifted against the jagged rocks and blew in my face. The wind tugged at me, icy fingers trying to drag me back toward the shining lake. My sword banged against my hip with every step. Ren's book in my pocket grew heavier.

I'd lost track of time in the blizzard—it could have been midday or midnight. But when I next raised my head against the onslaught of elements, a strange stack of rocks peeked out of the snowbank. I shivered, yet I was burning, sweating. The mountain rose on both the left and right of me, everything else shrouded in a veil of clouds.

I stared at the craggy formation. *A burial marker?* I shook the thought loose. No, it was something else. I knew what it was, but my thoughts were so slow. I rested my hand over my pocket. Over Ren's book.

My brain finally unscrambled, and I realized those rocks signaled the summit of the pass. I would have smiled had my face not been numb.

I crossed the summit of the Fjalls as the storm raged. A whole new set of muscles began aching on the downward trek—my thighs and back burned—but the staffs kept me from sliding off the mountain.

The landscape of white blurred in and out of focus before me as I pressed on, one foot in front of the other. Had I been hiking for hours or days? Either way, I must be close. The Wild's grasp on my mind stretched thinner on this side of the mountain, though its claws sank deep.

Another step, and the snow underfoot shifted. My heart lurched into my throat, and I would have careened head over feet had one staff not gotten wedged into a rock buried in snow. And had my grip not been frozen to the wood. My other staff tumbled downhill, pulling more and more snow with it until a small avalanche crashed into the trees below.

I gripped my staff and breathed for a moment. It had saved my life.

Once my heart had stopped racing, I continued, stepping as gingerly as I could. The wind finally calmed as I descended past the tree line again, and every breath got easier. Clouds still hung low, and the snow had turned to rain—but I wasn't going to get much farther on my shaking legs in the darkening night.

I was searching off the path for a place to rest, covering my tracks as well as I could, when a rock slipped under my foot and I tumbled forward. I rolled once, twice, coming to a stop only when my body slammed into something hard and rough.

Groaning, I pushed myself up on shaking arms. My ribs burned where I'd hit the tree stump. But ahead, a small rock overhang created a shallow cave. There were no signs of wildlife, and no vines, so I scooted down the ridge and crawled into the alcove.

My eyes drifted shut almost immediately from exhaustion.

Survive.

They snapped open. I carefully unwrapped my hands, nervous to see what damage had been done. My fingertips were white, but there was no black—the strips of the wool shirt and heavy cloak had protected them from the worst of the cold. I laid the strips out to dry and wished desperately for water. If I ate the snow, it would only freeze me from the inside out.

I pulled my arms from the damp sleeves of my tunic and wrapped them around my torso, trying to keep all my body heat together.

My eyes drifted shut again, and I couldn't fight it this time.

✦ ✦ ✦

I spent most of the night shivering, dreaming of the lake, of ribbon trees wrapping around me, falling asleep only to be jerked awake in fear I would forget again. That the vines had returned. But I opened my eyes to sunshine; the storm had run its course.

The narrow path wasn't much wider than an animal trail, but I followed it regardless—anything to get me out of the Wild faster. I tried to remember the map of Turia I had studied so long ago. I exhaled long and slow. I'd been so focused on getting out of the Wild, I'd forgotten that a whole new set of troubles awaited me. Mining towns dotted the western forests of Turia, and my light hair marked me as a foreigner.

Resolved to sort that out later, I ate the few shriveled wild strawberries I came across, again wishing for water. I'd traveled only a short way before the silence got to me. Birds weren't singing here. No squirrels chirping. Just creaking trees.

The Wild's magic seemed muted here, and though my mind was clearer, a feeling of being watched crept in.

I wasn't sure if the shadowman could have tracked me through that storm, but I darted off the trail and headed straight south. *Stay on the road,* everyone had said. But if the Wild was *protecting* me from the shadowman, its reach wouldn't extend to the roads.

In the forest, I pressed on. Still, I didn't cross any streams, and my throat ached with thirst. Every step away from the Fjalls, every step away from the Wild, the emptiness inside grew until my every thought stayed focused on it. My hands shook. The hole from the tethers threatened to consume me.

I didn't even hear the wolf until it lunged.

Instinct took over, and my walking staff came up, the only thing between me and the sharp fangs of the wolf. I used its momentum to roll back and kick it off, then swung my staff at its muzzle. It yelped and stood in my path, a menacing growl deep in its throat. Two other massive beasts stalked out of the brush to stand next to their leader. Their muscles rippled beneath their thick fur. They were so *big.*

I switched my staff to my left hand and eased my sword out of its scabbard. Sweat dripped beneath my tunic. My ring burned against my finger. I stepped back—once, twice. The wolves didn't follow.

My brow furrowed, and I stepped back again. The biggest wolf, the one in the middle, sat on his haunches. The other two lay down, their tongues lolling to the side. Their leader watched as I checked above to either side and behind me. But there were no other predators nearby.

Cautiously, I stepped forward. The biggest wolf stood. I retreated, and the wolf sat again. I ground my jaw together. Wretched Wild.

"I have to keep going," I said aloud, my voice shattering the cadence of the forest around us. The wolves stood.

Run, the Wild whispered again. *Run away.* I squeezed my eyes tight against the memory of the shining lake and ribbon trees. I wouldn't forget. I'd bear the pain of the tethers forever if it meant not forgetting Ren and my father.

Survive, Hafa had said.

My focus narrowed down to my sword, staff, and the wolves. I stepped forward. "Let me pass."

Their hackles rose once more. The biggest wolf lunged. I dodged to the side and brought my sword up, nicking its side, and threw my staff at the next wolf like a javelin, connecting with its neck.

I swung and ducked, lunging out of the way and trying to push my way past them. My blade was an extension of my arm, and power thrummed through me. Even so, my strength was waning too fast.

A wolf jumped at me from the side as I engaged the other two in front. My arm came up to block the attack, even though I knew the wolf's claws would rip it to shreds.

But the wolf never reached me. Instead, it flew back into a tree, landing in a heap. Yelping in pain, it scrambled to its feet and loped into the forest. The rest of the pack eyed me warily before following.

I studied the underbrush for more threats before falling to my knees, staring at my sword. Magic. I'd somehow used magic. But the tethers were broken. So how?

Then I remembered. The mage in the clearing. The vibrating heat as my ring had absorbed his magic that kept everyone else from moving. I studied the dirt-encrusted gem. I didn't feel anything in it—had almost forgotten about it, actually. But it had saved the energy.

My hands shook, and I stumbled back. Magic. Not my own, but I'd used it nonetheless.

I bent to retrieve my staff and gasped at a burning across my side. My staff had rows of gouges from the claws or teeth of the wolves. So did I. I winced and sat hard in the dirt. I gently lifted the torn layers of material away from my body. Three red streaks dripped blood between my protruding hip bone and my ribs.

I tore a strip from the bottom of my tunic and pressed it into my side, breathing through my nose when the world began to spin. The scent of the ribbon trees lingered in the air, churning my stomach. I put more pressure on the wounds, then pulled the cloth away—they weren't deep. I exhaled in relief, then slowly, ever so slowly, got to my feet.

I had to make it to Turia. Aleinn had died in my place. Hafa had died defending me. Their sacrifices wouldn't be in vain.

"Wretched, wretched Wild!" I yelled into the trees, and threw a rock into the brush.

The rock came bouncing back at me, rolling to a stop at my feet. The Wild didn't answer with words. But it watched. It was always watching.

I stumbled south, closing in on the edge of the Wild. I could feel it. Feel the Wild's desperation. Trees with newly sprouted leaves scattered among the evergreens joined the fight to keep me in. Branches snagged at my hair and cloak while vines twisted around my ankles, threatening to root me to the ground. I pulled my sword to fight them off, and though they flinched away for a moment, it wasn't enough to deter them.

After what felt like hours of chopping through the roughage, my shoulders and legs aching like never before, the Wild suddenly stopped fighting. The trees stood still; the vines lay dormant. No more exotic birds, no more curious animals.

I'd made it into Turia and out of the Wild.

And yet some unseen dread settled around the tightness in my belly. The same sense of unease as when I'd crossed the shadowman's blackened trail.

Someone—some*thing*—was tracking me. Waiting for me.

For the first time since watching Aleinn fall lifelessly to the ground, since hesitating while Hafa battled the mage without me, something besides fear and pain and desperation to survive filled me.

Rage.

I would not run away again.

CHAPTER NINE

My senses cataloged every snapped branch, every scurrying animal. There were no blackened trails nearby, yet I knew the creature tracking me wasn't natural. I crossed straight through a small clearing and left my cloak and gouged staff under a bush. When I passed into the undergrowth, I drew my sword and snuck around to the side.

The shadowman's foot didn't make a sound as he stepped into the clearing. Little sunlight filtered through the overhead branches, and he blended into the shadows as if he were part of them. He wasn't smudged, like the mage had been, but there was something overly precise in the way he moved. He held a black sword, and his cloak billowed in the still forest air.

My heartbeat echoed in my empty stomach, and my pulse throbbed against my wounds. Now that I'd left the Wild, the absence of its magic left me stretched thin, like a worn-out sweater. Did I have enough energy to fight another battle?

I inhaled slowly and let my focus narrow down to my sword and my opponent. We'd find out.

I slipped silently from the embrace of the trees, attacking when he drew even with me. The shadowman wasn't surprised; he simply turned and met my blade, then raised his other hand. Instinct took over from my practice with Master Hafa, and I lifted my ring hand. I staggered back from the shock of absorbing the burst of energy sent my way.

The shadowman charged when the blast didn't affect me. I blocked his swing and answered with one of my own. His offense came fast, but his swings were so precise they were predictable. My ring vibrated with the shadowman's magic—I could feel it now, outside of the Wild.

The tip of my sword wobbled with my shaking muscles. Master Hafa had taught me only to defend against magic, not to attack with it. When I'd used it against the wolves, it had been sheer luck. And my strength wouldn't last much longer.

I took a deep breath and visualized shifting the magic from the ring into the sword. When the shadowman approached again, I defended. I yelped and jumped back as a wave of energy blasted from my sword. The shadowman rippled like the surface of a pond, and the magic slowed him down for a fraction of a second, but then passed straight through him.

No. I pushed out the rest of the magic until there was nothing left. I panted, my sword growing heavier by the second. He wasn't winded—if he even breathed. And I had used up precious energy on magic that hadn't worked.

I released a long, slow breath, and raised my sword to Master Hafa's specifications. I wouldn't continue on, hunted by this *thing.* I had answers to find in Turia.

Our blades met again, and I spun, grabbing the hunting knife in my boot, then slashing at him with both weapons.

He parried my first three blows, but my fourth struck true. The edge of my knife disappeared into him without any resistance, then reappeared as he dissolved like smoke in the wind. His sword thumped to the ground.

I was alone in the clearing, but my heart still raced.

His black sword glinted dully, and I slipped my knife back into my boot and reached down for it. My hand stopped before I could touch it. I pushed against the invisible barrier until I realized it wasn't magic from the blade keeping me away; it was my ring's magic protecting me. And then, as I watched, the black sword disintegrated into dust on the forest floor, a small patch of dead grass the only hint that anything had been there.

I jumped back and sheathed my blade. Rested my hands on my knees. No uneasiness. No one following me. No Wild trying to trap me. The sun had just passed below the trees. I'd have an hour at best before it was too dark to see.

Food. And water. The need for them took over every other rational thought. It even filled the hole in my chest where the tethers had been.

I headed south again, hoping to cross a stream but not finding one. There was a blackberry bush to the left of my path, but when I searched under the leaves, my hands came away with only scratches; the berries had all been picked off. The wind rushed through the trees like a waterfall. The sound never led to water.

Survive.

The word echoed through me, but it had started to lose its meaning. I tried thinking about my time in the Wild, if I'd eaten anything at all. Hazy snatches of memory came back, of a handful of berries here and there, but the Wild's magic had tricked me into thinking I was full, the wretched place.

Exhaustion laced every muscle, every thought. But if I stopped for the night, I was afraid I would never get up. So I pushed on as the light faded.

The ground seemed to shift beneath me with every step. Then I tripped over a root, and fell head over tail down an embankment.

When the world finally stopped spinning, I lay in a patch of . . . onions? Sturdy green stalks in neat rows and a tantalizing aroma surrounded me.

My face and tangled hair were covered in dirt, a new ache sprouted in my ribs on the other side from the wolf scratches, and my ankle throbbed in time with my heartbeat. I didn't move, didn't bother to lift my face.

"Are you dead?" a voice whispered. Something nudged my leg. I groaned, and someone yelped.

My head snapped up.

Not a voice on the wind. Not a trick of the Wild.

A boy.

Maybe ten or twelve years old. Dark hair. Olive skin. Holding a stick like a sword.

"Mama!" he yelled into the night. "Papa! A girl fell into the onions!"

My head landed back in the dirt, and the world went dark.

✦ ✦ ✦

Liquid dribbled down my chin, pulling me from an odd limbo between wakefulness and sleep. Someone placed a cup against my lips and tilted my head back, and cool water chased warm broth down my throat, churning together in my stomach.

The air smelled like a combination of onions and spices I'd never tasted. I squinted against the firelight. Four sets of brown eyes stared at me.

A woman sat nearest, peace radiating from her like sunshine. She wore a simple faded-green skirt, gray shirt, and an apron whose original color I couldn't begin to guess. A thin yellow scarf wrapped around her ebony hair, which was pulled into a loose bun at the top of her head, with only a few strands of silver shining through at her temples.

A man stood behind her, his strong hand resting protectively on her shoulder. Same dark hair. A colorless shirt smudged with dirt covered broad shoulders accustomed to work.

The boy who'd found me, now without his stick, peeked out from behind the man, who could only be his father.

The fourth pair of eyes belonged to a small girl with black hair, holding a handmade doll. The girl's wide caramel eyes never blinked, and her mouth was stuck in a permanent O.

The woman tipped a ceramic bowl filled with red broth into my mouth. I drank greedily, slurping in as much as I could.

"Easy now, *carina,*" she murmured, like I was a young colt. Her accent was soft, her *R*'s rolling trills and her vowels longer.

A pang shuddered through me. *Did Gentry ever make it out?*

"It will take time for you to get used to having food again."

Time? Oh no—how long had I been here? I thought I'd left the Wild. But maybe I hadn't?

I jerked back, scooting until I fell off the bed I hadn't realized I'd been on. "I won't stay!" My ribs groaned and pulled, my ankle throbbed, as I tossed blankets aside searching for my sword. At least I had my ring. *Ren's book!* "Where is it?" I asked frantically, patting my pockets and bending to look under the bed.

"Where is what?" the man asked, taking a protective step to guard his family from me.

"My belongings! I can't forget again. I won't . . ." I ran my hands over the floor. Had I missed the brown cover in the dim light?

"Here," a small voice said. The boy held my sheathed sword and book out to me, a curious tilt to his head. "We weren't going to take them."

I froze, then grabbed them. He jumped away, and I bit my lip, brow furrowed, studying the family and the cabin I was in.

My staff lay on the floor by the bed I'd been on, which was similar to mine in Hálendi—a wood frame filled with straw, covered by a blanket. Everything else was foreign. The planks of the walls intersecting in corners, the fire in the side wall instead of in the middle of the room, the long, tall table pushed up against the wall by the cupboards. A door in the back hinted at another room, tucked by the fireplace.

"Where am I?" I asked, holding tight to my sword and stashing the book into my pocket. "How long have I been here?"

The woman tilted her head, a move that matched her son's. "You haven't been here more than an hour, carina. And you're in our *bosco*," she said, her eyes flicking to my hair.

"Bosco?" The word tasted foreign on my tongue.

"Our land," she said. "Our patch of trees, if you will."

"Not in the Wild?" I asked, and limped to the window. We were in a clearing, but beyond that, I couldn't see much in the dark.

"She talks funny," the little girl whispered.

"Hush," her father whispered back.

"The Wild?" the woman asked. "Of course not, carina. No one goes . . ." She took in my clothes and hair again.

Glaciers, I'd said too much. "My name is not Carina," I said, hoping to change topics.

The boy scoffed. "It's not a name."

The woman clicked her tongue at him, a sound I'd never heard, yet I knew exactly what it meant. "I am called Irena. My husband is Lorenz, and this is Carlo and Gia. I call you 'carina' because I do not know your name."

"I—" I tried to swallow, but my mouth was still too dry. The room started spinning again.

"Here, sit," Irena and Lorenz both said, coming forward and taking me by the elbow, gently guiding me back to the bed. "You are not well?" Irena asked, easing me down so I sat against the wall.

"My mama will take care of you," Gia said with a nod.

The corners of my mouth tipped into a smile. Not the Wild. They wouldn't force me to stay. I wouldn't forget.

Lorenz spread his arms, gathering his children and shepherding them toward the room by the fireplace. "Come, it's time for bed."

They protested loudly, though Carlo yawned and Gia rubbed her eyes with her little fists.

"What ails you, child?" Irena asked when we were as alone as we could be in the tiny house. She went to the long table, the skirt brushing against her calves much shorter than any in Hálendi. As she dumped water from the bucket into a bowl, the liquid caught the light from the fire. She washed her hands and wiped them on a cloth. The tasks awakened a memory I had pushed deep down inside: a memory of my mother with warmth in her arms.

What ailed me? The room went blurry as tears gathered in my eyes and trailed down my cheeks when I squeezed my eyes shut. My father. My brother. Aleinn, Master Hafa, Leland, all those soldiers who'd become my friends. My kingdom. My future. My present. It all ailed me.

When I didn't respond right away, a line of worry deepened in Irena's brow.

"May I have more water, please?" I asked, my throat scratching.

She filled a delicate ceramic cup and sat on a stool by the bed. I spilled some of the water, my grip weak, but managed to swallow most of it. It slid, cool and refreshing, all the way down my throat, and I knew I would never enjoy any drink as much as this simple cup of stream water.

I held the cup in my lap and leaned my head back a moment to take a few breaths. "Could I also have more food, please? Anything you have to spare?" It had been only a week, yet my voice was almost unrecognizable to me, like it had changed in the Wild, too.

Irena's hand brushed my shoulder—a delicate touch, yet so foreign—and she brought me a small chunk of bread from the kitchen.

"Don't eat too much, or you'll lose it all."

She watched as I tore off a small portion and put it into my mouth. An herb I hadn't expected burst over my tongue. Rosemary, maybe? I chewed slowly, savoring every moment. The woman chuckled. She probably thought I was . . . well, whatever the Turian equivalent of an Ice Desert wanderer was.

"I'm glad to see you appreciate my baking." Her eyes were still laughing.

I was too tired to smile or laugh with her. My chin tipped down, and my eyelids grew heavy, unable to resist the pull of this home. Heat from the fire wrapped around my aching body—not with numbness, like in the Wild, but with actual warmth.

"This is the finest baking I've ever encountered," I rasped out.

Irena helped me lie down as I struggled to stay awake. I knew I should thank her—they'd saved my life. But a part of me wasn't sure this wasn't a new trick of the Wild.

Her brown eyes lost their laugh. "I don't know what you are running from, child, or how you ended up on my door looking like the Wild chewed you up and spit you out, but you are welcome to stay until you are ready to get wherever you're going."

Would I ever be ready to leave this haven and face those responsible for so much destruction?

I had no family left, no kingdom. Now that my empty stomach and parched tongue were taken care of, I could once again feel the hollowness just under my heart. I didn't think it would ever go away. I wasn't sure I wanted it to. The pain was all I had left of my family. I remembered the longing I had sensed through my father's tether the day he had given me my sword. The thought flashed through my mind that maybe that was why my father had always clung to his grief—it was a way to be close to my mother.

A murky haze left over from the Wild blocked out my memories of my home, my kingdom, as if those experiences had been lived in a different lifetime. I wasn't sure who had come out of the Wild, but it wasn't the same person who had run away into it.

I was half asleep already when I murmured, "Jen—"

"What, carina?" Irena tilted her head in confusion.

I hadn't thought to give her a name other than my own. "My name," I said. "My name is Jen."

She held out her hand. I stared at it until I remembered—Turians greeted each other by touching hands.

"It's so nice to meet you, Jen."

I had nothing to offer these people, nothing left to give. But I touched my hand to hers. Her fingers squeezed mine, the pressure reassuring and gentle.

"It's nice to meet you, too."

I'd made it to Turia. Now how would I get to King Marko?

CHAPTER TEN

Vines reach like tentacles, cloaked shadows at the edge of my vision.

Muddy bodies with glassy eyes stare at the sky.

The mage slides his knife across Aleinn's neck. Again. And again. And again.

Haunted by nightmares, I slept off and on through the whole next day and into the early morning hours of the next. Each time I awoke from an awful dream, questions plagued me. Why had the mage targeted my family? Who was he working with? Where was he now?

How could I ever hope to defeat him if he found out he'd killed the wrong girl and came after me again?

I'd already had three cups of water from the bucket on the table and was slowly lacing my boots, my fingers stiff, when Lorenz emerged from the tiny room in the corner of the cabin. He shook his head and clicked his tongue at me, exactly like Irena had at Carlo.

"She won't like that, carina. Best rest a little longer." He grabbed a wide-brimmed hat from a hook by the door, added a log to the low fire, and, with a nod my way, plopped the hat on his head and ducked outside.

"He's right," Irena said from the door of her room. I startled and winced, breathing through the flash of pain in my ribs. "First, you'll need a bath. Then we'll see about your injuries."

"But—"

Irena flicked her fingers, cutting me off.

She set up a large tub right there in the kitchen, filled it with water carted from the stream and warmed with the fire. "I don't want to have to burn those blankets, and if you spend another minute in those clothes, I'm afraid that's what it will come to."

I wrinkled my nose and unlaced my boots slowly. A bath did sound nice.

"If you need help—"

"I can manage," I blurted. My hair would be a tangled mess, but I couldn't risk it. Not in Turia. Not with a mage who'd tried to kill me still out there somewhere.

She finished filling the tub, then shooed Carlo and Gia outside. "Change into these." She set a bundle of clothes on the floor by a towel.

"We'll be in the garden if you need us," she said as she shut the door behind her.

I exhaled in the peaceful silence. Within these walls, the forest chirps and buzzing I'd grown accustomed to were so far away. I stood with a groan and peeled off my layers, then huddled in the warm water, moaning. The wounds from the wolves stung, then settled. My eyes fell closed, and the heat soaked deep into my bones, unknotting my muscles.

My hair, on the other hand, took three washings to get the grime of the Wild out. And my ring had darkened a few shades with all the dirt embedded in the etchings and around the gem. My thumb traced the blue stone, and I flipped the ring around to hide the gem, though Irena and her family had probably already noticed it.

The water had cooled and turned an awful shade of brown by the time I got out, dried off, and put on some of the clothes Irena had given me. She'd left both a nightgown, and a skirt and blouse. I bit my lip as I tucked the blouse into the high-waisted faded-red skirt, trying to mimic Irena's style. The top was much too big on me, and because I was taller than her, the skirt was much, much too short, barely reaching midcalf. She'd left no stockings, and my cold feet were still bare. But it was better than sitting in a nightgown all day.

A quick knock sounded.

"Enter," I called after an awkward moment, wondering what I was supposed to say.

My practiced fingers braided my wet hair as Irena bustled in, little Gia toddling behind her. "It smells better in here already," she said with a laugh. She gathered my filthy clothes and dumped them into the tub. "Sit," she commanded. "Rest."

"I can help," I said, though I knew very well I had no idea how to wash clothes.

Gia came and took my hand, sitting on the edge of the bed. "Mama washes the best. We can't help yet."

Her tiny fingers wrapped around mine. How long had it been since anyone besides my brother had touched me? She kicked her legs, banging her feet against the wood frame. The side of my mouth quirked up. "Are we too little?"

Gia nodded solemnly. "But Carlo can help Papa in the fields. And I help Mama pick berries."

I squeezed her chubby hand and smiled. A sharp ache started in the back of my head to match the constant ache in my chest. My lips pressed together, and Irena, eyes trained on us, paused. "Lie back now, Jen. Gia, bring Jen some bread and the carrots we picked this morning."

"Okay, Mama."

Gia's shoulders raised proudly when she brought me the food.

"Thank you," I told her, mouth already watering. I tucked my feet under the blanket. "Your mama is lucky to have such a good helper." I stuffed the herbed bread in my mouth and bit off the end of a carrot, munching it all together.

Gia beamed at the praise, then addressed her mother. "May I play now?"

Irena chuckled, squeezing the last of the water from my trousers. "Yes, carina. But stay close."

Gia tore out of the house, her black curls flying behind her. How many times had Ren and I sprinted from the castle just like that? I swallowed the lump in my throat.

"She is perfect," I said to Irena.

She laughed. "A perfect handful, yes." Irena sobered, her finger poking through one of the tears in my tunic, from the wolves. "Let's get *you* patched up, then we'll worry about the clothes."

Irena started with the scratches over my ribs. They weren't deep, but she took a little jar from her cupboard and mixed the crushed herbs with water, then smeared them over the wounds, wrapping them with a clean cloth. I'd never seen anyone treat injuries this way, but Turians had always known more about healing than Hálendians.

"Where are you headed?" she asked as she applied a clear, thick cream to my nose and cheeks, where my skin had peeled from my time in the sun. She didn't ask where I was from. If I couldn't hide my origins—and I really doubted I could—I'd need a reason to be here. A new story, like the stories in the library back home.

I cleared my throat and leaned back a bit so Irena wasn't so close. The pungent smells of herbs I only vaguely recognized drenched the air. "Turiana. I'm looking for information."

Irena's head bobbed once, accepting my vague reply. She took rags that had been soaking in a purple liquid and wrapped them tight around my tender ankle, then placed my leg atop a rolled-up blanket on the bed. "The palace library is the most extensive on the Plateau. You can find near anything there."

I hoped she was right. Hoped that I'd find out if Marko had sent the mage after my family. Or how to kill a mage. Or what I should do next.

I lay propped up in the bed the rest of the morning, the ache from the tethers pressing against me, keeping the peace I could almost feel in this home just out of reach. I watched, numb, as Irena moved around, singing or humming with her velvet voice, using care-worn yet gentle hands to prepare a meal for her family.

Carlo came back at midday with warm milk that filled my belly enough to let my eyes finally close. The shaking in my hands had almost disappeared.

The nap wasn't long enough. I jerked awake, wincing at the boulder sitting on my chest after yet another dream about the shining lake in the Wild. I checked that my sword still rested nearby, that the knife still hid in my boots, my staff and cloak bundled next to them on the floor. That Ren's book was still under my pillow.

I needed to leave. Find out if Marko had ordered my family's death. Find the mage and the traitor who'd betrayed us. Hálendi's people, its history, sat on my shoulders, pressing me into the soft bed.

Clouds I couldn't see from my spot in bed opened, dumping enough rain to bring Lorenz and Carlo in early. The family settled into the tiny cabin, creating a togetherness I'd never experienced in my life. Irena smiled at the rain as Lorenz kissed her cheek and helped her with dinner, standing close enough to always be touching. Carlo stirred the contents of the blackened pot over the fire, and Gia played with her doll at the base of my bed.

Survive, or that gray monstrosity wins.

I'd survived. But he still won.

I'd leave when it stopped raining.

"Is everything all right, carina?" Irena's quiet voice caught my attention. Carlo eyed me from next to the fire.

I loosened my grip on my sword—my fingers had wrapped themselves around it—and forced a smile. "Yes."

"Do you fight?" Carlo asked as he stirred the stew. Irena's steady rhythm of chopping missed a beat.

I debated, but the sword had given that away already. "Yes." I wasn't sure what else to say, so I stayed quiet.

Carlo's long wooden spoon stopped stirring. "I've heard of

girls joining up, but all the girls I know just want to raise orchards instead." He wrinkled his nose. "Will you show me?"

I tilted my head. "Show you what?"

He gestured to my staff and my sword. "How to fight."

"Well . . ." My insides twisted, remembering muddy paths and sightless eyes.

Irena cut in. "She's still healing, Car."

He slumped back and stirred dinner again. When everything was ready, Lorenz pulled the long table away from the wall, and we gathered the mismatched chairs and sat around it together. Gia kept up a constant stream of chatter. Lorenz's gaze kept darting to me when he thought I wasn't looking. The feeling of being watched followed me into my dreams.

✦ ✦ ✦

The next morning—another nightmare had woken me long before the others—I explored outside the cabin until I found a quiet stand of trees next to their barn. The rain had stopped sometime during the night, though dark clouds hung low, nearly brushing the treetops. The wet ground sank with every step, resisting me every time I lifted my foot. I'd meant to do the stretches and exercises Master Hafa taught to build strength before setting out again. Instead, I stared at the trees to the north. Toward the Wild. Toward home.

Word of the mage's attack should have reached Hálenborg by now if anyone had survived. And if not . . .

A pair of black crows landed in a tree, shaking the branch with their weight. Did everyone believe me dead?

Soft footsteps approached from the house. I settled into a relaxed stance and tried to hide evidence of my heavy thoughts.

"Is it time for breakfast already?" I asked, infusing my voice with a lightness I didn't feel.

Irena leaned against a tree and eyed me without responding. My shoulders slumped under her gaze, but I couldn't seem to lift them again. The Wild pulled at me, even from afar. Beckoning.

"I don't know what's happened to you, and I'm not asking for details," Irena said, drawing my attention from the trees. "But you've a long life ahead of you, Jen. Don't dwell on your past—it's not where you're going." She wiped her hands on her apron and turned back to the cabin without waiting for a response.

Rain pinged against the roof again as we finished breakfast. I'd wait for this next storm to pass, then leave. Instead of working outside, Lorenz and Carlo sat around the fire. The boy whittled a figurine from wood, but Lorenz's concentration bounced between the fire and me.

"You could just ask her," Irena finally said.

My cheeks heated, and my fingers twisted in the coarse fabric of my skirt. Waiting.

"The man who owns the field closest to ours said he heard a rumor something was brewing between Turia and Hálendi."

The wind shifted outside, and rain splashed against the windows. Something was definitely brewing. But who had started it?

"He said the Hálendian princess never arrived."

I bowed my head, hoping they wouldn't see the truth. I still couldn't believe Marko would toss away centuries of peace between our lands. Couldn't believe he'd fabricate a marriage alliance just to kill us.

"Do you know anything about that?" he asked, a direct question I couldn't avoid.

My thumb rubbed against the gem of my ring, still palm-down. "I know a little." The rasp of Carlo's knife against his wood block stopped. Even little Gia perked up. "I don't know everything, but . . ." I swallowed. "I don't want to endanger you."

A sliver of guilt wormed its way under my skin. This harmless family wouldn't stand a chance against a mage, and I might be endangering them just by being here.

Irena reached for Lorenz's hand, and they shared a worried glance. Lorenz pressed his lips together. "Do you know if there will be a betrothal?"

My teeth clenched together hard, and I rubbed my forehead to erase the memory of Aleinn dressed in my cloak. "No, there will not." Not as long as everyone thought me dead. And I'd let them think that as long as a mage roamed the Plateau and a traitor hid in Hálendi.

Lightning flashed, briefly casting the room in sharp contrast. Carlo's wooden toy lay forgotten in his lap. Gia hugged her doll and watched her parents with wide eyes.

My brow furrowed. "Why does this disappoint you? You *want* a foreigner on the throne with your prince heir?"

Lorenz swiped his hand through the air. "Foreigner or not, we needed the alliance. Riiga has been threatening us from the south. Raising prices to import our crops. There's even rumors of mercenaries arriving there from the Continent."

"Glaciers," I muttered, mind spinning. With those circumstances, Marko would be a fool to break our agreement, to destroy my family. Hálendi might have been short on troops, but our soldiers' ability was unmatched. Riiga wouldn't dare instigate a confrontation if Turia were linked through marriage to Hálendi. "I . . ." My mind raced, flicking through possibilities. "I want to help, if I can."

The lines around Irena's eyes and mouth softened, but Lorenz's eyebrows dipped until they almost met in the middle.

I hurried on before he could dismiss me. "I need to go to Turiana anyway, so maybe I could . . . find a way to work for the king. Train soldiers." The words came out as I thought them, tumbling one over the other. "Or find out what happened with the princess, why she didn't come."

Lorenz shook his head. "No, carina, it's too—"

"I can do it," I said.

"I know you can," he said, his words startling me into silence. He did? With a glance toward the Wild and a small grin, he said, "I do not doubt your abilities. I only think you are so young to carry such a burden."

My thumb rubbed the gem in my ring, my braid falling over my shoulder as I lowered my head. I thought it would feel heavier, this responsibility, but my spirits lifted with a sense of direction. A path to take.

"I may be young, but it's a burden I'll gladly bear," I said quietly. The rain still pounded on the windows, wind still thrashed the trees, but their gloom couldn't reach me anymore.

Irena huffed. "It's a burden you can bear after you've healed a bit more. Your ribs stick out too far to carry much of anything."

Irena saw through my placating smile—I know she did. I'd need to leave much sooner than that.

✦ ✦ ✦

The idea came in the night, mirroring the crash of thunder that woke me. The servants in the palace in Turiana. Like Irena and Lorenz's gossipy neighbor, servants were always the first to know anything, had access to parts of the palace I'd never be welcomed in as a princess. I could find out if Marko had sent the mage, and if so, figure out how to defeat them both. Then I'd move on to the Hálendian traitor.

Knowing Lorenz and Irena's opinion on the prince heir marrying a foreigner wasn't enough to absolve Marko's involvement in the attack. Maybe other opinions held sway elsewhere.

My hand had wrapped around my staff when Irena's voice broke the morning quiet.

"Are you leaving us now, Jen?" I had pulled my pile of folded Hálendian clothing from the corner of my bed to change into, but Irena shook her head. "A girl in a gray uniform will stick out."

Lorenz emerged from the other room shaking his head. "You don't want to stick out."

Irena handed me a small leather bag—the same leather as in Hálendi, but instead of a drawstring and loops to attach it to a belt, it was square, with a flap to cover the opening and a long strap that fit over my shoulder and across my body. "For the clothes you came with," she said.

I took the satchel and held it to my chest. It already had a bit of wrapped food at the bottom. "Thank you," I whispered. The clothes, battered though they were, reminded me of home.

I tucked everything into the bag, then gathered Irena's castoff skirt and blouse and changed in their room, belting her skirt at my waist. I'd have to get used to all that fabric swishing around my calves. At least the storm last night had finally brought in warmer weather. I slipped Ren's book into the pocket of the skirt. My braid stayed tucked in my shirt, my knife in my boot. The boots didn't match my Turian apparel, but Irena's would never fit and I didn't have money for a new pair.

I debated how odd it would look to walk around in a skirt with a sword at my hip. In the end, I belted it on but tied a sweater Irena gave me around my waist to hide the weapon from view.

The whole family waited outside the cabin. Lorenz gave me a few precious coins and general directions to the village of Teano, where I'd hire a cart to Turiana. When he'd finished, I took one of his hands and one of Irena's in mine.

"I'll never be able to thank you both enough for everything that you have done for me and given me." Irena pulled me into a hug. Lorenz put his arms around both of us. We stood like that long enough to heal some of my brokenness, to ease a bit of the pain from the tethers.

To Carlo, whose hair still stuck up in the back and on the side, I handed my staff, complete with claw marks and the strips I'd used to protect my hands. His eyes went huge as he took the gift. "Thank you," he whispered.

I squeezed his shoulder. "I first learned to fight with a staff. Practice hard, and you'll do great things one day, Carlo."

Gia hugged my legs. I squatted down and hugged her tight,

breathing in her fresh-from-sleep scent. "Goodbye, little one." She leaned into her father as I stood, resting her head against his leg and waving to me.

Irena pulled the yellow scarf from her hair and wrapped it around mine, then plopped a wide-brimmed hat on top. "Stay safe," she whispered. "If you are ever near here again, please come see us, Jen. You've a light inside that brightens everything around you."

My feet didn't move when I ordered them to. I didn't want to leave this place. If I walked away from this clearing, from this family, I could never leave the path I was choosing. I had to be all in, or all out. A shiver trickled down my neck, but I shook it off. This wasn't like the Wild. I wanted to stay, but I wouldn't. I remembered.

Ren's smiling face flashed in my memory. The quiet moment I'd shared with my father the day before I left for Turia. My mother's soft smile and warm arms. Aleinn's loyalty and friendship. They resonated deep inside me.

I would find a way to avenge the death of my family, the attack on my kingdom. But I would do more than that. I would protect Irena and her family, and all families like hers. I knew a little of what the mage was capable of. I would not let him destroy our land, our people—regardless of which side of the border they lived on.

"I promise I will be careful. Thank you." I hugged Irena one last time, tousled Gia's hair, and stepped into the sunshine filtering through the trees.

I'd find a way into the palace, and I'd find the mage. I just had to make it to Turiana without incident. It couldn't be worse than the Wild. At least, I hoped.

In the King's Study

The king strolled toward the study after breakfast, Blaire trailing behind. He tapped yet another letter in his hands.

> *I am already moving the men in place. Riiga will have an intimate connection to Turia before the storm season sets in. There is no guarantee with the other factors, the other situation. I care only for the welfare of Riiga and its people.*

He pushed the door to the study open and threw the letter into the fire.

A woman stood as he entered, sparing only a glance for the letter burning in the grate. Her deep-blue gown and green sash accented her red hair and perfect complexion. A blood-red cloak hung around her shoulders.

"Who are you?" the king growled. "How did you get in here?"

"You sent for me, Your Majesty, and now I am here." Her

voice cascaded like a stream flowing over smooth pebbles, low and sibilant. She bowed her head and curtsied low.

He looked her up and down. "You are the mage Blaire summoned from the Ice Deserts?"

"I am Redalia, his messenger."

The king gestured for her to sit in a circle of chairs by the window. She chose the red velvet.

"Miss Redalia, this is my most trusted advisor, Lord Blaire." She inclined her head to him. "We have had confirmation that Hálendi declared war on Turia. We still have what you seek." Redalia's long, sharp fingernails scratched the velvet arm of her chair. "However, I need assurance your master won't interfere on the Plateau." The king crossed one knee over the other and stroked the ring on his smallest finger.

A spot of light reflecting from the high window trembled on the wall next to Redalia's chair. "I assure you, Your Majesty, his designs are not for the Plateau."

The king steepled his thin fingers beneath his pointed chin. "There are many rulers on the Continent, many lands that bicker among themselves. They are hardly capable of standing against a mage. The Plateau is a much better prize. So why does he settle for less?"

Redalia brushed her hands over the satin folds of her dress. "Let's just say there is a certain draw to the Continent."

She looked between him and Blaire. Blaire broke first. "Surely you understand our dilemma, Miss Redalia. We are bound by our allegiances and our geography with no opportunity to expand, and as a result our people are suffocated. Fighting and sickness run rampant. We *need* more of a foothold on the Plateau. And until we have that, unfortunately, we must hold on to our bargaining chip." His gaze stayed fixed somewhere around her chin.

Redalia tilted her head back, and a wave of red hair brushed her shoulders. "What assurance would you have?"

The king smiled. "I want him to send me something from the Continent. I want proof he's left the Plateau."

Redalia's left eye ticked ever so slightly. "I cannot offer you that at this time, Your Majesty."

"Then we cannot deliver your manuscript at this time." The king stood and gestured to the door. "Tell your master I would like to meet with him in person—not with a messenger, delightful though you are."

She stood and brushed her cloak behind her, a gold dagger winking from her side. "I will give him the message."

The king waited until the door had closed to speak again. "I do not trust her. Make sure the information is secure, Blaire. If she gets what she wants before we claim our land—"

"Of course, Your Majesty. I will make sure it is safe." He tugged on his robe and hurried out of the room.

Blaire didn't stop until he stood at the fireplace in his bedroom. A brick near the edge came loose as he tugged. But before he could get the block out, something—someone—laughed behind him. It was a soft sound, but chills crawled down his spine.

He turned. Redalia sat in a chair by his bed. She smiled as if they shared a secret.

Her hand caressed the gold dagger in her lap. "Show me what you've been hiding."

Blaire stared at the dagger, then pulled the loose brick from the wall completely and placed a tattered scroll on the table between them.

She stood and slammed her dagger into the table, pinning the top of the parchment in place, then gently unrolled the scroll. Her eyes scanned the page, a furrow marring her brow. Before Blaire could blink, she was behind him with her knife at his throat.

"This is the manuscript?" she snarled. "Where is the location of the Black Library?"

"I— Yes. It says right here, 'The Black Library is in a castle of rock inside a cave in the Wastelands.' "

"Which cave?" She dug the knife into his neck until blood dotted the blade. "What is this key it speaks of?"

"I don't know what it is," Blaire sputtered, "only that you must have the key to access the library." Redalia hissed, pressing into his throat harder, and he rushed on. "Wait, there's more!" Redalia eased the dagger away. "The location is stated more explicitly in Scribe Jershi's manuscript about the Gray Mage." He twisted so he could look up at her.

"And where, dear Blaire"—she bit out his name—"is this manuscript about Graymere?"

"I have tracked Jershi's travels." Redalia tightened her hold on him. "Only recently have I found he traveled to Turia to write and study. There is no other place the manuscript could be!"

"How certain are you, love?" Her voice quieted like the breath before a scream.

"I am positive! And the key is in Turia as well." Blaire was panting now, and sweat ran freely from his greasy hair. A trickle of blood trailed down his neck and stained his purple robe.

"And did you ever stop to think, Blaire dear, what the consequences would be when I showed up and you didn't have the location? Did you forget that, at your request, we just started a war in Turia, and that the entire palace will now be more heavily guarded than ever? I could have found the manuscript within a *day* if not for that!"

Blaire's face drained of color.

"It's you, isn't it! You're the Red Mage—"

She slid her dagger across his neck and then shoved it into his side. Blood gushed onto her hand, but she held the blade there until his life drained out of his eyes.

"Yes, it's me," she snarled. Blood soaked the front of her dress as she stalked away, but she preferred it that way.

CHAPTER ELEVEN

The road wound through patches of trees—boscos, Irena had called them—and wide open fields. New life bubbled from every corner of the land. Row after row of bushy plants—carrots, potatoes, and others I'd never seen—grew next to acres of spring wheat, still green. Low walls and irrigation ditches hedged the different crops. And there was always some source of clean water nearby I could drink from as long as the farmers didn't see.

I even passed through a few orchards, inhaling the rich scent of their blossoms and brushing my fingers along the soft petals as I walked by. The weather in Hálendi was too unpredictable for those, but when the carts rolled in from Turia it was a day of celebration. I couldn't imagine having such luxury every day.

I lifted Irena's blouse from where it stuck to my neck. The heat here sank into your skin, burrowing in as if you'd never be comfortable again. I understood the shorter skirts, now.

Farmers worked in the fields, backs bent like they'd been out for hours. My hat concealed enough that they hardly paid me any mind, but that itching between my shoulder blades returned. I brushed away the sensation and nodded at anyone who acknowledged me until I could breathe free amid the uninhabited boscos.

The houses here were mostly like Lorenz and Irena's—square, with peaked rooftops and brick chimneys—although some had two stories. They lacked the bright colors of Hálendian homes—no red or purple doors peeking through grass or snow; most here were just brown. But the land made up for that. Shades of green and yellow, splashes of white and blue and pink flowers.

Flies and bees tumbled through the air drunkenly from one patch of flowers to the next, and holes and burrows dotted the side of the road, though their inhabitants stayed out of sight. And the whole time as I walked toward Teano, I kept thinking that Turia wouldn't have been such a bad place to make my home.

When the stars finally emerged, I climbed a tree and tucked myself into its branches—high enough to be out of reach from anything on the ground, but not so high I'd break anything if I accidentally fell. The tethers didn't hurt quite as much as they used to, the ache diminishing a little every passing hour. The ache was fading, but the memory was not. I closed my eyes and drifted toward sleep. Regular food, water, and even the walking were slowly restoring my body. But would the scars ever fully disappear?

✦ ✦ ✦

I made it to Teano by midafternoon the next day, making good time through the fields.

It wasn't big enough to get lost in, so I wandered into the wide streets, inhaling the fragrance of purple flowers that climbed all over the buildings. Villagers meandered down the streets toward the center of town, so I followed, hoping I'd come across the market where Lorenz had said I could hire a cart.

The village was a giant oval, with shorter, smaller houses and shops on the outskirts, and taller buildings near the center, though none of them were more than three stories. I'd never been in a village on my own, and so many people watching me kept my nerves buzzing. Lorenz's directions had been vague; would someone figure out I didn't belong?

Irena was right—I would not have gone unnoticed in my own clothes. The women wore skirts and blouses, some long and bright, others shorter like mine, though it seemed the older the woman, the longer the skirt. Most wore scarves to hold back their dark hair, with long tails of color trailing behind them. Men of all ages wore trousers, and shirts with three buttons at the neck and no collar. They moved differently than Hálendians, not slower, but smoother, like each step was a dance.

A few gave me odd looks for my hat and boots, but most were busy talking to their friends, absorbed in some sort of village drama, as we all flowed inward. In the center, a *plat*, Lorenz had called it, opened, revealing a wide expanse of grass and gravel, and carts full of produce and other wares to sell. *Here* was the market—not along each street, like in Hálenborg.

A massive building made of ancient yellowed bricks loomed over the plat, with weather-beaten stone animals standing guard at the corners. I wandered toward it as I studied the contents of the wagons lined up and the shops lucky enough to occupy the space.

"I didn't think he'd really come," said a girl to her friend. They walked arm in arm ahead of me, both with bright skirts with embroidered flowers at the waist and perfectly curled hair.

The friend rose on her tiptoes. "I know! But my mother said that she heard from the innkeeper's husband that the prince would arrive tomorrow!" Her voice rose in pitch with each word until she was fairly screeching.

I stopped cold. *The prince?* A man bumped into my back, knocking my hat askew, then stepped around me muttering about distracted females. My stomach did a weird flip, and I fixed my hat. Part of me wanted to stay an extra day and see him. The rest of me sighed in relief that I'd missed him.

"Make way!" a booming voice shouted.

A horse and rider tromped straight through the plat, forcing villagers out of the way. The horse climbed directly up the worn, uneven steps of the large hall, and then the woman riding turned her mount to face the square. She took off her hat and slapped it against her leg, a frown marring her mud-spattered face.

A baby cried at a nearby stall, and the sour scent of something burning slithered through the air. The vibrant market had changed. I made my way toward the edge of the crowd, stepping slowly to avoid drawing anyone's eye.

"What has happened?" a man called out from the front. "What news?"

The rider closed her eyes and took a deep breath. "War!" she shouted.

Gasps and murmurs rippled around me.

The rider waited until the crowd quieted again. "We are at war with Hálendi."

War? Someone must have survived, then. And told the council what the mage had said about Marko sending him. I needed to get out of here. Fast.

Shouts erupted across the plat, everyone pushing toward the front, begging for more information. I snuck toward the nearest road, head down, and stepped hard on someone's foot.

"Hey! Watch it!" a woman said.

"I'm sorry." Reflex had me looking directly at her.

The woman blinked at my blue eyes and fair skin, her gaze darting to the stray hairs falling from Irena's yellow scarf.

I slipped sideways and ducked my head again as I shouldered my way out of the square, waiting for an accusation to rise behind me. But it didn't come. Not yet. I bumped into others as they hurried along the road going the opposite way, eager to see what the commotion was about, but I didn't apologize, didn't stop.

A dull roar came from the plat, the sound nipping at my heels. Curses ran through my head as I dodged down an empty side street. I followed it, almost jogging, my boots scuffing on the stone. I didn't know how to get to Turiana from here. Lorenz had told me how to hire a cart but nothing more. And even if I did make it there, the chance of anyone letting me into the palace, let alone hiring me as a servant, had dwindled to nothing if our kingdoms were at war now.

Dread trickled into me, an icy drip down my neck and into my lungs. I skidded to a stop, chest heaving from even that short run out of the chaos of the square. I closed my eyes. The shivery dread settled in the center of my chest. My hands shook, and I turned to face the alley I'd just come from.

Bright sunshine illuminated everything. There was no shadowman there. But I knew one was coming.

I took off in the opposite direction. How many of those creatures were there? And how had it tracked me?

Only one more street to the edge of the village. I glanced over my shoulder as I tore around a corner as fast as I could—and plowed into something. Hard.

"Oof," the thing grunted.

My hat flew backward, and I bounced off whatever I'd hit. Hands grabbed my arms, keeping me from crashing to the cobblestone.

"Whoa, are you all right?" a voice as smooth as a wide river asked. A brown stallion tossed its head nearby, its reins dangling where the young man talking to me must have dropped them.

"I—" My words dried up as I met his gaze. He was about my age, maybe a little older. His emerald-green eyes were startling against his olive skin and dark, curly hair—so brown it was almost black. A hint of stubble shadowed his jaw, and his thick eyebrows pulled low. His features weren't as sharp as my people's, yet he was undeniably handsome.

His eyes flicked over my face and widened, then met the gaze of the man standing next to him, older than us, with light-brown hair almost the same shade as his skin. The two stood apart from a larger group, everyone rushing to prepare their horses. The man's hand was on his sword, his narrowed gaze focused on my hair, which was now spilling from Irena's scarf.

My time was up. I twisted my arms out of the younger man's grip and shoved him into his friend. The boy fell back with a yelp of surprise, and I grabbed his horse's reins, leapt into the saddle, and kicked the horse's sides, not daring to look behind.

Rushing wind overtook their shouts as I pounded out of the village and into the surrounding fields, bursting onto a road leading I didn't care where, as long as it was *away*. I couldn't believe I'd just stolen a horse, but I'd had to do something.

After the first bend, where a hill hid me from view, I veered off the road onto a small path next to a field, flying toward a bosco, where I hoped I could hide. I finally glanced over my shoulder and groaned.

The two men had followed. They'd seen where I'd gone. How had the boy found another horse so quickly?

The dread again tightened around my ribs, squeezing until goose bumps rose up and down my arms. My knees dug into the horse's sides, patches of sunlight blinding me as he ran through the trees of the bosco.

My horse skidded into a meadow, front legs straightening so fast I almost flew over his head. My pursuers soon joined me, their horses sliding to a stop next to mine. They'd caught up, but that worry no longer took priority.

There, in front of us, two shadowmen waited, black blades drawn, rays of light beating down on everything but them. The horse danced under me, and I turned his head, ready to flee the other way. But another shadowman waited for us there.

My horse reared up with a scream, sending me tumbling. Its hooves pounded into the soft ground, churning the wildflowers into pieces.

"No, don't—" the older man started, but the boy had already dismounted. He hooked his arms under my shoulders and helped me scramble away from the stomping hooves. Both horses took off into the trees. The older man jumped down to stand between us and the enemy, and his horse bolted, too. Leaving us alone with the shadowmen.

"You shouldn't have followed me," I snapped under my breath as I shook off the boy's help.

He positioned himself between me and the shadowmen ahead, his hand resting on the hilt of his sword. "Of course I followed—you stole my horse!"

"We mean no harm!" the older man called, but our opponents' only response was to raise their swords.

The boy faced the first two shadowmen; the older man faced the one now at our backs. "You should go," the green-eyed boy said to me, his voice all edges and thorns, ready for battle. "Run." He didn't look nearly as scared as he should. The other man didn't, either.

Run, Hafa and Leland had said. But if I'd stayed and helped Hafa, maybe things would have been different.

I untied the sweater from my waist, tossed it aside with my bag, and pulled my blade from its sheath. The ring of metal echoed around us.

"*You* should run," I told the boy and his friend. I raised my sword, both hands gripping the hilt with white knuckles so the tip didn't shake. The shadowmen each took a step closer, herding us together.

One flicked his hand, and a blast of energy raced toward us on the wind. It was invisible to the eye, yet the boy ducked to avoid it. My left hand shot forward, absorbing the power into my ring.

"Watch out for their magic," I warned, and charged at the two attackers in front of me, my skirt trailing in my wake.

I didn't spare the men behind me a glance, only hoped they'd engaged the third shadowman fast enough that they weren't blown away.

My sword bounced from one black blade to the other, a fury of steel and shimmering air. My ring burned with the magic I absorbed as I tried to keep these two from using more of it against me or my unlikely fighting companions.

The ring of clashing swords from the other fight stopped suddenly. "Where did he go?" the boy shouted.

I couldn't chance a look back. My lungs heaved, trying to keep enough air in them as I parried strike after strike from the shadowmen. They were faster now that the third had disintegrated, and attacked relentlessly, pressing closer.

And then the two men were with me, drawing my opponents' attention away. The older man went around the right side, trying to draw one off.

"No!" I shouted.

I was too late. The shadowman lifted his hand, and the man flew back with a cry, landing with a thud and rolling in the grass near the edge of the meadow.

But he'd distracted the nearest shadowman, and I flicked my sword through his belly. His black blade thumped against the grass.

One left.

The boy stayed close to me, behind the protection of my ring. We moved like we'd fought together for years, reading each other's moves and adjusting as a unit. Something about his method struck a familiar chord. But I couldn't give it much thought, as this enemy fought in a fury of steel and shadow. Too fast for either of us to best.

Even two against one, we wouldn't win. Not like this.

The boy, almost reading my mind, eased away to our opponent's weaker side. The shadowman turned to release his magic, and I stretched to catch what I could. The boy ducked, but the shadowman had turned back to me. His blade swung while I was off balance, and I twisted to avoid the blow. My ankle wobbled, and I fell. A stinging pain shot through my stomach, but I'd distracted the shadowman enough for the boy to heave his sword through its neck.

The figure disintegrated like the others, its black blade falling to the ground.

The boy stood with his sword still raised, sweat trickling down the side of his face. The sun above him sent white spots through my vision, and I put my arm over my eyes.

He turned to where his companion had fallen. "Luc, are you—"

"I'm fine," the man wheezed.

A bee buzzed somewhere overhead, and a blade of grass tickled my cheek. Taking slow, deep breaths as the stinging in my stomach spread, I watched the boy from under my arm.

He reached for the black blade still shining in the grass.

"Don't touch it," I said, then groaned as a wave of nausea hit me.

He jerked his hand away. The sword dissolved. *"Cavolo,"* he muttered under his breath, then knelt by my side.

Everything hurt, especially breathing. But the shivery dread was gone, at least.

Warm hands cradled my shoulders to help me sit up. A sharp pain lanced through my stomach, and I gasped. I hadn't been cut that deeply. Why did it hurt so hideously?

Fabric shifted, and I felt my skin exposed to the cool air. I forced my eyes open and tried to inhale slowly as the boy gently pressed his finger near the wound. I pushed his hand away and tugged my shirt down.

"It doesn't look very deep." His gentle voice rolled softly over me. He wore what I assumed was a uniform—dark trousers, tall boots, and a loose shirt under a tan tunic that was more like a vest.

"I'm fine—it's just a scratch." My voice came out as a raspy growl. An icy pain began to radiate from the wound. I shook the fog from my mind and eased myself to kneeling, tugging Irena's skirt into place.

He sat back on his heels. "I'm only trying to help."

"Why?" I asked. "I stole your horse."

"I remember," he said, face carefully blank.

"Who are you?" I leaned to the side and sheathed my sword. The way we'd fought together . . . he seemed familiar, but I knew I'd never met him. I would have remembered.

He didn't answer, but stood instead and called out to his friend. "Still breathing, then?"

I scooted a bit farther away. Had he heard the announcement in the square? The ice in my stomach gripped me tighter.

The other man, Luc he'd called him, rolled his eyes and rubbed his chest. "Like you could get rid of me that easily." He kicked through the grass until he found his sword, then hobbled over with a wary eye darting between us. "I think I cracked a few ribs."

The boy stood and whistled for his horse. "This would have gone a lot differently if you hadn't stayed . . . ," He waited for my name.

"Aleinn," I whispered. My chest tightened, but it was the name I'd decided to go by until I was ready to meet the mage again. I'd made a mistake giving Irena a shortened version of my real name, and I didn't want anyone to trace me back to Irena if I could help it. Now, every time someone said Aleinn's name, I'd remember her sacrifice and my purpose. "And yours?"

"I'm Luc, and that's Teren," his companion blurted out.

Teren snapped his mouth shut on whatever he had been about to say, and Luc glared at him, an entire conversation passing in the space of a few blinks. When it seemed they'd made some sort of decision, Teren reached his hand out to pull me up.

I hesitated a long moment before accepting. My skin sparked where we touched, and I swayed. His other hand went to my waist, steadying me until the black spots in my vision cleared. The spark only intensified the longer his skin made contact with mine.

Luc cleared his throat, and Teren stepped away with his brow furrowed.

Wait. They were in uniform. A war had just been announced. Against Hálendi.

"Right, well, thank you both for your help," I said as I circled around them toward my bag and sweater. I did not need to be keeping company with Turian soldiers. The scarf around my hair itched with sweat.

Both men watched me, faces inscrutable, but they didn't try

to stop me as I passed them, and my breath released in a slow sigh. Until they started following.

"What were those cursed things?" Teren asked Luc, staying a step behind me.

"Do I look like a walking library?" Luc answered, shoving his sword into its sheath. He whistled loud and long, mimicking Teren's whistle from before. "Where are those *maledetto* horses?"

I slung my satchel over my shoulder and tied Irena's sweater around my sheath once again. Teren's eyes followed my movements, lingering on my sword. Or maybe my legs—I wasn't sure which. I ignored him and started walking back toward the road.

"Wait!" Teren called.

Branches snapped and birds quieted as something crashed through the forest, getting closer with every step. My hand went around my sword like it was moving through mud. But it was only their horses that trotted into the meadow—the one I'd stolen from Teren, and Luc's. The third, which Teren had ridden to chase after me, was nowhere to be seen.

They mounted their horses and walked them forward so they were blocking my path. I stopped, hands on my hips.

"We need to leave this meadow before something else finds us." Teren offered his hand again while Luc watched the outskirts of the bosco, where shadows danced under the trees.

My strength was leaching slowly out of me, seeping into the ground, but I said, "No, thank you. I'll continue on my own."

But when I tried to go around, Teren moved his horse to block my path once more. He dismounted, though Luc looked ready to strangle him.

"You're injured. We can take you to the best healer in the kingdom."

"I'll—" I swallowed and tried again. "I'll just go back to the village."

"I wouldn't go there right now if I were you," he said with a glance at my hair. So they did know about the war. And that I wasn't Turian.

Luc glared at Teren. "We need to go."

Yes, please go, I urged in my mind.

"I'm not leaving her here," Teren said.

Luc's eyebrows raised. "I wasn't suggesting that." A dark undertone laced the words. He glared my way like he was ready to tie me up and toss me over his horse if I held them up much longer.

Teren was right; I needed a healer. My hand rested on the hilt of my sword, but I wasn't sure I had the strength to draw it. And since they were in uniform, there was a chance they could get me into the palace. I wanted to get into the palace. Just not into the dungeon. Ice spread through my veins, pulsing out from the cut in my stomach.

First, the healer. I'd just have to be careful. My lips pressed together, and I nodded.

Teren looked like he still wanted to help me mount his horse, but I shook my head and settled into the saddle myself. My skirt had enough folds to cover my legs if I was cautious how I sat, but I missed my trousers desperately.

Teren mounted behind me, and my heart jumped at the close contact. I sat stiffly, the ice inside me spreading faster, as if battling the heat from his chest. He nudged his tired horse forward and shifted in the saddle. Maybe he was as uncomfortable as me.

"Lean back. If something else decides to chase us, we may need to run for it."

My arms and shoulders, my back, every place that touched him, ignited a new spark beneath my skin, but I tried to relax. I still didn't know why they were helping me, but as my thoughts swirled in my head like a blizzard, I decided I needed help more than I needed to know their motives.

Luc spoke from ahead. "Let's find that healer."

"There's another village due south of here," Teren said. "Let's see how far away we can get."

The words were innocent enough, but something about the way he said them had me wishing I'd had the strength to refuse their offer.

CHAPTER TWELVE

There's a man next to me on his horse, shadows blurring his face. He points to my left. I try to look, but my neck is stiff. My hands and legs are numb. I can't even blink.

The man grabs my head and turns it until I see a figure in a billowing gray cloak on the road ahead. My heart fills with dread.

I've been here before. On this road.

Except this time is infinitely worse. The figure in gray holds Ren in front of him with a knife pressed to his throat.

But that isn't right. Ren shouldn't be here. He's in North Watch. Dead. I try to call out to him, to draw my sword, anything, but I can't move.

Ren smiles and whispers in the grating voice of the mage behind him, "I'm coming for you."

And then the mage slits Ren's throat.

I gasped and forced my eyelids open, taking shallow breaths. Two shadowed eyes hovered above me. I tried to scramble away, but an arm tightened around my waist. I closed my eyes and pushed against the arm, but my vision was filled with Ren's spilled blood. My body began to shake.

"It was a nightmare. It's okay," a deep voice said. "Careful, or you'll open your wound."

I blinked the fog out of my eyes and found Teren's emerald eyes staring back. I gasped, trying to catch my breath. Ice ran through my veins. He rubbed my arm in a soothing motion, and I was momentarily distracted by his warm hand. He was lying right beside me.

"Aleinn . . ."

My eyes snapped up to his before I remembered that was the name I'd given him. His voice was gentle as he whispered, "You're safe now."

I let his words wash over me as I took in the rest of our surroundings. We were in a cottage very much like Irena's. Except the other man, Luc, lay on the floor at the base of the pile of blankets Teren and I were on.

Everything clicked into place. The meadow. The shadow-men. The ice in my wound.

I groaned and tried to sit up, to move away again, but Teren held my shoulder down.

I swatted at his hand, and he leaned away, hands open, palms toward me. "You need to stay still, or the bandage will shift and expose the wound." He lifted a shoulder. "If it doesn't stay shut, I'll have to stitch it, and sewing is not my best talent."

I grimaced and let my head fall back onto the pile of blankets attempting to be a bed. Cris had gotten stitches on his arm once when we were younger, and I'd watched. I did not want to go through that.

When he saw I wasn't going to bolt, Teren propped his head up in his hand like being this close to me didn't bother him at all. His shirt was open and loose at the collar—very different from the high-collared tunics in Hálendi. In shadows and highlights, the moonlight set off the strong line of his neck, his collarbone, and a triangle of chest. I had definitely never been this close to a man other than my brother and my father, and he was . . . strangely warm.

"I . . . What are you doing here?" I asked when he continued studying me like I was studying him.

"The blade was poisoned. You passed out, and we stopped, but by then the cut was ringed in white, with green spreading—"

"That sounds lovely," I said, wrinkling my nose. He laughed. "But I meant, what are you doing *in this bed*?" I raised my eyebrows and glanced at Luc by our feet.

He had the nerve to scoot closer. My freezing body was drawn to his heat, and it took all my willpower not to lean into him.

"Wintergrain root counteracts most poison, but works better when you're warm—the blood flows faster, taking the antidote to more of the body quicker." Then his voice changed, hardened. "Our kind hosts couldn't spare a log for a fire in these harsh springtime temperatures."

The cold fireplace lay empty in a side wall, near a battered door on uneven hinges, which led to another room. Looking closer, I saw that this cottage wasn't like Irena's well-kept home after all. Teren retrieved a small bowl from the floor.

"May I—" He swallowed hard enough his throat bobbed. "I should put more wintergrain on your wound."

I tensed but nodded. He had already done it once. He helped

me sit up, and I lifted my shirt just high enough to uncover the bandages. His long fingers brushed my skin as he pulled the wrapping down, and I shivered at the contact.

He jerked back. "Sorry, did I—"

"It's . . . f-fine. I'm fine," I stammered.

He blew out a long breath, then gently moved the cloth and scraped away the old root. I clenched the blanket in my fists, trying to remain still. He paused, staring at the scratches from the wolf, but he didn't ask about them.

When he put the new salve on, I sucked in a breath at the soothing sensation.

"Did that hurt?"

"No," I sighed.

He chuckled and tore a small strip off the blanket, folding it over my wound.

He hesitated. "Um, hold this here," he said, moving my hand to press on the folded bit on my stomach. I stiffened as his arms went around me to wrap the bandage, and I noticed again how loose his collar was. A shirt like that would leave you with a cold neck in Hálendi. But here, it was . . . nice.

"Are you a healer?" I asked.

He set the bowl on the ground and helped me ease back. Instead of lying next to me, he stayed sitting and pulled his knees up. I already missed the heat from his body, though Luc provided a warm spot by my feet.

"No," Teren said. "But I have studied under the best healer in the kingdom." The moonlight filtered in from behind him, so I could see only his dark, wavy hair and the bare outline of his features.

"Well, thank you for not sewing me up, then. I'd rather have a real healer do it."

He snorted, and I chuckled at the sound, then moaned at the tightness in my stomach.

"Let's call it even. We'd never have survived against those things and their shimmering waves in the meadow. What were you doing in Teano, anyway?"

His hands draped loosely around his knees, but he watched my reaction closely. For a moment, I'd been just a girl, and he'd been a boy interested in me for me—not for my position, not for my brother's title. It all came back, though. Uniforms, war, mages. Secrets. Death. Heaviness settled over my limbs. And what had he meant by "shimmering waves"?

"Aleinn?"

I flinched at the sound of her name on his lips.

When I didn't answer, Teren reached down again, this time for a smaller bowl of liquid. "Here, drink this."

I hesitated. "What is it?"

"*Now* you're worried about being poisoned?" His teeth glinted in the dim light as he laughed softly. "It's only water. Promise."

Teren held out the bowl with a questioning look, as if he knew I was considering my answer to his previous question. I sat up only on my elbow and took it, grateful for the interruption but not letting my fingers linger against his. I sipped the cool water and used the time to settle my mind.

"I was traveling to Turiana to visit a friend." *Or a betrothed.* I shivered, and a bit of liquid sloshed over the side. He took the bowl and helped me ease back again, and I was a little out of breath from the exertion and from his touch at the nape of my neck.

"Have you fought those things before?" he said. "You seemed to catch its magic with your hand. . . ."

I jerked up again. "My sword—where is it?" My skirt was twisted around my legs, but I patted its folds until I found Ren's book.

"It's here." He lifted a bundle from the floor next to him. "I kept it close so our hosts wouldn't steal it in the night," he grumbled.

"And my bag?" I questioned as I took my sword from his outstretched hand, feeling some of my strength return just from holding it. The strips were still wrapped around the stone in the hilt.

"Is the bag special?" he asked.

My throat tightened. Had they gone through it? Did they recognize a Hálendian uniform when they saw one?

I shrugged, trying to backtrack for reacting so strongly about my sword. "It was given to me by a friend." The bag was Turian, so he could make of that what he would.

He tilted his head toward Luc, still snoring softly. "You'll have to ask Luc how it fares as a pillow." He smiled and flicked my braid, which rested on my shoulder. "I don't think I've ever seen hair this fair—it's the color of ripe wheat." He paused and looked me in the eyes. "Where are you from?"

I pushed my nervousness, fighting to get to the surface, deep inside and hoped he wouldn't read the whole story in my eyes. With my hair and skin and accent so different from the Turians', lying would only raise more suspicion. "I'm . . . from the north," I stated, for that much was true. I racked my mind for a new topic and blurted out the first question I thought of. "If you aren't a healer, what are you?"

Luc snorted in his sleep, and Teren hesitated. Not for long, but the hesitation was there. "We are in the prince's guard."

Wariness crept into me. Something wasn't right about his response. My mind raced. I would need to tread a thin line between honesty and deception, but this man could get me into the palace if he really was in the prince's guard. If he was lying, however, I needed to be very careful what I exposed. I could land in the dungeon. Or worse.

"When we were fighting, you ducked out of the way of its magic like you could see it," I said. "Is that what you meant by 'shimmering waves'?" Someone shifted on a creaky bed in the room beyond ours, then quieted.

Teren lowered his voice further. "I've never seen magic before. I mean, I've never been anywhere magic has been used, so I didn't know I *could* 'see' it." He pulled at a stray thread on his trousers.

He glanced at the ring on my hand, which rested on my stomach. Instead of asking about it, he said, "Do you know what those things were?"

I chose my words carefully. "I've only had to fight one other. 'Shadowmen' is my own name for them; I don't actually know what they are."

Teren pushed his hand through his tangled dark hair. "Men made of shadow that fight with poisoned blades and use magic."

The beginning of a smile bloomed on my lips. "They are definitely the deadliest shadows I've ever encountered."

He grinned back and lay down. "Are you still traveling to Turiana? Or are you on your way home?"

A heaviness fell over me at the thought of home. And a little bit at the thought of leaving these two men behind. Teren and I both carried secrets. Too many secrets. And there was a war between our people, but we had fought the shadowmen like we'd trained together for years.

"I— Yes. I'm still traveling to Turiana." I'd stay with them to the healer's, and then I'd sneak away and find my own way to the palace. I wasn't sure it was the right move—I didn't have the head for strategy that Ren did.

Teren rested his hands behind his head. "Then let us accompany you. With the shadowmen out there, we'll stand more of a chance as a group."

"But we're going to the healer first, right?" I asked as the fuzzy haze of sleep started to creep in.

He paused—a beat too long. "Healer first."

My eyes were heavy with exhaustion. I should have stayed wary of this stranger next to me, but even with all the secrets between us, I felt something I hadn't truly felt in weeks: safe.

My eyes were shutting without my permission and my mind was full of wool. "I'm sorry for stealing your horse," I said, though I hadn't meant to.

He chuckled. "I'm glad you did," he whispered, and I wasn't sure I'd heard him right.

"Why can't I stay awake?" I mumbled, letting my body sink into the blankets.

"It's the wintergrain root." His voice was soft as he nestled down, too. "You need sleep to help your body heal. Don't fight it."

"I'm not fighting it," I slurred.

Teren's chuckle rumbled in his chest, his warmth beside me again. I shifted closer to him as I felt myself slipping into unconsciousness, unable to resist.

✦✦✦

The light filtering through the rough burlap covering the cottage's only window was still purple when I woke.

A cold ache throbbed in my middle, but it was localized around the wound. The rest of me was warm. I moved to try to get a better look around the cottage and saw Luc asleep on the ground, but the arm around me tightened. My back was pressed against Teren's hard chest. Heat rose in my cheeks. I pulled away enough to turn on my side and face him, but that only made it worse.

"Waitdon't . . . Whattimeisit?" Teren's face was inches from mine, his eyes still shut. He'd shifted even closer to me in his sleep, and I could feel his breath moving the strands of my hair. I lifted his arm from my waist. He stirred again, this time opening his eyes. I ran a hand over my hair to make sure my braid was still tight. His eyes followed the movement, smiling and blinking like he was about to fall asleep again.

"Wake up." I whispered, nudging his chest with my hand and becoming very aware of the muscles underneath. I snatched my hand back.

"Teren!" I hissed, trying not to wake Luc.

He blinked again, this time rubbing his eyes. We both sat up and scooted away from each other. "I . . . What? Sorry. Are you in pain? What can I get you?" He passed his hands over his eyes and hair. One side of his hair stuck straight up, and I couldn't help but stare at it, a smile creeping onto my face.

He fidgeted under my scrutiny and reached for the water. He cupped some in his hands, scrubbed it over his face, and then pushed his wet hands through his hair, making it stand on end in dark waves. My skin blazed, but I couldn't stop looking.

When he caught me, my blush reached the tips of my ears. His mouth curved up, with laugh lines crinkling around his eyes. His bottom teeth were a little crooked; it made me like his smile even more.

Luc coughed loudly and rolled over with a groan, and whatever moment we were sharing ended abruptly.

Teren nudged his friend with his foot. "What's the matter, old man—can't take a night on the floor?"

Luc stood and stretched, his back popping with the motion. "I'm going to wash up. Outside." He glanced at Teren as he walked by.

"I think I'll join him," Teren said, baring his teeth in an attempt at a smile. He rubbed the top of his leg. "Check the bandaging on your wound, and see if we need to rewrap it."

When they'd ducked out the low door, I untied the yellow scarf and ran my fingers through my hair, rebraiding it and wrapping the scarf back around it. Then I lifted the hem of my blouse. The bandage itself was mostly red. I breathed through my nose deeply once, then pulled the scrap of blanket away from the cut. It was only white around the edges, no green tinge anywhere. But a trickle of blood oozed out. I tore another strip off the tattered blanket and added it around the saturated one.

Teren and Luc stepped back into the cottage, and I yanked my blouse down, biting the inside of my cheek to keep from wincing.

"How is it feeling?" Teren whispered, casting a glance at Luc.

"It's good. Better today." I tucked my blouse into my skirt and slipped my feet into my boots, keeping my eyes down as I replied. I didn't want to waste more time sleeping off winter-grain root, and I definitely didn't want him sewing me shut. The sooner we got to a healer, the sooner I could get my bearings and get to the palace.

"If we're leaving before the farmer wakes up, I'd suggest we hurry," Luc whispered.

They helped me fold the blankets into a pile by the cold hearth, Luc muttering about niceties the whole time. They grabbed their vests and swords, and I slung my bag over my shoulder.

"Let's go," I whispered. The icy ache was already branching out again.

✦✦✦

"Are you doing okay?" Teren ducked his head toward mine so I could hear him over the pounding hooves and wind. I nodded, not sure he'd hear me if I answered out loud. Not sure he'd believe me.

We had been riding for a couple of hours, and my hips and legs ached as they readjusted to being on a horse and sharing a saddle.

We rode past more boscos and endless fields. The land here seemed older, softer. Like the elements had smoothed out the rough edges I was used to in Hálendi. Tall, skinny trees or low stone walls marked the boundaries between farms, and square cottages in stands of trees dotted the fields.

When we weren't passing through farmland, the long grass reached the belly of our horse, and enormous flowers dotted the countryside in bright reds, yellows, and blues. The only flowers that grew in the wilderness of Hálendi were small, hardy enough to survive the harsh winters and short summers.

Riding with Teren at my back, his arms cradling me, simultaneously eased the pain and made my heart beat faster. He didn't seem affected at all—leaning down to point out deer in a field or a hawk circling above us. I had to remind myself several times an hour that I didn't know who he was or, more importantly, what it was he was lying about. I knew Luc didn't trust me, but Teren's feelings were harder to guess.

"Let's water the horses," Luc shouted from ahead of us as he reined in his stallion near a river and a grove of trees with vibrant green leaves and tiny white flowers.

Teren dismounted, then waited as I slid off the saddle, holding my skirt down as I went. Between riding for so long and the icy ache spreading into my limbs, I fell into him as soon as my feet hit the ground. His arms encircled me, holding me up, for exactly three heartbeats.

I pulled away when I could stand on my own and hobbled to the stream by Luc. I all but collapsed on the bank, cupping my hands to the clear water, drinking it down, and letting the liquid coat my throat and stomach. Luc splashed his face and neck, but Teren dunked his whole head in the stream and shook out his hair, spraying water everywhere. I laughed and splashed him back, shivering, the ice inside swirling together with the heat from the sun.

Teren jerked to the side to avoid the water and locked eyes with me. A slow, appreciative smile tipped his lips up.

He was even more handsome when he smiled like that. Too handsome. My gaze dropped to the water, and I filled my hands, drinking as much as I could.

Luc cleared his throat. "We should . . . relieve ourselves." He nodded toward the grove. "So we don't have to stop again."

I was too tired to even blush as Teren nodded and headed into the trees. Luc stood watch, tense and ready for some animal to jump out, but there were only the birds chirping happily above. I waited on the bank with Luc and wondered how I'd extricate myself from their company once we'd gotten to the healer's.

The sun, fully risen now, was scorching me despite the skirt and light blouse Irena had lent me. My fur-lined boots didn't help anything, and I felt a bruise forming where my sword had bounced at my hip all day. I wiped the sweat from my brow and assessed the filthy state of my clothing. A shadow passed over me.

"Here," Luc grunted while holding out his hand. I grasped it and pulled myself up, trying to hide the stiffness in my back and hips and shoulders and side.

I nodded in thanks. I wasn't sure what to make of Luc. His hands were weathered, and his brown eyes lit with intelligence. He was loyal and protective, yet he also held some kind of authority over Teren, though it had its limits. Like an older brother. Like Ren. I sighed.

Luc broke the awkward silence. "Teren said you'd fought the shadowmen before."

I glanced to where Teren had entered the trees. "Just once."

"Do you know why your wound was poisoned and mine wasn't?" His stance was relaxed, but his eyes held a glint of suspicion.

My brow furrowed for a moment. "You were wounded?" I looked him over, and he shifted under my gaze.

"It was just a scratch," he responded, lifting the loose sleeve of his shirt to show me a shallow gash on his forearm.

My mind raced through the possibilities. "I assumed it was an effect of their black blades." Luc's eyes narrowed in suspicion, so I turned the question back to him. "Do *you* know why I was poisoned?"

"No." His response was short, and he took a step away, but only one. "I don't trust you, but thank you. For fighting with us against them."

My lips quirked into a half smile, and I touched a fist to my opposite shoulder with a nod before realizing that wasn't done here.

Luc noticed, but instead of commenting on it, he held my elbow and led me to a fallen tree so I could sit in the shade. "You look like you're about to fall over," he grumbled. "And you need a hat." He gestured vaguely to his face, and I realized my skin must be bright red from exposure to the sun.

I winced as I put a cold hand to my tender cheeks. "My hat is back in Teano."

He only grunted. "What part of Hálendi are you from?"

I rubbed the spot on my forehead where a headache was blossoming and shivered again. "Who says I'm from Hálendi?"

He scoffed. "My eyes say so, that's who."

I laughed and shook my head. "You don't trust me, and you haven't given me a reason to trust you, so you'll forgive me if I keep my past private."

Luc was about to reply when my senses snapped alert. The birds had quieted and grass rustled next to his leg. I pulled the knife from my boot and threw it in one smooth motion.

Luc jumped away and drew his sword with a yell.

"Stop," he commanded, the blade pointed at my neck. I raised my arms away from my body.

"Easy," I murmured. "Look where it landed."

He squinted at me but glanced down. His head jerked back when he saw my knife in a long green snake, and he lowered his sword to his side.

I slowly approached and kicked it to make sure the animal was dead.

"How did you . . ." Luc was breathing hard, blinking at the bright-yellow belly of the snake, which had been a foot from his leg. With bright colors like that, it had to be poisonous.

"Instinct," I said with a shrug as I pulled my knife out of the snake and wiped the blade on the grass, then tucked it back into my boot.

He blew out the air in his lungs in a gust and sheathed his sword. We both turned as Teren returned from the bosco. Luc gestured for me to go next, and I tried to keep my gait smooth as I searched for a private spot.

After finding relief behind a large rock, I lifted my blouse.

The bandage was now soaked with blood and sweat. I couldn't decide if I felt more cold or hot as nausea roiled through my stomach. I dabbed at the sweat on my forehead and tugged my blouse away from my sticky skin as I picked my way back to the meadow. I hoped we were almost to the healer—I didn't know how much longer I'd last on horseback.

"I don't think she was lying," I overheard Teren say by the horses.

I stopped out of sight and held my breath, straining to hear anything else.

"I heard what she said about the shadowmen last night," Luc said, and my jaw snapped shut.

He'd been awake while Teren and I spoke? *That sneaky little—*

"You have to admit she didn't tell you the entire truth. She didn't tell you why their magic didn't affect her. Didn't tell you *who* she was visiting in Turiana. She's lying to get us to trust her."

"Or she's telling enough truth to let us know she's on our side."

Someone adjusted the reins of a horse, and Luc answered so quietly I could barely hear him. He didn't sound angry or upset, just cautious. Worried. "Her sword is ancient, she's got a Hálendian uniform in her bag, and her kingdom just declared war on ours."

My hand wrapped around Ren's book in my pocket, and I leaned against the tree hiding me, its rough bark scraping against my cheek. I could run now, but I wouldn't get far—not in my current state.

"But the bag is Turian, and her uniform is old and patched."

My heart lightened the tiniest bit, but then Teren continued. "I'm not saying we should trust her implicitly, but she did kill those shadowmen. And maybe she knows something about Jennesara."

I breathed out slowly. He'd said my name with . . . disdain. Lorenz and Irena didn't have a problem with a foreigner on the throne, but maybe the palace did.

"What if she saw something, Luc? What if she has proof, or knows—"

A branch snapped loudly somewhere behind me, and they fell silent. I cursed under my breath, then rustled the bush next to me before walking into view.

Luc passed by on his way to the trees and stopped me with a hand on my arm. "Thank you," he said begrudgingly. "For the snake."

I shrugged, not sure I trusted myself to answer without snapping at him. He was right to be suspicious, but I was tired.

He held on. "You're bleeding."

I looked down at the darkened spot of blood on my blouse. I sighed and shaded my eyes from the bright sunlight behind him. "I can make it to the healer." My mouth stretched in an ironic smile. "I don't think riding a horse at a canter is helping, but I'll manage." His brow furrowed in what looked like concern. I gave him a pat on the shoulder. "You just worry about the long grass."

He snorted in response and stalked off with a smile. The change in his face was drastic—the light in his eyes intensified, and he was actually pleasant without the scowl.

I untied my bag from Teren's horse and collapsed onto the

ground nearby, rummaging for whatever food I had left from Irena. I didn't feel like eating, but I needed to keep up my strength. The last time I didn't eat, the Wild had nearly swallowed me whole. Wretched Wild.

Teren's eyes widened when I pulled a small crust of bread and some dried fruit from my bag.

"You had *that* in your bag this whole time?" he said as he sat in front of me.

He must have missed the food when they'd dug through it last night. I smirked and handed him a piece of the loaf, which he tore into. Luc returned and ate what little I had left to offer, while I finished off the smallest portion. Both Luc and Teren still looked hungry after all the food was gone.

Luc spoke up as he finished. "She's bleeding again, *diri*."

My head jerked up at Luc's words. I glared at him for betraying me and wondered what *diri* meant. "It's only a little," I said.

Teren sat up and reached out like he was going to lift my blouse right then and there. I slapped his hand away and pointed at him. "The healer can change my bandage."

Luc barked out a laugh. I watched them both. "What was the prince doing so far from the palace?"

Teren and Luc darted a look at each other, then at me. "Every year he visits towns in different areas of the kingdom," Teren answered. "Meets with town officials and talks to people, mostly. Teano was his next stop."

His next stop. It was a strange thing, to be so close to your fate yet miss it entirely. My father went out in Hálendi every few years, and Ren had gone once. I'd been so jealous that he'd gotten to see the kingdom without me that I'd never asked about it. Now I'd never get the chance.

"He'll be headed as fast as he can to the palace now," Luc said as he mounted his horse.

Teren glared at him, though I wasn't sure why, and led his horse to me. "Let me give you a boost so you don't reopen your wound."

When he touched my arm, the heat from his hand swept through my blouse to my skin, and it took me a moment to find words to respond. "Be careful. I don't want you stitching me up."

Teren braced his hands on my hips with a smile. I froze for a moment, still very aware of his touch, and stared at the hollow where his neck and collarbone met.

"Easy does it. Try not to twist as you go."

Oh, right. Mounting the horse.

I let Teren do most of the lifting. Once in the saddle, it was no time at all before he was right behind me.

"Ready?" His breath stroked my neck as he spoke low in my ear. I shifted to hide the shiver his voice sent down my back.

When we'd been trotting for several minutes—keeping a more sedate pace to rest the horses during the hottest hours of the day—I asked a question I'd been curious about ever since Teren had said my name.

"What happens to the prince now that there isn't a betrothal with Hálendi anymore? Do you think he's . . . relieved?"

Teren let out a gusty sigh behind me. "I'm not sure if 're-lieved' is the right word. He got out of an agreement with the Hálendians, but the Riigans tripled their tariffs for importing our goods, and farmers are panicking—if they can't sell their grain, they won't have enough to buy supplies for next year. The prince needs another betrothal in place to prevent Riiga forcing a connection by marriage."

I let that sink in for a few steps. "Even though his betrothed just died? There isn't a . . . mourning period or something?"

Teren's hands tightened on the reins. "The prince told me he didn't know her well enough to mourn her. Any correspondence from him went unanswered by her, tradition forgotten, and she even had her father sign the agreement on her behalf. Clearly, she didn't take an active interest in their union."

I pressed my lips together to keep from blurting anything out. But I wanted to. I didn't know the prince, whether or not he was a good person, whether or not we would have gotten along. Still, the idea of him thinking ill of me—of *dead* me—didn't sit right.

"If someone could prove our innocence to Hálendi, we wouldn't have a war to fight," Teren said. "We wouldn't have to rush into something. . . ."

Here it was. The reason he was giving me so much information. I had answers. I had proof, even. *Was* the proof. But the mage's knife across Aleinn's throat was too fresh. She'd sacrificed everything for me, and if I announced myself, offered myself up, it would only bring the mage to my door faster.

"You think Hálendi's council would listen to your proof if you had it?" I asked. Stalling for time.

"They'd better. We don't have enough soldiers to fight off Hálendi *and* Riiga."

I shivered and realized I could barely feel my hands they were so cold. There had to be some way, something I could say that would convince them to get me into the palace and avoid the dungeon.

"I may have information that could help you," I said hesitantly. Teren went perfectly still behind me. "But if I give up that information, my kingdom could see it as treason. I'd need protection, anonymity, in exchange."

A long moment passed before Teren spoke. "But you'd talk to the king?"

I nodded and swallowed, thirsty again, though we'd just drunk our fill at the stream. "After we find a healer," I whispered, and Teren shifted to look closer at my face.

"Luc," he called ahead. "I think we need to run for it."

I winced at his booming voice next to my ear, then lurched back into his chest when his stallion started to gallop.

Ice and heat pounded into my side with each hoofbeat. I tried to breathe deeply and focus on my surroundings.

My head ached, and the wound throbbed. I wasn't as cold as I had been before, but something else was wrong. My mind began swirling, skipping over thoughts like a smooth stone over water. Almost like in the Wild. I pressed my hand against Ren's book in my pocket.

Teren tucked his arm tighter around my middle, supporting more of my weight. I didn't have the energy to resist, or really do much of anything. He leaned down and had to shout to be heard over the whistle of wind through my ears.

"Do you need to rest?"

I shut my eyes as I tried to process his words. *Rest*. Yes, I wanted to rest. "No," I shouted as I turned my head toward him. "Keep going—I can make it." I winced at the lie.

"We're close, Aleinn." I could hear the worry in his voice, and turned so I could tuck my head against his chest for just a moment.

✦✦✦

A change in the horse's steady pace jolted me out of sleep. I shifted, twisting my body to balance out the ride. The shard of ice in my side flared out, fighting the heat I felt everywhere else, and I gasped and squeezed my eyes shut. Master Hafa told me once that tension spreads pain, so I steadied my breathing and tried to relax.

Colors blurred by as I focused on taking my next breath. Teren leaned down to say something in my ear, but I couldn't make sense of his words. I only saw the fading light and felt minutes, hours, ticking away. Every time he leaned down, I responded with, "I'm okay. Keep going."

The scenery and the sun's arc hazed by, slowing down and speeding up at odd intervals. I blinked once and found we were racing through a city much bigger than the villages we'd gone through. My head was propped up by Teren, tucked between his shoulder and neck. I caught glimpses of curious eyes, dark hair, and flashes of light from windows as we clopped through the winding streets. The sky was deepening to the purple before the black, and I hoped we were close.

I kept waiting to stop at the healer's shop, but when we got to a set of gates set in thick walls, we passed right through with just a shout to the guards from Luc. How well off was this healer?

Finally, finally, we stopped, and the world seemed to take an extra turn. I felt hands under my arms, pulling me off the horse, someone helping my leg over the saddle. I leaned against whoever held my arm and felt wetness trickle down my side. My breathing was shallow and fast, and my eyes were getting heavy.

A flurry of servants ran around us in a blur of drab colors. Shouts of "Your Highness!" and "Prince Enzo!" competed in a sort of dissonant melody, a muted chaos competing with the pounding beat of ice and heat and pain through my body.

But at least we had stopped. Instead of a healer's abode, a palace with huge windows and a turret sprawled in front of us.

Wait. The palace? They were supposed to take me to a healer first.

"Your Highness!"

I turned out of habit toward the old man who'd called out. He was looking our way, but not at me.

"Master Romo," Teren said, returning the man's greeting.

The world spun again, and I lurched into Teren's side.

"Cavolo, Aleinn!" He picked me up in his arms and faced the army of servants and stablehands. "Why didn't you tell me the bleeding had gotten worse?" The noise around us crashed into my head.

"Let me," Luc said. "You should meet with your father."

My hand squeezed the material of Teren's tan vest, and he held me tighter. "I'll take her to Yesilia first."

Who was Yesilia? And why was Teren meeting with his father?

Luc and the man Teren had called Master Romo carved a path through the people running about.

"Welcome home, Prince Enzo," Master Romo said with a bow, and opened the palace doors for us.

I blinked slowly, and my brow furrowed as I looked up and saw the set of Teren's jaw. "*You're* the prince?"

In the Hálendi Borderlands

The light came out of the pool itself, casting odd shadows on the cavern wall. Brownlok leaned over the edge, listening to the other mages through the still water.

"What do you mean, all your shades were defeated?" he said. "Who could defeat them all?"

Water dripped down from the moldy cave ceiling as he waited for Graymere to answer.

"The shades don't reveal any more detail than shadow through their eyes, and the land resisted my magic—Kais found a way to interfere, as usual. But we don't need to worry about some Hálendian coward."

A low hiss echoed through the pool, rippling the water. "And the other problem?"

"Taken care of." Graymere's grating voice echoed through the cavern. "Hálendi is stretched thin and ready to fall. We won't have any interference from the line of kings and their so-called magic. Redalia, do you have the location?"

The light in the cave took on the crimson hue of blood.

"That king is a power-hungry fool who yearns for trinkets when real glory is within his grasp." Redalia's normally sultry voice was sickly sweet and sarcastically sharp. "His advisor was quite the fan of mine, though, and thought he would impress me with his knowledge of *where* the manuscript with the location is—in the palace library in Turiana."

Brownlok's eyes narrowed under his cowl, but Graymere spoke first.

"*What?*" His rage tumbled around the cave. "Hálendi will attack Turia within the week! The entire kingdom will be crawling with soldiers suspicious of any foreigner."

"I took care of Lord Blaire—more quickly than he deserved, the snake." Redalia's voice, smooth again, calmed the reverberations in the cave. "His study also revealed a key of some sort."

Graymere hummed, a low, rumbling sound that sent loose pebbles cascading down the walls. "He *would* layer his treasure with tricks and traps."

Brownlok spoke up again, at last. "Let me go to Turia. I'm near, and could get into the palace to retrieve—"

A silvery laugh tinkled through the cavern, silencing him. "Don't fret, little Brown," Redalia said. "We won't need your heroics quite yet. The Contintent is weak, ravaged by its own wars, and *without* magic." The laugh danced through the cave again. "Perhaps we should just finish what we have started here and keep the Plateau for ourselves."

"The Plateau is irrelevant," Graymere said. "We would use up the remaining stores of our magic to conquer it, and without the replenishing power the Continent holds for those who know how to harness it, we would waste away within years. Besides, without Moraga, I will not be at full strength. Even if they are weak, we cannot afford to fail. We can conquer these children on the Plateau *after* we take the Continent."

"Of course, Lord Graymere," Redalia said serenely, before adding, "I heard another pined for Blaire's position next to the king. He may be of use to us."

"Good. Stay in touch with the king. His reward for releasing us from the Ice Deserts will come."

Redalia laughed. "Yes, Graymere," she purred, his name echoing in the cave.

"Brownlok, continue making trouble at the border," Graymere demanded before Brownlok could protest. "We'll have the map soon, regardless of Riiga's misstep. My followers are gathering once again. We move to the next part of the plan. The next kingdom to fall."

CHAPTER THIRTEEN

Light flickered beyond my eyelids. I was almost warm. I cracked my eyes open, wincing at what felt like sand beneath my lids.

Tall windows lined one side of the room, letting in the early light of dawn, and embers glowed in a big fireplace on the opposite wall. There were several beds in my line of vision, all unoccupied. A vacant stool rested beside mine. I shifted and felt my side stretch, but the pain I expected was barely there.

Where—

I groaned. Teren. Enzo, actually. Prince Enzo.

My mind jumped around, remembering the longest ride of my life, how no one had questioned our entrance through the palace gates, the shouting and chaos, and then his arms. He'd had to carry me. And we were technically betrothed. I squeezed my eyes shut in embarrassment as I remembered waking next to him in the cottage, how I'd lied to him.

And I would have to keep lying. I couldn't attract the attention of the mage. Not yet.

Even though I was surrounded by a palace of people, I was on my own again.

I lifted my shirt and peeked under the white strips of cloth wrapped tight around my middle. Two little black stitches marked my stomach now, puckering the skin together. My head fell back against the feather pillow. I was glad I'd been asleep for that part.

Along the wall, not far from my bed, a tall shelf was filled with odd, mismatched jars of herbs and concoctions. My nose itched with the combination of scents, each trying to overpower the others. There were two doors—one at either end of the room. One had two guards standing stiffly, glaring from afar. The other swung open as if my gaze had summoned the entrant.

A white-haired woman emerged, back bent with age, but eyes bright, even from across the room. She crossed to the guards and spoke briefly with them, too quiet to hear. One nodded and opened the door, where two more waited. A tiny part of me was proud at how many they'd posted.

The woman went to the shelf next, and gathered one small, squat jar and one tall, skinny one. Her scarf, instead of hanging down her back like those in the villages had, was wrapped with her hair into a bun.

She sat on the low stool next to me, brushed my hands out of the way, and lifted my shirt from my stomach. No greeting, no introduction. The guards, who had their hands on their swords, kept their eyes firmly ahead.

"Morning," I croaked. My hand surreptitiously checked my hair—still braided, still under the yellow scarf. The woman tracked my movement but didn't comment.

"I am Yesilia," she said in a quiet voice, yet the underlying strength in it reminded me of my father.

This must be the healer Teren—no, Enzo—had meant. He hadn't said the healer we were seeing was *in* the palace. Then I noticed my ring was gone. And my sword and bag, and even my boots. I frantically patted my skirt. Ren's book was gone, too. They'd taken everything.

She raised her eyebrows higher the longer she inspected my wound. "Your infection has healed very . . . quickly," she said. "Even for me."

I resisted the urge to touch my hair again. Yesilia glanced my way before she poured a few drops from each jar into a small bowl and swirled them together. Her eyes, piercing and green, met mine. "Drink."

I took the bowl at her command, swishing the contents a few more times. "Where are my belongings?"

She raised an eyebrow. No words. Barely blinking. I'd had my fair share of staring matches with stubborn courtiers, but this woman who mostly communicated with her eyebrows . . .

I took a sip of the liquid, and it burned like I'd swallowed evergreen needles. "What is that?" I sputtered out, wiping my mouth with my hand.

Her lips pursed like she was holding back a smile. "It will help with the pain." She gathered up her jars and returned them to the shelf, then slipped between the guards and out the door. By the time it shut behind her, the stinging had faded and left a coating on my throat that slowly filtered to my limbs.

When the sun had fully risen, the door opened and someone passed a tray inside. One of the guards brought it to me, eyeing me like a poisonous snake. I decided he could look at me however he wanted as long as he kept bringing trays filled with warm bread, some kind of mushy, grainlike soup with a delicious nutty flavor, and fresh berries.

Yesilia was gone for hours. In the Wild, there had been so much noise I almost hadn't noticed I was alone. Here, the silence was complete.

Somewhere within these walls, the answers awaited. Irena and Ren had both mentioned how extensive the palace's library was. On magic. Maybe even on tethers, even though mine were broken now. If I could find a way to stay, to be able to use that library, I could find a way to defeat the mage.

My father had often spoken of King Marko's cunning, that he could not be deceived or taken advantage of. Master Hafa had spoken of lesser magic manifesting in other kingdoms to balance out the magic in the line of kings of Hálendi. Maybe that was why Teren—Enzo—could see the shimmering waves. And maybe Marko's cunning was a form of magic as well. I'd have to be careful with what I said and did if I wanted to stay in the palace and out of the dungeon.

✦✦✦

By the time I'd eaten my midday meal, the silence and waiting had me pacing around my bed. I studied the jars on the shelf but didn't touch any—the guards watched my every move. I peeked behind the partially drawn curtains, but all I caught a glimpse of before a guard cleared his throat was a rose garden with blooms beginning to unfurl.

When Yesilia finally returned, her mouth was pulled into a

frown. She came right over to me, patted my hand gently, then left through the small door at the back—her personal chambers, I assumed—and clicked the door shut.

My sigh rang through the hall, and I sat on my neatly made bed. But only a few minutes later, a young boy stepped inside and approached me hesitantly.

"Miss Aleinn is invited to speak to His Majesty, King Marko. Does she accept this invitation?"

My heart jumped. The guards didn't acknowledge me. Yesilia hadn't *said* not to leave, so I replied, "Yes, that is agreeable. Thank you."

I eased off the bed and started to follow the boy, trying to smooth out the wrinkles in my filthy skirt as I went, but Yesilia bustled out of the smaller room with a bundle in her arms. "Wait, child."

The boy continued through the door, and the two guards left with him, though I was sure they weren't far outside. She set her load on a bed near the fire and waved me over. "You can't see the king with blood on you."

The clothes she'd set on the bed weren't mine. "If I could wear my—"

She flicked her fingers, brushing my words away.

"But—"

"There's no time for a bath, so this will have to do." She shook out a yellow blouse and a long blue skirt. I shimmied into the blouse and belted the skirt around my waist. The soft fabric flowed almost to my ankles and was beautiful, but I couldn't get used to the bright colors that were common here. I insisted on my boots instead of the Turians' more traditional sheepskin shoes. Yesilia's eyebrows drew together, but she relented, bringing my boots—and my ring, sword, and knife.

"And my book?" I asked a little desperately.

She tapped her finger against the side of her head, went back into her room, and brought it to me. I breathed a sigh as I wrapped my fingers around it, and it went straight into my pocket. "Thank you," I whispered.

She tilted her head—she had to have looked in it, seen it was blank. Ren's name was too faded to be noticed by someone who didn't know it was there. I didn't care if she wondered why I carried around a blank book.

Yesilia tapped my shoulder. "Letting you carry your weapons is a courtesy," she said as I laced my boots and tucked the knife in. "It took some convincing to get Marko to treat you as a guest. Don't waste my efforts."

She gathered my clothes and took them into her room. I snapped my jaw shut. She'd been gone . . . negotiating on my behalf? I ran my fingers through my hair, twisting the braid back and tucking it under Irena's scarf. A quick check in a small mirror by the fireplace, and I was as ready as I could be.

The door wasn't locked, and when I left, the same boy waited for me, and all four guards escorted me through the corridors of the palace. Everything here shone like it had spent a lovely day in the sun. Beautiful mosaics of colorful tiles lined the polished floor, with pots growing plants *inside.* High ceilings and delicate stonework arched overhead. I was so focused on the stunning details of the palace I tripped down a small step.

Luc waited at the doors of the throne room. "I'll need your weapons, please."

I slowly unbuckled my sword, brow furrowed. They gave me my weapons, only to take them away again? That didn't seem like courtesy to me. I handed it over.

Luc grunted at my ring. I rolled my eyes and handed it over as well. "Don't lose that," I whispered.

He raised an eyebrow and waited. I let out a huff and took the knife from my boot and laid it in his hands. In Hálendi, you could be presented to the king *with* your weapons—it was expected, even. Then again, every courtier in the room would have been armed. My father most of all—with his magic.

"That's all I have, I swear." I thought I saw his lip twitch, but his face was stony as I passed through a large set of doors. He followed me in, carrying my weapons, and my four guards took up position around me.

The room was grand but nearly empty. Archers watched from the upper balcony, and on the main level, next to gold banners hanging all the way from the high ceiling to the polished stone floor, guards stood with swords drawn. A raised dais at the far end held two figures—the king, seated, and his son, standing tall next to him, his hands clasped behind. I couldn't help but notice his confident stance, the fine fabric of his crisp shirt, the gold embroidered vest, and the gold cuff just above his elbow that signified his status as prince heir. He'd definitely grown into the family nose.

A small group of advisors sat on gilded chairs at the base of the dais, all wearing what looked like long robes that were open at the front, revealing their shirts and trousers or skirts underneath.

I marched toward the king, keeping to the middle of the four guards. In a pinch, they'd serve as protection against any nervous bowmen.

As I approached the dais, I slowed and bowed with my hand fisted at my shoulder, then dropped to one knee. I probably should have curtsied, since I was in a skirt, but it was too late now. My mind flew through different scenarios, each one worse than the last.

"You may rise." The king's voice was deeper than I expected. He wasn't thin, but he didn't have the bulk or harsh lines of my father. He seemed almost soft. But then I noticed his eyes—sharp and clear, as if they saw everything.

"My son has told me that you claimed to be traveling from Hálendi into our kingdom to visit a friend. Is that correct?"

I spoke carefully. "That is what I told your son, yes."

Murmurs rippled through the advisors, and their haughty stares burned into me. That, at least, I was familiar with.

King Marko's lips twitched, and he tilted his head. "My son has also told me he thinks you weren't being entirely truthful with him."

"Your son has good judgment." The king's lips twitched again with a glance at Teren—Enzo. My palms began to sweat. Had I given something away?

"Would you care to enlighten us as to what actually happened?"

I nodded. He asked for what had happened, not who I was. "I was part of Princess Jennesara's caravan on the way to meet her betrothed, Your Majesty." Truth. I needed to keep it simple. "We had been traveling in the Wild for almost two days when we were attacked." I tucked my hands into the folds of my full skirt to hide their trembling.

"Filthy men wearing tattered brown uniforms came out of the Wild and surrounded us, along with a magic wielder in a gray cloak on a gray horse." I took a deep breath and forced myself to continue. To remember what I'd tucked away. "The mage immobilized everyone in the clearing, told us the Hálendian rulers were dead, and then he . . . he slit her throat." I felt my grief slipping out before I could pull it back in. "Before I could get to her. Before I could do anything," I whispered.

The mage had said something to her. His lips moved in my memory, almost clear enough that I could make it out.

An advisor in a garish purple robe coughed, drawing me out of the memory.

"General Leland, who was leading the party, saw a chance for me to escape and pushed me into the forest." I paused and felt my eyes slipping toward the prince's, but forced myself to focus on the king. "The mage did not seem like one who would leave any survivors."

King Marko leaned to one side, his elbow on the arm of his throne, and rested his chin in his hand. This was the moment Yesilia had spoken of. *Don't waste it,* I told myself.

"I failed to protect her, Your Majesty. I would like your permission to stay so I can find a way to defeat the mage."

Someone's shoe clicked on the tile floor. A robe rustled. *Chin up, Jenna.* I held the king's gaze, and there almost seemed a tangible connection between us.

He stood, drawing every eye. Every eye except Enzo's. His gaze hadn't left me since I'd entered the room.

"I agree that you should stay," was all he said before turning and passing through a door behind the dais, his golden robe billowing behind him. Enzo followed him.

My stomach turned into a ball of writhing snakes. Had I failed? He hadn't said *where* I'd stay. Would it be in the dungeon? Luc came to me and took me by the elbow. But instead of leading me back the way we came, he took me to a side door and through a small, dark hall that widened, not to the entrance of the dungeon, but to another room. The king's study.

Marko already sat behind his desk, his gilded robe hanging from a hook by the door.

Enzo sat in one chair facing his father's desk, and the king gestured for me to take the other. Luc stood between us. He had my weapons, but didn't return them. Marko's guard was stationed just outside the door, and I was glad we would keep this conversation as private as possible.

"The mage attacked two days into the Wild?" Marko started the interrogation.

"Yes." I clasped my hands in my lap. "It was on our second day in the Wild."

Marko studied what looked like a map spread over his desk. "Still within Hálendi's borders, then."

Enzo shifted in his chair to face me. "Your general pushed you into the *Wild*? That's not an escape. That's a death writ."

I stared at my hands, rubbing the strip of white on my finger where my ring had been. "I wish I had stayed and fought," I whispered.

King Marko pursed his lips as he weighed my words. "I have heard of your skill with a sword, but would that be enough to stop a magic wielder?"

"I have weapons suited to fighting magic, Your Majesty. They were given to me to better protect the princess." The king leaned forward, so I continued. "The ring absorbs magic, and the sword expels it. I do not know much more, only how to use them."

"My son also says you were attacked by shadowmen."

Enzo stretched his leg in front of him, and I struggled to keep my thoughts focused on our conversation and not on him—my betrothed. He didn't look upset at all that I'd held back from him, just curious. And maybe a little hopeful that I'd be his proof of Turia's innocence.

But Hálendi couldn't know I'd survived. Not yet.

"One of them chased me in the Wild, but the Wild . . . protected me." I shuddered.

"Protected you?" Luc said from behind me. "The Wild?"

I folded my arms and rocked back in my chair. "It . . . I don't think I can explain it," I said. Would Marko prod for more information? Would he believe me if I told him?

After a long pause, the king said, "Tell me about the shadowmen."

I released my pent-up breath. "I only know that they can wield magic, their black blades are poisoned"—Luc shifted behind me but didn't interrupt—"and I've killed four. I don't know how many there are, or where they come from, but I imagine they are a creation of the mage."

There was a long pause after I finished my narrative. I sat stiffly in the chair and didn't fidget.

Marko leaned forward, piercing me with his sharp eyes. "The Hálendians claim we are responsible for the princess's death, as well as the deaths of Shraeus and the prince heir. Do you know why they say that?"

"The mage said *you* had sent him, Your Majesty."

And if the Hálendian council knew that, it meant someone else had survived.

He tilted his head. "And do you believe that?"

I paused and considered my next words carefully. "Everything I've learned since entering your kingdom, the people I've spoken with, the long history of peace with Hálendi, and your personal friendship with King Shraeus, gives you little motivation to initiate a betrothal just to start a war."

Marko raised an eyebrow.

"If you had wanted to get out of the betrothal, you would have bargained your way out of it, and probably come off a lot richer." I shrugged.

Marko smiled. "You are correct to assume I did not order the assassinations. But if you had come here and found out I was responsible?"

Luc and Enzo both tensed.

I blinked. "I would have avenged my king." I said it looking straight at Marko, but he didn't flinch.

"And now?"

"Now I want to figure out how to destroy the mage." I leaned against the armrest, my stitches itching in my side.

"But why do you want to stay in Turiana?" Marko asked.

"I've heard your library has the most extensive collection on magic."

"Yes, but even so, you think *you* can defeat him?"

I nodded once. "I've seen the mage, seen his face. I've fought his shadowmen twice and won. I know how they fight, how they attack. If I could find something to give me an edge, I believe I could win."

"You barely lived through your last encounter with a shadowman," Enzo interjected.

I met his gaze. "I watched the mage kill those around me. I have nothing to lose. And besides, who else stands a chance against him?"

Enzo stared at me, searching my eyes, assessing.

Marko spoke again. "How do I know you aren't an assassin sent by Hálendi to end the war before it begins?"

Enzo didn't speak up to defend me, and neither did Luc. I started to sweat. I hadn't killed them on the way to Turiana, but I hadn't known who they were, either. And my weapons would suggest I was more than just a guard.

The king didn't speak, waiting for my defense.

I scoured my brain for something I could tell him that was the truth but wouldn't reveal my identity. My gaze snapped to his, and I hoped he really *did* have magic to discern the truth, because otherwise I had no proof.

"I've never killed anyone before."

A slow smile grew on Marko's face, and he leaned back in his chair. "Even with such fine weapons?"

Ice and snow, I couldn't tell if he believed me or not. Was he testing me? Or teasing me? I smoothed out my skirt as my mind raced. "Hálendi's ambassador, Lord Ernir, could vouch for me." He would reveal my identity, but that would be better than being locked in the dungeon.

Unless it brought the mage to Marko's door.

"The ambassador was called home over a month ago and is no longer here," Marko responded with narrowed eyes. "Which is unfortunate, considering we could have used him to communicate with Hálendi."

My brows pulled down. "He never returned. And as far as I know, he wasn't called back. He couldn't have been, with the snows still pounding the Fjalls."

Unless it had been in the first message sent with my father's acceptance of the betrothal visit. But that didn't make sense, either. Having an ambassador within Turia's palace would only help the wedding negotiations go faster. Where would the ambassador have gone?

I rubbed the fabric of my skirt, waiting for the king's decision. Would he believe what I'd said even though I'd concealed much of the truth?

Marko steepled his fingers under his chin and pondered my statement for what seemed like ages. "Yesilia vouched for you."

Next to me, Enzo sucked in a breath. But what did that mean, she *vouched* for me? "The . . . the healer, Your Majesty?" I asked.

He started rolling up the map on his desk. "She claimed we would be wise to keep you close, not only as a defense if the mage ever attacks here, but also because we are at war with your people." He tied the map and scooted it to the edge, then leaned his elbows on the clean surface. "And as I couldn't talk her out of it, and as Yesilia is my mother, I rarely deny her requests."

My breath hitched. His mother? Marko was spinning his web around me, one gossamer strand at a time, tossing and turning me until I didn't know which way was up and was too trapped to ever escape.

"So, Miss Aleinn, you will stay with her, you will do as she says, and if you step out of line even once, you will be locked away in chains until we find a better use for you. Are we in agreement?"

I scrambled to catch up. I believed that Marko hadn't sent the mage. But then who was the mage working with, and why had the blame been tossed on Turia? I couldn't go back to Hálendi with a mage and a traitor loose, and, as a Hálendian here, I'd never be accepted outside the palace. I had no other options, so if staying with Yesilia meant I could find a way to stop the mage, I'd do whatever the king asked of me.

"We are in agreement, Your Majesty," I hurried to say, with a fist to my shoulder. Best of all, I *wasn't* going to the dungeon—as long as I did what Yesilia said.

CHAPTER FOURTEEN

I wasn't exactly sure what the king had in mind when he'd said I'd be under Yesilia's care, but scrubbing pots was not it. She had me cleaning every bowl, spoon, and pot in the healer's chambers, and I'd been sent from his study just yesterday. She'd made no mention of allowing me into the library, and I hadn't found a way to bring it up yet. But I'd need to find a way there soon, even if I had to sneak out at night.

"Did you know you have a visitor, Your Majesty?" I asked Yesilia as I rinsed the scrubbing brush in a pail of filthy black water.

She set the bowl she'd been drying on a stack on the table next to us.

"I am just Yesilia now, child. My father's reign was long, and the throne passed from him to my firstborn," she said, wiping her hands on a towel. "Now, what's this you say about a visitor?"

I pointed with the brush to an empty bed near the fireplace. "Underneath."

Yesilia's hands went to her hips, and a girl, maybe eight or nine years old, popped out from under the frame.

"Mari!" Yesilia chided, though she laughed when she said it. "Did you escape your nurse again?"

The girl's wild black curls bounced up and down as she nodded. "They'll never find me in here." She dusted off her dress, smearing the dirt in even more, and skipped over.

Watching the girl as carefully as she watched me, I handed Yesilia another bowl.

"Perhaps you should have stolen an apron before escaping," Yesilia said, raising an eyebrow.

The girl shrugged and laced her small hand into Yesilia's. "I wanted to see the Hálendian." She smiled brilliantly at me. "I'm Marietta," she said in a conspiratorial whisper, holding her hand out to me.

I wiped my hand on a mostly clean towel and reached over the tub of water to take her hand. "I'm the Hálendian."

"Such trouble." Yesilia clicked her tongue at me. "Marietta, this is Aleinn, and you will address her properly."

Marietta rocked forward onto her toes, staring unabashedly at my hair. "Yes, Grandmother."

Wait. Grandmother? This must be one of Enzo's sisters, then.

"Why did you run from your nurse, little one?" Yesilia asked as she flicked a curl from the girl's face. It bounced right back, and Marietta blew at it.

"All anyone can talk about is the ball. It's boring. I never get to go, and I never get to eat anything—except what I snatch from the kitchens."

"Ball?" I said, water dripping down my elbow. "You're having a ball even though . . ." I wasn't sure I should discuss a war with Enzo's little sister.

Marietta shrugged and plopped down on the floor next to Yesilia. "Mother says it's not polite to invite yourself into other people's homes, and Chiara says the nobles want to throw their daughters at Enzo. He's strong, but I don't know how he'll catch them all." Her face twisted like she was thinking it through, then she shrugged.

My brush slipped off the edge of a bowl and plunked into the wash pail, splashing me with dirty water. I sputtered and wiped it off. Enzo had told me he needed a betrothal in place. I just didn't expect to feel . . . upset . . . about his moving on. But that was before Enzo was also Teren.

The door opened, and a girl nearly the same age as me bustled in, a whirl of swishing skirts with the scent of lilacs wafting in with her.

"Grandmother, have you seen— Oh!" The girl stopped short when she saw me. She was graceful and beautiful, with classic features, olive skin, and wavy deep-brown hair. "I apologize for bursting in. I—" She saw Marietta hiding behind Yesilia. "Mari, your nurse has been looking everywhere for you!"

And then the queen herself swept in. And *I* was up to my elbows in bubbles.

"Chiara, did you find— Ah, good morning, Yesilia. Marietta," she said in a tone that meant a lecture was coming. "You must stop hiding from everyone."

Marietta widened her stance with one hand on her hip. "I'm not hiding from *everyone*. Just from people I don't want to find me."

A laugh bubbled up my throat that I quickly changed into a cough.

Queen Cora's lips pursed at her daughter, but her eyes twinkled. "Come along, Mari."

Chiara held out her hand to her sister. "Come on, you can practice drawing with me." Her staring at me was more subtle than Marietta's, but it was still there.

Mari's eyes lit up. "With the black stuff?"

Queen Cora finally let a laugh escape. "Just make sure you change into your oldest apron first. Your maid almost quit when she saw your dress the last time you played with charcoal."

My chest ached—not from the stitches or the wolves or from scrubbing pots. They were so easy with each other.

"It may be too late to make much of a difference," Yesilia said, and nudged my elbow so I'd continue washing.

Queen Cora let out a heavy sigh. "Come, Mari, come." She crossed to her mother-in-law, giving her a tight hug. "It was nice to see you, Yesilia. Aleinn . . ." She nodded to me, and my broken heart thumped hard once.

All three of them left, and the room was somehow darker than before, though the same amount of sunlight was streaming in. I wiped my nose on the back of my arm and scrubbed harder at a particularly stubborn spot.

Yesilia put her hand on my shoulder, and I wiped at my nose again. "What is it?"

I patted my forehead with my other sleeve and sat back. "I miss my family," I said quietly, staring at the door they'd gone through. "Do you have any jars on the shelf that can cure that kind of pain?"

Though I was taller, she put both her hands on my cheeks so she could look me right in my eyes. "There isn't a jar, but I do have something that helps." Then she wrapped her thin and surprisingly strong arms around me. I tucked my head into her shoulder and held on.

✦✦✦

As I ticked down the hours left in the day, Enzo's sisters and mother weren't my only visitors. While I was cleaning off the shelf that held all of Yesilia's remedies, various men and women stopped by, purportedly for one ailment or another. The advisor I'd seen in the throne room—still wearing the purple robe—stepped inside but didn't bother to approach the healer, didn't fabricate some excuse. He just watched as I put back all of her jars exactly to her specifications; then he slipped out when I didn't acknowledge him or drop anything under his scrutiny.

There were others, people who truly sought Yesilia's care. They ignored me, and I watched as the king's mother expertly applied her knowledge of herbs and medicine.

By the time the evening meal was brought in for us, I could barely keep from falling asleep in my soup. After I'd finished, Yesilia showed me to my bed and checked my stitches and the wolf scratches. She put a cup with a warm blend of herbs in my hand. As I drank, her eyebrows scrunched and she poked me.

"Ow," I mumbled sleepily, and set the cup on a small, spindly table nearby. "What is it?" I took a peek at my stomach. It looked almost back to normal, so I wasn't sure what she was worried about.

"Nothing," she said, and shook her head. "Rest. You've earned it."

✦✦✦

I'd meant to stay awake, to sneak out of the healer's chambers and find the library. But the sky was starting to ease out of night when I woke up, throat dry. Yesilia had refilled my cup, and I drank every last drop.

My other clothes—my uniform and Irena's skirt, sweater, nightclothes, and blouse—were folded neatly on the empty bed next to mine. Irena's bag leaned against the pile. I pulled the trousers from my uniform but left on my yellow blouse. It was too hot here for high collars, and I didn't want to be too Hálendian. I switched Ren's book from my skirt to my trousers. There wouldn't be time to wander the halls looking for the library, but I was sure I could find somewhere to practice, to clear my head so I could think. Yesilia hadn't told me not to leave, and I needed to see something other than these four walls.

Yesilia's door was cracked open, so I tiptoed over to it, reached my hand in, and lifted my sword off the hook on the wall. I belted it around me, breathing a sigh of relief when the ring was tied to one of the strips around the hilt. Wearing them both calmed the anxiety tickling my insides. The door out into the hall squeaked a little, but the guard stayed fast asleep.

It took a few tries to get out of the palace, but eventually I found a door leading to the crisp morning air. I tilted my face to the sky and breathed deep the scent of a sleeping world.

I jogged around the perimeter of the palace to warm up.

A large grassy field surrounded the main palace, with stone buildings and flowering gardens spread throughout. I could just make out the wall—thick and imposing—beyond the farthest buildings. The ground dropped away on its other side, and the only entrances were two ramps that led from the city up to the royal compound. The back side of the palace was also protected by the wall, but the land dropped off so steeply that there could be no way in or out.

I crossed the grounds to a barnlike structure near the barracks. It had to be the practice grounds. I slipped inside the building, and the smell of dust and wood and sweat hit me hard. Master Hafa's domain. One he'd never rule again. I bowed my head and touched my fist to my shoulder before stepping into the center of the ring.

It was still too early for even dim gray light to filter through the dingy windows, but I didn't need light to stretch and spar. I knew the moves with my eyes closed.

I unsheathed my sword, relishing the feel of the worn leather hilt in my hand again, and started on basic attack positions, moving against the ghosts of my past. Yesilia had sewn me up better than I thought possible—it didn't even pull where she'd stitched. My mind filtered through everything I'd been through the past month, and I let it all flow out of my body through my sword.

I was swinging and turning, moving to the steps of my favorite dance, when my sword connected with something solid. A loud clang resonated throughout the barn. I jumped back, sword ready. When I saw it was Enzo, alone, I stumbled and tripped, falling into the dust.

"Hello." Prince Enzo sheathed his sword with a wide smile. "I'm glad to see you've recovered." He held his hand out to help me up.

Of course it would be him here, now that I was out of breath and covered in dirt. With a glance at the gold cuff on his arm, I wiped my hand on my trousers and let him pull me off the ground.

"I could have hurt you." I sheathed my sword and tugged on my braid, unsure of what else to say. This was the first time he had approached me after two days of silence. After I'd admitted I'd lied to him.

"You should be practicing with a wooden sword." He raised his brows and leaned toward me ever so slightly. I had to look up to meet his green eyes.

"I . . . I didn't know where they were." I dragged my eyes away from him and stepped back. "Isn't it a little early for you to practice? And without Luc?" I winced at my attempt at small talk.

He went to a closet in a dark corner I hadn't noticed before and returned with two wooden swords. He tossed one to me.

He frowned and swung the sword through the air a few times. "I needed to work out some energy before meetings start for the day. Luc is probably still asleep. Or getting really mad that I'm not in my chambers." He gave me a half smile and scuffed the toe of his boot in the dirt. "I . . . I'm sorry I couldn't tell you who I was."

"I understand why you couldn't." Better than he could imagine. We had both kept secrets. I tapped the practice sword against my leg. "I was waiting to tell my secrets to someone more important than a mere guard." I smirked at him.

"Ha!" He lifted his sword. "Go easy on this 'mere guard,' then."

I laughed. "Are you sure you're ready for this, Your Highness?" I pushed out the title awkwardly.

"Please, just call me Enzo. You did, after all, spend the night in my bed."

He laughed as my cheeks blazed red.

"You mean *you* spent the night in *my* bed." I lunged at him, but he dodged my first move. I stepped to the side, circling him, confident in my skills. There were many things I wasn't good at, but I knew how to fight.

We parried and attacked and defended, each of us controlling our responses, holding back a little, testing weaknesses and strengths. The way he moved, the sequence of his swings, reminded me of Ren. I stumbled at that thought, but Enzo didn't take advantage of my misstep. Ren had said my betrothed was boring and pompous. Knowing my brother like I did, I could see why he thought that—Enzo had enough confidence to rival his. A flash of longing caught me off guard. If only things had been different.

Enzo stepped back a few paces and pulled up the bottom of his once-crisp shirt to wipe the sweat from his face. My gaze caught on his strip of exposed stomach.

I ducked my head, pretending to dust off my trousers, before he could catch me staring. We were evenly matched—with his strength and longer reach to my speed and experience—but I didn't have the endurance I'd had before the Wild.

"You know," I said, panting. "If you weren't holding back, you would have won the bout already."

"I thought the point was to get you back in shape, not beat you." He leaned over and rested his hands on his knees.

I laughed a little. "In that case, I think I'm done for today." It was almost dawn, and I needed to return to Yesilia's before that lazy guard woke up. I handed him my wooden sword, hilt first.

He straightened and took it, then stepped into my path, stopping me short. I caught a whiff of sweat and dirt, and something purely him. "How did you become like this? So focused with a sword?"

I debated for a moment. Our wedding date might have been set by now if it weren't for the mage. Maybe it was because I knew he didn't like Jennesara, but I found I wanted to tell him. I wanted him to know a little of who I was, and even why.

"My mother died when I was young." I started stretching out my arms, an excuse to do something with my hands. "My father was busy with his responsibilities, and I was left mostly on my own." Enzo's head tilted with sympathy, but I didn't want his pity. "I did have an older brother, though. He taught me everything he was learning so we could spar together. We would sneak to our own hidden spot and practice. When my brother's teacher heard about it, he invited me to learn from him as well." I smiled at the memory and watched the golden dust floating through the musty barn.

"By the time my father caught wind of it, I could already beat half of his guard, so we—my brother and I—talked him into letting me continue."

"His guard?"

I tensed at the mistake and thought furiously for some

way out. "My father was in charge of some of the troops in Hálendi." I shrugged and tried to come up with something to divert Enzo from this topic, worried that he was adding another piece to my puzzle, but he saved me the trouble.

"Won't your family worry with you being here?"

All the air left my lungs in a rush. "No. My brother is— My brother died, not long ago. My father had already passed away." Enzo's boot crunched in the dirt as he took a step toward me, but I took two steps back without looking up.

"I should be going, Your— Enzo." I took a shaky breath, eyes on the floor. I touched my fist to my shoulder. My head was not where it should be for talking about my past.

I turned and hurried out of the barn, glancing back once I reached the door. Enzo watched me with a half smile and a furrowed brow. He was the man I was betrothed to. But as long as the mage roamed the Plateau, I would need to stay vigilant. Enzo had a way of pulling secrets from me.

✦✦✦

When I got back, the guard still slept, his head lolling at an awkward angle. I rolled my eyes at him, snuck back in, changed into the long blue skirt and switched Ren's book into the skirt pocket. The floor creaked as I inched my way to Yesilia's room, my sheathed sword in hand.

Her door opened with a whoosh right as I reached it. I stood there, arm outstretched, frozen. Yesilia took the sword from my hand and replaced it on the hook in her room. "You won't need that here." She glanced at the ring I'd settled back on my finger, then bustled past, leaving me blinking in her wake. Had she been watching? Did she know I'd left? It hadn't been expressly forbidden. . . .

A man burst into the room holding a small child in his arms.

"Please, help! My son, he was shaking and his skin is burning with fever!"

Yesilia pointed at which bed she wanted him in, then shooed the man to the other side of it. She assessed the boy—felt his stomach, his forehead, even put her ear to his chest to listen to his heart. "Fetch the catnip and honey," she said. The man didn't move. She looked up. "Aleinn? Did you hear me?"

I froze for a moment—she wanted *me* to help? I ran to the shelf and picked out the jars—I knew where everything was from when I'd cleaned yesterday—and brought some extra scraps of cloth for good measure. While Yesilia ground the herb with her pestle, I gathered water from the giant pot over the low-burning fire.

Yesilia nodded and went to work. A half hour later, the boy was comfortable, and the father was calm, sitting by the bed, dabbing a cool cloth on his son's forehead. I returned the jars to their places. Yesilia had managed to get the fever down faster than anything I'd ever seen.

"Sit," she told me, and pointed to a table with two chairs by her shelf of remedies. I perched on one while she gathered two cups, filled them with hot water, and sprinkled some herbs and honey in, swirling them both as she sat across from me. "I see the way you watch when I work," she said. My leg bounced under the table. "You can ask anything, you know. What I do. Why I do it."

I licked my lips and blew on the cup she handed over. "How does it work? How do you know which herbs to use?"

She sat back and folded her age-worn hands around her own cup. "Knowing which herb comes from a lot of years of experience," she started. "But the key to any good healer isn't in their supply cabinet."

"It's not?" I asked.

She shook her head and took a sip. "It's your ability to focus your mind on what you want to do. You want the body to piece itself back together, to heal itself."

"But that little boy got better so quickly. Back home, he would have been suffering most of the day with fever, if not longer." A tiny voice whispered in my mind, wondering about my mother, about how precious time had been spent looking for a healer, for anyone who could help.

"Just as every person is different, so is the timing for each individual, and that can even depend on how willing the body is to get better."

How willing? Who would want to stay sick?

She smiled like she knew my thoughts, but continued without addressing them. "Children are usually fast healers, but you, child, healed the fastest I've ever seen."

I took a long drink of the hot liquid. It burned my tongue, and the bitterness stole my breath, despite the added honey. She hadn't outright said she suspected anything, that I was unusual. Yet she studied me like my tutors devoured a brand-new book they'd never read. What Yesilia said about healing, about focusing the mind, and the willingness of the body to change, it sounded . . . it sounded an awful lot like magic.

"I've heard tales of the royal family in Hálendi, that they

can . . . could"—I took another gulp—"do something similar. The prince heir, in particular."

She leaned forward and set her cup on the table, eyes bright. "When Kais enchanted the Ice Deserts, his magic awoke the land itself." My hands started to shake at hearing my people's history from her lips. History I'd only recently learned from my father and brother and Master Hafa.

"You mean the Wild?" I set my drink on the table and tucked my hands in my lap. *The shining lake. Forgetting the pain. Forgetting.* I shivered and focused on the hard chair beneath me.

She nodded. "Over time, the magic awoke in the people as well. Nothing extreme like what had been on the Continent—that magic sleeps. But extra abilities and propensities, some for healing or for farming the land, others for becoming a warrior or protecting others."

Yesilia had magic. That was what it all came down to. Yesilia, and if what she said was true, others here in Turia. I leaned forward, my elbows on the table, my head in my hands. If the mage hadn't attacked, if everything hadn't fallen to pieces, this would be my home. A place full of people who might have accepted me—white streak and all.

Yesilia paused, her eyes growing heavy. Her shoulders dropped.

"Are you all right?" I asked. She hadn't looked this tired since I arrived.

She yawned. "I am well, child. Healing like that takes its toll on this frail old body, that's all." She pulled herself to stand and gathered both our cups. "Marko tells me not to overtax myself, but I know my limits. I know when not to force it."

She turned away, but I called out. "What happens if you use

too much?" I wished I had my drink back, something to hold to keep from fidgeting. Yesilia studied me again, assessing, a graveness in her countenance I'd not seen before. She couldn't know my secret, could she? She'd never even glanced at my hair.

"If you use too much of yourself, your body won't have enough energy left to maintain its own basic functions." She tipped her head down, staring into my eyes. "If you use too much, you die."

The door to the healing chamber burst open. "Lady Yesilia!" a frantic woman called out.

Yesilia went to meet her. I stayed by the shelf, Yesilia's words echoing in my mind. No one had mentioned that little fact. Maybe that was the one good thing about the tethers being broken. I adjusted a jar, wondering which herbs this woman would need.

"You must come," the woman continued. "Their Majesties are attempting to finalize the menu for the ball, and cannot decide. They've asked you to come and help."

Yesilia heaved a long-suffering sigh. "All right, I'll be there." She turned to me and took my elbow. "Come along, child. I have some books I'd like you to find in the library while I'm away."

I stumbled after them, the guards casting me wary glances when I left the chambers. As we got farther into the palace, tapestries of wide fields and wild red poppies covered the walls, with bits of green growing in nearly every corner. I'd never seen so much life *inside* before. Servants darted up and down the halls, most carrying linens or crates of decorations, others running faster with messages. We hadn't held many celebrations at the castle in Hálenborg, and I'd never seen such a frenzy over a ball before.

I had the turns memorized by the time we reached the large mahogany doors of the library.

"Master Romo can help you, if he's in," Yesilia said as the frantic servant rocked on her toes with a nervous glance at me. "Stay here until I collect you. Don't wander," she finished.

Did she know about my escape this morning? Either way, she'd led me exactly where I wanted to be.

"Take your time," I whispered as I stared at the beautifully carved doors, with part of a tree on either side.

Yesilia chuckled and turned the corner, and for a brief moment, I was alone in the hall.

I wasn't sure I could walk in. Facing this library made me long for the one at home. But Ren wouldn't breeze into the room looking for me. A servant passed in the hall. I felt his eyes on my back, so I lifted my chin and pulled the big doors open.

The smell was the same; the dust was the same. It even felt the same. It was two stories tall, with a wraparound balcony, accessed by a wide stairway. Heavy golden drapes hung next to enormous windows, which allowed light to bounce around the room, illuminating the tables and chairs in the middle, and the many shelves fanning out perpendicular to the outer walls.

"May I help you?"

The voice startled me, and I bumped into the doorframe, which I hadn't yet passed all the way through. An old man with white hair looked on with kind, curious eyes. His skin was wrinkled and weathered from years in the sun, but he stood tall.

"Yesilia sent me to get these books." I held out the scrap she'd written the titles on.

He cocked his head, taking in my accent, light hair, and fair skin. Instead of demanding proof, he nodded and pointed out the different sections of the library. "I am Master Romo, Miss Aleinn. If you need help finding anything, please let me know."

I wasn't surprised he knew who I was—word always traveled quickly between servants.

Wait. He seemed familiar, but I couldn't— *Oh*. The day I'd arrived. He'd been in the courtyard; he'd addressed Enzo by his title. "Aren't you the steward?"

He dipped his head. "Yes, I am head steward, but I am keeper of the records as well." He smiled, the wrinkles deepening around his eyes. "I would know where any of the more unusual manuscripts are, if you find you need direction."

I nodded and followed him into the room, shoving down the memories from my past that pushed up emotions I couldn't afford to feel.

Master Romo showed me to the section where the books on herbs and other remedies were. I thanked him, and he went back to his corner, studying a massive tome, which occupied almost an entire table. Yesilia's books were in the middle row of a shelf almost twice as tall as me. I pulled them down and tucked them under my arm. A book on the row higher caught my eye, and I ran my finger down the design on its spine—a sword pressed into the leather. There was no title, only the name of the author in the lower corner. Jershi. The name rang familiar, but I couldn't remember why.

I pulled it from the shelf, opening the worn binding carefully. *Magical Lore,* the title read, *History and Usage, Vol. 1.* The memory came, sharp and clear—this was the Turian scribe I'd read about on my birthday, the scribe who'd studied magic.

Half of the shelf in front of me, and the entire next two

shelves, contained his writings. Dark, aged spines, worn with weather and use, called to me. Much of the rest of the row looked to contain works on magic or history, too. My jaw hung slack at the abundance of information available. It would take ages to search through everything. But I had to find the answers before the mage found me.

CHAPTER FIFTEEN

I sat back in the hard, wooden chair and rubbed my eyes with the palms of my hands. I'd been tucked away in a corner surrounded by old, decaying books and fragments of manuscripts for hours. It had to be nearing dinner, and I'd skipped the noon meal, though Master Romo had offered to request a food tray. I didn't want anyone to remember I was still here, didn't want to be banished to the healing chamber again.

If what I was reading was correct—and I had no reason to doubt it—we were in big trouble.

According to Scribe Jershi, there were three original mages and an apprentice that the first emperor on the Continent, Emperor Gero, fought against. Gero defeated the Black Mage, the leader of the evil mages. Then there was the Red Mage, who was known for a gold-hilted knife and unnaturally red hair—some thought it was stained with blood from all the souls the mage had tortured out of their bodies.

Last, there was the Gray Mage, whose apprentice was known as the Brown Mage. The Gray Mage was the most cunning of all the mages of that time, save only the Black Mage, and notoriously slippery. His was the only name mentioned in the text: Graymere.

He rode a gray stallion and was known for his shade mages—echoes, elements of his energy who wielded black swords and did his bidding. They could even use magic—nothing as complicated or deadly as Graymere's, just a shadow of his power.

Just like the shadowmen in the forest.

And there were more notes on the black blades. The first stated that they would react as poison to the magic inside anyone pierced by the blade. The second warned that anyone who tried to wield a shade mage's weapon would become a shade mage, too, forever bound as a slave of the Gray Mage. I shivered, remembering how my ring had pushed my hand away when I tried to pick up the unnatural sword in the forest, how close Enzo had been to touching the one in the meadow.

Graymere had been banished to the Ice Deserts. The scrap of burned parchment had hinted at magic being used against Hálendi's troops near that wasteland.

The dread swirling inside hardened into a knot at the base of my throat.

Could the gray-cloaked mage be the original mage from Gero's day? Would he have survived all these centuries since the Great War? But if he was with me in the middle of the Wild, someone else had killed my father and brother—both had died at nearly the same hour, miles from my caravan. Could *three* mages be in play?

Magic, Jennesara, is not always predictable, Master Hafa had said.

I bit the inside of my cheek and closed my eyes. The mage had said something to Aleinn, before he . . . I swallowed and gripped the rough table, its edges digging into my palms.

The mage had pulled her hair back, leaned close. His lips had moved. I saw it clearly now, etched as it was in my brain.

I told you I'd have my revenge, Kais.

My hands shook as I peeled them away from the table. That didn't seem like something an imitator would say. It seemed like—

"Aaaeeii!"

The high scream pierced the silence. I jumped up, knocking my chair over. A streak of dark brown ran at me. I reached out, grabbed my assailant around her middle, and turned her upside down, pinning her arms against her torso.

"I think screaming gives away the attack, Marietta." I spoke casually, like I was simply commenting on the youngest princess's style, but my heart pounded wildly. Marietta smiled, a dimple in one cheek, her face turning red and her corkscrew-curly hair hanging to the floor.

"I thought adding a scream would do nicely in the library. They say Hálendians are all great warriors."

I laughed and let her ankles go, folding her over so she could stand right side up again. "Not *all* of us. You nearly had me, but it would take a greater surprise to catch me off guard."

She just smiled wider and stuck her hand on her hip, accepting my challenge. "I'll get you, Leinn, when you least expect it!" Then she waggled her eyebrows and sidestepped out of view into the next aisle. Her footsteps squeaked as she snuck into the hallway.

I chuckled and bent down to right my chair when a soft sniffle emanated from somewhere within the library. I wouldn't have heard it had I not been listening to Marietta leave, but there it was again, followed by a shuddering breath. Someone was crying. I glanced in the direction of the sound, and then back at the book I had been studying.

Greymere. I shivered thinking that the evil man I'd barely escaped from had a name. The original mages. I was a descendant of the man who chased them into the Ice Deserts, who banished them. The Gray Mage—Graymere—coming after me was more than an assignment. It was personal.

The next sound was small, like a nose being wiped. I sighed, added the book to Yesilia's pile, and carried all three with me. I crept up the stairs and padded across the stone floor toward an alcove. The heavy drapes had been partially drawn—open enough to let in the sunlight, closed enough to conceal someone.

I peeked around one of the gold panels and saw Chiara, alone on a window seat, weeping silently into her hands.

I took a deep breath, stepped behind the panel of fabric opposite her, and sat, folding my legs while she composed herself and wiped her eyes with a wet handkerchief.

"Aleinn, I— What do you want?" She sniffed and brushed away the last of her tears. I wasn't sure what to say, so I stayed silent—when it had been me weeping alone in the castle, I'd only wanted someone to listen.

"Enzo told me how you saved him from that shadowman," she murmured, folding the handkerchief into a small square. "Thank you for that."

I leaned back against the wall and adjusted the books on my lap. "He saved me as well—we fought together." My finger traced the books' spines. "Do you want to talk about whatever happened that made you want to hide away?" I asked hesitantly.

She unfolded and refolded the handkerchief. "It's nothing, really. I'm fine. Just something someone said." She sniffed again and watched my reaction, waiting to see if I would accept that answer and move on.

I scratched my hair under the yellow scarf and smiled, pretending I spoke to other girls my age all the time. The window looked out over a maze garden. Neck-high green shrubbery wound in a pattern that created several private alcoves, a gurgling fountain the prize in the middle.

Chiara had inherited her father's piercing eyes. She took my measure in the quiet window seat. Deciding if she would trust me or not. I held my breath until she spoke.

"I feel trapped sometimes," she whispered.

A warm sort of tightness bloomed in my chest—I knew what a privilege it was for her to trust me. How few people I had trusted. I kept my gaze outside.

"Not trapped in a physical sense—I love my home and my family," she continued, and leaned her head against the bookshelf behind her, the soft evening light reflecting off the drapes, cocooning us in a world of solace and gold.

"I feel trapped by who I am supposed to be, who I want to be, and who people expect me to be. I want . . ." She glanced up at me, and I nodded. "I want to be able to be who I am without people throwing their expectations on me to be either more or less. I want room to make mistakes and grow, without people judging and laughing at me."

I didn't have any answers, but how often had I felt the same? Ren had always managed to cheer me up, so I shrugged and did my best to imitate him. "If you give me their names, I can take care of them, Princess." My lips twitched. Would she hear the joke?

She half sobbed, half laughed in response. "I doubt my father would approve." She wiped her nose again. "It's not only that. I hate how much calculation goes into every conversation, every 'chance' meeting. I feel like I can't be my true self around most people, because it would scare him off—scare *them* off, I mean."

She took a deep breath and got a little bolder. "I feel like around *certain* people I have to hide who I am. Like my title alone is all I can be. If I were to add my personality onto that, I would somehow be less . . . desirable." Her shoulders rounded in on themselves, and she brushed a stray lock of hair aside. Her normally tame waves were disheveled, like she had run here fast.

I paused for a moment, sifting through my thoughts. I wished Ren could be here—he always gave me the exact advice I needed. "Princess—"

"I don't want to be a princess right now. It's Chiara, please." She smiled tentatively. She looked so young, curled up on the window seat, her hair falling around her, her hands smooth, and her eyes lit from within. I didn't know how old she was exactly, but I don't think I had looked like that ever in my life. Not since losing my mother, at least.

"How old are you? Fifteen?" It was incredibly impolite to ask, but our cocoon made me drop propriety.

"Sixteen, actually. And . . . you?"

With a sharp ache, I missed Aleinn's warm smile and the confidences we'd shared. "Seventeen."

She grinned, and we shared something in that awkward

moment of normalcy, like a secret channeled between us, connecting us together. Connecting us as friends.

"My brother used to tell me that there will always be people who want to tear you down," I said. "When they'd laugh at me or make me feel inferior, he'd always bump my shoulder and say, 'Chin up. They lose their power when you stop giving it to them.'" I lost myself in the memories. Of Ren defending me, strengthening me, helping me be more than I would have been on my own. Something fluttered where the tethers had been.

"Your brother is a smart man," Chiara said, breaking the moment.

I blinked my eyes open—I hadn't realized I'd closed them—and tried to smile but didn't succeed. "He was." Her brow furrowed in confusion, then her eyes widened in sorrow.

I turned back to the window and willed a tear not to fall. "Don't tell anyone about him, please. Although I think he would have liked you." I shifted the books in my lap so I could unfold my legs and stand. "Do you have an attendant or someone else I should find?" Yesilia had asked me to stay in the library, but I didn't want Chiara to have to brave the busy hallways on her own, not with puffy eyes and a red nose.

She took a deep breath and straightened her shoulders, reaching up to repin her hair. "My guard is . . ." She frowned, and my senses heightened. "I don't want to bother him."

I shifted the load in my hands. "Well," I started, hoping I wasn't overstepping our newly formed friendship. "I think Yesilia forgot to retrieve me. Would you walk with me back to her chambers?"

Chiara straightened, the first true smile on her face since I'd heard her sniffling. "Of course! My grandmother is a wonderful healer, but she's a little forgetful when she gets focused on something."

We headed out of the library together. Every servant—and a few nobles—who passed by eyed me suspiciously, but Chiara glared right back at them. When we reached the healing chamber, the door was cracked open, no guard in sight.

"If you ever need someone to talk to, you know where I am," I said, hooking my thumb back to the door.

She waved and turned, her step lighter than it had been before.

I shifted the books under one arm, then entered. Whether my enemies were the original mages or not, I still had so much to study. I hoped Yesilia wouldn't make me clean—

"Aleinn!" Enzo stood at the shelf with his grandmother.

I stopped in my tracks. Luc, lounging in a chair near the door, raised his eyebrows at me.

"I . . . Hello," I said, then cursed inwardly at the inane greeting.

"There you are," Yesilia said as if she hadn't abandoned me. She was holding a long scroll filled with tiny writing. "It's about time you returned. Your dinner is here." She pointed to the table near her room, where a plate sat, heaped with thinly sliced meat and thin noodles I'd only ever had once before, and a pile of green and yellow vegetables.

I carefully made my way to the food, set the books on the corner of the table, and positioned my chair so that I could see the room while eating.

Yesilia and Enzo resumed their conversation on the other

side of the room, and from what I heard, it sounded like a lesson on herb combinations. Enzo had said he'd been trained under the best healer in the kingdom, but I didn't expect him to be in here for lessons the day before the ball where he'd choose a new betrothed.

I ate quietly but enthusiastically, though the food was cold and the noodles stuck together. My gaze kept straying to Enzo. More often than not, he was already looking my way, and I jerked my head back down. The third time it happened, Luc cleared his throat.

I finished my food hastily, then tucked my nose into one of the books I'd brought back. The words squished on the page until I couldn't decipher a single thing, but at least I wouldn't get caught sneaking a glance at the prince again.

I wished I could tell him about my worries. That I thought there were two other mages besides the one that'd attacked me. That I had no idea what they were capable of. That their vendetta was personal. But my concerns only firmed my resolve—I couldn't reveal my identity, and I wouldn't stand in the way of Enzo making a new marriage alliance.

When he left, with Luc ushering him out the door without giving us a chance to speak, I could finally breathe again. Yesilia watched me closely, but I slipped into her room and changed into a nightdress, then drank the cup of water she'd left near my bed and curled up, falling asleep almost instantly.

✦✦✦

The next day, I'd helped Yesilia with a series of health complaints from various people, determined to busy myself until I could sneak away to the library again and not think about the ball. Or anything involving the prince's romantic prospects, for that matter.

When there was a lull midmorning, she turned to me. "Usually stitches need to stay in for a week or two, but I believe yours are ready to come out now."

My eyebrows shot up. Cris's stitches had stayed in forever—or what had seemed like forever back then.

Lifting my shirt, Yesilia snipped the first thread, and I sucked in a breath as she began easing it out. To distract myself from the odd tugging sensation, I shut my eyes and asked something I'd wondered about.

"My mother died a long time ago," I started. Yesilia freed the first thread entirely. "She was perfectly healthy, and then one evening she complained that her chest hurt, and that she was having a hard time breathing."

Yesilia clipped the last stitch and began to pull. I went on, needing to know. "Do you . . . Could you have helped her? If you had been there?"

Yesilia sighed as she gathered the threads and threw them into the embers of the fireplace. "Like I said before, child, it depends on the person. But some things happen no matter how hard a healer tries to prevent it." Her lips pursed and she finished softly, "I don't think I could have helped your mother."

I tucked my shirt back into my skirt. I wore Irena's clothes today, so I could wash the others. Even if Yesilia couldn't have helped my mother, I wished there were more healers like her in Hálendi. Maybe, if I ever got the chance, I could ask King Marko about that—sending skilled healers to train my people, or letting me stay and learn longer from his mother.

The door burst open, and Mari, panting, bolted into the room, then slammed the door shut behind her. I reached for my sword, but grasped only air, forgetting that it was in Yesilia's bedroom.

"What's happened?" I asked, pulling Mari behind me in case an intruder came crashing in.

Mari bent over, hands on her knees, trying to catch her breath.

"Are you hurt?" Yesilia asked.

Mari shook her head.

"Is someone else hurt?" I asked.

Again, she shook her head. "It's Chiara. Her cabbage-headed guard was whining about missing some sort of contest in the city. He kept whining and whining until finally Chiara dismissed him for the day."

I looked at Yesilia, then back to Mari. "So you ran all the way here? I'm sure Chiara knows—"

Mari shook her head so hard her curls bounced into her face. "Tonight is the *ball.*"

My brow furrowed, but Yesilia was rubbing her chin. "What does that have to do with anything?" I asked.

Mari sighed like I was trying her patience, a sigh I was sure her mother had given *her* many times. "There will be all sorts of people here tonight. Father told us to be sure our guards were close. Chiara's guard knew that. He shouldn't have been whining—he knows his duty."

Yesilia took a seat in the rocking chair by the fire. I tried to keep up with Mari's logic and remembered Luc lounging here the day before. "You each have guards? Even in the palace?"

Mari nodded. "It's been that way for almost a year now. No one will tell me why."

Yesilia didn't comment, but the serious set of her mouth told me enough. Almost a year. Before the raids started on Hálendi's borders. "Okay, so we find someone else to—"

"You, Aleinn," Mari said. "I want you to guard her. You protected that other princess."

The mage's knife sliding across Aleinn's throat crashed into me. "I don't—"

"Yes," Yesilia said. "You will do this."

"But I—"

Yesilia stood and dragged me toward her room. "Mari, send for a bath, and find her a dress."

"A dress?" I asked. "If I'm going to guard her, I'll need my sword. A uniform would be—"

Yesilia tipped her chin and stared down her nose at me. "Which uniform, child? Are you to be a Hálendian in a Turian uniform, or a uniformed Hálendian in a kingdom you are at war with?"

She had a point. Mari was already gone, running back down the hall. "How can I possibly help her without—"

"You still have that knife in your boot, yes?" she asked.

I opened my mouth, then shut it. "Yes."

Yesilia nodded and started tugging at the scarf around my hair. I twisted out from under her grip. "Wait," I said, hands out as I backed away. "I can bathe myself and do my own hair."

She flicked her fingers at me like it didn't matter either way. "Yes, of course, child."

A row of servants trickled in with buckets of water. Mari

must have told them who the bath was for, because none of them had been warmed in the fire first.

By the time I was cleaned up, Mari had found me an outfit. A simple cream blouse with a neckline in a deeper V than I was used to; a thick embroidered belt with a golden clasp in the middle; and a skirt the color of raspberries that flowed to the floor, a wide swath of cream embroidery along the trim. It was beautiful—and would hide my boots.

I braided my hair carefully, weaving a matching ribbon through the strands and winding the plait at the base of my neck. It wasn't elaborate enough for the occasion, but it would have to do. My ring was my only adornment, and I kept the jewel facing my palm.

Mari waited impatiently, and grabbed my hand the moment I'd dressed, dragging me toward the door. I looked back at Yesilia, pleading for any last-minute advice. She just bobbed her eyebrows and chuckled.

We raced through palace until we arrived at Chiara's chambers. Mari's sister was a sight to behold. The basic garments were the same as mine, but the fabric, a deep emerald, fairly shone in the firelight, and the embroidery was a masterpiece. A crown of gold leaves adorned her dark hair, and gold strands looped from her temples, down under her ears, and up into the elaborate curls at the back of her head. A bracelet of smaller shimmering leaves wound up her arm like a delicate vine.

"Thank you for this, Aleinn," Chiara said as her maid pinned the final curl. The young girl bobbed a curtsy and left, eyeing me the whole time.

When she'd gone, I folded my arms. "Why did you dismiss your guard if your father insisted he be here?"

Chiara bit her lip and wrung her hands. She paced to her mirror and back, the dark green of her dress a sharp contrast to the abundance of peach fabric in her room. "I figured if he wasn't going to be invested in his duty tonight, it would be better not to have him. And he really wanted to—"

"You always let him bully you." Mari jumped onto Chiara's bed belly-first, her feet dangling off. "Nurse always tells me I can't go outside just because I want to. You shouldn't let him go just because he wants to."

It seemed like an old argument between them that I did not want to take sides in. I wished I had my sword to rest my hands against so I didn't muss my skirt.

"It's not a weakness to care about others and their wants," Chiara shot back at her sister.

"Have you talked to your father about this?" I said before they could wage a full battle. "Or your brother? If you don't trust him to do his job . . ."

Chiara shrugged and adjusted her bracelet. "I've attended plenty of balls alone. Besides, my father and brother are worried about other matters."

About Hálendi, she meant. And Riiga. I sat by Mari on the bed. "Well, you aren't alone anymore. What do you think, Mari? Are you going to sneak in with us?"

Mari snorted and hopped to the floor. "Hours of watching ladies gush over my brother? No, thank you. I'll be in the kitchens." She gave us a little salute and skipped out of the room.

Chiara and I both started laughing once the door had closed. But that was one aspect I hadn't thought of when I'd agreed to this only an hour ago. Enzo was looking to find a new bride. Now I'd have to watch him pick her.

In the Turian Countryside

His companion slept fitfully next to him, their horses tied up nearby. He couldn't sleep at all, though the trees swayed and the stream chattered and the moon drenched them in an ethereal light. This was proving more trouble than expected. It shouldn't be this hard to find one Hálendian.

And he *would* find her.

CHAPTER SIXTEEN

Glass doors covered an entire wall of the ballroom and opened onto a terrace overflowing with trailing flowers. More blooms—and even trees—clustered together along the edges of the dance floor.

I'd thought the colors of the gowns in Hálendi were bright; those had nothing on the vibrant dresses of Turia. It seemed every woman had entered a contest of who could wear the most blinding shade.

Chiara kept me close, our elbows linked together. She flaunted my presence many times, warning away those she didn't want to speak with. I longed to escape into the greenery.

Everywhere we turned, the benefits of an alliance with the royal family were being bandied about, as though Enzo were only a cart of coal to be traded and used. If I ever defeated the mages and found the traitor who'd set my family up to be killed, perhaps . . .

My stomach sank into my toes. Even if I did tell Enzo who I was, we could never be together. I was now the ruling heir of Hálendi. The throne was meant to be Ren's. I'd never envisioned *myself* sitting on it, but duty to the kingdom came before all else.

I caught a glimpse of Enzo with a young woman on his arm, a burst of color and radiance. He was beaming at her, until his gaze found mine, almost like he had sensed me watching. He raised an eyebrow.

I tore my eyes away, but the image was already seared into my mind. Now I'd have to watch others court and flirt with the man I had come to consider as a friend. Who could have been mine, but would never be.

It was going to be a long night.

The entire room smelled of roasted pheasant, and memories of home filled my mind. Escaping from fancy dinners with Ren. And my father? I didn't think the cracks in my heart would ever heal where he was concerned. We had just begun to understand each other. I wondered if I'd ever get to go back. If I'd even survive until the end of the year.

Once the first man braved my presence and requested a dance from Chiara, others followed suit, and I was left to stand against the wall, straining to keep the swirling pair in sight. Nobles circled close by once, sometimes twice, to get a better look at the stranger in their midst. It didn't bother me; I'd dealt with stares before, with whispers.

"Excuse me," a man said. I stepped out of his way, but he didn't move.

He also didn't say anything else, so I said, "Did you need to speak with me?"

The man pressed his lips together in what might pass for a

smile if your face was numb from cold. He wore a purple tunic and pointed shoes.

His accent finally registered. Not Turian. Not Hálendian.

He still wasn't speaking, so I ignored him, searching until I found Chiara again. She was leaning away from her partner as they danced. Only a tiny bit, but it was there if you knew what to look for. If you'd also learned that same trick. Enzo crossed their path, drawing my gaze along with him until I forced myself to refocus.

The man next to me cleared his throat, but I didn't pay him any attention. He'd speak when he was ready, or he wouldn't.

"The princess is a picture of benevolence, wouldn't you agree?" he finally said.

I kept watch on Chiara. "Yes, she is."

He sniffed. "To invite you to this ball, even as protector, when your people are no longer welcome here, is quite the peace offering."

My eyes flicked to his briefly, and only years of practice kept the disdain from showing on my face. How had he known I was here to replace her guard?

"She is, as you said, a picture of benevolence." It was something I'd done for years—instead of playing the courtiers' games, I'd toss their own words back at them. It always made them furious, and it kept me from having to dissect everything they said.

"You would do well not to tread on her benevolence too much, Hálendian." He stalked off, a path opening in the crowd as he made his way closer to the king and queen on their raised dais overlooking the crowd.

Marko had seen our interaction. He was still watching me, with arms folded.

"What did Ambassador Koranth want?" Chiara had reappeared at my side, standing a little closer than before.

I scowled and scanned the crowd. "What happened to your last dance partner?"

Her mouth dropped open, then pursed shut. "He asked me to walk with him in the garden tomorrow," she said, attempting a smile for any listening ears. "Would you accompany us?"

Meaning she didn't trust her guard to return, let alone to protect her.

"Yes, of course."

She visibly relaxed, turning to take in the rest of the party. "Meet me in the maze garden after breakfast."

I wanted to tell her I'd walk her down, but I nodded. Maybe she wanted it to look more like a chance encounter. I dropped my voice. "Couldn't you just refuse him?"

Her smile became forced to any who looked closely. "He's Riigan. I did not want to cause offense. Not now."

Enzo, resplendent in a long gold embroidered vest and polished boots, stopped in front of Chiara. His eyes snagged on mine, though, and for a long moment, no one spoke.

"Well, brother," Chiara said, rising on tiptoe to see over his shoulder. "Have you found your future wife yet?"

I averted my gaze and tucked my hands into the folds of my skirt. He made it so easy to forget—his new betrothal, the mage, everything. But forgetting was dangerous.

"No, sister, I have not," Enzo replied, a tightness in his voice belying his light words. He tipped his head toward me. "What is *she* doing here?"

Chiara's hands went to her hips. "My guard was unavailable, so I asked Aleinn to take his place. Just until he gets back."

Enzo took in a deep breath, his shoulders rising with the motion. "And did you think what that would look like? The Turian princess with her Hálendian friend?"

More and more sets of eyes turned our way the longer the three of us spoke. "Yesilia told me to come, so I did," I said. Enzo's mouth snapped shut.

"Koranth spoke to her," Chiara said, tipping her head toward me.

Enzo rubbed a spot above his eyebrow. "I saw. Did the Riigan ambassador have anything interesting to say?"

"That I should not take advantage of Chiara's *benevolence*." I held my hands out to my sides.

A muscle in Enzo's jaw ticked. He reached up to run his hand through his hair, but stopped the motion halfway there.

I lifted a shoulder. "He doesn't bother me. I'm used to . . ." I trailed off when I realized what I was about to say, to give away.

Enzo noticed my slip. Opened his mouth like he would ask me to finish that sentence.

"I think Mother wants you to keep dancing." Chiara nodded behind Enzo, toward the dais.

Enzo let out a sigh, then pasted on a wide smile, showing off his crooked bottom teeth. He bowed low to us, and when he rose, locked eyes with mine. "Will you do me the honor of this dance . . . Chiara?" His gaze shifted to his sister when he said her name.

A breeze from the terrace found its way in, lifting the hairs on the back of my neck. Chiara took his hand, and they assumed their position on the dance floor. But when he turned his sister into his arms, he was staring past her, right at me. I clenched my skirt in my fists, wishing I could be anywhere but here.

Though Chiara had her fair share of partners long into the night, Enzo favored almost every woman there with at least one dance. Except me. I understood it. Agreed with it.

But by the end of the ball, the courtiers waited with bated breath for an announcement, and he hadn't chosen another betrothed. He claimed he needed more time.

When I'd finally returned Chiara to her rooms, I was too tired to do anything but drink the cup of tea Yesilia had left on my table and crawl into bed.

And while a tiny seed of hope took root that he hadn't chosen someone, I couldn't give it light, couldn't let it grow. He was no longer an option for me.

✦ ✦ ✦

A shaft of light streaming through the window gouged into my eyes the next day, waking me from a deep slumber.

I blinked.

Wasn't I supposed to be somewhere? I shook my head.

A bitter taste coated my mouth.

Chiara. I should be with Chiara right now.

I stumbled out of bed as a sense of urgency swooped into my fuzzy mind. I fell against the table as I put on my boots, knocking my cup over and spilling its remaining contents onto my yellow scarf I'd left folded there last night. My sword. Where was . . . I shook my head again trying to focus. Yesilia's room.

I meant to be quiet but crashed against the door. It banged against the wall, but her room was empty.

It took me two tries to get my sheath fastened around my waist. Piercing brightness poured through the hall windows when I left the healing chamber. Had I ever slept this late?

A few passing servants gave me a strange look, but I ignored them and tried to get the thoughts in my brain to align. I had to meet up with Chiara. I found her room after two wrong turns and pushed open the door. It was empty. Her bed was made.

Then I remembered.

Panic coursed through my system, clearing out the cobwebs enough to find the missing piece: She'd asked me to accompany her. Didn't trust her guard for the meeting with that Riigan.

I sprinted into the hallway, skidding to a stop at the nearest window. The light speared into my skull as I searched the grounds.

"Can I help you, Miss Aleinn?"

Romo's concerned eyes took in my disheveled appearance.

"Chiara. Where is she?" My words were slurred, and my thoughts kept slamming into a stone wall.

Romo's eyes narrowed, but he pointed toward the east staircase. "She was headed toward the gardens a half hour ago."

The maze! I turned and almost plowed into a maid carrying a pile of linens. I dodged around her, slammed into the wall, stumbled down the stairs, and burst out the side door of the palace.

Heat already thickened the air, coating my skin in a thin layer of sweat. Luc stood at the entrance to the hedge garden. I almost missed it, and turned sharp. Too sharp. The gravel under me shifted. I put out my hand to keep from falling. The small rocks bit into my palm, but the pain only focused my mind more as I ran. My skirt snagged on a bush, and I cursed, snatching the extra fabric into my fist.

Enzo stood with a pair of young ladies in one of the alcoves in the maze, but I picked up my pace and hurtled by.

"Aleinn?" he called. But I was listening for something else, something out of place.

I took corners blindly, using my instincts and something that felt like a tether to guide me. And then I heard it—a shrill cry, cut off sharply.

A high wall of shrubbery with a bench at the bottom lay straight ahead. The sound had come from the other side. I sprinted down the path, leapt onto the bench, and vaulted. Time seemed to slow, then stop, as I jumped. For half a heartbeat, I was frozen above the hedge in the act of pulling my sword from its sheath. The man she'd danced with last night held Chiara, one hand around her waist, the other over her mouth. She stood frozen, wide-eyed, fingernails digging into his flesh. Another man, armed, guarded the entrance to the little alcove.

Time sped up again. I landed on my feet, sword drawn, and slammed my hilt into the arm the man had wrapped around Chiara. My momentum forced all three of us to the ground, and I pushed Chiara away as I rolled. The princess scooted back from her captor and started screaming. The man writhed on the ground, holding his now-broken arm.

My sword was already swinging toward the shoulder of the second man. He barely raised his blade in time to deflect mine, but managed to block it and my next two swings. My third struck true, though, and cut deeply into his leg. He yelled and staggered to his knees. I hit the side of his head with the hilt of my sword, knocking him unconscious, then kicked his sword away.

Chiara had stopped screaming. My breaths were too loud, the sun too hot. Luc skidded into view in a cloud of dust.

"I should run you through right now." Enzo's threat came with a menace that I'd never heard in his voice before. He stood by Chiara with his sword drawn, gold cuff glinting in the sun, the tip of his blade at the throat of his sister's attacker. Chiara held on to Enzo's free arm, keeping him between herself and the other man.

Fog seeped back into my mind as my heartbeat tripped and raced, unwilling to settle into a normal rhythm. A bird's sharp trill pierced the air above, and for one awful moment, I thought I was back in the Wild. Something was wrong.

My hands trembled. The world tilted, and a half-done braid fell over my shoulder. My sword clattered to the ground, and all I could think was that Master Hafa would have my hide for losing my weapon. Luc's hand on my elbow steadied me.

"Aleinn? Are you injured?" Enzo asked in a too-loud voice.

I shook my head, and the motion sent the ground heaving. "No."

I pulled my arm from Luc's grasp, leaned away, and vomited into the bushes.

"I told you the maze gardens were a bad idea," Luc grumbled.

The acrid smell made my nose burn, and I scooted away from the hedge and lay on the ground.

Palace guards arrived then. They pulled the man beneath Enzo's sword to his feet and dragged him, and his unconscious companion, toward the palace. The man was moaning and holding his broken arm, but Enzo instructed the guards to take them both to the dungeon before seeing a healer.

Enzo approached me—with Chiara still cowering next to him—and picked up my sword. His thumb brushed over the leather strands covering the gem in the cross guard. But I couldn't find the energy to stop him.

He knelt and slid my sword into its sheath at my hip.

"Please don't carry me again," I whispered. "I think I'd rather just stay here and sleep in this wretched heat."

He smiled and looked at Chiara, who sighed with relief.

"Let's get you up. We'll just . . . help you walk." Enzo took my hands and pulled me to standing, and the momentum carried me too close to him. I swayed for a moment with my hands in his, and a soft breeze pulled at several loose strands of my hair.

He brushed the strands away from my face, his hand feathering over my cheek. I leaned into his touch with a soft sigh.

"Aleinn?"

I blinked slowly, like a butterfly priming for its first flight. My thoughts jumbled around, and my hair—

My hair! I stepped away on shaky legs and started fixing my braid.

Enzo raised his hand like he would reach toward me, but turned to his sister and Luc and cleared his throat. "Come on. Let's help her back to the palace, where she can be sick in peace."

✦ ✦ ✦

It took ages, with me stumbling between them, but we eventually made it. Chiara's room happened to be on the third floor. Three miserable sets of stairs to climb. But once we made it to Chiara's room, Luc stationed himself in the hall, and I collapsed on the floor just inside the door.

"Leinn? Come lie on my bed, it will be much more comfortable." Chiara touched my shoulder, but the cool tile felt good against my flushed skin.

"No. I . . . I'm . . . This is good. Don't worry about me."

Enzo must have noticed our informality, but he didn't comment on it. His jaw had been set since the garden.

The door flew open, and Queen Cora burst into the room, leaving her attendants in the hall. Word always spread quickly in a palace, whether you wanted it to or not.

"Chiara? Darling, are you okay? What happened?" She gathered her daughter into her arms and sat with her on the bed. Chiara burst into tears.

A fresh wave of nausea rolled over me, and I groaned and draped an arm over my mouth. Enzo stood halfway between his family and me, and his fists clenched and unclenched as he took stock of the situation.

He straightened his vest with a deep breath. "Okay, Chiara, can you tell us what happened?"

She sniffed and wiped her nose on her handkerchief. I stretched until I could kick the open door closed. Chiara didn't need any more rumors spreading than what I'm sure had already been started. Enzo's warm gaze found mine, and he nodded his thanks.

Chiara took a deep breath, and her mother pulled her closer.

"Last night, Lord Sennor invited me to walk in the gardens today. I didn't want to offend him, so I agreed and—"

"I don't recognize the name. Where are his holdings?" asked Enzo.

She swallowed. "He is from Riiga. A visitor staying with Ambassador Koranth."

The prince growled and started pacing.

"Enzo," their mother said in a calming voice. "If Riiga is involved, we had best talk to your father about all of this before we make any hasty decisions."

The queen held Chiara tight, stroking her hair and letting her cry on her shoulder, tears dripping onto the queen's finery. I pressed my cheek harder into the cool stone.

"I asked Aleinn to accompany me," Chiara continued. "We were all to meet in the garden, and I tried to stall as long as I could, but Aleinn hadn't arrived and Lord Sennor grew impatient for our walk to begin. Nothing was amiss until he pulled us into that alcove in the maze garden. He grabbed my wrist and tried to kiss me and . . ." She put her face down, and her cheeks flushed.

Anger boiled inside me, but Enzo looked like he was about to fly out the door and break Sennor's other arm before I had the chance.

Queen Cora took her daughter by the shoulders. "Chiara, listen to me. You have nothing to be ashamed of. You are not responsible for the reprehensible behavior of someone else." Her mother, though soft-spoken, defended her fiercely.

Chiara sniffed. "I cried out for help, thinking someone would be nearby, but Lord Sennor overpowered me. I tried to fight back, but he was too strong." She wiped her nose again. "That was when Leinn appeared out of nowhere and tackled him. Then Enzo was there, and I . . . I don't really remember much beyond that."

"Where was your guard?" Enzo asked, pacing back and forth.

She gulped and shrugged. "He begged me to let him have the night off last night, so I let him. And . . . he never returned this morning."

Enzo turned to me. "Why didn't you meet her?" he demanded. "Did you drink too much last night?"

My arms were shaking, but I raised myself to sit against the wall. "I don't—" I squeezed my eyes shut, trying to get my thoughts in the right order. "No. Only the tea."

My heart paused for a beat, then thumped hard and started racing like a jackrabbit being chased by a wolf. The blood drained out of my cheeks, and I lay on my side while my heart found its rhythm again. I combed through my memory, trying to find anything out of the ordinary, any reason my head would be pounding and my heart tripping.

Queen Cora spoke up from where she held Chiara. "Enzo, send for Yesilia, please."

Enzo stood stunned before making his way to the door. He sent one of his mother's attendants for the healer, then knelt by me. "Are you sick, then?"

I shook my head, then squeezed my eyes shut when the world kept spinning. Moments—or was it minutes?—passed before I could form words again. "I'm sorry I wasn't there, Chiara. I'm sorry you—"

Yesilia burst into the room so fast the door would have hit my crumpled form had Enzo not put his hand out to stop it.

"Where is she? Is she alive?" Yesilia asked, breathless.

"Chiara's fine, Grandmother," Enzo said, but Yesilia dashed to *my* aid, falling to her knees quickly for someone so old.

She took my face in her hands, lifted my eyelids, listened to my heart.

"Yesilia, what—" Cora started, but Yesilia shushed her. She shushed the *queen*.

I groaned, and Yesilia snapped, "You be quiet, too." I laid my head on the tile while her ear was pressed to my chest.

She sat back on her heels and tapped my forehead. "You are lucky you aren't dead."

Another wave of prickling nausea hit, and I clutched my stomach. "I don't feel lucky."

"What do you mean?" Enzo asked. He helped Yesilia to her feet. "What's going on?"

Yesilia's eyebrows arched higher than I'd ever seen them. "You could say that." She folded her arms and stared me down. "The cup by her bed, the one I always leave for her, had nightshade in it."

Enzo went perfectly still.

"Is that bad?" I asked weakly.

He ran both hands through his hair. "It's a poison. If you eat it, there's no antidote."

Chiara whimpered. "What do you mean? Is Leinn going to die?"

Yesilia put her hands on her hips. "She should be dead already. She must not have had a very strong dose," she said, eyes narrowed. "Have you vomited yet?"

"Yes," I groaned.

She nodded once. "Then there's a chance you'll recover, though it might not be pleasant."

"Bring her here, on the bed, where she can rest," Queen Cora said, patting a space behind her and Chiara.

Enzo eased me up, and he and Yesilia helped me onto the soft peach silk. Yesilia slipped off my boots, and the knife tumbled onto the floor. She shook her head, muttering about Hálendians, and tucked it back in.

"You stay here," Enzo said, pointing at Chiara. "I'll post guards at the door." He shoved his hands in his pockets. "And, Leinn, don't you leave, either."

"But—" Chiara started to protest.

"Chiara, I need you to look after Aleinn. And, Aleinn, even drugged, you could handle anyone who comes after my sister."

I only had energy to nod.

"Someone in this palace is trying to cause trouble. I'm going to find out who and why. Until then, both of you stay in this room."

He stalked into the hall, startling his mother's attendants, and I let Chiara and her mother and Yesilia fuss over me, glad to let someone else shoulder the burden for once.

✦ ✦ ✦

"You should be dead," Yesilia whispered once we were alone. The queen had gone to find the king, and Chiara said she wanted a nice hot bath to wash Sennor's unwanted touch away.

"But you said—"

She cut me off. "I know what I said. But there were enough

remnants of nightshade in your cup to kill a full-grown man even *after* however much you drank. And the poison's been in your system since you fell asleep." She tapped my forehead again with her bony finger. "You should be dead."

I sat up and swallowed water that Yesilia had drawn herself. If I wasn't dead—and I didn't think I was—what had protected me from the nightshade? Could she mean . . . Had it been my magic? Was it capable of stitching me back together, even without my knowing I'd been poisoned?

She leaned closer, her minty breath filling the air. "Listen, child. I'm not asking you to reveal your secrets. But I *am* telling you that someone tried to kill you last night."

Glaciers. It wasn't the mage—he'd not be subtle about it. So who had tried to assassinate me this time, the second attempt on my life in under a month? And what would they do if they found out I'd drunk the poison they'd left yet didn't die?

King Marko's voice sounded from the hall, ordering the guards to let him in. He burst through the door, accompanied by Enzo. I sat up and scrubbed my hands over my face, wishing I had my scarf to hold back my messy braid.

Enzo pulled up a chair, and Chiara came in from the bathing room and hugged her father, then settled on the edge of her bed with her feet tucked under her. King Marko stood, a hand on her shoulder, like he was ready for battle.

"The good news," King Marko said, "is that Lord Sennor was under the impression that you, Chiara, had encouraged his advances."

"What?" the princess squeaked. "I would *never* encourage that type of behavior. And how is that *good* news?"

I put my hands behind my head. "It could mean he was being fed false information by someone else," I said.

If that were the case, there should theoretically be a trail to follow. But it would also mean a lot of planning and preparation had gone into Sennor's meeting with Chiara, and that we were dealing with a threat more integrated into the palace's network than I would have ever thought possible.

But what were they after? And more importantly, who else in the guard couldn't be trusted?

Mages and traitors in Hálendi. Assassins in Turia. Restless Riigans. Could they all be connected?

Enzo sat back and crossed his legs, his ankle resting on his knee. "Exactly. We don't think he was lying, so I'd go with the puppet theory. Luc is searching Sennor's room. Perhaps something there will lead to the instigator."

"And his guard?" I'd be interested to see what information they could get out of him. He'd been waiting for an attack.

Enzo leaned to one side, resting his arm on the chair. "We haven't been able to glean anything from him yet. But I'm hopeful we can get him talking. His belongings will be searched as well. When we've finished, they will both be escorted from Turia."

"But how will this affect our kingdoms' relationship?" Chiara asked, rubbing a spot on her blanket. "The only reason I accepted Sennor's invitation was to avoid offending Riiga."

Marko squeezed his daughter's shoulder. "Ambassador Koranth was full of his usual bluster. I will handle Riiga. In the future, if you feel uncomfortable, you decline."

Chiara swallowed thickly, then nodded.

I added Ambassador Koranth to my list of people in the palace to watch. "What about Chiara's personal guard?"

Enzo shook his head. "He still hasn't returned."

Chiara rested her chin on her knees. "I can't hide in here forever."

Marko kissed her head, then started toward the door. "You will tell anyone who asks that you had a headache today. We'll find you another guard, and—"

Chiara shook her head. "I want Aleinn."

Me? I'd barely gotten there in time; I'd almost failed her. Failed *another* friend. Yet she asked that I protect her? Standing with her would put me in a more visible position. Could I risk it? Then again, it wasn't likely anyone would recognize the Hálendian princess who never left her castle.

Enzo put both hands on the armrests and pushed himself up. "Luc could find someone . . ."

Marko shook his head, studying me like he had in the throne room. "How did you know Chiara was in trouble?"

I lowered my hands to my lap, twisting the silken blanket between my fingers. "I don't know, exactly. A lot of little details that added up. Something just felt . . . wrong."

His lips twisted to the side as he thought, but he eventually nodded. "You will take care of her. We'll find you a uniform—I want everyone to know she is guarded, and that her protector is . . . vigilant."

He strode out of the room, a dark thundercloud of crackling tension.

Enzo sat by his sister, slinging his arm around her shoulders. It reminded me so much of my brother my heart threatened to trip out of rhythm again.

"If you need anything," he told her, "Aleinn will be close by, and I'll always have your back, no matter what, okay?" She smiled and nodded against his shoulder.

I quietly got up and put on my boots.

"Aleinn?" Chiara asked. The tiniest sliver of fear threaded into her question.

"I'm just going to the healing chambers, then I'll return," I said, and slipped out. I felt too much like an intruder. I couldn't watch her and Enzo without remembering Ren and the million times we'd shared a similar moment. I couldn't watch them without remembering that I would never have another moment like that with my brother again.

I took a deep breath and leaned against the wall next to the door, closing my eyes against the grief that flared up. And then I took another. My hand found my pocket and wrapped around the book that always stayed with me. The door suddenly clicked shut.

"Leinn?" He said the name like a question, and I opened my eyes, but I wasn't sure what question he was asking. Searching his face, I wasn't sure if he knew, either.

I smiled, though I knew it didn't reach my eyes.

"You miss your brother."

My smile faltered, and I nodded. I didn't have the energy for more than that. I ached for my father as well. For my home. I couldn't escape the pain from the tethers.

He didn't say anything. I think he knew there was nothing that could be said just then. We were standing in a hall, after all.

"Thank you," he whispered. My lungs were tight, and my mind was trying to catch up to what he was thanking me for. He took a step closer and touched my arm, his deep-green eyes pouring into mine. "I owe you more than I can ever repay. As does my sister."

One moment he was there, so close I could feel the heat from his body, his touch like fire on my arm. The next he was striding down the hallway like he'd rather be anywhere else. I took a shuddering breath and wondered if I was still feeling effects from the poison.

Either way, every time I saw him, spoke with him, he made me wish for something that could never be.

CHAPTER SEVENTEEN

Ren's name had completely faded from his book. I cradled it in my hands as I sat on my new bed in my new room—which was more of a closet, really—next to the princess's suite. The brown uniform I wore itched against my legs, the trousers tighter than I was used to.

I pulled Irena's bag from the shelf on the wall and unlatched the flap. My old gray uniform. Irena's sweater. I kissed the cover of Ren's book and tucked it between the folds of fabric. They'd be safer in Yesilia's room, but I couldn't bear to part with them, despite the threat from whoever had tried to poison me.

A tiny mirror hung by the door, and I checked that my braid had stayed tight. I already missed the scarf. Chiara, as princess, would garner attention wherever she went. I, as her Hálendian guard, would share that attention. If Graymere found out I was still alive, he would come for me. And now that I was more visible, I worried over just how soon he'd get here. But at least Chiara spent some of her day studying in the library. I needed to find out everything I could about the Gray Mage before I faced him again. Before it was too late.

I gathered the books Yesilia had had me borrow for her and stepped into the hall to await Chiara. A tiny clock had started ticking in the back of my mind. It had been three days since I realized the mage had a personal vendetta against my family. A week since Enzo, Luc, and I had killed his shades, and almost a month since Graymere had attacked.

A month. What had the mage been doing? What did he want, other than revenge on my family?

Chiara's door opened. I quieted my thoughts and straightened my posture. Two maids came out and they both nodded respectfully. My brow furrowed, and I stared after them as they made their way to a back stairway.

"You've earned their favor," Chiara murmured. "For saving me."

I tilted my head. "Oh." I'd never in my life been respected by servants. They must really admire Chiara for me to be so quickly accepted. "We start in the library today, right, Princess?"

"Yes, but please call me Chiara," she said, and walked down the hall toward the main stairs. I almost told her that as her guard I couldn't, but how many had told *me* that? How many times had I wished for *one* solitary person who wasn't a relative to call me by name?

We entered the sanctuary of the library, and Chiara went to a table in the corner with her tutor. I tracked my way back to the shelf I'd taken Yesilia's books from. I didn't know where to start. Which other books to choose.

"Can I help you find something?" Master Romo asked from the end of the row.

The time had passed to work out Graymere's mystery on

my own, and Yesilia's words about healers and magic in Turia swirled in my head. With a deep breath, I said, "Yes, actually. I . . . I'm looking for anything on the ancient mages."

Romo set his load of books down nearby. "Information on magic, or on the original mages from the Great War?" He came over and eyed me closely.

"The original mages," I replied, and gripped my one book harder but handed him Yesilia's two to reshelve in the correct place.

"I see you've already read some of Scribe Jershi." He put Yesilia's books back in their spots, then set his hands on his hips, eyes lit with the challenge of finding information. "This is the bulk of his work." He tapped his finger against his mouth. "Mages, you say?" He pulled out several books and handed them to me, then retrieved a few more. I led the way to a table where I could see the door and Chiara, set my load down, then slumped into the chair, hands on the table.

So many books. I'd never get through it all before the mage found and killed me.

"If you tell me what exactly you are looking for, I could help, Miss Aleinn," he said as he added his stack to mine. Romo took a seat and waited. Longing for home stole my breath—how many times had my tutors, or even Ren, offered to help just like this?

"Thank you, Master Romo. But I . . . I don't really know."

He pointed at a few books in front of him. "Well, these carry the history of the mages, who they were before the Great War." He touched another. "Their warfare tactics. And this one, a particular favorite of mine, tells of their powers and artifacts. Or—"

"That one," I said, taking the last book he'd mentioned from the stack. I twisted the ring around my finger in my lap. "Why is it your favorite?"

He scooted the tome closer to me and stood. "Read it." His eyes gleamed as he went back to work.

I flipped it open, my finger dragging down a page and flipping to the next as I skimmed the information. When Chiara finished her lessons, I'd have to stay with her—

My breath caught in my throat.

> *The mages stored power—and sometimes some of their life force—in artifacts. When wielding these artifacts in battle, their energy would then be twice what they normally had access to. The Black Mage wielded a crystal staff, the Gray Mage wielded a silver sword, and the Red Mage wielded a gold dagger.*

I rubbed my forehead and put my elbows on either side of the book. "How could anyone hope to win against such a force?" I whispered.

> *Channeling power into an artifact both strengthens and weakens the mages, however. Though they are stronger with their artifacts, they are weak without them. A mage without an artifact becomes like a broken vessel trying to hold water: the faster you pour water in, the faster in leaks out, and the wider the cracks become.*

The mage in the Wild, the Gray Mage. His scabbard had been empty. He'd used a knife on Aleinn, and a borrowed sword on Hafa.

Emperor Gero defeated the mages after he stole both the crystal staff and the silver sword, which were then used against them. The Black Mage was destroyed; the rest fled.

Fled here. To the Plateau. And Kais followed.

Ice and snow and all the glaciers. Graymere's scabbard had been empty. He wanted his sword. He was looking for the mages' library.

The burned note I'd found so long ago had mentioned a search for it, a search my father hadn't authorized. I put my hand over my mouth and sat back. Had the traitor in Hálendi been working *with* the mages? And then they'd declared war on Turia because . . . Well, I wasn't sure why.

"That must be some book if the most vigilant person on the Plateau didn't notice me come in," an all-too-familiar voice said as the prince pulled out the chair Romo had been in.

I checked on Chiara—still studying. "I . . . yes" was all I could say. Between the mages, the assassin on the loose, and Enzo choosing a new betrothed, I needed to keep him at a distance.

He rubbed his hand on his leg. A door shut somewhere on the balcony. "Listen, Aleinn, there's really no good way to tell you this."

My heart sank. What else could go wrong? "Tell me what?"

"Hálendi has launched their attack at Fjall Pass."

My face crumpled at this news, and I bowed my head. So soon? How had they mobilized their troops to cross the Wild so quickly? Unless the traitor had been planning this for some time. And if the traitor was in league with Graymere, did that mean *he'd* be nearby as well?

He set his hand on my back, a reassuring weight, and then it was gone. "I just wanted to warn you to be careful."

I nodded, numb, even as everything spun out of control. "I'm sorry."

He let out a sigh that ruffled the pages of my book. "It's not your fault they decided to attack."

I closed my eyes and turned my face to the sun trying to shine through a thin layer of clouds. It *was* my fault. They were fighting because my father and brother were dead. Because they believed me dead. But I couldn't reveal myself yet. Graymere's scabbard had been empty, but even so, he'd defeated Hafa as though the weapons master were a novice.

Enzo's touch on my shoulder brought my gaze back to him, but he held in whatever he wanted to say. Chiara was with a different tutor now—they spoke quietly, their soft murmuring creating a hum of privacy around Enzo and me.

"Where is Luc this morning?" I asked, trying to forget the warmth of his hand.

"He's working with Yesilia to dispatch healers in preparation for refugees and wounded soldiers throughout Turia."

I pursed my lips and nodded. As prince heir, Enzo would probably be responsible for the war efforts here—organizing the shelter, food, and water stores.

Again, he looked like he wanted to tell me something. Instead, he nudged my open book. "It's a tale of some forbidden romance, isn't it?" He tugged on my braid, teasing me like Ren used to do.

My surprised laughter escaped, and it echoed around the quiet room. He smiled and sat back in his chair, folding his arms across his chest. A forbidden romance was the first thing he thought of? Did he, could he, feel this connection between us?

"If only it were," I sighed. His eyes caught mine and held them. I ran my hand across the book, debating what I should tell him. "It's about the ancient mages from the Great War."

He exhaled and rested his arm on the table. "With Riiga and the council and my sister's attack, I'd almost forgotten about the mage."

And the ball, too, I added internally. *A new betrothed.*

"How serious are the problems with Riiga?" I asked. "Do you truly think the incident with Sennor was a deliberate attempt to start a war?" I winced. "I mean, *another* war?"

Enzo nodded, leaning back in his chair and stretching out his legs. "I do. Koranth has been meeting with my father's advisors in private. *Weekly.*"

I raised my eyebrows. "And King Marko allows this?"

Enzo ran his hands through his hair, making the curls stand up all over. "We can't afford to agitate the Riigans too much."

Turia's land was wide and well protected, with the Wild to the north and the cliffs to the south. "With Hálendi's attack," I said, "now would be the perfect time for Riiga to strike."

"Exactly," he said. "But I don't want to worry about that right now." He leaned back again in his chair as if he didn't have anywhere else to be, although I'm sure he did. "Did you find anything helpful in the book?"

I fiddled with the end of my braid as a sharp ache swelled inside—I was alone, even sitting next to the man I should feel closest to.

"I think we aren't dealing with just any mage." I took a deep breath and lowered my voice, even though no one was close enough to hear us. "I think he's one of the Black Mage's original followers. Graymere."

"I—" Enzo paused. "Is that even possible? He'd be centuries old."

I pulled a different text closer, and we leaned over it. My shoulder brushed his, and fluttering erupted in my stomach. "The description of the Gray Mage—Graymere—matches the man at the ambush exactly."

"It could be a coincidence. Someone trying to create more fear by impersonating him."

I nodded once and flipped the page quickly but carefully. "Yes, but hardly anyone knows about the mages of old. It's not exactly common knowledge. And look at this description of Graymere's shades."

He scooted his chair closer to mine so he could read what I pointed to. His eyes went wide.

"So you think Graymere found a way to be preserved ever since the Great War, and is making some sort of move *now*?"

I tugged at the loose collar of my uniform. "I . . . Well, yes. I do."

He ran his hand over his mouth. "Cavolo," he cursed. "We definitely don't have the resources to fight against Riiga, Hálendi, *and* an ancient mage."

I mindlessly ran my hand down the length of my braid, and he followed the movement with his eyes. "And there might be more than just him," I muttered, wishing I knew exactly what we were facing.

"How many more?"

I swallowed and wrapped my braid around my hand. "At least two."

He cursed under his breath. "But why kill the Hálendian royal family?" he said. "And why now?"

I explained the legend of the mages' library, how it was thought to hold the remnants of magic from the Great War. How Graymere's scabbard was empty. "We always heard about it as some mystical treasure—the magic of old. But if it truly does exist and contain the mage's artifacts, it's more of a curse than a blessing."

He looked at the books surrounding us and rubbed the back of his neck. "Where would some place like that even be hidden?"

I thought about the maps I had studied, how much uncharted territory there still was on the Plateau. I straightened my shoulders. "Well, there's got to be information on it somewhere. Every buried treasure needs its hiding spot marked. We just have to find the record of it."

Enzo touched my hand. "I can't get away much from meetings and other . . . events," he said with a grimace, "but I'd like to help."

"Do you think we should tell your father?" I asked. There were so many pieces in play; all three kingdoms rested on a precipice, and even the smallest nudge could send the whole Plateau tipping into chaos.

He sat forward, rubbing his thumb along the textured parchment. "No, not yet. I want to gather everything we can first, and then present all the facts to him when his counselors can't dismiss the evidence."

"Okay." I bit my lower lip. His gaze settled on my mouth, and my stomach tightened. I knew my duty, and I knew his. Yet I couldn't push him away. "Are you busy now? I can show you what else I've found."

He deliberated only a moment. "Show me."

We pored over the books together as I caught him up on what I'd learned so far. He picked up another book and cracked it open, and we sat together in silence as we searched for anything else on the mages I'd missed that could be used against them.

"Look here," he said, and pushed the book closer to me. Our shoulders touched again, and a shiver ran down my spine. I shook it off, hoping he wouldn't notice, wishing I could ignore the feelings he stirred. "It says that Gero was the Black Mage's brother, and that they both passed their magic on to their sons. Gero's son, Kais, formed the magical barrier in the Ice Deserts so no one could leave unless they were pure in heart or summoned by another."

Gero's brother was the Black Mage? I closed my eyes and twirled the end of my braid. "So . . . the Black Mage's son was the Gray Mage, wasn't he?" I didn't need to see it on the page to know it rang true.

That meant Graymere was my cousin . . . sort of. My skin crawled at the thought of sharing blood with that monster. That's why he'd said what he did to Aleinn. That's why his first step after being freed from the Ice Deserts was to come after my family.

"He was," Enzo said. "But what is this key it talks about?"

"What?" I leaned in. Along the side of the block of text, in the margin, was a faint, handwritten note.

Two make up one, the key to the door.

Two kingdoms to hide, to be found nevermore.

I put my chin in my hand. "The two kingdoms must be Hálendi and Turia. The first king of Riiga hadn't left Hálendi when the mages' library was formed."

He rested one hand on the back of my seat and the other on the table. The sunlight filtered down from the window, wrapping us in a quiet embrace. One I never wanted to leave.

"My father told me a story once," Enzo started, staring at nothing. My shoulder nearly touched his chest, and I barely breathed so I wouldn't startle him away. Did he realize how close we sat? "That when the mages came—I think he meant Kais, not . . . not Graymere—Turia was ruled by Queen Oriana. My father told me that she formed the first friendship with the king of Hálendi, even went on a journey with him to see the Plateau, to decide what land she would give him. My father said we must strive to maintain our friendship with Hálendi. He didn't say why, only that it was important—"

"Your Highness," a young girl stood, out of breath, next to Enzo. "Yesilia sent me to fetch you."

He nodded, and the girl hurried off. Enzo reluctantly rose.

Right. The war at the border. For a few blissful moments,

I'd forgotten that there were soldiers at the pass, fighting because my father and brother were dead. Because they believed me dead.

"I'll see you soon?" he asked as he began backing away. Something flickered across his face, and it was the same expression Ren wore when he needed to tell me something I wouldn't want to hear. But maybe I was just reading my own emotions in his face.

Perhaps Enzo could be my ally in figuring out how to stop the war, how to defeat the mages. The desire to tell him who I was swelled until the words filled my throat.

Chiara laughed with her tutor, breaking me from my thoughts.

The weights stacked on my shoulders pulled at the muscles in my neck. I hated that there were people dying on the border, but bringing the mage—or mages—into Turia would make everything worse. No, if I wanted to tell Enzo everything, I would have to destroy Graymere first.

I lifted my chin and nodded. "Soon."

CHAPTER EIGHTEEN

"First, you'll put one arm around my neck and pin my arms with your other," I instructed Chiara. After the lessons with her tutors, we'd gone back to her chambers, and now she stood in front of me fidgeting with a pair of trousers she'd borrowed, rocking from one foot to the other. Mari watched from Chiara's bed, excitement lighting her eyes.

"If your attacker is behind you, where would he be vulnerable?"

She scratched her neck. "His face?"

"And his stomach! Elbow him there!" Mari bounced up and down.

I smiled at her exuberance. "Yes, those are both options, but only *if* you can get enough leverage. You also have the arch of your attacker's foot, the knees, and the groin. But overall, to escape, you'll need to either offset your attacker's balance, or cause him pain."

Chiara took a shaky breath. Learning the basic principles of hand-to-hand combat had been her idea. I'd practice with her as much as she wanted if it meant she could get out of a bad situation going forward.

"Surprise will be your best weapon." I had her hold me from behind, and demonstrated slowly as I explained. "Lunge to the side, hook your other leg behind both of his, and either toss him over your leg, or roll him onto the ground." I started the roll so she got the idea, but didn't finish it, as I didn't want to hurt her.

"Then what?" She stepped away and put her hands on her hips. Determined to see it through.

"Well, you either run or you fight. Your best bet would probably be to run, because you're usually unarmed and hopefully you'll be familiar with your surroundings."

She nodded, as if storing the information away.

"Okay, let's practice." I smiled with reassurance as I wrapped my arms around her waist, pinning her arms. "What are you going to do?"

She screamed loud and high, and the door burst open, a very flustered brother charging in, followed closely by Luc. Sword half-drawn, Enzo skidded to a stop so fast that Luc ran into him. I let go of Chiara and Mari jumped off the bed in front of us and pulled what looked like a dull kitchen knife out of her boot. When she saw it was just her brother, she lowered the blade and started laughing.

Chiara snorted, trying to contain herself, and then I lost it. It wasn't until the three of us girls had tears streaming down our faces that we finally caught our breath. Luc rolled his eyes and retreated into the hallway, snapping the door shut behind him. Enzo stood with his hands on his hips, sword back in its sheath.

"Do I even want to know what is happening in here?" he

asked, looking between us. "And I don't think you should have that knife, Mari."

She shrugged and tucked it back into her boot. "I need to be prepared for anything."

Which only made me laugh harder. With the weight of what was coming looming over the palace, it felt good to have something to smile about.

"Leinn is teaching me how to defend myself," Chiara said.

Enzo folded his arms and nodded. "That's a good idea. How is it going?" He guided Mari back to her perch on the bed and sat next to her.

Mari imitated him, doing her best to look stern.

I gave Chiara a questioning look. "Ready?"

She smiled and nodded, turning to face Enzo. I moved around behind her and put my arms around her again, pinning her. She made gentle motions, trying to mimic what I had shown her. But she couldn't get me off balance enough to throw me. I sighed and let her go.

I caught sight of Enzo holding back a laugh. Inspiration struck.

"Your Highness," I started. He stopped laughing. "Come over here and grab your sister from behind."

His eyes got some of their spark back. He stalked around behind Chiara, rubbing his hands together mischievously. She shifted, and her eyes darted to mine.

"This will be good," I told her. "You can see how much force will be required. I give you permission to do whatever you can to break free. Outside of this practice, you'll only have one shot to get away."

"Take him down!" Mari was back to bouncing on the bed.

Enzo wrapped his arms around Chiara, engulfing her, and pinned her to him. I smiled as she squirmed, testing his grip. A shiver raced along my skin when, unbidden, my mind slipped back to the farmer's cottage when I'd woken with Enzo's arm around me. I refused to let my mind wander any further.

Chiara struggled for a moment, but she didn't lunge far enough to the side. She pushed her head back against his chest and stomped on his foot, but not hard enough.

"You are stuck. And now he knows your tricks."

Enzo let her go, and she looked at the ground, discouraged.

I put my hand on her shoulder. "Chin up, Chiara. It was a good first try—it takes some time to learn this. We are practicing now so you can escape when it really matters."

She looked up with determined eyes. "Show me."

I tugged on my braid. "What do you mean?"

She pointed to me and her brother. "Enzo, grab Leinn. I want to see how to get away."

Mari stood up on the bed, arms in the air. "Yes! I want to see Leinn take out Enzo!"

My eyes widened. "Uh, I'm not sure that would be—"

"What's the matter, Leinn? Afraid you won't be able to beat me?" Enzo smirked, green eyes sparkling.

I rose to the challenge. "We'll want a little more space. Chiara, you might want to step toward the wall."

She skipped to the bed with Mari and bounced next to her. I gestured for Enzo to approach. Before we even touched, his warmth engulfed my form, and then his solid arms came around me.

"Ready?" he whispered in my ear. I shivered, and a laugh rumbled through his chest.

I tried to focus. I did. But he smelled like books and sunshine and, faintly, of crisp apples. I'd sparred with hundreds of men before, but no one had ever incapacitated me with their scent alone.

Chiara leaned over and whispered something to Mari, who giggled. I snapped back into the moment. All right, they wanted to see how to get out of his grip? I'd show them.

I lunged hard to the side, throwing Enzo off balance, then slipped my other leg behind both of his. We were in a crouch now, and I hooked my arms under his knees, then used my hip as leverage to toss him backward hard enough his feet flew over his head and he landed on his stomach. He hit the ground hard and coughed, forehead pressed against the rug.

"Yes," Mari whispered, almost reverently. She and Chiara's jaws had gone slack.

"You don't have to go easy on me, Your Highness," I said, smirking down at him.

He groaned and stood, then rubbed the back of his neck. "You were poisoned yesterday—"

"They won't go easy on your sister."

He looked over at Chiara and Mari, then back to me. "Again."

I stepped up to him.

"Are you sure I won't hurt you?" he whispered as he re-wrapped his arms around me.

I tried to focus on what he was saying instead of his embrace. "I'll be fine."

He tightened his hold and widened his stance so I couldn't pull the same move again.

This time I kicked my heel up to his crotch, but he moved his hips back before I connected. I lunged to the side while he was off balance and slipped my leg behind his. Before I could toss him again, he adjusted his hold and *tickled* my stomach. I shrieked a laugh at the unexpected contact and he rolled us back, caging me underneath him.

I should have thrown my fist at his throat, should have done something, anything, besides let him pin me, but his green eyes held me captive. The rest of the room faded. His gaze flicked down to my mouth. My breath caught in my throat. I grabbed a handful of his shirt, inching him closer. For once, I found myself okay with being trapped.

Mari finally broke the tension by yelling a battle cry as she climbed onto Enzo, trying to wrestle him off me. I jolted out of the moment, rolled them both to the side, and sat up.

The door opened, and Luc stuck his head in. "Enzo? We've really got to get—" He stopped when he saw us all on the ground.

Chiara walked over and whacked her brother on the back of the head. "You cheated."

He cleared his throat and stood, throwing Mari over his shoulder. "Sorry, Luc. Just teaching my sisters a lesson." Mari tried to break free but couldn't escape his grip.

Luc's eyes flitted to me, still on the ground, and then back to Enzo. "What kind of lesson?"

I groaned and stood, then extricated Mari from Enzo. "Just teaching Chiara to defend herself."

Luc's frown was warm and genuine. "Good idea." Then he waved Enzo out. "We've really got to go, diri."

"Go?" I asked, tucking my hands in my pockets.

Luc ducked back into the hallway. Enzo glanced between his sisters and me like he couldn't make up his mind what to say. "I just came to let you know that our departure has been set: we'll be leaving tomorrow."

His words caught in my mind. Mari folded her arms and sat on the floor, and Chiara's smile melted away.

"You're leaving?" I asked, feeling more blindsided than I probably should have.

"My father, mother, and I are going to Lord Hallen's estate to . . . meet with some courtiers."

My brow furrowed. The Hálendian army was attacking at the pass: Why would the prince heir leave the palace? And why hadn't he mentioned this when we'd spoken in the libra— *That look. Like he'd wanted to tell me something.*

Chiara rolled her eyes and fell into a chair by the empty fireplace. "We aren't in court, Enzo." She turned to me. "Because the Hálendian princess is dead and he didn't choose someone at the ball, our parents want to throw Lady Cynthia Hallen at him. *Esteemed* Councilor Hallen's daughter."

My head jerked back to her casual reference to my death. "Oh, uh, of course," I said to cover my awkwardness. From the way Chiara had said Cynthia's name, it sounded like she approved of her as much as I did.

Enzo tipped his head toward me subtly. "Chiara, that's no way to talk about the princess—"

She shrugged, but her voice softened. "She never bothered

to answer anything herself, and she never came to visit, even though her brother did. I'm glad you don't have to marry her."

I snapped my jaw closed, and my cheeks heated. Then another part of Enzo's announcement registered. "You *and* your parents are leaving the palace? For how long?"

He winced and rubbed the back of his neck. "The estate is only one day west of Turiana—"

"*One* day," Chiara interjected, "and yet they are leaving Marietta and me here." She huffed and folded her arms.

"It's going to be a special form of torture, I assure you. Especially when there are . . . other pressing matters I need to attend to." He watched me intently, trying to communicate something with a look, but I was already moving toward the door.

"Excuse me, Chiara. I'll let you speak to your brother privately." I bowed and walked stiffly out of the room, letting the door click shut behind me. The mages must be my focus now.

My chest ached at the thought of Enzo courting the beautiful daughters of the Turian nobility. My little room down the hall waited for me, a sanctuary from a future that would never happen, memories I would never have if Enzo wed another. But something uneasy sat in my gut. A whispered warning.

I turned back toward Chiara's room just as Enzo exited, and we barreled into each other. He grabbed my arms, steadying us both.

"Sorry," I said, looking up at him. His hands tightened almost imperceptibly, then he blinked and released me.

"Did you forget something?" He tipped his head to Chiara's door.

"Something doesn't feel right about this," I said.

Enzo looked at Luc, who was speaking with someone down the hall. He grabbed my hand, and the contact startled me so much I let him pull me around a corner and into a small sitting room, where he quietly closed the door.

He took a few steps away from me, then stopped, his back to me. Golden light illuminated every corner, every shadow in the room. A sofa and chairs were positioned near the windows, but we stayed by the door.

His shoulders rose and fell with a sigh. "The council prefers Cynthia, but"—he faced me, looking pained—"nothing will be decided right away."

"It's not that." Though that was part of it. I was jealous of a woman I'd never even met. I rubbed the spot beneath my rib cage, where the tethers used to be. "I don't have a good feeling about you and your parents leaving the palace. Someone tried to poison me and compromise Chiara only yesterday, and we don't know who. We don't even know where the mages are, or what their plan is. You'll be on the road, an easy target for anyone to attack."

He sighed. "It has to be done."

My jaw clenched. "But it doesn't make sense. Why not invite *them* to stay *here*?"

"Because troops are amassing at the southern border. There have been reports of villages inundated with Riigans and mercenaries from the Continent."

"Riiga is readying to attack?" My mind raced with the implications. Could they have somehow known Hálendi was about to break the peace? Or did they act when an advantageous situation appeared?

"Koranth has been meeting with nobility, and we don't know how much influence he's gained. My father fears Ambassador Koranth will push me into an alliance with Riiga if another match isn't set."

"So you're going to Hallen's estate to keep Koranth and those loyal to him out of the decision without starting another dispute." Yet another mess caused by my silence. He needed a betrothal to keep Riiga away. And I was right *here*. But, of course, my own throne separated us. "Enzo, I—"

Fear choked me. Visions of the mage's power—how he'd held everyone frozen, his blade across Aleinn's throat—rose in my mind. It could be Chiara next. Or Enzo himself.

"What is it?" he asked when I paused.

"Never mind." I ground my teeth. I couldn't tell him yet. Couldn't risk the mage attacking me here. "But it's too dangerous. I don't think you should go."

"We are taking a large contingent of men. We'll only be at the estate for a week. Besides, we'll be traveling with most of the palace guard. Anyone would be a fool to attack us, magic or no."

"Take me with you. I can defend against magic." I paced back and forth, imagining all the ways this trip could go wrong.

He held my arm to stop me, and suddenly we were so close I could count his long, dark eyelashes, name every constellation in his eyes. Our breath mingled together, and I wasn't sure if he pulled me in or if I pulled him, but somehow, impossibly, we were closer.

"Leinn, I need you here," he whispered. "I don't trust Koranth being so close to my sisters, but he's a necessary evil at this point to keep Riiga from attacking. I have to know that my sisters are protected. I *trust* you, Leinn."

His other hand came up, hovering just over my cheek. Tingles and sparks raced along my skin, and when his hand finally made contact, I went still under his touch.

"I *need* you"—he stepped closer until there was only a sliver of space between us—"here."

He stared at my lips, not moving, our breaths coming faster as we stood on the edge of a cliff. My heart told me to leap into the oblivion, that Enzo was the right choice.

His head came down toward mine, and he moved his hand from my arm to my hair. Right over the white streak I'd hidden my entire life. The mark that would identify me to the world, to the mages. The mark that now signaled my duty to the throne.

I stiffened, and Enzo studied me. What did he see? Did he understand what I couldn't figure out myself?

I yearned to erase what distance still separated us. To see if his lips would taste like apples. Instead, I rose onto my toes, turned his chin, and kissed his cheek, my lips lingering, memorizing the feel of him. "I'll protect your sisters, Enzo. Stay safe."

He straightened, his hands brushing my skin as they returned to his sides. He inclined his head and stepped around me to the door. He adjusted the cuff on his arm and flexed the hand that had rested on my cheek, then slipped through the door.

My legs threatened to buckle beneath me. I held on to the arm of the nearest chair and eased into it. My eyes squeezed shut, and I rested my head in my hands, elbows on my knees. I'd never felt like this toward anyone. But Enzo was no longer mine to have.

✦✦✦

"Where could she be?" I asked as I checked under the beds in Yesilia's empty chambers. She'd gone to Hallen's estate as well—Lady Hallen had requested her presence. Mari had gone missing before Enzo, his parents, and Yesilia had left this morning, and Chiara and I had been searching for her most of the day. I kept telling myself she was too young to be a political target, that she was just hiding.

Chiara leaned against the doorframe and shrugged, chewing her way through a kind of fruit she'd called cherries. I'd tried one, and then immediately eaten ten more. "She'll come out when she's ready," she said, and spit a seed into her handkerchief.

I was almost glad Enzo was gone. In the library yesterday, and again in that sitting room, I had been contemplating telling him who I really was. Now he was on his way to look at another possible new bride. As if he were picking out a new sword. I told myself he was only doing his duty and following the counsel of the king and his advisors. And I could never marry him anyway. I had run out of time. But I'd promised him I'd protect his sisters. Which I couldn't do if I couldn't find them both.

I looked over to Chiara, surprised at her good cheer. "You're not still upset about being left behind?"

"What Mari doesn't know is that with the king and queen gone, we won't be held to our schedules. I can spend as long as I want reading, and we can spend hours in the gardens—as long as the summer rains hold off for the week." She flashed a brilliant smile over her shoulder as she practically skipped down the hall toward the library.

I followed Chiara, eager for more time in the library as well. Still, I scanned the hallways as I walked, wondering where an eight-year-old would hide. If Mari didn't show up soon, I worried I'd never find her.

The doors to the throne room flew open and banged against the wall. I pulled Chiara behind me and put a hand to my sword, then realized it was Marietta who had blown out of the room. I knelt down, and she threw herself into my arms, sobbing onto my shoulder.

"Mari? What happened? Are you okay?" Relief at finding her and worry at the source of her tears turned in my stomach.

Chiara rubbed Mari's back while craning her head into the throne room to see if someone else was there.

Marietta sniffed and wiped her nose on my shirt. She peered up at us with red eyes and soot smudged on her dress and cheeks.

"I've been hiding all morning, and no one has tried to find me. Mother and Father left me here alone. Everyone always leaves me!" she wailed, and buried her head in my shoulder again.

I held her tight. "Marietta . . ." My voice was soft but firm. I waited for her to look at me before continuing. "I am here. I won't leave you." I knew how it felt to be left behind.

Chiara jumped in as well. "Mari, we *have* been looking for you everywhere." She smiled softly at her younger sister, who was finally calming down.

I brushed her hair out of her face. "You're better at hiding than everyone in the entire palace is at finding. Even *we* failed."

The timid edges of a smile appeared, and she laughed a little. "I am the bestest at hiding."

"How about this?" I stood, putting my hands on my hips.

"Why don't you stay with us until your parents return? We can spend the rest of the day in the library. And maybe we could have some adventures tomorrow?"

Marietta's eyes grew wide, and her smile stretched across her face. "Oh, yes, yes! Could we?"

Chiara laughed and took her hand. "Of course, Mari. We'll go exploring!" They skipped down the hall, arms swinging. I grinned. One less thing to worry about.

✦✦✦

Chiara stayed curled up on a stuffed chair by the window, reading romances and fairy tales. Master Romo had laughed when Mari had asked him if there were any secret doors in the library, but she'd spent the rest of the afternoon searching every corner anyway.

I tugged the collar of my brown uniform away from my neck—Turia was wretchedly hot even in the end of spring—and pulled yet another book from a stack on my table as I tried to find Graymere's weaknesses and where the mages' library might be.

One thought kept circling in my mind: the tethers had broken within minutes of each other. It had been Graymere who attacked me in the Wild. So someone else had assassinated my father in Hálenborg, and another someone had killed Ren in North Watch.

If the Red and Brown Mages were indeed working with Graymere, and all three sought the mages' library, what would be their next move? Did they already know where it was? Did they have the key?

I'd found the book Enzo had been reading from yesterday, and was flipping through it, looking for anything more.

Two make up one, the key to the door. Two kingdoms to hide, to be found nevermore.

Was it even talking about the mages' library? But the burned note I'd found so long ago mentioned a key as well.

Something else on the page seemed to reach up and pull my gaze down.

The Black Library:
A stockpile of the learning and weapons of the Black Mage and his followers. The location is unknown, but is rumored to be the final resting place of Moraga, the feared sword of Graymere, the Gray Mage.

This had to be the mages' library, though Black Library seemed a much more appropriate name, considering what it contained. I closed my eyes and tilted my head back, trying to remember exactly what the burned note had said. Something about destruction, strange magic.

The key must lie in Hálendi.

I shook my head and stared at the book again. It said there were two parts to the key. Two kingdoms.

I went over what I'd guessed so far. Graymere was looking for his sword, his power, turning the kingdoms against each other so he could find the Black Library. And then what?

Revenge. He had taken that out against my family. Would

he take back his land—the Continent? I doubted there would be anyone who could stop him from taking anything he wanted if he had his sword.

I found the next book in the stack and turned pages, reading as fast as I could, but stopped when I got to a drawing. Two circles—one larger, the smaller one inside, and shaded in between, like a ring, or a wheel. And there were markings on it, seemingly random dots. At the bottom was the word *Turia*.

The markings were familiar somehow. Something from home, from before the Wild . . .

I gasped, then covered my mouth with my hand. My father's Medallion had markings just like this on the back of it. Ren had shown them to me, that day in the library before we left.

Two kingdoms to hide. Enzo had said that Oriana and Kais had traveled the Plateau together.

Two make up one. I couldn't be sure, but it looked like this ring, with its matching markings, would fit around the Medallion.

The key to the door.

Ren had taken it to North Watch before he'd been killed. Which meant the mages already had one piece of the key. My stomach jumped and danced, and my hands started to shake.

Where was the other? It must be in Turia somewhere. I drummed my fingers against the book, wishing that I could just ask Enzo. Why did he and his parents have to leave *now*?

"I'm starving!" Mari called down from the balcony.

Chiara laughed. "Let's go find dinner."

Ren's curses ran through my head in a loop. If the mages already knew where the Black Library was, the Turian key would be the final piece to unlock. Even if they didn't know, they'd need this part eventually.

Mari was jumping down the stairs two at a time; Chiara marked her place.

The book in front of me was massive—too big to hide. But I couldn't leave this here when there were unknown threats in the palace. I slipped the knife out of my boot and lifted the back cover. Romo wasn't looking, but Chiara and Mari were on their way. One deep breath, and I pressed the knife into the page, exhaling when it punctured the parchment. Then I slid the knife along the spine until I'd freed the illustration.

I slipped my knife back into my boot as I finished closing the book, then quickly folded the parchment. I tucked it into my pocket just as Chiara and Mari got to my table.

"I told Cook to make cake for dinner," Mari was saying. "Do you think he'll do it?"

I forced a smile, my hand clenched tight around the folded illustration. "I'm sure he will at least make it for dessert, Mari."

A fist-sized rock had lodged in my stomach and its weight was now spreading to my limbs. If the mages knew the rest of the key was in Turia, they'd be heading here soon, if they weren't already. While Enzo and the king and queen were at some lord's estate.

And if the mages found the Black Library, there wasn't much chance of anyone succeeding against them. I thought again of Scribe Jershi's description of the mages when they'd lost their artifacts. Broken vessels. Our only chance to defeat the Gray Mage would be before he found his sword.

The image of Graymere holding Aleinn flashed in my mind.

But instead of pushing the vivid picture away, I studied the mage—the blackness in his eyes, his long fingers gripping the knife. Inside me, something seemed to grow, to reach out to the mage from my memory. Something where the tethers had been.

I shook my head, and the connection broke.

We needed to find the Black Library before he did. And destroy it.

"Coming, Leinn?" Mari asked, her hand in Chiara's.

Enzo's request to keep his sisters safe echoed in my mind.

I gathered my books and placed them on the nearest shelf, glancing back once as I walked into the hall with them. I'd hide the illustration in Ren's book in my room. And when Enzo returned, we'd have to have a talk with his father. We had to keep Graymere from finding the Black Library. Even if that meant revealing that he'd killed the wrong girl.

CHAPTER NINETEEN

Worry about the mages and sickness at the thought of Enzo courting Lady Cynthia had kept me awake most of the night. Thunder had shaken the palace, while lightning split the sky into ribbons. Then the rain had started. I had watched it pound against the window, trying to think of what I could do from the palace to prepare for the mages.

"Come on!" yelled Mari, pulling my thoughts to the present. Her voice echoed in the dim, cool hallway. For once, I wasn't sweating from the heat everyone else seemed to take in stride.

"How much farther to your most secret hiding spot? I'm getting hungry!" Chiara's voice didn't bounce quite like Mari's, but there was no one around to hear her. The late morning sun hid behind low billowing clouds that tumbled over each other as they dumped their rain. We hurried to catch up to Mari's skipping pace. The sconces hadn't been lit in the halls, and the murky light made me shiver. *Where* is *everyone?*

More light filtered inside as we crossed the main entrance to the palace. The foyer was long and tall, with windows stretching three stories high. The floors gleamed with polish, but today, the tiles seemed to douse the light instead of reflect it.

Something outside moved. I went to the window to see who would be out in such miserable weather, while the sisters continued.

I squinted through the rain streaking along the glass. Men in dark cloaks ran toward the palace. One figure rammed his sword through a guard without missing a step. Sharp, icy prickles swooped from my fingertips to my heart.

There were no shouts, no screams, no alarms ringing. Just silent progress through the mud to the palace entrance. To us.

My mind ground to a halt, and my throat closed. There was nowhere to hide, no room or closet to duck into.

"No!" I choked out. I sprinted toward Chiara and Mari, slipping on the polished floor like I was moving in slow motion. They stopped in the middle of the grand open foyer and turned, frowning in confusion.

I got my footing and barreled into both of them, pushing them into the corner.

"Aleinn?" Chiara started. "Wha—"

I turned to the doors and drew my sword, and the sisters fell silent. There was no way the men about to explode into the palace wouldn't see us and kill us on the spot. My focus narrowed to the front doors, my heart pounding out of my chest.

The door splintered. Chiara and Marietta flinched at the crashing boom that filled the empty room. Windows all along the corridor smashed as men poured into the palace, spreading like darkness. Mud and rain and water splashed onto the tile floors, seeping into the grout and staining everything brown red.

I raised my sword.

That's when I felt it. Something pulled where the tethers had been, just below my rib cage. A warm shimmering wave I couldn't quite see rippled out from my middle. It covered me and the princesses, cocooning us in a muted cave. I could still hear swords clashing and people screaming, could still see the men streaking past us, but everything was muffled and smudged as if we were underwater.

Chiara and Mari stayed silent behind me, their shallow breathing matching my own. Every strip of leather on the hilt of my sword dug into my palm. Though sound couldn't reach us, the coppery scent of blood mixed with fresh rain and dirt swirled together until I could taste them.

It feels like rushing, Ren had said. But this, to me, was . . . clarity.

We hid in that corner for what seemed like ages as chaos surrounded us, undetected by the soldiers still streaming into the palace, shouting, and searching the halls. Most of the fighting took place farther inside, but we watched as some servants tried to fight back or run. They were all captured or killed.

Who had attacked the palace in the middle of the day, and why?

Every inch of me wanted to jump out and fight the invaders, but Enzo's words reverberated inside. *I have to keep the princesses safe.*

When the steady stream of men passing through the broken front door finally trickled away, sounds of the intrusion still came from other floors and wings of the palace. The muscles in my shoulders trembled to keep my sword up, and the shield around us flickered. We needed somewhere to hide. I turned to Marietta and knelt beside her, whispering fiercely.

"Mari, where is your very best hiding spot?" She was shivering and staring at the broken door. I grabbed her shoulder. "Look at me, Mari. Look only at me." I took a deep breath in and out, and she mimicked me. "Where is your hiding spot? Is it close?"

"Right around the corner." She blinked and swallowed hard. "The main drawing room."

I shook out my hands, then raised my sword once more. "Let's go."

As I took a step forward, Chiara and Mari right behind, the shimmering shield around us flickered again, then dissipated. The magic that had shielded us from being seen—wherever it had come from—had completely drained me.

I listened, then turned the corner into the hallway. A man leaned against the wall right in front of us, his sword lax at his side, but his eyes went wide. I reacted on instinct, though my initial swing was sluggish.

He parried my first blow. I dodged his attempt at a swing and sank my blade into his chest. Something flickered within, something dark and powerful. My sword sliced between his ribs and the soft flesh beneath them, stopping at bone on the other side. I stood there long enough to watch the surprise, then the life, drain from his eyes. He fell back, but I held on to my sword tight. Blood dripped from its tip onto the polished floors. I tried to breathe in, but my lungs had turned to ice.

I had killed a man.

"Leinn—" Chiara's frightened whisper didn't penetrate my shock.

Mari tugged on my hand, and a shout from the direction of the front doors pushed me to action. I wiped my blade on the brown tunic of the man now staring lifelessly at the ceiling and led the princesses through the first doorway on the left, the main drawing room.

I closed the door, but I could hear a group of men coming toward us from the foyer.

"Come on." Mari's frightened voice pulled my attention to the empty fireplace. It was grand, extending from the wall several feet, and almost tall enough for me to stand upright in. The commotion outside the room grew louder.

She reached up and pushed on a brick in the mantel. A small door opened on the side of the fireplace, near the wall.

She waved for Chiara and me to follow her. We ducked through the hidden door, clicking it shut just as the drawing room filled with clomping, laughing, shouting men.

I slumped against the closed door. The invaders were boasting about their victory—they hadn't seen us. I shut my eyes but opened them with a start when my mind replayed the sight of the life draining out of the man's eyes. And the flicker of something within me that had stirred while killing him.

A set of small hands rested on my cheeks, and I focused on Mari's face. Only the tiniest bit of light filtered in from a slit in the floor. Mari and Chiara watched me with worry on their faces. I held my finger to my lips. They settled down on the floor, and we waited, listening to the men.

We were in a small alcove between the fireplace and the walls. There was enough space for the three of us to sit shoulder to shoulder, and it was long enough that we could lie completely flat. The ceiling was too low to stand up straight, and the walls were dusty, bare wood and stone.

I killed him. My thoughts careened through fragmented

moments. My stomach dropping when I saw the soldiers running toward the palace. My sword sliding through that man's flesh. The magic shielding us from being seen. The blood staining the ground, my sword.

"—find the princesses, but do not harm them," a voice in the drawing room said. "When the remaining guards are locked in the barracks and the servants locked in the dungeon, we will begin your search."

Pounding steps faded into the hallway, but we remained still.

"I received your letter. I hope you are impressed with the loyalty my men have shown." He sounded different, but I knew Koranth's smooth voice. The condescending lilt when he'd spoken to me at the ball. Who was he talking to, though? What men did he have?

"The position you desired in Riiga recently became available. I'm sure Janiis will reward you for your help in this matter," replied a voice I'd never heard. It was soft and deep, like the glassy surface of a lake with no bottom.

A feather-light stirring caressed the spot where the tethers had been, but I pushed the feeling away. It wasn't Graymere's voice. Yet chills still skittered down my neck.

"But between the weakness at the west gate, letting someone escape to warn the king, and your lack of ability to find the princesses, I am beginning to doubt your desires, Lord Koranth. I thought Riiga's reward was important to you."

"It was only one man—"

"It only takes *one*!" The other voice yelled, knocking dust from the walls around us.

"Everything I have done is for the welfare of Riiga. The king will see that," Koranth snapped, moving farther from our hiding spot. "Please make yourself comfortable in a guest chamber. I'm confident we will soon find what you seek."

"But we will not have as much time to search as I expected because of your failure," the man continued. "You must . . ."

A door clicked shut, and their conversation faded.

Riiga had attacked the palace? Were they mad?

Mari fiddled with the ribbon on her dress. I shook my head and put a finger to my lips. We needed to be sure there was no one in the room before we moved or made any sound.

I tried to make sense of what had happened, what we'd need to do. Everyone would be searching for the princesses soon, when they realized they hadn't been captured in the initial assault.

Our hideout was on the ground floor, which was ideal, but we had no access to windows. Regardless, we'd never make it by the guards at the wall. And then there were Koranth's men positioned throughout the palace. We were trapped.

The surge of energy rushed out of me, leaving me even more drained and empty than before. I blinked slowly, trying to stay awake, to keep from seeing the man's death again, from feeling the horror and power I had felt in that moment, but I couldn't fight my body's exhaustion. The magic, or whatever had shielded us, had left me gutted. I gestured once more for the princesses to stay silent, and then my chin hit my chest.

✦ ✦ ✦

When I woke, everything ached, but I felt less empty inside. Chiara and Mari were whispering to each other as they sat on the floor across from me. My entire body groaned in protest as I shifted on the stone floor, bringing my knees up. Whatever had shielded us had emanated from the place where the tethers had been. My ring hadn't been warm like it had been when I fought the shade mage. The magic hadn't come from my sword. It had come from me.

But the tethers were *broken*.

Then I remembered the icy wound from the shade mage's blade that wouldn't heal—my wound had been poisoned, but Luc's hadn't. The black blade had reacted to my magic, even though the tethers were no longer there.

I closed my eyes and focused inward. The pain was still there, but something else was as well. A connection—faint like a single silk thread—and an emptiness. I'd thought feeling full in the Wild was a trick of its magic, but what if it was the Wild's magic itself filling me up?

Whatever power I had used today, I was now completely drained of it. I silently cursed my lack of knowledge. My father said using magic was like exercising a muscle. I'd have to hope that it would rejuvenate with rest, because I had no idea how to fill my reserves on my own.

"How long was I asleep?"

"At least an hour," Chiara whispered. "No one else has entered since Koranth and the other man left."

Mari spoke up this time with an even quieter whisper. "Koranth sounded different."

"Different?" I lowered my voice to match hers.

"He sounded . . . mean."

It had been Riigans visiting Koranth who had attacked

Chiara in the garden. Koranth had made a point to speak to me when I'd attended the ball. Marko and Cora and Enzo had left the palace to avoid Koranth's influence. Was Koranth also responsible for Chiara's guard abandoning her? I cursed under my breath.

"Does this have something to do with the tariffs?" Chiara asked into the darkness.

"Tariffs?" I asked absently. Koranth had to have soldiers positioned at the gate—there had been no warning from the outer wall of an attack. How many more Turians had he bought?

"Riiga tripled its normal tariffs on our grain, and the farmers are starting to panic."

I nodded in the dark. Enzo had mentioned that when we first met. Riiga pressured Turia from the outside with the tariffs, and Koranth pressured from the inside with a forced union.

The wide, scared eyes in front of me reflected what little light seeped into our hiding place. *Keep the princesses safe.* Gritty, dried blood scratched against my hands, and I scrubbed them against my trousers.

"I'm not sure what Koranth is after, but your safety is our priority," I told them. "We'll find a way to escape—we just need to be patient and smart. This will be a grand adventure." I tried to lend excitement to my words. I had spent over a week surviving the Wild alone. The initial fear that had paralyzed me was not something I'd easily forget. I had to keep the princesses positive and calm if we were to get out of this alive.

"Leinn?" Mari's quiet voice almost blended in with the blackness around us.

"Yes, Mari?" I rubbed my eyes with my wrists, trying to

figure out what to do next. We couldn't trust anyone—there was no telling how many servants and guards Koranth had bought out. We were trapped in a tiny hidden nook with no food or water. There was no chance of making it out of the palace, through the gates, and into the city without being caught.

"How did you keep the men from seeing us?" Mari asked timidly. Was she afraid of me? Should she be? "They ran right by. Some looked right *through* us. Was that magic?"

I remembered the power I'd felt as the life drained out of the invader's eyes, and I tugged on my braid. Years of keeping my secret made me hesitant to share where the magic truly came from. And if they *were* captured, I didn't want them knowing.

"I'm not exactly sure, Mari. I knew I wanted to keep you safe, but I don't know how I did it, or if I can do anything else. When my father gave me my sword and my ring, he said they were special, but he never told me exactly how to use them." I missed my father and Ren with a fierce ache. They knew about the tethers, about magic. They would have known what to do.

"Have you done it before?" Chiara's voice was braver than Mari's, like she thought this was something out of her fairy stories.

"No, nothing like this."

"Why did your father give you those?" Mari asked, scooting forward so she could sit cross-legged.

I licked my dry lips. "I used to guard the princess of Hálendi." It was mostly the truth.

"Enzo's betrothed?" Chiara asked, shifting.

"Yes. I was given these heirlooms to better protect her."

"But, Leinn, the princess died." Mari's quiet, innocent voice cut my heart into shreds.

My tongue stopped any reply—I wouldn't lie to them. I took a deep breath instead. "I will do everything I can to keep you both safe. But I need you to stay close by me and do exactly what I say."

I felt more than saw them both nod in agreement. I needed something else to think about besides my lack of ability to save Aleinn. "Okay. We are hidden safely here, so we may as well stay. But we need food and water. Maybe if I practice, I could shield myself again and make it to the kitchens. I would only be gone for—"

"Wait, Leinn," Mari said. "I have food here."

My mouth dropped open at the same time Chiara hissed, *"What?"*

"I . . . I keep some, so if anyone comes into the drawing room while I'm hiding, I won't get hungry." She wiggled closer to me, reached onto one of the exposed beams, and pulled out what looked like a bowl. "It's only dried fruit and nuts. Things Cook wouldn't mind me snitching from the pantry."

My dry lips cracked as I started to smile. We were hiding with the single person who knew every nook and cranny of the palace. Who had a secret stash of food.

Then she pulled something else from her makeshift shelf, felt for my hands, and set something supple and leathery in them.

My lips cracked even more as they stretched into a full smile. "Is that . . . water?" I asked.

"Yep," she said, puffing out extra air on the *p*. "It's not very fresh, though."

I laughed softly. "Mari, you are a wonder."

Chiara hugged her tight, and we set the bowl and the water back on the shelf to save until we needed it.

We were trapped and alone, but Mari had just bought us time.

✦ ✦ ✦

There had been constant movement in the palace all afternoon. We'd been keeping still in the hot, cramped space behind the fireplace for hours with no end in sight. It seemed the drawing room was now a strategy room for setting guard rotations and discussing any murmurings of uproar from the servants who had been kept out of the dungeon to wait on them.

Around what I thought might be dinnertime, the room finally emptied. The minute I whispered that we should stretch while we could, Mari popped up, reaching her hands above her head and shaking out her legs.

"I thought they'd never leave!" she said. "Can we eat now?"

I was closest, so I pulled out the bowl and water. We cracked the door open the tiniest bit, and though there wasn't much light, the cool air lifted our spirits. We each ate only a small handful and took a few sips of water. I coughed when I drank—the water tasted like a stable, but at least we had it. The sisters stared at the bowl after I set it aside.

"We can't eat it all today because you'll want food in the morning," I whispered.

Mari's stomach grumbled in the quiet. She stood and leaned against the wall. "What do you think Mother and Father and Enzo are doing?" she asked. My stomach protested this time, but not for lack of food.

"Probably dancing. Or eating a marvelous feast." Chiara

tipped her head back and closed her eyes. "Roasted pheasant, maybe."

Mari rubbed her belly and nodded. "Enzo's probably been talking with all the most beautiful ladies, too. I just hope he doesn't pick someone mean. Sometimes the beautiful ones are the meanest."

"I'll bet there will be lots of nice, pretty people." Chiara bumped my shoulder as she moved closer to the open door and fresh air. "But he didn't choose someone before. Maybe he won't have to choose someone now."

I pulled my knees up and rested my arms on them. The sisters kept talking, arguing about the merits of curly hair versus straight hair in whomever Enzo would choose, and I tried to block them out. I could tell whatever well of magic I had was slowly filling, but I was still so tired. Thinking about Enzo only made me more tired, so I turned my thoughts to escape, instead.

"Do you know of any secret doors through the outer wall, Mari?" I interrupted.

She sat cross-legged, drawing absentmindedly in the coat of dust on the ground. "No, I've never found one, but I don't get to explore outside the palace very often."

"What about your magic?" Chiara asked. "Couldn't you hide us while we walk out the front gate?"

My fingers found my braid, smoothing the strands. "I don't know," I said. "I still feel weak from the last time. I don't know if I'd be able to hold it long enough."

"I know, the dungeon!" Mari blurted, and Chiara immediately shushed her. We held our breath, waiting to see if someone had heard, but everything remained still.

"Is there a place to hide there?" I whispered, though I wouldn't risk retreating deeper into the palace unless we absolutely had to. I'd rather not make it easy for them to lock us up.

"That's just an old rumor, Mari," Chiara said. "And if there *was* something there, it's collapsed by now."

"It's not collapsed!" Mari insisted. "I found it last year, and it was fine."

Chiara choked and sputtered. "You what?"

I inched closer to them. "What are you talking about? What's in the dungeon?"

"A tunnel," Chiara said. "A *rumor* of one, anyway."

Mari folded her arms. "It's a way out. There's a secret door in the dungeon, and there's a tunnel that leads to the hill at the back of the palace. It was drippy and wet, but it wasn't collapsed."

My mind raced through the possibilities. I didn't know if I could get us out the front gate, but the path to the dungeon might be less dangerous. "You said it was passable last year?"

"Yes," she whispered. Her bouncing legs bumped into mine. "Let's go! What are we waiting for?"

"Not so fast, Mari," I said gently, settling my hand on her leg. "Even if the tunnel is passable, we'd have to get to the dungeon unnoticed, sneak past the guards there, and then be on our own wherever it deposits us. There hasn't been time for word to reach your family yet. Besides, who knows how much of a holding Koranth has in the city?"

I took off my vest, folded it, and gave it to Mari to sit on. "We are still safe here. We have food and water. Let's stay hidden a little longer and try to get some rest."

Chiara agreed immediately, and Mari relented. I shut the secret door, and we all tried to scoot into separate corners, but it didn't matter how we lay, the space was too small to not be crowding someone. Mari fell asleep first, her slow breaths settling into the walls, then Chiara.

I shut my eyes and swallowed hard, reaching inside toward the empty place by the broken tethers. Something stirred, swirling along with the frayed ends of my family, like an ember waiting to catch fire. But what could I do with it? If this was my well of magic, how could I get it to shield us again? And would it work for as long as we needed it while we were exposed? I shuddered at the thought of all the things that could go wrong if we left our hiding spot. Then again, there was plenty that could go wrong if we stayed.

At Lord Hallen's Estate

Graymere stood, an orchard of trees and men behind him, the rising sun before him. The manor house jutted from the land, ivy dripping from its walls, gardens pristine, fresh with dew. All was quiet. Too quiet.

The stables should have been full, the yard bursting with tents and animals and servants. But there was no king here, no queen, and no prince heir.

He stalked past his men, who silently awaited their next command. By the time he'd reached his horse, every new apple on every tree had shriveled.

The shadows swirled at his feet, and he raised another shade, black blade shining against the sun now blazing over the fields. In his mind, his vision split, one half showing the dying orchard and stately manor, the other a blurred, hazy version of the same dull landscape. He would not fail. Could not.

"Find him."

CHAPTER TWENTY

Something tapped against my foot, pulling me out of sleep. Muffled voices spoke in the drawing room. I blinked slowly, exhausted all the way to my bones. The tapping at my foot came again—Chiara's foot nudging against mine. A muscle in my neck twinged when I lifted my head, and I rubbed the sore spot. Chiara and Mari sat along the wall, awake already.

"—a guard from Hálendi. She arrived just over a week ago. I tried to have her removed from her post, but the poison didn't affect her like I expected it to."

All vestiges of sleep fled. It didn't even surprise me to hear confirmation that Koranth had poisoned me. I ground my jaw, wishing I had kicked out the man's teeth at the ball.

The chilling voice from the day before answered. "A week?" He paused. "You think this guard from Hálendi is the reason your men cannot find the princesses?"

"I do. She is . . . unnaturally skilled."

"Tell me, Lord Koranth . . ." He paused for several long moments. "Does she carry any unusual weaponry?"

How could he know that? My blood turned to ice. Whoever was outside knew who I was, that I wasn't dead. Fear paralyzed me. Chiara and Mari watched me mutely, brows furrowed.

"Why?" I could hear the suspicion in Koranth's voice.

"I want to know exactly what we're up against." I heard something like papers being shifted around.

Their voices faded, like they were walking toward the door once again. "Lord Brownlok, we will find the princesses, and the manuscript. We will tear the palace apart until we do."

"Rest assured, if I don't find what I seek, I will tear it apart myself," Brownlok replied before the door fully shut, burying us in silence once again.

Brownlok. I pulled in a shaky breath. His voice so similar to Graymere's. Could it be? I squeezed my eyes shut, but I couldn't block out the truth I felt in my bones. Brownlok had to be Graymere's apprentice.

A mage.

In the castle.

And he knew who I was.

I rubbed my palms over my face. We waited silently several minutes, sitting side by side, listening for any sound. Koranth wanted to connect Riiga with Turia, possibly using Chiara to do so. Was that the reward Brownlok had spoken of yesterday? But Koranth wanted the princesses. Brownlok wanted a manuscript.

The library. I slapped my palm against my knee. He was searching for the Black Library. And all my research on the mages was conveniently stacked on a shelf in plain sight. I rubbed my forehead, my palm stinging. The illustration of the key wasn't there, at least. It was in my room, tucked in the folds of Ren's book, hidden in Irena's bag under my bed. But did they even need the illustration? Was he searching for something else entirely?

"Cavolo," I whispered under my breath, tapping my forehead like I'd seen Yesilia do.

I was stuck here, in this hole. I couldn't fight everyone by myself, and I couldn't trust anyone in the palace. Any magic I had was depleted. I didn't know how to use it against a mage, anyway.

But if Brownlok was still searching, it meant he hadn't found anything. Dread swirled inside me, so I focused on the only thing I could do. Keep the princesses safe.

"How did he know about your sword, Leinn?" Mari whispered.

"I don't know." I pushed down the panic. "But I think that man, Brownlok, might be a mage."

The sisters shrank down, cowering. Maybe I shouldn't have told them, but they needed to know what we were up against.

I stood, crouching under the low ceiling, leaning against the wall. If the king attacked the palace, they would have to fight a mage. I could help fight from the king's ranks, but only if the princesses were already safe. And I wouldn't put it past Brownlok to burn the castle to the ground on his way out once he found what he was looking for.

I pushed at the magic, but nothing happened. Tension coiled my muscles tight. I focused my thoughts on making my hand invisible, but it didn't feel right.

I lifted my chin. I could do this. I *had* to do this.

I breathed in through my nose, letting all thoughts escape as I exhaled. The calm that usually came before battle, the oneness of mind and body, seeped into me. I imagined reaching in and pulling out a silky thread of the liquid magic, then wrapping it around and around my hand. Chiara gasped, and I opened my eyes. My hand was gone. I flexed my fingers, but I could see nothing. A smile spread across my face as I looked up.

I released the magic, breathing hard.

"We need to get out of here. Today."

"You said it's too much of a risk," Chiara protested, eyeing the little door nervously. "We can last a bit longer until help arrives."

"You're right, we could last a bit longer. But sometimes it's better to take a risk now than be forced to take one when we're thirsty and starving and more likely to make a mistake."

"But—"

"If your father attacks the palace, there's a good chance our hiding place could get overrun or destroyed before we escape," I said. I held out Mari's bowl, and we each had a few more bites and another swallow of stable water. "Sometimes you have to take a risk."

Chiara and Mari looked at each other, then back to me. "Let's do it," Mari said, and nodded once, definitively.

Chiara rubbed her hands together. "When are we breaking out of here?"

"Tonight," I said, trying to smile. We'd be up against guards, Koranth, and a mage. I put my hand on the hilt of my sword and pulled a little magic out, hiding the sword from sight. It would have to be enough. I would have to be enough.

✦ ✦ ✦

The drawing room had been quiet for over an hour. Night had fallen, and we'd eaten the last of the food and drunk the last of the water. The door to our hideout was cracked open in front of me. But I crouched in front of it with my hand tight around the hilt of my sword. Hesitating.

I hadn't been able to protect Aleinn. Had run instead of fighting with Hafa. *If I'd stayed, maybe* . . . I shook the thought away. Behind me stood two sisters who felt like family, and I would not fail them.

The door creaked as I eased through it and checked every corner of the room. Empty. Now we had to get into the hall without being seen.

I wrapped a thread of magic around myself and poked my head out, ready to push the girls back into hiding. Clear. They crept out behind me, and we headed toward the back stairs. Our cautious steps echoed unnaturally, and even the slightest swish of fabric carried farther than it should have. The palace was eerily empty, though somewhere in its walls our enemies waited.

Footsteps approached, one set. We ducked into the shadow of a plant and a settee, and I focused on the magic within me, fanning it out, shielding us from one man with tired, slow steps. Sweat trickled down my back. He walked right by our hiding spot.

I could hear others in the large banquet hall, their voices rising over the rain beating against the glass and leaking over the tiles in the hall, but no one was coming closer. We dashed up the servants' stairway to the third floor, where Ren's book hid in my little room.

Had I made a mistake bringing the princesses out of hiding? The shield around us flickered once, and Mari slipped her hand into mine. Her touch resonated within me, strengthened me. I took a deep breath and buried my doubt.

I heard the two guards before I saw them. I pushed Chiara and Mari into my tiny room. The men were already in the hallway, so I didn't shut the door. The guards paused to look out the window at something.

Go, I urged silently. Eventually, they continued down the hall. When they were out of sight, I dove under my bed, grabbing Irena's bag. I dug through it, pulling out the clothes and pocketing the book, the illustration still tucked safely inside.

"That's all we need?" Mari asked.

I put my finger over my lips and nodded. "What's the fastest way to the dungeon from here?" I whispered.

"Follow me," Mari said, and we all went back into the hall.

The palace was quiet. Too quiet. Urgency bled through the tiles of the floor, pressing us on, down hallways I'd never seen. But Mari knew them.

"Wait," I hissed as Mari tore around a corner. I was only a breath behind, but she was already in the next hall, a servant near the end staring right at her. My magic responded, wrapping around all three of us. The woman gasped, then rubbed her eyes.

"What is it?" a man in uniform asked, his voice gruff, his hand on his sword as he came out of a room.

The woman shook her head, opened her mouth, then shut

it again. "Nothing. I thought I saw something . . . but there's nothing there."

My heartbeat pounded in my ears as we stood, frozen against the stone wall of the hall.

The man stared right through us. "Better send a message. Lord Brownlok told us to alert him if anything strange happened."

He walked closer, his boots clicking on the tile. All three of us held our breath as he passed. The servant shook her head again and went down a stairway.

I took Mari's hand, and we ran down the passage, then tiptoed down the stairs behind the servant. When we reached the bottom, we stopped. Only one corridor was left before the stairs to the dungeon—the long servants' hallway. I snuck a look around the corner. It was empty. I dropped our shield and leaned against the wall. It had been over a day since I'd eaten anything more than a handful of nuts. My throat ached with thirst.

We kept to the edge of the hall, treading as softly and swiftly as we could. It seemed like it took an hour, step by careful step, to make our way to the end.

No light pierced the darkness of the narrow staircase that led to the dungeon, no way of knowing what awaited us at the bottom. I looked back down the hall once more, desperate for any other way.

Echoing footsteps approached. I still had magic in me, but the exhaustion and lack of food were draining me faster than I'd hoped.

"The steps are likely to be steep and uneven," I whispered, "so don't go too fast." I pulled the dagger out of my boot and handed it to Chiara. "Mari, stay in the middle. Chiara, if someone comes up behind us, defend your sister."

She took the dagger, shifted her grip on it, and nodded once.

"There will be at least one guard in the dungeon. Maybe more. Stay against the wall and let me handle it. Let's go."

I took each step deliberately, feeling out the edge with one hand braced against the wall. After the first turn in the spiral stairs, a few loose pebbles scattered and fell over the edge. The plink of rock against rock was quiet, but I tensed, waiting for someone to rush up the stairs in the dark. No one came, but I brushed the steps clear with my boot after that.

Halfway down, I felt a stirring in my middle, like a ripple or a shock wave passing over us. Urgency vibrated again where the tethers used to be, a pulse from a single silken thread inside. I picked up my pace down the last turn, dread settling over me.

A torch at the bottom of the stairs cast shadows over a damp wood door to the antechamber. There was no grate, so I crouched to the floor to look under the crack. I spied table legs and those belonging to a single chair, but nothing more. If there was a guard, he wasn't there.

I adjusted my grip on my sword and pushed the door open. I was wrong.

A guard sat on the single chair I'd seen, his feet propped up on the table. He leapt to his feet, his eyes widening as the princesses filed in behind me. There was no point in hiding behind my shield—he'd seen us, he'd run to get Brownlok, and I'd rather fight him than a mage. So I saved my magic, my strength.

Murmurs rose from the occupied cells as Chiara and Mari ran to an open cell against the wall, and I charged at the guard.

He was fast, but I dodged his first blow and swung at his legs. He met me sword for sword, rebuffing my attack. This wasn't some mangy recruit—this was a fully trained palace guard. I stepped back, letting him spend his energy while I defended. Exhaustion slowed my movements, but he was getting sloppy. I was darting forward to disarm him when I felt the shock wave again, this time so powerful I stumbled back, missing my opportunity to end the fight.

Something fluttered in my middle—another tether? I gasped as the need to escape filled me. I recognized the feeling. I'd felt it in the Wild, and again in Teano.

I was being followed.

If I didn't make it into the tunnel and get the princesses to safety, we'd be trapped.

I parried a blow and danced around the man, testing his range, swinging faster and harder. I blocked his attack and twisted, leaving my left side exposed. He took the bait and sliced into my arm. The wound burned, but I finished the turn and pushed my sword into his exposed ribs. Muffled cheers sounded from within the cells as I watched the life drain from his eyes, and the darkness inside me unfurled and stretched.

We needed to leave. Now.

I pushed my foot against his chest and yanked my sword out, then wiped it on the bottom of his filthy tunic. I swallowed against the newest image that would torture my dreams.

The dungeon was nothing more than a low rock ceiling, a dirt floor, and a row of wooden doors with a square of grating in the middle. No sign of a tunnel out. "Chiara? Mari?"

The door to the stairwell shattered, and a wave of energy

blew through the room. The table slammed into me, lifting me off my feet and into the wall. My head filled with stars as I crumpled to the floor, and it took three tries to fill my lungs with air. I raised my head, and my stomach dropped.

A cloaked figure, fluid and dark, filled the doorway, the light from the torch glancing off. A shade mage.

He lifted his black sword and glided into the room, sweeping a hand at the fallen chair between us. It flew into the stone wall, splintering into pieces. He waved his hand at me next, but I was ready this time and punched my left hand forward. Power surged into my ring and seeped into my core.

I stood, and our weapons met with muted clangs. The shade mage blended with the shadows in the room, flitting around, attacking from every angle with magic and sword. His blade cut through my uniform, but I danced out of reach of its poison. Mari's frightened face was at the forefront of my mind. It couldn't end like this. I couldn't leave her at this shade's mercy.

Blood dripped down my arm from the guard's blow, covering my ring and hand. I was slowing down, physically and mentally. The focus that I needed in a fight was eluding me. My throat was a desert of sand and rock; I didn't have enough water in my system to even sweat. I could feel my body overheating. But still I fought, defending against blow after blow. This shade was faster than the ones I'd met in the forest. He blocked me almost before I attacked, like he knew me.

I reached to parry his blade, but was late to catch a blast of magic. A glancing blow to my left shoulder struck with enough force to shove me against the wall. A bone crunched. Blackness and light swirled together in front of me as pain vibrated out.

I tried to stop his next attack, but he slashed his blade into my thigh, right below the pocket that held Ren's book. I slid down the wall, unable to move or even think from the pain in my shoulder and the ice in my leg.

"Hey! We're over here!" Chiara stood just inside a cell, holding my dagger with a trembling hand.

The shade mage turned before I registered what was happening. *No*. I reached out with my hand, sword still clutched in it, and the door to the cell swung shut with a bang.

I pulled myself up, balancing on one leg. My left hand was fisted across my stomach, useless from the agony in my shoulder.

"You have more power than I expected in one so young and inexperienced."

The shade's murky voice grated down my spine. He lifted his hand, and an invisible force crashed against me, pinning me against the wall.

I couldn't breathe. My ribs started to ache from the pressure. The shade mage took slow, measured steps toward me. His features were blurred, but his menace oozed into my mind, filling it with despair.

The shade leaned closer. "You will never—"

A blinding light flashed in my vision, and the force smashing into me vaporized. The shade's shriek echoed off the stone walls.

Chiara stood before me, holding a torch in shaking hands. "Where—" She stopped when she saw me.

I was on my feet but leaning heavily against the wall. My ring burned hot, and the shard of ice in my leg was already spreading. I didn't want my blood in Mari's nightmares, but could I hide only my injuries? I closed my eyes and focused on accessing the magic in the ring—fanning it around my form, shielding my injuries from sight, keeping the poison at bay. My body wanted to be healed; I just needed to get the magic to stitch it back together.

Mari peeked out from the cell, knife in hand. "Is he gone?"

I slid to the floor to rest my leg while I could.

"Chiara," my voice barely scratched out of my throat. "Get the keys from the guard and release everyone in the cells."

Instead of obeying my orders, she put the torch back in its sconce, tore a strip off her skirt and started wrapping it around my wounded leg. I gasped as she tightened it. The wound throbbed with every beat of my heart. But at least I was still alive. I would get the sisters out of the palace.

Mari was at the end of the room brushing at the dirt on the floor. "The door is here!"

Chiara unlocked the cell doors and servants piled into the anteroom, too many people with nowhere to go. "Sneak back into the palace in small groups," she said as she ushered everyone toward the walls to make space. "Hide until my father returns."

Master Romo was the last out of the cell. "The king is camped in the valley. We will arm ourselves however we can and fight when the time is right." A murmur of assent rippled through the dungeon. I squeezed my eyes shut and a tear slipped down my cheek, a mix of relief and pain. The king was here.

I tried standing but fell back with a gasp. Romo and Chiara pushed their way to me. Romo sheathed my sword, and Chiara lifted my uninjured arm around her shoulders to help me stand.

I paused for a moment, scraping my thoughts together. "How did you know the king . . ."

Romo tapped his ear. "Even in the dungeon, servants hear everything."

They helped me limp to where Mari brushed dirt from the floor, exposing the square outline of a wooden door.

Romo took a torch from a sconce and held it out to Mari. "Hold it high, Princess." She hefted it with both hands. Romo tugged the door open, dirt raining into the gaping hole. A few stairs were visible in the dim, flickering light. "When the king attacks, we'll be ready."

Romo turned to me. "Shall I accompany you, Miss Aleinn?" he asked.

I shook my head. "The king needs you inside. If you can, get to the barracks. The remaining palace guards are prisoners there."

"Be careful," he said as he gripped my elbow.

"You too." I wheezed out a cough and leaned against him for a moment before letting him help me into the cramped tunnel. My ribs screamed and my shoulder ached as I stooped. Ice slammed through my veins from the wound in my leg, fighting against my magic. I looked up at Romo, and nodded for him to shut the hatch.

The blackness of the tunnel closed around us. We leaned toward the torchlight and hobbled forward until we could stand in the main tunnel.

Pain fogged my mind, but I saw Enzo's face in the darkness, the trust in his green eyes that I would protect his sisters. Shade mages were Graymere's specialty, and the newest one had found me fast in the dungeon. Was he nearby, working with Brownlok? The key illustration sat against my leg like a millstone. We needed to get to the king as soon as possible. But first, we'd have to cross a camp full of soldiers I wasn't entirely sure we could trust.

Mari frowned and bit her lip as she watched me limp. "Can you make it?"

I was running out of energy as I poured magic from my ring into my shield, but I couldn't let Mari see me injured. I needed her to keep moving forward, to keep believing we were going to get out of this.

"She'll make it." Chiara slipped under my good shoulder, wrapping her hand around my waist. "Let's go find our family."

CHAPTER TWENTY-ONE

Mari went ahead of us, clearing the rocks from the center of the muddy tunnel. Rotting wooden timbers braced the roughly hewn walls. Every breath of the humid, muggy air sent knives into my cracked ribs. I couldn't use my arm—my shoulder had to be broken. I leaned heavily on Chiara, each step forward excruciating.

Little by little, the tunnel lightened. We caught a breeze of fresh air, and after one final turn, we reached the end. A huge boulder disguised the exit, with trailing plants covering everything.

The land dropped away, rocks and scrubby bushes scattering the slope to the valley below us. If there had once been a path down, all evidence of it had long been erased. We rested for a moment while Mari scrambled down, looking for the easiest route.

The shield around my wounds flickered. Chiara watched me, eyes wide with worry. The farther Mari explored, the worse I felt. Emptier.

"Chiara. I think you should go on without me. Find Enzo."

I couldn't catch my breath, and my words came out haltingly. "You can send . . . someone back. Later." I leaned my head against a rock.

"No, Leinn. We aren't leaving you."

Mari came back, bouncing on her toes. "I saw the tents! Father's here! But . . ." She bit her lip and studied my slouched form. "But there isn't an easy way down."

The magic in me brightened, a tiny flare as Mari took my hand and helped me stand. The edges of my vision went white, and the blood drained from my head. But after a few breaths, I could see again.

Chiara took my knife from Mari's boot and pressed the tip into her skirt at her waistline. The fabric was filthy, and though it had once been a rich blue, it was now a grayish brown. She ripped the top layer from the waistband, leaving a plain cream-colored one underneath.

"What are you—" I started to ask.

Chiara fanned out the fabric. "You can sit on it, and we'll pull you down."

She set her jaw, brows furrowed. I didn't have the energy to get her to relent, so I let her help me sit on the make-shift sled.

My relief didn't last long. As we started downhill, rocks bit into my backside, and one particularly vicious bush snagged in my hair, pulling the leather tie from my braid. But with every new jolt in my leg and ribs and shoulder, my mind wandered further, recalling something warm . . . someone warm . . . next to me.

"Leinn?" Mari called, trying to get my attention.

We'd reached the bottom, a grassy field between us and the sea of white tents. So many. How would we find the king among all of them? How could we trust any of the soldiers between here and there?

Mari knelt next to me and took my face in her little hands. "You can do this, Leinn. We need you. I believe in you." My magic stirred, and the ice faded the tiniest bit.

I licked my lips and swallowed. "I don't know who is still loyal to your father, so we'll stay together, and I'll shield us."

"Do you have the strength for that?" Chiara whispered. Her skirt was streaked with brown, there was a long tear in the hem, and dark smudges circled her eyes.

"We can make it," I said. I'd survived several attacks from mages and a week in the Wild on my own; I could survive this. I held out my hand, and Chiara pulled me up, looping her arm around my waist again. Mari's hand held my elbow. "Let's go."

The smooth grass waved against my legs as we limped toward the tents. There was magic in the ring still; its heat warmed my finger. I used its magic instead of my own and threaded it around us, weaving a thin shield. One I hoped would get us to the king.

The sun hadn't risen yet, and most still slept in their tents. Watchmen stood guard along the periphery of the camp, but they kept their focus toward the city, toward the threat.

There wasn't a clear path to the center, where Chiara thought her father's tent would be. So she led us, zigzagging through the stomped-on grass, around small firepits.

I wished Enzo would appear before us, or Luc, or anyone I

could trust, so I could hand the sisters over and stop trudging over this cursedly uneven ground.

"That's father's tent," Chiara finally whispered, pointing to one much larger than the others.

Mari lifted the flap, and we stumbled inside. Enzo stood behind a table with maps spread over it, speaking with his mother and father. Luc was pacing off to one side.

"Stop!" Enzo growled. Instead of the warm welcome I'd expected, he drew his sword and leapt over the table, angling himself between us and his parents.

Luc drew his sword but looked around in confusion.

I squeezed my eyes shut—I'd forgotten that Enzo could "see" magic. I let the shield dissolve, and Mari raced to her parents.

Cora's strangled gasp broke the tension. She met Mari's embrace, and pulled Chiara in. Marko put his arms around all of them, then pulled Enzo in, too.

"My darlings, what's happened to you?" Cora asked. She was laughing and crying, keeping a hand on both daughters, unwilling to let either go.

"We had an adventure, Mama!" Mari said. "You'll never—"

The room spun around me, and I seemed to float to my knees. I looked up, and Luc was helping me, keeping me from falling on my face.

"How did you escape?" I heard Enzo say. "And why do you smell like fire and mold?"

"I'm so glad you're safe," Marko whispered.

Luc eased me to the ground, somehow sensing to be careful of my shoulder. He couldn't see my wounds; the magic still threaded tightly around them. I tried to release it, but it was like when I'd clenched my hand around my sword too long and my fingers didn't respond to let go.

"Leinn?" Enzo's voice came from so far away.

A hush fell over the tent like a too-heavy blanket as everyone's attention turned to me. He stepped around his sisters and knelt by my side.

"What's wrong with her?" he whispered.

Luc's gaze flicked over my body. "I don't know, diri. She's holding her hand funny, but there's no wound. Her breathing is too shallow, and she feels like ice."

"She's hurt." Chiara's words twirled together like dancers who'd drunk too much. My eyes fell shut, and I let them.

"What's happened, Leinn? What's wrong?" Enzo's hushed voice asked, hands now cradling my face.

"Mother, take Mari out, please," Chiara said, her voice full of authority. "And find Yesilia." Shuffling footsteps left the tent, and the ice spread into my chest. I let the quiet wrap around me like a shroud.

Someone stroked my hair, and Chiara's voice said, "Leinn. You got us back to our family. We're safe."

"Safe," I muttered, trying again to pry the magic away, and slowly opened my eyes.

Enzo stroked the side of my face. "I'm here."

The magic finally slipped away like a leaf in the wind. His ragged inhale was the only sound in the tent.

I didn't have to look down. I knew what they saw.

My left arm was bent at the wrong angle. A gash in my other arm spilled blood onto my hand. Blood soaked my shirt, though most of it probably wasn't mine. My leg, with its makeshift tourniquet tied around it, and a slash with white edging and green veins.

Enzo's gaze traveled back to mine. He brushed my hair from my face. Chiara dashed to the tent flap and called for the healer to hurry.

Then Enzo froze. Lifted a section of hair, letting the strands run through his fingers. Studied my face.

"Jennesara?" he whispered so softly I barely heard.

Enzo knew. His betrothed was alive.

"Well, she's not an assassin, then," Luc muttered from somewhere above me. Then a blanket was pressed to my leg to stop the trickling blood, and I let the darkness waiting at the edge of my mind consume me.

✦✦✦

Strong arms lifted me gently, and cool water trickled into my mouth and down my throat. Sharpness pulled at my arm again and again, and the greatest flash of pain I'd ever known seared through my shoulder.

I felt everything, but I couldn't find the strength to function or care. My job was done—Chiara and Mari were safe.

Something else nudged the back of my consciousness, something else I was supposed to do.

The darkness was numbing. I was shutting down, slipping away, getting colder and colder.

Then I felt warmth in my leg replace the ice, and the warmth was next to me, surrounding me, pulling me away from the numbing ache of darkness.

From far away, a deep voice whispered, "Stay with me."

Only then did a different blackness wash over me.

✦✦✦

The white-hot fire in my ribs jolted my mind back into consciousness. A groan escaped my lips, and I cracked my eyes open. The flaps of the tent had been lifted, letting a cool breeze ruffle against my side while the sun beat down and heat rolled through everything.

Enzo's face came into focus. He knelt by me, gently lifting my head with his hand, and brought a cup to my lips. He had a line between his eyebrows, a fixed question. I sipped the warm water, and he laid my head back on the pillow. I leaned into his touch, my body reacting on its own.

"You could have told me," he whispered.

Sunshine filtered through the white tent and filled it with light. But I couldn't read him. Couldn't tell if he was mad I'd lied while his kingdom suffered. If he'd ever forgive me. If he even cared that his betrothed was still alive.

A muscle in his jaw jumped, and he rubbed his hand through his hair. "I'll be back," he sighed, and I realized I'd waited too long to speak.

"Wait." My mind jumped in fits and starts, and, *glaciers*, everything hurt. "I wanted to tell you. But I watched Graymere kill everyone I was traveling with. If I revealed who I was, where I was, I was afraid he'd find out. I couldn't bring him here and watch him kill your family, too."

Enzo settled on the floor, his head in his hand, elbow on his knee. "So you're alive. Jennesara," he said, testing my name out. "I can't—"

King Marko marched into the tent, and Luc, who'd been stationed just outside, untied the flaps and let them close us in.

Marko took my hand—on the arm that wasn't strapped to my side—and bowed over it. "Thank you for protecting my daughters, Al—Princess." He carefully set my hand on my stomach, then folded his arms over his chest, every inch the king. "But my men are dying at the pass, and you are playing guard in my palace? What really happened on your journey here, and why didn't you say who you were?"

I swallowed down the guilt until it lodged deep inside me. "The mage." I closed my eyes and took a breath. I had to make them see. "The mage said that my family was all dead because of you, before killing my maid instead of me."

Enzo got up and began pacing the small tent. I missed having him by my side.

"She was wearing my cloak." My breath rattled in my chest. "I should have stayed and fought, but our general told me to escape into the Wild. I had to survive and find out who had turned against us and why. If the mage had known I'd survived, he would have come after me here. In your palace."

Enzo stopped pacing, but all I could see was his back. I couldn't tell if he believed me.

The king's voice was icy. "And you didn't think you could trust me not to reveal your identity?"

"I do trust you, Your Majesty." Something caught in my throat, and I coughed. I gasped and coughed again at the pressure on my ribs. Enzo turned, his face an unreadable mask, and drew water, then tipped me up so I could drink. He moved away once I'd caught my breath. Stood next to his father.

"There is more happening on the Plateau than we realize, Father. Lei—Jennesara thinks there are actually three mages, and—"

"And now *you* have been keeping information from me?" King Marko glanced between us with his piercing gaze.

I pulled in more air, gathering energy to respond, but Enzo spoke first. "She found evidence in the library, and shared what she had learned. It was I who suggested we wait to tell you."

His father's jaw clenched in frustration. "Tell me now."

The tent flaps snapped as wind snaked through the camp. Enzo faced his father. "It's something Jennesara was looking for. She has a theory that the mage who attacked her wasn't some new radical who'd learned magic. She believes he was an original follower of the Black Mage from the Great War."

Marko's expression froze.

I cleared the dryness from my throat. "The mage who attacked in the Wild matches the description of Graymere—the Gray Mage. He could conjure shade mages—projections of his desires and powers in shadow. The text mentioned a Red Mage and a Brown Mage, too. And both my father and brother were killed at the same time the Gray Mage was with me."

"How do you know it was at the same time?" he asked roughly.

I swallowed. "I've always had a sort of connection with my family. I could feel it, that they were dead."

Marko frowned and turned to his son. "When were you

planning on informing me of your theories?" His voice was calm. His jaw and shoulders, though, were tense with disappointment.

Enzo folded his arms across his chest. "When I had more than just a fragment of a theory of who they might be or what they might be after. I didn't want the idea dismissed by the council until I had enough proof to back up the claims."

His father sighed, and the tension in the tent eased slightly. "And one of these mages is in my palace now?"

The white ceiling of the tent spun around. I closed my eyes, but the world still turned. "He's working with Koranth, who bribed palace guards." I paused to catch my breath, and the silence in the tent swirled and thickened with each passing moment.

"Chiara and Mari said you used magic to shield them from the invaders." King Marko's gaze, fierce and determined, cut to mine. "But Hálendi's secondborn does not inherit magic."

My hair was fanned out behind me, an answer in itself. "They do not. But I did." I tried to get my thoughts in order, to fight against the sleepiness the wintergrain root on my leg wound produced. "A shade mage came after us in the dungeon—" I shifted and winced, remembering his murky voice, a crushing wall, the ice.

"Cavolo," Enzo said under his breath.

I nodded stiffly. "And if Graymere sent a shade after me, he knows I'm here."

Enzo tousled his curls. "And if the mage comes for you now—"

"We are vulnerable camped on this field." The king's gaze

locked with Enzo's. "We need to retake the palace immediately."

He swept out of the tent without a backward glance.

Enzo hesitated, and I took in a rattling breath. "Did Chiara and Mari tell you—"

"Yes," he nodded, and took a step closer. Knelt next to me. "They told us about the west gate and where the guards and servants are."

"Take . . . my ring." My thoughts and words slurred together as the herb in my thigh fought the poison, as my magic sputtered inside me.

Enzo hesitated but peeled back the blankets and reached for my left hand. It was curled on my stomach, blood etched in the creases.

"Your knuckle is swollen. I won't be able to get the ring off." He gently stroked my hand and tucked the blankets up again. He gathered my hair and brushed it back. Fingered the strands. Shook his head. "Lei—Jennesara, we've got numbers. They won't have a chance."

"Please, it's Jenna," I rasped. "And Enzo?" His mouth twitched up. "Find Koranth for me."

He chuckled and helped me drink a little more water. My eyes fell closed, and I thought I heard his breath hitch. Something cool brushed against my forehead, and my eyes flew open again.

"Enzo?" I wanted—needed—to ask so much more.

"I'll find Koranth," he said firmly.

Exhaustion pulled at me, and my eyelids fluttered. We needed time to figure everything out. Time we didn't have. "Be safe."

Yesilia bustled in with an armful of fresh bandages and Luc poked his head into the tent. "We need to go, diri."

Enzo's footsteps retreated as sleep prowled closer. But before he ducked out of the tent, I could have sworn I heard him say, "I'm here, Jenna. Don't give up."

In the Kingdom of Turia

The noon sun baked the earth outside as the west gate inched up. Its creak scratched over the grass and across the empty outbuildings, echoing off the palace walls.

Brownlok's horse tossed his head, but didn't flinch at the men surrounding him. Rows of King Marko's soldiers entered the breached gate, but there was no force to meet them, no resistance in the outer courtyard of the palace.

"Wait," Brownlok commanded.

Silence filled the air, ready to burst at the slightest prick.

The mage checked his saddlebag one more time, tightening the strap. He'd risked too much to lose now.

The soldiers were getting closer. The men around him shifted on their feet, breathing loudly. Brownlok inhaled, pulling energy from all around, focusing it into a single speck. He exhaled, and a boom shook the earth, followed by the shriek of splintering glass and wood.

He'd opened a gaping hole in the palace.

Shattered glass reflected the harsh light. Beams, doors, and twisted furniture marred the front lawn. The king's groaning men littered the ground, flattened by shrapnel. Those who'd survived the explosion now raced to stop the barrage of Brownlok's men who sprinted toward freedom on the other side of the palace's wall.

The mage urged his horse through the wreckage and chaos of fighting. On the other side of the field, a boy held back his friends, watching the mage with the proper respect. A boy with the king's mark on his vest. Brownlok turned his hooded face toward the prince heir and smiled as he dipped his head in greeting.

Graymere would have killed him. But Brownlok didn't care about revenge on a people so far removed from him. Killing them wouldn't bring back his family.

Even so, the boy would never be king. Not if Brownlok could help it.

CHAPTER TWENTY-TWO

Two healers had carried me on a makeshift bed into Yesilia's domain once we'd retaken the palace. It wasn't an experience I wanted to repeat. As dusk fell, they'd transported me carefully through the wreckage at the front, where our hideaway in the drawing room had been completely smashed.

I'd been in Yesilia's chambers ever since, with a fire burning bright at all hours, blankets piled on. She'd helped me change out of my ragged Turian uniform and into a men's tunic large enough to ease my broken arm through, pairing it with a long skirt so she'd have easy access to my leg. She muttered about investing in a bookshelf as I transferred Ren's book from my uniform to my pocket.

The latest batch of wintergrain root still pulled the poison from my body, and my wounds pulsed with my heartbeat. Every time I fell asleep, I dreamed of the men I'd killed, so now I didn't dare close my eyes. My ribs ached, my left arm was still useless, though the swelling had gone down, and I needed to get out of the palace, or the mages would find me again.

Yesilia mixed herbs and tended the fire, checking on the injured soldiers spread out on the surrounding beds.

I shifted on my cot and ground my teeth to keep from groaning. I still felt that *something* stirring inside me—I was being hunted. I couldn't fight, and I couldn't lead them here.

Enzo hadn't come by yet, though I'd been here for hours. I told myself he was busy, that he'd have a lot to look after with a broken palace and captured men. But we'd left everything between us in shambles, and though we couldn't be together, I wanted him to understand, needed him not to hate me.

"Yesilia?" I croaked.

She hurried over and felt my forehead. "Yes, child? Do you need more willow bark tea?"

I shook my head. The willow bark would help me sleep, which would help me heal and replenish my magic, but I needed information. What had Brownlok found? Did he have both pieces of the key? Graymere's shade had failed. Would the mage himself come after me next?

"I need to go to the library." I kept my voice quiet in the still room.

She tilted her head, one eyebrow raised. "Well, you can go as soon as you can get there on your own."

She checked a woman on my other side, who'd needed stitches from the explosion.

Yesilia was no help. She knew very well I'd never make it there on my own. I closed my eyes to try and pull magic from my core and drag it into my shoulder, to stitch the bone and muscles back together. I felt a tingle of warmth and then a growing heat spreading in my arm.

The door opened with a commotion, breaking my concentration. I sighed in frustration as the warmth disappeared, and glanced over.

Enzo.

He was finally here. Never taking my eyes off his slow approach, I sat up as much as I could. He greeted several soldiers on his way, his gaze always coming back to mine.

When he reached my side, I almost thought he was going to reach toward me, but his hands remained clenched at his sides instead.

He didn't say anything.

I ran my finger over the rough wool of the blanket. "Did you find Koranth?"

He smiled, but it didn't dim the exhaustion in the dark smudges under his eyes. "Someone else found him first. He's being escorted to Riiga's borders tomorrow. He claims to have been *coerced* by magic into helping Brownlok."

I huffed at the obvious but clever lie. "And the southern border?"

"Stable."

"And"—I swallowed my anguish—"the northern border?"

His lips pursed. "Our line at the pass broke. We are holding at the edge of the Wild. Hopefully with the soldiers we used to retake the palace returning to ranks, Hálendi won't make more progress."

"I'm sorry," I whispered.

Enzo dropped to his knees, and his fingers brushed the back of my hand. All thought fled as my heart pumped.

"I—" He broke off with a curse. "You could have told me."

It was the same plea as yesterday, and it stung, though I knew I wouldn't have acted any differently. But no matter what unresolved issues we had, I needed to find answers about the mages before Graymere came for me. Yesilia was busy with someone on the other side of the room. "Will you help me?" I whispered so quietly he had to lean closer.

"What did you want help with?" he asked. His crisp apple scent washed over me, stealing my thoughts.

I bit my lip, and his eyes followed the motion. "Take me to the library."

His mouth opened and closed. "I . . . What?"

I sat up a little more, wincing as my ribs protested. "I have to see what Brownlok uncovered. And"—someone behind him moaned—"I want to talk without an audience."

His head dipped, and for a moment I thought he'd refuse. But he peeled back every blanket except one, then slipped one hand under my knees, the other under my shoulders.

I held back a groan as he stood with me, the blanket draped over me, walking as fast as he could around the beds. Luc stood as we neared the exit.

"What are you—"

"Open the door," Enzo hissed, "or Yesilia's going to catch us. And Jenna's too heavy to run with."

Luc snorted but obeyed, and all three of us hurried down the hall to the library. He set me down in front of the doors, keeping his arm around me.

"I'm glad you're okay," Luc whispered, and took his position outside the doors, now hanging loose on their hinges.

"Thank you," I whispered back. I pulled the blanket around

my shoulders and limped into the library with Enzo's arm supporting me.

The tables and chairs had been righted, but books were strewn all over the floor. Stars shone through the tall windows, bathing everything in a soft glow, our only light. How would I ever find anything in this mess?

I pointed to the shelf where I'd found Jershi's writings, and Enzo helped me over. There were a dozen or more books missing. My stomach sank. What had Brownlok found? My arm and leg started to throb.

"Enzo . . . ," I said, but he started to speak at the same time. "What was it you wanted to say?"

"I—" He cleared his throat. "Why didn't you answer *yourself* when the betrothal was presented? Why did you let your father answer when I invited you here?"

I leaned heavier on him, and he carried me to a sofa that had been slashed down the middle, but most of the stuffing was still intact.

"I didn't *let* him answer." I eased back into it with a grimace. His brow furrowed. "I didn't know I was betrothed to you until the eve of my seventeenth birthday, two days before I left for Turia."

He sat next to me, several inches between us. "How could you not know?"

"My father didn't tell me. There was—*is*—a traitor in the castle. My father suspected something, so he didn't tell anyone. No one knew about the engagement. Not even the council."

"*Cavolo.*"

"Yeah, cavolo." I leaned back, surveying the damage around

us. "Yet somehow, the traitor discovered the secret. With enough warning that a mage was waiting for me in the Wild, and for my brother in North Watch. My father and I were the only ones who even knew Ren was going to split off from our party and travel north, yet the mages found him."

I wanted to slump, but the motion hurt too much.

"I didn't think your father could accept a betrothal without your consent," Enzo said, watching me carefully.

"Well, he did."

Enzo put his arm on the back of the couch and rested his head in his hand. His hair tumbled everywhere, and his jaw was shadowed with stubble. "Yet you came anyway?"

Our gazes caught and held. "Yes. Hálendi needed troops."

He leaned the tiniest bit closer. My ribs ached as my breathing sped up.

"Enzo, I . . ." Once the words were out of my mouth, I wouldn't be able to take them back. But whether or not I said them, they'd still be true.

"Wait," he said. He put his hand on my cheek. "Whatever you are going to say doesn't seem good. I just want one more moment," he whispered.

His hand slid behind my neck. He leaned in, cradling me with one arm around my back, the other in my hair. A feeling of rightness washed over me. My hand wrapped around his wrist, my fingers on his racing pulse, and he turned what I'd thought to be a hello into a conversation. His lips caressed mine gently, carefully, mindful of my injuries. I cursed the mages to the Ice Deserts—Enzo was finally here, *kissing me,* and all I wanted was to press closer, but my body was too broken.

When he pulled away, my chest hurt from more than just cracked ribs. How could I walk away, knowing this was how he kissed?

I squeezed my eyes closed and spit out the bitter words. "I'm the ruling heir."

His forehead still rested against mine. "What?"

"My father and brother are dead." I leaned back and rubbed my hand over my eyes. "If we ever sort out the mages. If I can find the traitor who betrayed us . . . I'll be crowned queen of Hálendi. You'll one day be king of Turia. We . . . we can never be."

Enzo's shoulders fell with a great exhale. He took his arm off the sofa and leaned on his knees. Pushed himself up and kicked a few torn pages from his path, paced to the nearest shelf and back, then threw himself next to me, closer than before.

"I don't even know if they'll want me as queen," I whispered. I rubbed my hand over the sling Yesilia had fashioned, tracing the bumps in the strips of bandages.

He took my hand and held it in his. Calmness settled in. And when he brushed his thumb over my palm, gooseflesh raised on my skin. "Why not?" he asked.

I laced my fingers through his. "There was a royal family once who had two children inherit magic instead of just the firstborn. They warred over the kingdom, the secondborn trying to kill the first." He nodded for me to continue. "Everyone has always been wary of me. I didn't act like they thought a princess should. They were afraid I would inherit magic. I—" I swallowed. "They might claim I had something to do with—"

I didn't finish, but I didn't have to. A muscle in his jaw ticked, and his grip on my hand tightened. But his eyes were still soft in the starlight.

"Did you always know you had magic?" he asked.

"No—yes. I don't know." My hand trembled in his, and I couldn't look at him. "I've kept this secret my entire life. It's . . . hard to talk about."

"We don't have the same superstitions about magic here in Turia, Jenna."

I stilled, and he tipped my chin until I met his gaze. "You don't?"

"Magic is just magic. What tore apart the Continent ages ago was brought to our land, yes, but along with the evil mages came good men to combat them. Magic in an ally is an asset. In an enemy, it is not." His smile bloomed, crooked and perfect.

The fear inside me that had been knotted for years loosened. "I've always had a . . . connection . . . to my family. I call them tethers." He scooted closer so his knee pressed against my leg. "I don't know much about it, but somehow I can feel what they feel—their anger, sadness, joy, pain. But I've kept the connection, the tethers, hidden my whole life. I wasn't allowed to learn about magic in Hálendi, especially not as the secondborn heir."

He brushed his fingers down the hair I'd hated for years like it was a precious gift. "Can you feel those connections with anyone else?"

"I think I'd somehow formed a tether with my maid. She was my closest friend besides Ren. So maybe, if I have a special relationship with someone, one can form." Aleinn's tether had been so fragile I hadn't realized it was there until it broke. But it had been there. Would I have developed one with Enzo?

"And what happens if someone . . ."

"Dies?" I finished what he wouldn't. "It hurts. Like being torn apart from within. That's how I knew my father and brother were dead when I was in the Wild. I felt my father's tether break, then Ren's." It didn't hurt so much to talk about my family now.

"I'm sorry," he whispered. He let go of my hand, and I instantly missed it, but he wrapped an arm around my shoulder and held me.

"Can I tell you something else?" I asked. He nodded. A breeze lifted a page into the air, and it danced like a puppet without strings. I was done lying to Enzo. I wanted him to know everything, even if it hurt to say. Even if we'd never be together.

"When the invaders had gone to other parts of the palace, your sisters and I turned the corner to escape into the drawing room. There was a man there. All I saw was the sword in his hand, and I just . . . reacted. He— I—" I needed another breath before I could forge on. "I watched him die. Felt my sword cut through him. I—"

Enzo stopped me there. "You were doing what I asked—you were keeping my sisters safe."

"I killed the guard in the dungeon, too," I whispered.

"He would have killed you if given the chance, Jenna."

I understood, but I knew it would take time before those memories wouldn't haunt my dreams. Still, it was a relief to tell him, that he accepted me.

His fingers played with my hair, which Yesilia had tied back with a strip of leather. Not in the usual braid, for once. "After the attack in the dungeon, when you were so injured, why did you use your magic to shield your wounds from Mari?"

I leaned my head against his shoulder. "Mari had asked me

what happened to the other princess, the one I was supposed to guard but had failed. I didn't want her to think I'd fail her, too. I didn't want her having the nightmares I now have."

"You were protecting her. Her innocence."

"Yes, exactly. Everything had been one grand adventure for her. I needed to keep it that way so she could keep going. I didn't make it to Aleinn before the mage slit her throat." I pushed the guilt and grief deeper inside. "So I shielded my injuries from Mari."

"But you could let the shield go once you got to me?"

A soft smile played at my lips. "Before you left, you said you trusted me with your sisters. That's what kept me going, your trust in me. I couldn't let you down—I needed to get them back to you."

He brushed his hand over my cheek, and I leaned into his touch. "And you did. You brought them safely home."

"Enzo, it's hopeless." Even saying the words made me want to scream and rage at the world.

He kissed my temple. "We'll figure this out."

I leaned my head on his shoulder, but I wasn't sure there *was* a way to make this right. I cursed the mages once more. They'd taken everything from me. Again.

✦ ✦ ✦

I wanted to dream about Enzo's kisses, but mages and death filled my mind instead. We'd searched the library for as long as I could and still came away empty-handed.

The hole where my magic was stored was filling slowly, and as it did, I pulled threads to different parts of my body, urging the muscles and bones to heal. But it wouldn't be fast enough. I needed to leave. Soon.

And where was Enzo? It was hours past breakfast, yet—

"Leinn!" Mari whispered from right beside me. "You'll never guess—

I startled, then groaned as everything I'd been working to heal jostled and burned anew.

"I did it! I did it! I surprised Leinn!" she squealed with glee.

Chiara touched my shoulder, trying to keep back her smile while Mari did a little wiggle dance. Her happiness was contagious, and I laughed with her once I'd caught my breath.

But my conscience twinged. They still didn't know my true identity. So far, the only ones who knew my identity were the king, Enzo, Luc, and maybe Yesilia, though she might have guessed my identity long ago.

"What will I never guess?" I asked Mari as I dragged my legs over the side so I could sit.

Chiara rolled her eyes and folded her arms, waiting for her sister to spill the information. Mari was hopping from foot to foot. Most of the other beds were now empty, offering a bit of privacy, but not much.

"There is a visitor from the north. He just arrived, and Chiara blushes every time he's mentioned." She leaned closer and whispered loudly, "She thinks he's handsome."

I smirked at the blush rising on Chiara's cheeks. A man from the north? I wondered if Irena and Lorenz would know him. "What does your handsome man look like?"

A dreamy smile appeared on her face to go along with her rosy cheeks. A smile that reminded me of the girls who used to follow my brother around the castle.

"He's so tall. Taller than Enzo! And he has deep-blue eyes and the most amazing golden hair with a white streak."

It couldn't be.

The door to Yesilia's chambers flew open, banging into the wall. I lurched to my feet. It couldn't be. I'd felt his tether snap.

There, outlined in the doorway, a man with golden hair froze. His clothes were worn and dirty, and mud was caked on his boots. But a familiar smile bloomed across his face.

Ren.

I took a halting step toward him, my legs refusing to obey my command to run.

"Jenna!" His voice carried across the room and, like a memory I had long since forgotten, went straight into my heart and curled up to stay. He jumped over the nearest bed and wound his way to me.

"Ren," I whispered. My leg gave out on the first step, but I caught myself on the table and started running as best I could.

We crashed together, and he gathered me in his arms. I cried out, both from pleasure and pain. It was a small price to pay if it meant my brother wasn't dead. I burrowed my head against his chest and wrapped my good arm around him, listening to his heart pound.

"You were dead," I sobbed. He held me close and whispered soothing words into my hair. I finally pulled away, enough to see his dirt-streaked face, his blue eyes bright with tears, a smile splitting his face.

"Father?" I whispered. If the tethers had been wrong about Ren . . .

Ren's face fell, a deep sorrow in his eyes. I laid my head on his chest again and held him tighter. When my father's tether had snapped, it had felt just like when my mother died. But Ren's tether hadn't just snapped; it had shredded.

I could hear Chiara and Mari whispering behind us, and finally noticed the others who'd entered with Ren.

"Cris!" I said with a laugh, and wiped my nose on the back of my hand. His clothes were as dirty as Ren's, but his face didn't light up to see me.

He only barely smiled, looking more sick than anything. "What happened to you?" Cris said.

Enzo pushed his way forward. "Careful. She's injured."

Ren frowned and took me in—my limp, my arm wrapped to my side in a sling.

"Ice and snow, Jenna. What did happen to you?" The blood had drained from his face, leaving him paler and more haggard than he'd been before. He was thinner than before, too.

"Ren, shall I go?" Cris asked.

"Go?" I said, "You just got here."

He scuffed his boot against the floor. "I can take a message to the general. Stop the war."

My hand fisted in Ren's tunic. The war. My brother was alive. *He* was the ruling heir.

I met Enzo's gaze with wide eyes, and he chuckled, seeing that I'd finally figured it out. He asked Ren, "Why didn't you send a message to your people as soon as you crossed into Turia?"

Ren rubbed the back of his neck. "At first, it was because everyone said Hálendi blamed Turia for Jenna's death. But the longer we were in Turia, the more I couldn't figure out why you would attack us. And I wanted proof that Jenna was alive."

Yesilia came up behind my brother and smacked the back

of his head. "You are undoing all of my hard work! Come, children," she said with open arms. "Come to my room for your reunion, and we'll see what damage you've done." She peered at Ren's hair closer and raised an eyebrow. "Or perhaps you can undo the damage yourself."

Ren's cheekbones tinged pink under her scrutiny and my lips pressed into a smile. Cris touched his fist to his shoulder, then slipped out while Yesilia told Luc to accompany Chiara and Mari so they could tell their mother who'd arrived. Chiara glanced back at me right before she went out of sight, her brows pulled low. I hoped she'd forgive me once I explained everything.

Ren and Enzo helped me sit on Yesilia's bed, and my brother knelt by my side. He brushed my hair out of my face. "No braid?"

I shook my head and stared at him, drinking in the sight.

"It's really you." He touched his chest and lowered his voice until I could barely hear it. "I knew you weren't dead."

"Me?" I wiped my nose again. "You were the dead one."

He raised his eyes and looked over my injuries once more. "Are you sure about that?" I bumped his shoulder, and he shook his head. "Let's see what we can do about these wounds, and you can tell me what happened."

Who cared about healing? I wanted to know how he'd found me, how he'd known I wasn't dead. And how he was here. Alive.

In the Kingdom of Turia

"Brownlok has betrayed us." Greymere stood in a bosco away from the camp of his men. He'd expended so much energy to get them here, and now it was all wasted.

Redalia scoffed and brushed her silky hair, her bare shoulders glinting in the moonlight as she stared at the pool of water in her room. "He was useless anyway. We can track him to the Black Library, kill him, and take his power for ourselves."

Graymere flicked his hand, and a boulder flew into a tree, shattering the trunk. "If his impulsiveness hadn't forced the royals to leave the estate early, I could have destroyed their entire family and everyone loyal to them in one attack. The fool!" His yell echoed into the darkness.

Redalia laughed, the tinkling sound dissolving into the night. "Well, you've always known Brownlok's potential. Maybe you shouldn't have left him in the borderlands for so long."

"He is no match for me," he snarled. "Stay in Riiga. Get their council under control and find what you can on the Black Library. Kais would be a fool if he didn't protect it with enchantments."

Redalia's face twisted in anger. "Do not speak his name," she hissed. She paused, smoothing her face from any sign of her outburst. "You have a rogue mage and a very-much-alive brat with too much magic. Let me help you. I have my dagger, and without Moraga—"

Graymere growled and threw another boulder. "I can handle the girl. She is untrained."

"You must take her power, or we will never make it to the Black Library. Even my powers are fading on this magic-forsaken Plateau, and you saw what happened to our fellow mages in the Ice Deserts. We need to get to the Continent soon, or our powers will fade completely." Redalia's voice was hard in the night.

"I have kept us alive on my cousin's land for centuries for *one* purpose." Graymere stopped pacing and looked into the pool, his eyes lit with rage. "I will finish what I started."

CHAPTER TWENTY-THREE

Enzo pulled up a chair next to me, his knee brushing mine. Ren glared at him, then bobbed his eyebrows up and down at me while holding back his grin. Tears welled in my eyes again. My brother was back.

He set his hands on my shoulder. Intense heat started on the surface. The longer he kept his hand there, the deeper the heat penetrated, until it felt like I'd been lying in the sun for hours. My bone shifted into place, and the muscles around it relaxed. My head dropped as the pain left.

"What else?" Ren asked.

"Her ribs, a cut on her arm, and her leg," Enzo listed off.

"Start with my ribs," I said. If Ren tried healing my leg first and the shade's poison drained his magic before it was fully better, I wanted my ribs taken care of, at least.

"How are you here?" I asked, taking in his dirty, wavy hair, the bruises under his eyes. Cris had looked even worse.

Ren sighed. "I was almost to North Watch when I had a dream. It was . . . There was a woman in red. She was fighting with Father, almost like she was playing with him, waiting for something. Then she stuck her hand out and pulled his life out of him."

He touched his fingers to my sternum and closed his eyes, and my ribs stopped hurting. *Could that be the Red Mage?*

Ren leaned back and ruffled his hair. "The Medallion . . . I can't explain it, but I knew something was wrong. Cris and I broke off from our party, and the first town we came to had already heard the news—the king was dead. Cris said if something had happened to the king, then I would be a target as well, so we headed south to Turia instead, assuming Marko would give us asylum while we figured out what had happened."

I'd have to thank Cris when I saw him next; I'd asked him to keep Ren safe, and he had.

He told us how he'd made it through the Wild on Miners' Pass, how he'd arrived expecting safety but instead met with war.

"We searched from town to town by feel alone—trying to understand the Medallion, why it kept pushing me onward when everyone said you'd died."

"Your tether broke," I said softly. He moved his hands to my leg, and I hissed when the ice fought against the heat. More color drained from his face the longer he worked on me. "I thought you'd died."

His brow furrowed, and sweat beaded on his forehead. His skin lost more color, until it was almost gray. I pushed his hands away. "That's good enough." There was still ice in my leg, but it was already so much better. Yesilia came in with a tray of lunch for all of us, and passed around cups filled with sweet water before she bustled out again.

"Tell me," Ren said, when all three of us had settled on the bed, our backs against the wall, our feet dangling off.

Enzo and I relayed all we could about the mages, the war, about everything that had brought us here. While we talked, Ren ate like he'd been starving for weeks. With a jolt, I realized he might have been.

"I don't know how the tether would break," Ren said when we'd finished. "I guess it's possible the mage could manipulate your magic, break it himself. I've never read about it, but maybe that knowledge has been lost since their time."

"You're alive," I said. "That's all that matters."

Enzo sat forward. "I've given you all the time I can," he said apologetically. "If you'll both come with me, I think my father will want to speak with you." His hand brushed against mine and squeezed. I was glad he'd let Ren and me speak privately first, but he was right. It was time to end the war. Even if I had to leave the safety of the palace to do it.

✦ ✦ ✦

With Ren at my side, his arm around my shoulders as we walked toward the council room, I hoped I could somehow mend his tether. It was there inside me, but still a mess. I'd have to try once the ice in my leg stopped draining my magic.

The dread, the feeling of being hunted, was sharpening.

Enzo, walking on my other side, kept glancing between us, his dancing eyes reflecting my elation. My brother was back from the dead. And I was no longer the ruling heir of Hálendi.

But our kingdoms were still at war, with Hálendi's forces

advancing over the soft Turian soil, propelled by a traitor we still hadn't identified. And the mages were still after the Black Library.

The cane Yesilia had thrust into my hands and insisted I use thumped in time with our march down the halls. A guard halted us at the door.

"I'm sorry, Your Highness," he said, addressing Enzo. "His Majesty is meeting with his advisors and asked not to be disturbed."

Enzo straightened, but Ren winked at me and stepped forward. "Surely King Marko would appreciate knowing that Prince Athåren of Hålendi is ready to negotiate peace."

The guard's eyes widened and he stuttered incoherently.

"Ice and snow! Glaciers move faster than you," I grumbled. I pushed him out of the way with my cane and opened the door, Ren and Enzo close behind.

"—lendi's forces have forced our men back again. The fighting is now only three days from the palace. The good news is that they are keeping the land intact rather than razing everything."

"So they can keep it for themselves, no doubt," muttered the man nearest to the door.

I cleared my throat. He blinked up at me and sank into his chair while outraged whispers rippled through the room. Men and women sat around a long table with papers scattered across it.

Another man pushed his chair back and stood. "What is the meaning of this?" He took in my brother's fair hair but didn't bother looking past his ragged appearance. "Are we taking on yet another Hálendian guard?" He sneered, but Ren just smiled and tilted his head toward King Marko.

Marko stared at my brother. "Can it be?"

Ren nodded, and Marko stood to address the council.

"Lord Hallen, I believe it has been some time since you have been acquainted with King Shraeus's son—Atháren of Hálendi."

Murmurs rumbled around the room as those at the table craned their necks to get a better look at the heir to the Hálendian throne. So this was Lord Hallen, the *esteemed* councilor whose daughter had been approved for Enzo.

"And I believe you already know his sister, Princess Jennesara, who has taken refuge in our palace since her attempted assassination."

Silence swallowed the room, broken only by Lord Hallen choking on his reply.

I spoke up in the lull. "We need to get to the front lines, Your Majesty. We can stop the war."

"No!" Lord Hallen shouted. "We would be delivering our best chance at negotiating a treaty into our enemy's hands! How do we know they will really stop the fighting?"

Ren folded his arms over his chest. Enzo dragged a hand down his face. I clenched my teeth in an effort to keep from lashing out.

Hallen was the man who'd lured the king, queen, and prince heir out of the palace, though the timing was actually good, since if they'd been in the palace when it was attacked . . . My thoughts ground to a halt. The timing was almost *convenient*. The palace guard had been a skeleton of its usual numbers.

Perfect for Koranth and Brownlok to infiltrate the most secure location in Turia.

King Marko stared down his advisors. "Would anyone else like to support Lord Hallen's proposal to use the prince heir and the princess of Hálendi as hostages?"

I wrapped my hand around the pommel of my sword and held my cane tighter as muttering skipped around the table. But no one said a word.

"Good. You will all keep your positions a little longer."

I had never seen King Marko so livid.

"Councilor Hallen?" I blurted out, my slick hand gripping my cane tighter. I could be wrong, but the timing of everything had been too perfect. And Brownlok had been livid that someone had escaped to warn the king because he wouldn't have as much time to search the palace. Like he knew how long they'd be gone.

Hallen grabbed the back of his chair. "What?" he bit out, all politeness forgotten.

I tilted my head in pretend nonchalance. "Are you in league with the mages, or with Riiga?"

No one moved.

Marko's jaw clenched tight and Enzo eased closer to me.

"You know nothing," Hallen snarled at me. But it wasn't a denial. He wasn't dumb enough to lie in Marko's presence.

"Guards, escort Hallen back to his chambers and see that he stays in them," Marko said, his voice like steel.

Hallen didn't fight it, but Ren and Enzo stepped in front of me as Hallen and the guards exited. None of the other councilors made a single sound.

"I need to speak with the prince heir privately," Marko said to his council, eyes flashing. "You are excused."

The advisors stood as one and filed out until it was just us and the king. Marko rubbed his hand against his forehead. "I should have seen it. I just didn't want to."

I didn't know what to say. None of us did.

My brother finally cleared his throat and stepped forward. "Your Majesty, Jenna is proof that Turia wasn't involved in the assassination plot—you've housed her and protected her for weeks. We must put a stop to all of this."

King Marko studied my brother. "Are you sure General Leland will listen to you? I've tried communicating with him several times, but he's never sent back a reply."

"Leland is alive?" I interjected. I owed Leland my life; he had helped me escape when Graymere attacked.

Marko nodded. "He is the one leading Hálendi's attack."

I pulled out a chair and sat, stretching out my throbbing leg. "He must have been the one to report what the mage said in the Wild. That you were responsible for the death of my father and Ren."

Marko folded his hands on the table. "Prince Atháren, why didn't you stop the fighting once you'd crossed into our land? We obviously didn't kill you."

Ren scratched at something hanging around his neck.

"Glaciers!" I pulled him into the chair next to me. "You still have the Medallion?"

"Yes?" His brow furrowed, and he glanced at the king and Enzo.

I tapped my hand on the table. "Before Brownlok attacked,

I found a book. It talked about the Black Library." I glanced at Ren. "The mages' library."

Marko stood so fast his chair almost toppled over. He didn't speak, just gripped the back of the chair, his knuckles white.

"Enzo and I found out there really *is* a key, like the note I found in the fireplace said. But that there are two parts—one in Hálendi, one in Turia. I think . . . I think the Medallion of Sight is Hálendi's part of the key. I thought the mages got it when they killed you."

Marko cursed under his breath. "Did the book show what the key looked like?"

I pulled Ren's book from my pocket. The cover cracked as I opened it.

"Is that—" Ren started.

I nodded and unfolded the page I'd cut from the book in the library. Enzo came around the side of my chair to see it closer, and Ren and Marko leaned in. "I assume it would fit around the Medallion—"

Marko cursed again and strode out of the room. We all looked at each other, then scrambled after him. I jammed the page back into Ren's book and tucked it in my pocket as we went, Yesilia's cane tucked under my arm.

"Father?" Enzo called down the hallway.

"In here!" Marko called from the open door of his study. He ripped the tapestry from the wall behind his desk as we piled in. A tiny box was embedded in the stone wall. The box was open.

Marko wrenched it open the rest of the way and stuck his hand in, drawing out some papers, a few jewels, and dumping them on his desk. He reached in again, jamming his fingers into the back, but they came away empty.

He fell into his chair. "He found it."

"Found what?" Enzo asked.

"I didn't know it was the key," Marko touched his forehead and closed his eyes. "My grandfather only told me to keep it secret. It was Turia's to protect, and I failed."

Ren leaned forward, bracing his elbows on his knees. "I think I missed something."

Marko heaved a sigh. "When your people first came from the Continent, King Kais and Turia's queen, Oriana, chose the location to exile all of the mages' learning into, per Gero's command. They created keys, one-half given to each kingdom to guard, so that no one kingdom would ever be able to find it on their own." He gathered the other items and returned them to the box in the wall. "My grandfather told me all of this, and told me to keep the artifact safe, but I didn't know they were connected. Didn't know it was a key."

My hand clenched around the smooth top of my cane. "So now Brownlok has Turia's key."

Ren lifted the Medallion out from under his tunic. "But we still have the Medallion."

The king unrolled a map onto his desk. "I know that a map exists, but I don't know where it is. It's not in our library," he added when my jaw dropped. "My grandfather told me the mages' library was somewhere in the Wastelands, but there's no path through, no way to find it without all the keys."

Enzo's hand rested on my shoulder, squeezing gently. "We could try, though, right? We have an idea where it is, and a key. We can't let the mages find it first."

Ren's heel bounced against the floor. "My father told me he'd heard an account of a woman who'd traveled in the

Wastelands. She'd said it was a barren land that stretched as far as the eye could see, with red sand monsters and no water. If we don't have a map—"

"It doesn't matter if we have the map," I said, and they all turned to me. "We don't have the rest of the key. But the mages don't, either. We need to stop the war first, repair the divide between our people. If we don't fight the mages together, if they find the Black Library first, we'll never survive."

Marko sat back. "You're right. We can figure out this Black Library business after." His fingers formed a steeple under his chin. "It's getting late, but I assume you'll want to start for the front lines as soon as possible?" he asked Ren.

My brother sighed and nodded, no trace of his usual carefree exuberance. He'd never looked so tired.

"First, you need to bathe and change," I told him. "Then we're both going to the front lines."

"Jenna," Ren started, "I can go alone. I—"

"No. There are mages trying to kill us. And Graymere would just as soon kill you as me. I've fought his shade mages. I know how to use the artifacts father gave me to protect us. Graymere is going to try to kill me no matter where I am or where I go. There's no guarantee I'll be safe if I stay in the palace, especially since Brownlok destroyed the front of it. I can't hide forever, and I'm done running."

"Jenna, you can't be seriously considering this." Enzo kept his voice low. "Your leg—"

"If he's coming after me, I won't draw him to the palace or to your family." I tapped my cane against the floor and spoke carefully. "We need to stop the war. I'm living proof the Turians didn't attack us. People are dying needlessly."

Enzo began pacing. My brother rubbed the Medallion.

"I'm not sure you should go in person," King Marko finally said. "Not both of you, at any rate. Something feels off about this."

An icicle of fear inched down my spine at the thought of leaving the safety and comfort of the palace. But Aleinn had stared death in the eye. She knew what she was doing and why. The mages might find us on our way, but if I had a chance now to end the war, then I needed to take it.

"I am going. If we go together, they'll have no choice but to stop fighting immediately."

My brother rubbed the Medallion again, brows furrowed. "I agree with Jenna."

"I am coming, too," Enzo spoke up from beside me. King Marko's eyes darted to his son, but Enzo continued, deflecting the refusal he saw coming. "As the Turian heir, I can help present a united front. I can authorize an immediate truce."

My leg ached from sitting so long, from the tension inside me. I wanted Enzo to come—I remembered how seamlessly we'd fought against the shade mages in the meadow—but if anything happened to him . . .

"The moon is full tonight. If you leave after dinner, you can still make good progress." King Marko stood, the hollows under his eyes more pronounced than when the day started. "I'll send word to prepare the horses."

✦✦✦

Ren left with Marko to find some extra clothes, and supplies for the journey. Enzo and I walked slowly down the hall, the thump of my cane reverberating along with the echoes of the pounding hammers at the front of the palace.

Enzo hadn't said anything since we'd left his father's office. He ambled silently with his hands in his pockets, staring at the floor. I cleared my throat. "How long will repairs take?"

He stopped, his boots squeaking against the tile. I faced him, leaning on my cane. He took my arm, glanced up and down the hall, and tugged me through the closest open door.

"How many sitting rooms do you—"

My breath caught as he pulled me to him, closing the distance between us. He wrapped one arm around my back when I stumbled, and dug his other hand into my hair. Then his lips were on mine, kissing me like he hadn't seen me in months. He tasted like a fresh apple, still warm from the tree.

My cane dropped to the ground, and I wrapped my arms around his neck, tilting my head to get closer, closer. All sense of anything but Enzo faded away—his hands, his arms, his body against mine. He ignited a fire within me that I had never felt before. I reached my hands into his hair—his beautiful dark, curly hair—and the fire inside only grew hotter.

I don't know how long we had been kissing when I pulled away from him, afraid I would either melt or turn to ash. I kept my arm looped around his neck to keep him close, and he rested his forehead on mine.

"Hi," he whispered.

I chuckled. "Hi." I brushed my thumb along the purple shadows under his eyes. "Have you even slept since retaking the palace?"

He leaned into my hand. "The thought of the mages coming

after you again is pulling at the edges of my sanity." His chest rose and fell against mine. "We lost servants and soldiers. My sisters were almost captured. You almost died, too, Jenna. And now—" He swallowed.

He was afraid. Not of being with me, but of losing me. His bottomless green eyes revealed his worry, fatigue, and sorrow, but buried deep beneath those, I found what I was looking for. I eased his face closer to mine, and whispered the words he had once whispered to me in a white tent as I faded away.

"I am here, Enzo. And I won't give up."

He leaned into my palm. "I still want to give us a try, if you're willing." He played with a lock of my hair, then tucked it behind my ear. "We *are* technically still betrothed."

"I'd like that," I whispered, and brushed a brief kiss against his lips. He pressed forward as I pulled away, prolonging the kiss into something soft and slow that sent a shiver of delight from my toes up to my scalp.

"Cavolo," I muttered. "You're good at that."

He pulled me back to him, a dangerous glint in his eye. "I like it when you curse in Turian."

Footsteps sounded in the hall, and he groaned. I pushed him away and laughed. "You need to get ready to go, and so do I."

His gaze darkened and his smile faded, but he kissed my cheek and scooped up my cane. Patting down his hair, he strode out into the hall. I stared after him, the white-hot frost of dread edging the hope blooming inside me. We had to find a way to beat the mages. We had to.

✦ ✦ ✦

Chiara's door loomed in the darkening hallway. I couldn't leave without explaining why I hadn't told her my identity. The look she'd sent me after Ren arrived had festered in the back of my mind all day. I'd talk to Chiara, then I'd find Mari.

My knock echoed. Most everyone was eating dinner or preparing things for our journey. I'd tucked everything from Irena's bag onto the shelf in my little room, along with Ren's book with the now-useless illustration—then thrown an extra uniform to take with me in the bag.

I tapped my cane against the tile. Would Chiara answer?

Mari cracked the door, then threw it open with a smile. "Leinn! Or"—her brow furrowed—"Jenna?"

Chiara watched me warily from the settee. I sent her a strained smile. "Can I come in? I'd like to explain."

Mari waved me in and shut the door, pulling me to sit.

"Why did Athåren call you Jenna earlier today?" Chiara asked. "And in the tent, I thought I overheard Enzo say . . . Are you really—" She cut off with a glance at Mari.

I wrung my hands together in my lap. "I am."

Chiara's brows shot up, but Mari tilted her head. "You're what?"

A smile twisted my lips at her innocence. "My name is actually Jennesara."

"Then who's Aleinn?" Mari asked.

I rubbed the leg of my trousers and focused on Mari so I wouldn't have to see Chiara's reaction. Would she forgive me?

"Aleinn was my lady's maid, my friend," I told Mari. "She saved my life in the Wild." I looked to her sister. "I'm sorry I couldn't tell you who I was."

Chiara's foot tapped against the floor. "And Athåren is your brother, not your—?" She broke off with another glance at Mari.

I tipped my head back and laughed when I caught her meaning. "Yes. My *brother.*"

"Wait." Mari said with a serious expression. "That means you and Enzo . . ."

Heat rushed into my cheeks. "Yes?" It was an admission and a request for permission.

She tugged a tight curl bouncing by her cheek. "This is . . . perfect!" she squealed, and jumped on me with her arms tight around my neck.

I wrapped my arms around her and hugged her close. Chiara laughed and joined the hug.

She pulled away first. "So have you kissed yet?"

A blush raged on my fair skin. Both sisters squealed.

"It wasn't—"

A jolt of overwhelming panic stole my breath. The edges of my vision sparked, and a deep echo of dread ran through me. The mysterious tether inside me hummed with something dark and evil. There was no shock wave or eerie silence, but I knew, just as I had known in the dungeon: he was here.

I scrambled off the settee, pulling the sisters with me. My cane bounced against the tile.

"What is it? What's wrong?" Mari asked.

"You've got to get out of the palace! He's coming—Graymere is here!"

I drew my sword, and they scrambled after me as I raced into the hall. An explosion somewhere downstairs shook the walls. A framed mirror smashed to the ground, shards scattering everywhere. I skidded to a stop. A beat of silence passed before the chaos started.

The few servants in the family wing burst into the halls, along with guards and attendants, some running toward the explosion, some away. One young maid stopped and looked at the princesses behind me, seeking guidance or reassurance, I didn't know.

"Go!" I yelled at her, at all of them. "Get out!"

I closed my eyes, focusing on the tethers. Ren's was mostly broken still, but I was looking for the tether that somehow connected me to the evil hunting me.

I found it. And I remembered that Graymere was technically my cousin. My family.

I'd somehow developed a tether with him.

Another group of servants from the upper floors sprinted past us. The walls shook again, an aftershock or maybe more destruction.

I looked to the left, where I knew Graymere would soon appear, and turned right, pushing Mari and Chiara in front of me. The shaking had stopped. Distant yelling started.

"Get to Enzo and find Ren! Tell them Graymere is here," I yelled as we ran.

I glanced down the now-empty hallway as we turned the corner. Chiara screamed just ahead, but the sound was cut short. I slid to a halt and, sword ready, pushed Mari against the wall. Koranth had Chiara locked in his grip, one hand around her waist and one covering her mouth. Behind him, servants crowded past, trying to get down the narrow stairway.

Mari kept her back pressed against the wall, but reached down and pulled my knife from her boot—the dagger I'd given Chiara before we'd escaped through the dungeon. It shook in her hand as she pointed it at Koranth.

"Well, well," Koranth sneered. "If it isn't the troublesome trio."

"How did you get in?" He was supposed to be on his way to Riiga. His sword wasn't drawn, but I couldn't attack him without endangering Chiara. I willed Mari to stay against the wall, to not do anything rash with that knife.

"You of all people should know how fast word travels among servants, Jennesara. Especially word of your miraculous escape."

The spark of anger in Chiara's eyes was the only warning before she lunged to the side, slipped her leg behind Koranth's, reached under his legs, and tossed him. His robes billowed around him, and he landed hard on his stomach. She stood stunned at what she'd done.

I pushed Mari at her. "Run!" I yelled.

They skirted the clogged stairs and raced around another corner. Koranth pulled himself to his feet, but didn't follow them. And he still hadn't drawn his sword. I lunged at him, but he brought both hands up. I lifted my ring hand by pure instinct and staggered under the force of the magic Koranth sent at me.

I stepped back, as shocked that he had used magic as he was that I hadn't been affected by it. He raised his hands again, but a spear of pain pierced my leg and I fell against the wall.

The voice from my nightmares spoke behind me.

"Find the others. This one is mine."

Koranth glared at me, then chased after the princesses.

The Gray Mage stood alone in the hall, his black eyes pulling in the light from the sconces.

A sword was sheathed at his side.

"Princess." His voice wafted above the chaos around me and left a metallic taste in my mouth. "We are fortunate to meet a second time."

I pushed away the memory of him slashing Aleinn's throat. A wisp of darkness unfurled within me. This time, I embraced it. "We won't meet again, Graymere."

He raised his hands, and I lifted mine as well. An explosion of magic blasted into me, pushing me back a step, but the magic caught in my ring, turning it hot against my skin.

When his attack didn't work, his gaze narrowed on my hand. He snarled and, stalking toward me, drew a long silver sword from his scabbard.

My breath caught in my throat. Had he found Moraga?

But Turia's seal was branded on the pommel at the base of the hilt, and I exhaled. It must have belonged to a palace guard. And behind that sword's scabbard was another. Still empty.

"I have been waiting for centuries to be summoned from the Ice Deserts and regain my power." He raised his blade, his black eyes bottomless and his cloak billowing in the dead air. "You will not stand in my way."

Shouting started behind me, from the hall Chiara and Mari had escaped down. *Had they—*

The tether connecting me to the mage pulsed with pain, anger, darkness. I stepped away from the wall and faced him. I didn't know if the sword my father had given me would be enough to defeat him, but I would try.

"Ren, she's here!"

I heard Enzo's shout, but I couldn't turn to him, couldn't warn him to run. The ring of metal on metal started behind me—Graymere must have brought company. Palace guards streamed up the stairs, pushing the servants out of the way in their rush to meet the mage's men.

Graymere only smiled. Chills grated down my skin as the shadows in the hall slithered toward him, pooling at his feet. They billowed up, swirling like black fog until they took human shape. Their swords formed next, and glinted off the candlelight when they solidified.

"The girl is mine," he whispered to his shades. "Kill the young kings."

I glanced back in time to see the shades running toward Ren and Enzo as they tried to get to me.

"Your brother should have been dead long ago," Graymere said. "I thank you for bringing him here."

The darkness inside me grew, and I clenched my teeth against a response. I raised my sword and tried to find the single-minded focus I needed, pushing away the distraction of the surrounding battle.

Graymere's form wavered in the dim hall. He would have to divide his power to fight me and control the shades. If I could keep his attention on me, Enzo and Ren could defeat the shades faster.

"Nice sword, Graymere," I taunted. "I bet you're missing yours about now."

Disdain twisted his features, and a blast of something black and writhing tried to strangle me from the inside. From the tethers. I stumbled back, breathless from the hatred Graymere had pushed into me. He glided forward, his sword striking like a snake. The clanging of our blades reverberated off the stone walls and into my bones. Darkness from his tether bled into me as he attacked, fighting against my magic. I countered with a swing at his side, but I was too slow.

His blade nicked my shoulder and broke the connection at last. We circled each other. I was panting; he was smiling.

"It's easier when you focus on the tethers, you know," he said, holding a conversation as if he weren't trying to kill me. I was still out of breath, so I humored him.

"*What's* easier?"

He smiled. "How do you think I tore the connection between you and your rat brother? How do you think I found you in the dungeon? Hundreds of years in the Ice Deserts gave me plenty of time to figure out how to access our family's bond."

We paced around each other until I could see my brother and Enzo still fighting the two shades. Guards fought alongside them, keeping the mage's men at bay.

"I could teach you how to use your magic, Jennesara. You could be great."

My eyes snapped back to his. "Great like you?" I scoffed. "No, thank you."

His evil brimmed on the edge of my consciousness. I conjured every good and light thing I could think of—Enzo, Chiara, Mari, my brother, my father—and I pushed against that evil.

Graymere's chin tilted down. "So be it."

He attacked again. The metal and musk of battle faded. Magic swirled within, the power growing and pushing at its confines, the light inside me battling his darkness.

The mage swung at my legs and flung his magic at me with his other hand, but I twisted away. The moves that Master Hafa had taught me came back effortlessly. I wasn't thinking; I only acted, my body taking over with its own memory. The magic Graymere pulsed out was sometimes hot, sometimes cold, and sometimes weighted like lead. And sometimes it made my ring vibrate unnaturally. I had to stretch and change directions to catch it all, but the more magic I caught, the hotter my ring became, adding to the magic burning inside.

My sword stayed in sync with his, meeting his blade each time he attacked. I channeled strands of magic into my arms, my legs, willing the tingling burn of focused power to strengthen my muscles and quicken my reflexes.

We twisted around each other, spiraling in our own personal dance. But I could never get close enough. So I shielded myself and became invisible, changed directions, released the shield, and swung again.

Graymere's face shone with sweat now, but it took everything I had just to meet his blows. His evil pushed harder against the light inside me, hollowing me from the inside out. My leg ached, but I swung and dodged again and again.

He stepped back from the fight and prowled around me. I watched, balanced to spring away.

"My cousin's artifacts will not give you the strength to defeat me, young one," he snarled. The hand at his side spread wide and reached toward me. I felt something start to tear, as if I were being pulled out of my body. I gasped and lifted my hand—the ring snapped the connection—then shielded myself from view to get a few steps farther away.

The battle between the mage's men and guards edged closer.

Graymere gnashed his teeth and pulled a shadow from the wall. It morphed into a black blade. Now with a sword in each hand, he swung his head from side to side, searching.

"You can't hide from me." He waved his black blade in a wide arc, blasting the stone walls and sconces.

He lunged at me with both swords flying. I spun, the ice in my leg pulsing with every heartbeat. I dropped the shield to conserve what magic I had left.

Sweat ran down my back. The mage kept advancing, faster than I could summon my magic. I saw his black blade undercutting my guard and pulled my sword down to block it. But that left my side exposed, and his silver blade sliced into me. I braced for the pain I knew was coming, but he groaned and stumbled back before he could push the blade deeper. His black sword disintegrated into nothing and he snarled a curse I'd never heard.

The clang of a sword hitting the ground reverberated in the hall behind me. Ren shouted, "Where did he go?"

One shade down. Now Ren and Enzo could fight the last remaining shade together.

But could I last until then? Blood trailed hot and slick down my side and shoulder. My leg throbbed. Graymere grinned and wiped the sheen of sweat from his brow. His brown-clad men edged closer as the palace guard attempted to keep them from gaining ground.

Graymere had been honing his craft for hundreds of years, waiting to unleash his power again. And I was all that stood in his way. Even if my sword and ring had once belonged to Kais, they wouldn't be enough. I wouldn't be enough. He'd find the Black Library. And the world would fall.

Graymere's edges blurred, and hopelessness surged into me as he advanced. He let out a primal scream and raised his sword.

In that moment, I saw a vision of what he would do, what the world would become after he killed me. I saw Ren's death and Enzo's, my kingdom of warriors enslaved. I saw—

Survive. Master Hafa's voice echoed in my mind.

I saw Mari's face as she took my face in her sooty hands. *I believe in you.*

The look in Enzo's eyes right after he'd kissed me.

The last hug I gave my father.

I shoved Graymere's evil out of my body, following the path of our connection, pushing the love and the light closer and closer to him.

Our blades met with a crack that should have broken the walls. I pulled down the barriers around the magic inside, letting it fill every part of me as I swung my sword. I fought for my father, for Aleinn, for all the people I couldn't save. My ring was like fire, its magic flooding me with speed and strength and agility.

The Gray Mage pushed my blade away and stumbled back out of my reach.

I caught a flash of Luc and Enzo fighting off a circle of men—the shade must have disintegrated—but I kept my focus on Graymere.

The connection between us was weakening, but his well of evil seemed endless. And I was nearing the edges of my magic.

One of Graymere's men swung his club at my head from the side, and I barely deflected it. Another advanced in his place, forcing me away from Graymere. I kept swinging, but there was always another club, another sword, in my way.

Then I felt something pressed into the back of my trousers.

"Mari said to give you this." I recognized Ren's voice. He engaged the men in front of me, drawing their attack away, defending my back against a wave of others pushing down the corridor.

I shielded myself and ran, falling onto my knees to avoid the swinging clubs, sliding toward Graymere. I cut off the magic to my shield and slashed my blade through the fabric of his gray cloak and into his thigh, giving him a wound to match mine. The darkness inside me whispered to keep hurting him, to give him a wound for each of my own. He parried my next swing, and I rolled away so I could stand and face him again.

He snarled and limped toward me, swinging his blade. My magic burned and stretched, pushing me faster.

The darkness whispered again, to make him pay for what he had done to me, to my kingdom. To my father.

He lowered his silver blade and blasted magic toward me. I had to reach to catch it, and he swung at the gap. I twisted, putting all my weight on my injured leg. He slid his cross guard down, tangling it with mine and pulling me close.

"You and I aren't so different, cousin," he growled with a sneer. "But you cannot win."

"I already have," I whispered. I yanked the dagger from my belt and plunged it between his ribs, into what was left of his shriveled gray heart.

I remembered how I'd felt in Irena's home. How Yesilia had vouched for me. My father's embrace, Ren's support, Enzo's love, Chiara's friendship, Mari's trust, Aleinn's sacrifice. I took every good memory and shoved it into him through the tether, banishing his darkness once and for all.

We may have shared the same blood, the same power, but I was not like him and never would be.

His eyes glossed over, and the tether connecting us snapped. A wave of energy blew me off my feet and into the wall. The impact sucked the air out of my lungs and left my ears ringing. I sat there dazed, staring at the men in the hall who had also been flattened by the wave. My hand still clutched the dagger

I'd plunged into Graymere's heart. I dropped it next to me and wiped his black blood off my hand. I would never allow myself to become what he had become.

Two hands came down on my shoulders. I flinched and brought my sword up.

"Easy—it's me," Ren said in a soothing voice.

"How many times do I have to tell you not to do that?" My eyes closed in exhaustion.

Ren moved his hand to my side, where blood was flowing out, and a gentle warmth blossomed on the surface. When he took his hand away, the bleeding had stopped.

I sighed in relief. "You are a lot faster than me at that."

Ren chuckled and kissed my forehead. The palace guards—and Luc—were corralling the mage's soldiers who were trying to flee. Graymere's body sprawled across the floor, his lifeless eyes staring right through me, his gray robes splayed out around him.

"Jenna!" Enzo fought his way through the crowded corridor. He knelt and took my face in his hands.

He didn't say anything, only grinned his perfectly imperfect grin and pulled me into a hug. I closed my eyes and welcomed the safety I felt in his arms.

"Easy, Enzo." Ren pulled him away. "She used a lot of magic in that fight."

Enzo held my shoulders, looking for more wounds. Ren glared at his hands.

"I'm okay," I replied with a chuckle. "Just tired."

He and Ren helped me stand, then the world tilted as Enzo swept me into his arms. "Let's find a place for you to rest."

I refused to wait any longer, so they let me rest inside a carriage. A jolt in the road woke me sometime near dawn. I was tucked up against Enzo, with Ren on the bench across from us.

We were racing as fast as we could along Turia's roads heading north, a storm brewing behind us. Luc and a handful of others rode alongside our caravan.

I stretched and took inventory of my limbs—they hurt, but they were all there. The mage's blast had collapsed part of the palace, and while the carriage was being prepared, Ren had helped Yesilia heal those caught in the rubble. He had fallen asleep the moment we left the palace.

Enzo's arm tightened around my shoulder. "How do you feel?"

"Like I've been smashed between a waterfall and a rock." My voice was rough like sand. "But I'll live."

He smiled and brushed his lips across my cheek. He shot a wary gaze at Ren, and I laughed.

I leaned my head against his chest. "Mari and Chiara?"

"I was buckling on my sword after the explosion when they burst into my room saying that Koranth was chasing them and that Graymere was here. I sent them to Ren's room, the next door down, and waited. I surprised Koranth and wounded his shoulder, but he escaped down the side stairs before I could catch him." He paused, and foreboding filled me. "He had a shade blade, I think."

"Cavolo," I muttered. "That must be how he used magic against me when we first met in the hall, before Graymere got there. I assumed anyone who picked up a black blade would turn to shadow like the shades, but . . ." I shrugged.

"If he was Graymere's shade, he must have died when you killed Graymere, but no one has found a body yet." Enzo was trying to reassure me, but I don't think either of us was convinced. "My father said they'd burn Graymere's remains and seal away the ashes."

We rode in silence for another hour, watching the dawn rise and letting Ren sleep. There was no time to waste if we wanted to get there before the day's battle started.

The sun had almost crested the hills in the east when we alighted from the carriage into what had once been a wheat field. Clouds billowed to the south, blowing ever closer. We hurried through the camp to sounds of breakfast preparation and groans from the injured. A trail of wide eyes followed us—two fair-haired Hálendians and the Turian prince heir with an entourage of soldiers created quite a stir.

A man directed us to Lord Carver's tent. He and five high captains were studying a map of the land and the positioning of Hálendi's troops.

"Gentlemen," I said, interrupting their conversation. "I'd like to introduce you to my brother, Prince Atháren, future king of Hálendi."

The men stopped muttering as Ren put his fist to his shoulder out of respect and nodded in greeting. "We have come to negotiate peace."

Grins broke through the mud and blood caked on the captains' faces, but Lord Carver remained stoic. "And how do you plan on doing that when your generals are on the other side of the line?"

It was Enzo's turn to convince. "We will meet them for parley. Will you come with us to advise, Lord Carver?"

He ground his teeth but nodded. "You can bring five to a parley—"

"I'm the fifth," Luc said, and no one argued with his glare.

Carver buckled on his sword and summoned a flagman to raise a white flag. The boy rode into the trampled field separating the two kingdoms' troops while Lord Carver, Enzo, Luc, Ren, and I waited at the edge of Turia's line. Gray clouds hung low over the field.

"This will work, Enzo," I whispered to him as the rider reached the middle of the field.

But the twang of an arrow sounded from the orchard that housed Hálendian tents. The flagman fell from his horse with a cry, the white flag fluttering into the mud and the horse bolting down the line.

Murmurs rippled through the Turian camp, a sound of hopelessness that died away and sank into the mud. My jaw went slack. "I don't . . . How could they . . . ?"

A sharp wind started. Ren had his hand on his sword like he would take on Hálendi's entire army. Luc and Carver were straining to hold him back.

"What do we do now?" one of Carver's soldiers whispered behind us.

Enzo put his hands on top of his head, eyes traveling the length of the Hálendian line, searching for another solution.

It was a white flag. How could those cowardly little—

I yanked the leather strip from my braid and let the wind untangle the strands. "Let him go, Luc." Ren shook them off and stood next to me, but I put my hand on his when he tried to draw his sword. "You heal the flagman. I'll take care of any more arrows." I drew my sword and adjusted the leather strips to uncover the gem, the blue tint shining as the sun crested the hills beneath the clouds.

"You can't—" Enzo started, but I shook my head.

"This is our fight. We end this today."

Luc put a hand on Enzo's back. "Let them go, diri. She'll come back."

Enzo's jaw clenched, but he nodded.

I took Ren's hand, and a shield of magic surrounded us. Shouts broke out from Turia's men behind us. My magic was still replenishing, but I had enough for this.

"I'll get us there. You heal him."

Ren nodded, the veins in his neck bulging as he stared at our line.

We crossed into the swath of muddy field that served as a battlefield. The dead had been carried off in the night. Their blood still stained the ground.

My brother knelt in the cool mud next to the moaning flagman. The arrow had sliced deeply into the flesh of the boy's shoulder. Ren knit it together, then whispered, "Run back to the line."

The boy didn't hesitate, just got up and bolted for safety.

I let the shield around us flicker and go out. We stood, brother and sister, facing our countrymen, Ren's hands braced on his hips, my sword at the ready. A breeze lifted my hair, snapping like another white flag in the wind.

"Your king requests parley!" Ren bellowed toward the Hálendian camp.

No arrows flew from beyond the trees. No sound broke the silence.

Then, a single man emerged. Running to us. When he got close enough to see who we were, he fell to his knees. "Your Majesties!" A shout raised behind him, and cheers echoed through the field. Birds startled into flight at the edge of the orchard, black wings flapping against the wind.

The Turians remained silent.

The Hálendian man approached, but before he could say anything, Ren said, "The accords say you may bring five to parley. We will bring three more."

The man—I recognized him, now, as Leland's top captain—bowed and stuttered that of course we could bring three more.

I waved, and the rest of our group—Enzo, Carver, and Luc—stepped into the battlefield. My heart pounded harder, my instincts screaming at me to not let Enzo anywhere nearby.

The emissary led us into the trees, and a wave of shocked sounds rippled through the camp, slowly at first, then faster as soldiers stepped out to gawk.

My shoulder blades itched from the stares aimed at our

backs as we walked through the Hálendian camp. Enzo stayed close beside me.

A familiar palomino horse stood outside the general's large round tent, a wreath of white flowers around her neck.

"Gentry?" I blurted out, elated to see my horse had survived the Wild.

The emissary licked his lips, his gaze darting to the horse. "The general came back from the Wild riding her after you . . . He brought her as a reminder of what we fight for."

I rubbed Gentry's nose. "I'll bring you a treat later," I whispered to her. "After I deal with these ice heads." She nickered and pushed her nose into my neck.

The emissary cleared his throat and opened the flap. He wouldn't look at any of us.

"I don't like this," Luc whispered.

It was too late to turn around now. I held my head tall as I entered the large round tent behind Ren, the others following.

A table separated us from General Leland, who had a group of muddy warriors, his high captains and lieutenants, with heavy eyes and bloodstained hands standing behind him. Their eyes widened when they recognized Ren and me.

Cris stood next to Leland, eyes fixed on the floor.

"Prince Atháren, it really is you." Leland moved his hands to his hips. "And Princess. I thought it impossible you could survive on your own in the Wild."

I frowned at his greeting. And why would Cris not even look at us? "King Marko has protected me in Turiana these past weeks, General. He was not responsible for sending the Gray Mage against us. It's time to stop this war."

Leland stilled. A smile spread across his features, the blood flecks on his face transforming the gesture into a gruesome sight. "Ah, yes, my lady. We can send a runner to the council and—"

"Turia is not at fault for the death of my father," Ren said. "There is a greater threat we must face." Ren's shoulders straightened, and his eyes flashed as they made contact with each man and woman in the tent. "Our ancient pledge is to protect the people of this land, not fight against them."

"Nevertheless," said Leland with a casual shrug, "we will need the council's permission to cease fighting."

Leland's high captains remained grim statues, but some of the lieutenants fidgeted, murmurs rippling through the tent.

My brother shoved Leland's table, tipping it over and scattering the papers that had been stacked on it. Leland's captains reached for their swords, but no one drew their weapon.

"You do not need the council's permission, and you know it, General," Ren snapped. "You shot down a white flag! *I* am—"

"What is *this,* Leland?" My quiet voice silenced everyone. I bent to retrieve a stack of letters that had fallen at my feet. A scrap with burned edges slipped out from the pile and fluttered to the ground. My hands shook. The note I'd left with my father.

But the other notes were whole—and in the same handwriting. Several of them mentioned a Black Library. That was a term I'd never heard of in Hálendi. But one the mages would know.

Enzo picked up another stack, brown flecks staining them. These were addressed to Ambassador Ernir. "The ambassador never returned to Hálendi," Enzo whispered, but his voice cut through the tension in the tent. "And you have his letters. With blood on them."

My eyes darted between Leland and Cris. "Why didn't you tell them we were alive, Cris?"

The general pinched the bridge of his nose. "You said you had handled the problem, Cris."

What? He couldn't mean—

Cris swallowed. His gaze finally shifted from the ground. "There has to be another way . . ."

Ren shattered the silence with ringing metal as he drew his sword and swung at Leland.

Cris pulled his own blade and blocked Ren's strike. "Wait!" he cried.

Ren's chest heaved, but he didn't attack. "What is going on, Cris?" he asked. "You are like a brother to me." Ren's voice cracked. "Tell me Leland didn't mean what I think he means." His hands whitened around his hilt. Enzo touched my back, clenching the fabric of my shirt.

"You never understood!" Cris screamed at Ren, and I flinched at the sudden sound. "You had everything I ever wanted," he snarled. "A family who loved you, the respect of the kingdom—"

"Silence!" Leland shouted. He rubbed his forehead and sighed.

Cris stopped talking, but he didn't lower his sword.

Ren spoke with deadly calm. "Leland, as future king, I command you to cease—"

"You have no power to command *my* army." The general's face twisted.

Enzo took a step closer to me, but I couldn't move. My brother was here. I was alive. That was supposed to stop the fighting.

"I told Graymere I would take care of the problem," Leland said, "and I will." His men stirred behind him, but the general's calm voice stilled the ripples of whispers. "You are not the king yet, young prince."

Leland jerked his chin down, and Cris swung his blade toward Ren's chest. My heart stopped as everyone around me sprang to action. Three high captains lunged for Ren. Luc and Carver drew their weapons, and the lieutenants tried to stop the captains from behind.

I never saw Leland's hand tightening over the dagger at the side of his belt.

Suddenly, Enzo yanked on my shirt, pulling me backward and diving in front of me. Leland's dagger, aimed at me, ripped into Enzo's side instead.

I fell in slow motion, watching the blade slide deeper and deeper, sinking until the hilt slammed against his ribs.

Luc's sword ran Leland through.

Enzo's eyes were closing as I screamed his name and gripped his shirt in my hands.

He opened his mouth, and I leaned down to hear him over the melee, but no sound came out.

"Enzo!" A pool of deep red spread around him. I pulled the dagger out and pressed my hands against his wound. The blood flowed freely, soaking into the etchings on my ring.

Yesilia had said . . . focus on getting the body to piece itself back together.

My eyes slammed closed, and I dug into my depleted well of

magic, trying to push it into Enzo, to will his body to heal. His deep-green eyes were shockingly bright against his gray skin. He was dying. There was too much blood. Too much—

"No, Enzo, stay with me," I sobbed, trying to keep his wound closed, to keep his blood inside. "Ren, help!"

Luc pulled his sword from the general's chest, and blood splattered against the white tent wall as his sword met Cris's. Ren dropped to the ground. He shook his head, hands open, palms up. "I-I'm not at full strength. I don't think I can heal him."

"Try," I begged. "Please try."

Ren swallowed hard, then covered my hands with his. The shouting and the scent of blood and dirt assaulted my senses.

Leland—a man I had trusted, my father had trusted—had tried to kill me. And now Enzo, who was only here because of me, lay dying under my hands.

Focus.

I again dug deep, my magic pulling at Enzo's flesh, willing it to come together. But it wasn't working. There wasn't enough; I didn't know how to heal, and I was still too drained.

Ren panted. "There's too much blood."

"No!" I remembered my fight with Graymere, how I pushed back through the tethers. "I can help you," I whispered as I closed my eyes, pulling my focus inward.

"What?" Ren leaned into my shoulder, weakening.

"Keep going, I . . ." The shredded tether. It hadn't snapped with death—it had been Graymere's magic that disconnected it. I pulled what magic I had, wrapping it where the tethers were, letting it soak into Ren's.

A jolt ran through me—my connection to my brother

stitched together, not as strong as it once was, but a thin thread emerged from the broken tethers. I took everything I had and pushed it along that thread. To Ren.

He muttered something next to me, but I was too deep inside myself to comprehend. Yesilia's warning came back to me, to not use too much of myself. But I didn't care. Enzo could have every last ounce of my life force, as long as he lived.

"Jenna, stop!" Ren pulled me hard enough that I sat back on the ground.

Enzo's blood pooled on the ground around us, and his skin was still gray. But his wound had closed and his breathing had eased.

"You did it," I said, slumping against Ren.

He panted next to me, his wonder danced along our tender connection. "We both did. How did you . . . What was that?"

I shook my head. It had worked. "I used the tethers to give you what magic I had left."

"Glaciers," he muttered. Ren's emotions shifted to something heavier, and I followed his gaze. Papers scattered the ground, soaking up blood. Cris was gone, Leland's body lay next to us. Three of Leland's captains knelt, hands at the backs of their heads, with a lieutenant guarding them. Luc and the others from both camps had banded together around us, gripping each other's shoulders.

Luc knelt down, his jaw tense, a question he couldn't ask screaming from his eyes.

"I can't know for sure," Ren said, "but I think he'll recover."

Luc slumped in relief, and the men in the tent released a collective sigh, a few patting each other on the back.

I looked at the Hálendian captain with the highest rank who hadn't fought against us. "Captain, there are mages loose on the Plateau, and if we don't unite forces, we'll all be destroyed. The war ends today."

The captain placed his fist on his shoulder and bowed. "Yes, Your Highness."

Ren pulled himself up, grasping the hand of Lord Carver. "We need to get Enzo comfortable here. We can't take him injured into the Turian camp without causing an uproar."

Lord Carver nodded once. "I'll return and deliver the news. We can meet again at noon and discuss the details of the treaty." He glanced at Enzo again. "But if Prince Enzo doesn't recover from this—"

"He'll recover." I brushed the hair from Enzo's forehead, but I kept thinking about General Leland. He was working with Graymere. He'd betrayed my father. So why, then, had he saved my life? Why would he—

And then I remembered what he had said. Master Hafa had shouted that I would never survive in the Wild, and Leland had pushed me to go anyway. *"You think I don't know that?"* he had said. Then he'd burst into the Wild, his murderous gaze fixed on me. *He'd* been the lone survivor.

I pushed away the sorrow and betrayal, and kept hold of Enzo's hand as two men lifted him, carrying him to a new tent and settling him onto a bed stuffed with straw. My body was shutting down from the toll of the magic. I'd drained everything for the second day in a row.

Another stuffed bed was hauled in for me, but I climbed next to Enzo and pulled his arm around me, hoping my warmth would keep him from the cold darkness he'd saved me from before. Luc stood aimlessly at the door of the tent, watching the Hálendians work. "Luc?" He snapped to attention, the lost look fading away. "Keep us safe."

He nodded once and folded his arms over his chest as Ren crawled onto the second bed. Luc ushered everyone out, then took up his position outside. The first raindrops pinged against the trees above the tent. The storm had arrived. But I fell asleep knowing I'd given Enzo all that I could.

"Don't give up," I whispered.

CHAPTER TWENTY-SIX

Rain still pattered against the canvas roof when I woke curled up against Enzo. His skin looked better, no longer gray, after only a few hours of sleep. Luc spoke with someone outside, and I eased up and sat on a cushion by the bed. Ren stepped into the tent, brushing water off a borrowed cloak. I gathered Enzo's hand in mine—I couldn't bear to sever contact completely. Not when he'd been so close to death.

"Did you already meet with Lord Carver?" I whispered.

He nodded and sat on a rickety stool in the corner. Enzo's fingers brushed against my hand, and my eyes flew to his. He was still pale, but his soft smile lit me up inside. The tight fist squeezing my lungs loosened. He'd awoken.

"What happened?" he asked.

I swallowed; I couldn't speak over the lump in my throat, so Ren answered. "You were as good as dead, Enzo. That dagger was in up to the hilt."

Enzo looked to me and cleared his throat. "You healed me?"

"Ren and I together," I whispered. He'd been so close to death.

Enzo, sensing how close I was to falling apart, turned the conversation to Ren. "You said you met with Lord Carver?" His voice was raw, so I helped him sit up, propping pillows behind him, then ladled water for him from the bucket by my feet.

Ren nodded. "We negotiated a truce that we'll both take back to our councils to be ratified, but we are moving forward with an immediate end to the fighting. Oh, and I hope you both don't mind, but I set a wedding date for you."

Enzo choked on the water he'd been drinking, and I almost dropped the ladle into his lap. Ren's lips twitched once before he broke out into a laugh. I threw the ladle, and he fell off the stool trying to dodge it.

"Word of advice, Enzo?" Ren said as he brushed dirt off his backside. "Don't sneak up on her."

Enzo started to laugh, but held his side with a groan. A soldier ducked in, bringing food, and we split it among ourselves.

While we ate, Ren explained that those whose land had been destroyed by troops were to be compensated from Hálendi's treasury, and Hálendi would allow Turia use of its port without a tax for the next ten years. I knew Turia could have asked for more, but Ren and Lord Carver wanted to keep relations as amicable as possible—they both understood there were too many unknown pieces still playing on the Plateau to squabble over details.

My brother had somehow transformed into a king.

So many unanswered questions still lay before us. Something bothered me, though. "Ren, why did everyone think you'd died?"

Ren scrubbed his hands over his face. "The lieutenants said Leland told everyone he'd received a message saying my body had been found near North Watch." Ren sighed. "No one ever saw the message, though. Father must have suspected something when he sent me away in secret. And now I have no general for my army, and who knows how many counselors and captains are still loyal to him." His shoulders slumped. "If Hálendi doesn't want me, can I come live with you in Turiana?"

"Chin up, Ren," I told him. "You'll figure it out."

He laughed, but his eyes were still dull.

"So you're returning, then?" I asked. I'd just gotten him back, but he had a whole kingdom waiting for him. And we'd need Hálendi's strength to combat the new risk to the Plateau. "There are still two mages on the Plateau. Brownlok and the Red Mage."

"Don't remind me." Ren groaned. "We'll need to work out a plan with King Marko, figure out what to do about the mages and the library, how to best combine our resources. But, yes, then I'll need to go home."

"We may have another issue, here," Enzo said. "Didn't Kais use magic to form a barrier between the Ice Deserts and our people?"

"Cavolo," I muttered. I'd forgotten that little detail. "They could only be released if someone summoned them. Do you think Leland . . . ?"

But Ren was shaking his head. "How would he have known how to? Or that there was even a chance they existed?"

My stomach sank. "So someone else on the Plateau is in league with the mages."

"And two mages were looking for a key," Enzo said. "And maybe a map."

I had to hope that they didn't have a map yet, that wherever

Kais had hidden it was secure. Because if all they lacked was the Medallion, that meant they'd come after Ren next. And I wouldn't be able to protect him if he was in Hálendi.

Ren leaned forward, elbows on his knees "So we find the mages and kill them."

I shook my head. "The only reason the mages are still alive is because Kais *couldn't* find them."

"We could at least try, though." Ren scrubbed a hand over his face. "Maybe we should destroy the Medallion." But his words lacked conviction. The Medallion, after all, had been our father's and had served Hálendi well for years.

"I don't think we should destroy the Medallion—what if the mages somehow find the library anyway?" Enzo said. "As long as it's there, someone will always try to find it and use it."

An idea started buzzing in me. "Okay, but what if *we* try to find it?" They stared, brows furrowed in a look so identical I wanted to laugh. "If we find the Black Library first, we can destroy it."

"How?" Ren asked.

I shrugged. "I don't know. But Graymere's sword is there. The Black Mage's crystal staff. They might have enough power to do it."

Ren shook his head. "I meant, how will we find the Black Library first?"

Enzo slipped his hand into mine. "Maybe there's something in the library here. A clue that would help us."

"Possibly," I said. "Brownlok came here to search for something in the library, after all. Maybe he didn't find it. I can help you look."

Ren nodded, then cleared his throat. "About your . . .

betrothal," he started, rubbing his neck. "I know it was originally arranged to bring troops to Hálendi, but if you don't want to, I won't force either of you into this. We'll renegotiate. Find another way."

Enzo tilted his head. "I've told Jenna want *I* want." He spoke to Ren but kept his eyes on me.

I squeezed his hand and nodded to my brother. "I choose Enzo."

Enzo whooped and tugged me closer so he could kiss me on the cheek. His look said it would have been my lips, but my brother was glaring at him again.

Ren stood, pulling himself up like he'd aged a decade in the past day. "We can send runners out, see if we can find the mages. And if not, we can try for the Black Library." He shook his head. "But not today. Both of you need rest." He pointed between me and Enzo and glared. "Rest."

I flicked my hand at him. "Go find a meeting to interrupt."

Ren laughed and walked into the rain.

Enzo lifted his hand to my hair, finding the white strands and twirling them around his fingers. "We'll get through this together."

I closed my eyes and leaned my forehead against his. "Together," I whispered back.

In the Kingdom of Riiga

It was dark in Riiga, but Redalia did her best work in the dark. She spun her blade in her hand and paced in the sand. She had felt his death, had felt his power leave the world. She'd wanted the Continent just as much as Graymere had, but now everything had changed.

They would pay for Graymere's death.

All of them.

ACKNOWLEDGMENTS

When I was younger, I didn't want to be a writer when I grew up. But I loved reading and making up epic battles in my backyard and staring out the window daydreaming as my family drove to visit cousins every summer. Over time, I realized how important words are, how powerful they can be. I eventually became an editor so I could help other people's words shine, because making up my own was too difficult.

And then I turned thirty. I don't know what it was that changed, exactly, only that I felt like I had words to share, that I wanted to add my light to the world. So I did a scary thing: I filled a blank page with words. I finished a draft. And it wasn't any good, but I got feedback and tried again (and again 16x). Holding this book in my hands fulfills a dream I didn't know I had.

Reader, we can do hard things. But we can't do them alone.

To my fantastic agent, Laura Crockett, who has exquisite taste in books, thank you for taking a chance on me. We changed characters' names and slashed POVs and broke Word, and look at how far we've come. Thank you for your patient guidance and organizational skills. Also, thank you to the entire TriadaUS team, to Brent Taylor for selling foreign rights, and to Dr. Uwe Stender for creating an agency that feels like a family.

Monica Jean, you believed in this story and in me, and championed us again and again at every stage of the publishing process. Thank you for asking why now, and why not now—you helped me see clearer and dig deeper, and I cannot thank you enough for your enthusiasm and skill. I couldn't have asked for a better editor to start my publishing journey with.

To the entire team at Delacorte Press, thank you for working tirelessly to make this book the best it could be: Beverly Horowitz, Tamar Schwartz, Cathy Bobak, Nathan Kinney, Drew Fulton, Audrey Ingerson, Alex Hightower, Kris Kam, Megan Mitchell, Megan Williams, and Jenn Inzetta. And thank you, Alex Dos Diaz, for bringing Jenna to life through your art, and Regina Flath, for designing the most beautiful cover I've *ever* seen. To my copyeditors, Alison Kolani, Colleen Fellingham, and Elizabeth Johnson, you are wizards, and I declare you the best copyeditors in all of publishing. You made me love my story again, and you deserve to achieve all the wildest dreams of your hearts.

I also want to thank the members of my amazing writing groups for reading my garbage and helping me turn it into not-garbage: Becca Funk, Camille Smithson, and Spring Rain; Adelaide Thorne, Amy Wilson, Brittany Rainsdon, Kelly Hamilton, Marla Buttars, Rebekah Wells, and Sarah John. You are all so talented and kind, and I appreciate your friendship more than I can say.

Even though I was an editor and not a writer when I started going to conferences, the writing community in Utah welcomed me with open arms. I will be forever grateful to Abbey Romney for taking me to my first Storymakers Conference, and for giving me the courage and encouragement to finish the draft.

To my beta readers, thank you for giving my words a place

in your life and for helping me improve as a writer and a person (get ready for a long list of names, because this book went through a *lot* of drafts, and a *lot* of people gave me wonderful feedback): Abbey Romney, Amy Thompson, Becca Funk, Cameron Flanders, Camille Smithson, Claire Thompson, Cortney Pearson, Diana Thompson, Diane Thompson, Heather Godfrey, Janie Maxfield, Kathryn Thompson, Kelly Hamilton, Kristie Christensen, Lindsey Abplanalp, Lisa Johnson, Lorraine England, Megan Hirschi, Pamela Thompson, Simone Headden, and that one person I forgot (just kidding, there's probably five). Also, thank you, Courtney Packer, for answering my random questions about horses at one o'clock in the morning.

To summarize, book covers really need to be bigger to accommodate the name of everyone who helps create them.

Also, a huge thank you to the Delacorte Mavens, fellow Roaring20sDebuts, and Class 2K20 authors for sharing your wisdom and support as we swim the open waters of publishing. You are all rock stars.

Writing had to happen in the pockets of life, and I'm so grateful for my neighbors and family for loving my kids while my brain was entrenched in the Plateau. (Pamela Thompson, Dianne Flanders, and Amelia Smith, I'm looking at you.)

To my mom, thank you for showing me how powerful kindness is, and for teaching me to love unplanned stops on road trips. Becoming a writer was definitely an unplanned stop. To my dad, thank you for knowing everything about everything and sharing your wisdom with me. You were Google before Google was cool. To all of my extended family (Dan, Kathryn, Claire, Oscar, Ivy, Lisa, Jacob, Ruby, Violet, Mike, Amy, Holly,

Jack, Diane, Mark, Dianne, Breanne, Kevin, Luke, Sam, Emma, Kyle, Aaron, Rowan, Collin, Berlyn), thank you for your influence in my life—I love you all.

Cason, Siena, Milo, and Bexley, you are the most magical, wonderful children I could have been blessed with. Thank you for putting up with Deadline Mommy and bringing pure joy into my life with your stories and backflips and laughter.

Cameron, eternity won't be long enough. Because of your support and love and your faith in me, you've helped me become more than I ever dreamed I could be.

And finally, to you, reader. Thank you for sharing this journey with me. You are more amazing than you know.

The Hálendian crown is safe, but the battle for the Plateau has only just begun.

Turn the page for a sneak peek at the sequel to *SHIELDED.*

Ren

The flowers on my father's tomb had withered and died two months ago. And though it was my duty to replace the flowers, to remember my father's life, those dried husks remained.

The white entrance to the castle's crypt arched over my head, beckoning me in as it did at least once a day since I returned to Hálendi.

I clenched a cluster of the season's last blooms in my fist, their fragile stems already broken.

This was my duty. Whether or not I accepted my father's death, or wished I'd never left for North Watch to protect the border, or taken the Medallion from him when he'd offered it, this was my duty. To care for his tomb. To honor his life.

Black ash stained the stone walls above the dimly lit sconces on either side of the archway—the perpetual flames standing guard to the tombs of the kings. They'd started carving my section of the crypt the day after my coronation.

Down here, the crash of light and sound from the dining hall were a distant memory, though my stomach still swirled with cider. After a full month of parties and dinners to celebrate the commencement of my reign—festivities the kingdom couldn't really afford—one would think I knew my limits. Yet here I stood, swaying.

I took a few deep breaths, hoping the cool air would clear my head. The Medallion rested against my chest, right over my heart. It had warmed during dinner, a tingling sense of foreboding that was gone before dessert had been served.

The Medallion had been like that ever since I'd left Turia. Warm, then cool. Warning, then nothing. It had been nudging me for the past two weeks, but toward what, I couldn't decipher. It was a key to the Black Library, but my father hadn't told me about that. He'd said the Medallion would guide me, help me detect deceit. He was supposed to teach me more, but . . . we'd run out of time. The last advice he'd given me was to trust it. But how could I if I didn't understand it?

My stomach lurched again, like it couldn't decide if it should eject its contents. The Medallion warmed again. If it was *poison* coursing through my system and not cider, deep breathing wouldn't exactly help. But my magic would protect me.

It was time to pay my respects.

Orange petals shook to the perpetually cold ground, and a puff of breath escaped as I relaxed my grip on the flowers and stepped into the crypt.

I'd slipped away from my ever-vigilant guard and left the party because I couldn't pretend to laugh and charm anymore. I was too tired to carry my father's kingdom tonight.

The rough ceiling arched from one stone column to the next, and with each step I took past the kings of old, their stone coffins tucked away in the shadows, the columns trapped more light behind me until everything was more shadow than flame.

My parents lay side by side now, and would evermore. Both entombed in coffins of the whitest stone, casting an unearthly glow in the dim, wavering light.

The little stool I'd hidden behind my mother's tomb fourteen years ago remained untouched in its alcove. The jumble of emotions inside me pushed for release, but I couldn't sit and chat. Not tonight.

Although I'd been training to become king my whole life, I couldn't seem to manage anything. I'd thought it would be easy to step into my father's role and lead our people. But his assassination and Leland's betrayal had left the council in shambles. Leland's war with Turia fractured the peaceful relations we'd maintained with them for centuries. We'd signed treaties, but the damage would take much longer to heal.

Jenna had had to remain in Turia—her wedding to Enzo a promise of peace. I clutched the poor flowers tighter. She could handle herself there, but I wished she were here next to me. Wished my sister could help me with *this* burden.

Two months since burying Father. One since my coronation. Yet nothing was secure—not the council, not the kingdom. My stomach heaved. Not even my own castle, apparently.

I stood silently in front of my parents' tombs. I couldn't ask *why* or *how* or what to do next. Not again. Not when the answer was unending silence.

Countless bundles of dried flowers adorned the flat surface of both coffins. I hadn't laid a single petal of my own yet. As their heir, it was my duty to care for them, to place offerings from our world over their remains.

But it had been two months of unanswered questions and broken flowers tossed away.

Tonight, instead of pleading for guidance, my gaze slid from my father's tomb to my mother's. She used to ruffle my hair whenever I'd run by her, and I still remembered the bright sound of her laugh. If I'd been there when she passed, she wouldn't—

Gravel crunched behind me. One step, then two.

The fresh air hadn't cleared my head as well as I'd thought, because as I spun, I didn't quite dodge the knife slashing toward me. It tore through my dress jacket and tunic, then through my skin.

I slammed my forearm into my assailant's arm as a burning trail blossomed across my stomach. Someone else reached around my neck from behind, choking my airway. I leaned back into him and brought both legs up, kicking the knifer as hard as I could in the chest. He grunted and rolled away as my lungs screamed for air.

I tucked my leg up and slipped a knife out of my boot, then jammed it into the thigh of whoever had been stupid enough to attack me in the land of the dead.

This is the closest I'd ever be to my parents now, and at least here, in this place, I wouldn't let them down.

The arm around my neck fell away. I yanked my dagger from

his thigh, then forced my elbow into his gut. I had time for one gulping breath before the assailant's blade slashed at me again. I jumped back, tripping over the man who'd tried to choke me. My backside hit unyielding stone and a spasm shot up my spine. I rolled to my feet and deflected his next attack, slicing my blade through his forearm, then shoving my elbow into his face. He spun into a kick. But my knife was there first, slashing through his calf muscle before he could connect.

He fell to the ground, his scream rattling in my aching head. I kicked his weapon, and it spun into the shadows. My chest heaved and dark splatters of blood marred my once-fine jacket. Both attackers wore the gray uniform of the king's guards—*my* guards.

I pressed my hand against my sputtering heart—the Medallion had fallen out from its hiding spot. I tucked it back under my tunic, hoping neither of my attackers had seen it.

"Arrest him!" a high-pitched voice yelled, adding to the banging in my head.

Lady Isarr stood under the crypt's arch, one long fingernail pointed directly at me. A whole troop of people crowded around her, pushing their way in, with gasps from the wide-eyed courtiers, shock and anger from the guards she'd conveniently brought along.

Well, this complicated things a bit. My opposition was moving openly.

"Do not screech at your king, Lady Isarr. My head is already pounding, and I need to think," I said, rubbing my temple.

"What have you done, Your Majesty?" Isarr breathed out, oil dripping from her words like I'd never heard before. "You've murdered them!" she accused, spreading her arms to indicate the two groaning men sprawled at my feet. The men who clearly weren't dead. But who'd clearly wanted *me* dead.

The Medallion warmed against my chest, but I didn't need its help to sense her lie.

My dagger hung limp at my side, dripping blood into the cracks in the stone. The guards Isarr had brought in her entourage rushed to their fallen comrades.

"May I ask, Lady Isarr, why you and your associates are visiting the crypt at this hour?" I asked as I wiped my blade on my trousers. I'd known most of these people my entire life, yet they would charge me with murder?

Her hand flew to her chest. "We heard yelling and came at once!"

My eyebrows shot up and I stared down her entourage. "You heard yelling through all this rock?" I shook my head. "Try again."

Some in the crowd shifted. Others watched Isarr, to see how she would respond. The man on her immediate left and the woman on her right—her best friend and her known lover—didn't flinch. Loyal to Isarr, then.

She'd been relentless at the dinner parties over the course of the month, always pursuing me, always on the hunt. I thought I'd known her, her type. A harmless title chaser. Yet something in her countenance had changed. As though a mask I hadn't known she was wearing had fallen off. The worst part wasn't seeing her true nature. It was that I hadn't realized she'd been wearing a mask in the first place.

I studied her and those she'd surrounded herself with. Pieces clicked into place—snippets of conversations I'd overheard in the halls, looks, messages. She'd done well, filling her witness pool with some who were loyal to me, as well as those who would support her.

Isarr tilted her chin, looking down her long nose at me. "You *killed* those men," she said, her words snaking toward me.

I nudged the guards surrounding the man who'd tried to choke me to the side and slowly knelt, one knee digging into the unforgiving rock. A tremor racked my hand as I covered his wound, which bled more than it should have. "Not yet, I haven't."

A wave of unease moved through the crowd. There—a darted glance, shuffling feet. More were involved than just Isarr. But how many? I didn't sheath my knife.

"Your Majesty," one guard started, leaning toward me like he thought I would hurt the injured man. Well, hurt him more than the knife I'd stuck in his thigh.

"If you want him to live, stand back," I snapped.

The guard swallowed, but retreated. I turned my focus inward, on the man's wound. My skin prickled at the risk of diverting all my attention into the healing magic that flowed from my hands. But I needed him alive—for questioning, and to prove my innocence. And because Hálendi didn't need more death.

My surroundings faded to a dull murmur. My focus narrowed to his skin knitting together, the veins reconnecting. Energy flowed out of me and into this man who'd tried to take my life.

My vision spun as I pulled my hand away, and the watchful crowd came back into my peripheral vision. I pushed against my knee, forcing myself to stand tall, shoulders back.

Another guard, a silver knot on his uniform, inspected the other would-be assassin, who lay on the ground, still groaning, clutching his calf as others tried to wrap it. Isarr had brought a captain. One recently instated since I'd had to clean out the ranks loyal to General Leland. He shifted his feet, his eyes darting everywhere, one hand on the hilt of his sword. "Sire, according to law—"

"Am I not allowed to defend myself from assassins?" I cut in before he could commit treason and accuse me of murder. I'd give him *one* chance to show his loyalty.

The captain swallowed so hard I could see the bob in his neck. Hesitant. Not part of the plot, then.

Isarr clucked her tongue. "But how to prove it was defense? They are wearing *your* uniform, Your Majesty. Why would your own guards attack you?" She smiled as though she'd proved her point.

And she had, in a way. Proved that the list of those I could trust had dwindled far indeed. Ever since my closest friend, Cris, had drawn his sword and attacked me in the tent on the Turian front line, my friends and allies had fallen away in betrayal one by one. My stomach clenched and swirled until I thought I'd be sick. Who would be next?

They wanted proof of self-defense? Fine. I gritted my teeth and unbuttoned my dress jacket, then hooked a finger under my blood-soaked tunic, lifting it slowly. A red slash—not deep anymore, but long—slanted along my stomach from ribs to hip. Blood still dripped from it onto my trousers.

Gasps rang out so loud that the urge to laugh bubbled up. Everyone already thought me a murderer, though; I wouldn't add crazy to the list. I wished again that Jenna were here—not only did I need her support, I desperately wanted someone to laugh with. To talk to. One single person I could trust not to shove a knife in my back. Or stomach, as the case may be.

"As I said, am I not allowed to defend myself? Now, what is your excuse for interrupting my mourning?"

Isarr's reaction was slight: a lift of her chin, flashing eyes that had once lured me into a dark hallway for a kiss.

I kept my growl back, but only just. "Unless, perhaps, you orchestrated the assassination attempt? And conveniently brought your *friends* as witnesses?"

The courtiers behind her began to whisper, and more than a few stepped back, no doubt remembering in a new light whatever Isarr and her companions had said to lure them here. Distancing themselves from the guilty.

Isarr's narrowed gaze focused on the man clutching his calf. "If either of them die," she said, nodding to the attackers still on the ground, "you'll have to stand trial before the council." Her lips pulled up into the barest hint of triumph.

I smirked, and though it wasn't wise to taunt her, I couldn't help it. "Haven't you heard, or did you just forget, Isarr," I said, intentionally leaving off her title, "I'm a *healer*."

My cursed hands wouldn't stop shaking as I brushed my fingers over the assassin's calf. His cries immediately quieted even as my reserve drained. I lifted his trouser, and instead of a knife wound, there was only a line of pink skin. He could keep the cut on his forearm.

Silence dropped heavy over us, weighing as much as the castle over our heads.

The courtiers and guards bragged of Hálendi's magic. I wore the white streak in my hair prominently. But *seeing* magic was another matter altogether. And now that I'd revealed how strong my magic actually was—beyond healing a scrape or an illness—the next assassin would no doubt account for it.

Glaciers, I was an ice-headed idiot. I could blame it on whatever my cider had been tainted with, but I was also tired. Tired of secrets and betrayal and deception. And I wanted these men to spill the names of every courtier who'd funded this little endeavor.

"I wonder what sort of tales they have to tell the council," I said, tilting my head and pushing up to stand, my hands covered in blood, red and brown smears that would take ages to scrub away. "You want to accuse me of anything?" I asked the guard who had knifed me. He shook his head so hard his hair fell into his face, but he never took his eyes off his newly healed leg.

I turned to the captain. "I trust you can handle arresting these men, Isarr, and"—I pointed to the man and woman at her side—"those two?"

He nodded once, touching his fist to his shoulder.

No one said anything as the guards took hold of Isarr and her friends. Her simpering, lust-filled facade was completely gone now. Only rage remained. Rage that she'd been caught.

How many more in the castle watched and waited for their chance to dethrone me? How many more would bow to me as their king, only to light my boots on fire?

Guards moved to lift the assassins into the hall, and courtiers moved to get a closer look at their healed wounds. So many people. Shuffling feet and crunching gravel and whispers.

I wiped my forehead with my mostly clean sleeve and jerked my arm back to my side. "And, Captain, get everyone out of here!" I said, my voice rising to a shout at the end. Another wave of dizziness passed over me. "This is a crypt, not a gallery!"

My parents' tombs rested still and ever silent behind me. Watching all of it. Everything. All around me, broken stems and mangled orange petals lay scattered and crushed into the dusty floor.

Space. I needed space.

Bodies pressed against me as I pushed toward the exit. Dresses and shoulders too close. And *why* in all the glaciers was it so blasted warm down here?

My guard, Kaldur, pushed his way against the crowd.

I blinked and his hand gripped my elbow. "Your Majesty?"

I'd snuck away because I didn't need protection. And I didn't—I needed a witness. But if I ever wanted to keep the sliver of freedom I still had, he couldn't see my trembling hands.

"Kaldur, it's barely fall," I said, my lips twisted into some semblance of a smile as my stomach heaved and twisted. "Tell the castle steward we don't need fireplaces lit at dinner just yet. I've been abominably warm all evening."

Kaldur clenched his jaw and took several calming breaths before answering. "Sire, you really should allow me to accompany you when you decide to visit the crypt."

I didn't have a witty response to that, because he was right. I should have. I thought I'd be safe here, that the hallowed ground would be respected. But just like so many other things, other people, I was wrong.

I allowed Kaldur to escort me back to my chambers, more

to assuage his fears than mine. My enemies would regroup after tonight. I cursed myself again for showing my hand.

Kaldur checked everywhere, even behind the long blue drapes and under my bed, before taking position beside my door.

"You are not standing there all night," I said with a frown.

He straightened. "Yes, I am."

My chest tightened and my breaths came faster. *Wait, hold it in a bit longer.*

I stalked over to him. "No, you're not." I took his arm and shoved him out the door, then locked it behind him. He took up position outside, grumbling curses I couldn't decipher.

I rested my back against the door. Kaldur could grumble all he wanted, but he wasn't staying in here while I was asleep. No one was.

For good measure, I slid a side table in front of the door and perched a vase on its edge. A warning before the next knife came for me.

They'd been so close. Had I turned a half-second later . . .

My stomach squeezed. I stumbled to my bathing chamber and retched into an empty bucket. I wiped my mouth on my sleeve and braced my hands on the edge of the bucket. The servants would have to remove the mess tomorrow—no one was coming into this room tonight.

There had definitely been something in my cider. But the question remained: Was it part of Isarr's play against me? Or were others plotting to kill me?

I left the foul-smelling bathing chamber, yanked off my dress jacket, and fell into the chair next to the empty fireplace. The jacket had been embroidered with painstaking detail, and the buttons carefully sewn in two neat rows down the front. Now it was torn and smeared with blood and dust, with three buttons missing. I tossed it in the corner, then used an almost-clean patch of my tunic to wipe away the red caked on my torso, then tossed it as well. The last of the skin on my stomach knit together as I watched, leaving only a tiny pale scar.

I traced my finger along it, hating and loving my magic. My body healed itself without a thought, yet two people I loved dearly lay in the crypt beneath my feet. My magic hadn't prevented my best friend from betraying me. I shoved away any thought of Cris, lacing my fingers together until they stopped shaking.

I tilted my head back against the chair, exhaustion from healing the two men and myself finally claiming me.

A searing heat flashed against my chest, hotter than I'd ever felt. I snatched the Medallion away from my skin, expecting to see a brand mark where it had rested. But my skin remained unmarred. I ran my finger over the tiny notches and bumps on the Medallion's back, over the intricate runes carved into its front.

Had my father known a mage was coming after him? Coming after the key to the Black Library? Is that why he'd given me the Medallion before I'd left for North Watch?

Foreboding trickled along my skin. The Medallion remained hot.

"Oh, sure, *now* you warn me," I muttered into the empty room.